NINETY-EIGHT SABERS

ELIZABETH BROADBENT

Undertaker Books

Copyright © 2024 by Elizabeth Broadbent

All rights reserved.

No part of this publication may be reproduced, distributed, or transmitted in any form or by any means, including photocopying, recording, or other electronic or mechanical methods, without the prior written permission of the publisher, except as permitted by U.S. copyright law. For permission requests, contact Undertaker Books at info@undertakerbooks.com.

The story, all names, characters, and incidents portrayed in this production are fictitious. No identification with actual persons (living or deceased), places, buildings, and products is intended or should be inferred.

Book Cover by Erick Worthington & Elizabeth Broadbent

First edition 2024

MORE BY ELIZABETH BROADBENT

"South Carolina is too small for a republic, but too large for an insane asylum."
—James Louis Petigru

For Joey Oppermann

NINETY-EIGHT SABERS

CHAPTER 1

ASH

Summer sulked low and heavy over Cypress Bend. Ashby Trenholm held his father's hand, determined to mark his last heartbeat. The room smelled of sickness, of age gone stale, and only cicada-hum broke the afternoon's sullen inertia. He waited. Time stretched into the unimaginable. Once more, he thought of calling Sullivan; once more, he didn't. His younger brother hadn't come home for a decade, and the old man hadn't spoken since he left. Ash hoped for a gasped goodbye, a deathbed miracle.

None came.

Wet button-down clinging to his back, he shifted in the wingback chair. Death seemed too formal for a polo shirt, and Cypress Bend's air conditioner had died the day before. Sullivan should have been there. His first cousins Rhys and Olivia should have been there. All had refused, and he couldn't ask it of Elliot.

Truluck Trenholm would die regretted by no one, least of all his sons, nephews, and nieces. Those who might have missed him, the ones Rhys and Sullivan had called The Cypress Bend Ancients of Days, were long gone, other than Great-Aunt Alda. They remembered Ash's father as a laughing boy rather than a drunken Confederate archivist, a child more sinned against than sinning. Maybe Ash's cousin Henry would miss him. His father always had loved him best.

Before Henry came, he'd loved Sullivan best: the strong son, the son who could breathe. Ash hadn't carried his inhaler for years, but he remembered its heft and bulk bulging out his pocket. A son who turned blue wasn't worth his father's time, but a son who turned blue wasn't worth his blows, either. Ash could never decide which was worse.

The man in the corner stood silent, as if he kept his own vigil. Dark-skinned, eyes on the floor, he said nothing, but he never did. Ash ignored him, though a bitter, familiar misery descended. He looked away and wished one more time that the man would leave them alone.

His father's heart stumbled. The air hung stagnant, still. Ash waited, but it did not beat again. Carefully, he covered the old man with a sheet. An odd sense of betrayal lingered. He should have felt it.

"Does that make you happy, finally?" Ash asked the man in the corner.

But as usual, the man in coarse cotton pants and a plain shirt gave no reply.

Death might have eluded Ash, but its ugly offices remained. He stood, and his four German Shepherds rose. With his soaked button-down, sleeves rolled, and clumped-up dark hair, he probably looked red faced and sweating as a Southern country lawyer, but it couldn't be helped. "It's done," he told the white-habited nurse in the hallway, a second cousin once removed. She would call Lower Congaree's only funeral home. Arrangements had been made long ago; they were identical to those for every Trenholm Ash remembered. He would summon the family from whatever escapes they'd managed—Charleston, Richmond, wherever Sullivan wound up. Ash would find them all, no matter what their opinion on the cameras, the strangers, the money; they would come if he needed them.

His brother Sullivan had left for good on another day when the heat mooned low and claustrophobic over the farm. They'd gathered to celebrate Sullivan's and Rhys's twenty-first birthdays; Trenholms clumped through the house in familiar constellations. Babble ebbed and crested, cousins and uncles, great-aunts and second cousins. Pale and shaking, one of the barn boys slipped in. *Mister Trenholm,* he said in a low voice, Sullivan close enough to hear. *It's Jet.*

Sullivan pricked up like a hunting dog. The rangy bay Thoroughbred was his favorite. Ash's father flung a linen napkin and cussed loud enough that Olivia clapped her hands over Elliot's ears. *Like the others?* he asked.

Yessir. Another cousin somehow, youngish, the groom had probably planned on joining the party after he finished throwing hay. *Uncle Truluck, I went out to the back field to bring him in this morning. He was grazing under the Boundary Tree, and three identical men stepped out from behind him.*

Silence thick as summer heat had fallen over the party; Ash's stomach roiled sickly at both the inevitability of the groom's story and his relatives' prurient horror. They loved to be scared by Cypress Bend, and drew grim satisfaction from bearing its tales: *I went out to the farm yesterday, and you'll never believe what happened.*

Those men, they were wearing these old-fashioned clothes, the groom said. *And they moved at the same time, like puppets, like these weird dancers, and they reached up and tipped these old-style hats, and I blinked, and I swear no time passed at all, but then the sun was going down and Jet was at my feet.*

It's just like the others, Uncle Truluck. One ear missing, one eye, tongue and—and— He glanced at Olivia—*stuff between his legs removed, belly slit and things taken out, no blood. All the cuts look like they were done with a laser and there's no blood at all.*

Several people gasped, probably distant Trenholms, relatives less familiar with Cypress Bend's atrocities. Six Thoroughbreds had been killed identically in the four years previous, each neatly eviscerated. The bodies were drained of blood, often in broad daylight, and there were never any witnesses.

Deliberately, Sullivan set down his birthday cake. They always had two cakes, red velvet for him and coconut for Rhys, though their birthdays were two days apart. *No,* Sullivan said. *I'm sorry, Rhys. I'm done here.* With no word to anyone else, he strode out.

What was that about? their father asked, always disbelieving at his children's sudden flashes of will.

Sullivan's leaving. Rhys disappeared, presumably to talk him out of it.

Well, let him, goddammit. Their father stabbed another piece of cake. *Damn fool thing, walking out of your own birthday party.*

Twenty minutes later, a car door snapped the afternoon's pale silence, and Sullivan's Tesla receded down the Avenue of Oaks. Ash considered it a more eloquent goodbye than his brother could have mustered. Their father crumpled to his chair and shouted for everyone to leave. Not long after, he dragged himself to bed, suffered a stroke, and never spoke again. Ten years later, his death would call Sullivan home. Only heirs who attended the funeral would inherit.

Ash scrolled through his phone.

Money tugged harder than blood. His brother would come.

CHAPTER 2

SULLIVAN

Sullivan was drunk. He hadn't answered Ash's calls, but he'd listened to the voicemail. His father was finally dying, that bastard; he'd hung on far too long. Alcohol would soothe whatever scars broke open. There were too many—childhood's visceral terrors, a house of Southern reliquary, parental furies vicious and sudden as the farm's regular lightning strikes. They'd played a game called Confederate Assassin then. His father gave them black-and-white print-outs of Lincoln and William Tecumseh Sherman; they taped them to a dartboard. *We can't do this,* Sullivan had thought when he came home from college, suddenly appalled. He'd hidden the dartboard under his bed. But he'd accepted most of the madness as patriarchal fiat, Southern barbarities perhaps a shade worse than usual, but nothing he could rightfully complain about. Then Ash brought in reality TV. In that rank invasion, Sullivan realized something about his family was deeply, irrevocably fucked.

Far too cold, his therapist's office had smelled of incense; a desktop waterfall plashed in a corner. *You know that show,* Paranormal Gone South? Sullivan had asked.

I've seen it, the woman replied, and her guarded tone revealed a fan. Maybe, like so many of them, she adored Ash's Southern-boy good looks and Carolina accent; maybe she liked his oddball mix of traditional ghosthunting and off-the-wall tech-bro wankery. Or maybe, like so many others, she wanted something to believe in, no matter how dark.

Ashby Trenholm's my brother, and I grew up on that farm, Sullivan said. It would have been liberating if it weren't so nakedly horrible. *Everything that happens on his show? It's real, and it's worse than they show. Lightning strikes that place at least once a year, and the ghosts of enslaved people stand in the corners. They never speak.*

Thank God she'd believed it instead of locking him up.

When Sullivan's phone tolled, he knew. Childhood had left him with a sixth sense, or perhaps the mathematics were too simple. His father was dying; Ash would call when it ended. After a deep swallow of bourbon, Sullivan muted the TV, and his brother's UFO lecture dropped to silent mouthings.

"He's gone," Ash said when he picked up, no hello, no preamble.

"I know." Sullivan downed another slug of bourbon. It had ceased to burn.

"You're drunk, aren't you?" Ash asked. Sullivan pictured his brother in a suit jacket, pacing Cypress Bend's dimmed upper reaches. Tourists didn't see it, and it likely looked the same as Sullivan remembered, crossed sabers on gray walls, converted oil lamps atop antebellum tables. On television, Ash wore frat-boy khakis and a Gamecock polo shirt; he gestured at a screen in their father's old office. Sullivan's brother had stuffed it with tech, moved in an antebellum dining room table, and dubbed it "HQ."

"So what if I'm drunk?" Sullivan asked.

"You have to come home."

"I know."

"Where are you?" Ash probably asked so he could calculate times, distances.

"Don't worry about it." Sullivan sucked his bourbon like mother's milk. He might as well spend the afternoon drinking. Savannah wasn't far from Cypress Bend, that old house sunk in the swamp forest of Legare County, South Carolina, but Ash didn't need to know that. Sullivan hadn't seen his brother in ten years, at least in person. TV Ash pointed to a white speck on stilled surveillance footage. Noticeably larger and brighter than the stars, it didn't belong.

"You could at least tell me where you live." Pure Ash: that haughty tone, already aggrieved.

"You could at least accept my unwillingness to share that information, mostly so no tabloid reporters knock at my door."

Like he'd expected, Ash didn't answer.

"Uh-huh," Sullivan said. "You know exactly how I feel about it. I've been through enough hell." Sullivan drew another swig of liquor. "So, how's the media whore thing working out for you?"

"Don't." Ash sounded more tired than annoyed.

But for the first time in years, Sullivan had his brother on the phone, and he couldn't resist. "Haven't seen any real live ghosts on that paranormal whatsit yet. Do they still come, or are y'all too pussy to show more than those EMP-whatever recordings?" His accent thickened when he drank, and Savannah only encouraged it.

"Sullivan. You know some of the stuff is too messed up for primetime—"

"What about y'all's 'disc-shaped phenomenon?' I swear to God, Ash, if I took a shot every time you said 'disc-shaped phenomenon,' I'd be dead."

"That's rich coming from you."

The pointed viciousness sounded more like Olivia than Ash. Caught mid-swallow, Sullivan nearly choked. Liquor stung his throat, and for a long, sick moment, he shut up. "I'm surprised y'all can film at all," he said finally, honestly. Unexplained equipment failures and malfunctions plagued *Paranormal*. Anything electrical had a short life at Cypress Bend—phones failed, batteries corroded, appliances broke. Trenholms were used to it. "How often do the cameras break?"

"We manage," Ash snapped.

"What about lightning strikes? You have any of those lately?"

"Stop it." His brother sounded weary, as if he'd reconciled himself to a battering.

"When's the funeral?" Sullivan finally asked.

"Probably Saturday."

"I'll be up Friday." Somewhat viciously, he poked his phone and ended the call. Sullivan drew a long pull of liquor, collapsed on his couch, and wept.

CHAPTER 3

OLIVIA

When the three-note ringtone sounded, Olivia punched it off and excused herself from the Charleston cocktail party. The women were nodding flowers in pastel dresses; the men wore seersucker and bow ties. She felt fleeting regret for her brother Rhys, up in Virginia—Richmond held off liquor til an unimaginable eight p.m. Safe on the veranda, where Charleston's sea breezes would swallow her words, she tucked her blonde hair behind her ears, then redialed. "Henry?" she asked.

"He passed, Livy. I'm so sorry." Distance crackled Henry's voice. Legare County was a hundred miles and a world away from Charleston.

"It's fine, Christ. I knew it was going to happen, and it's not like I'm sad about it." Wind lifted her hair and ruffled whitecaps on the harbor. If she looked long enough, she'd spot dolphins. Tourists loved the dolphins. They didn't realize that Charleston Harbor teemed with sharks.

"When someone dies, you tell people you're sorry," Henry told her.

Trust Henry to say the polite thing. "What's Ash doing?"

"I think he's calling Sullivan. It just happened—I heard him telling the nurse. He hasn't even come down and told me yet."

Olivia weighed which questions to ask. She had too many of them, and Henry couldn't talk long. "Was Elliot there? I mean, when it happened?"

"No," he said. "She's on the patio with the parrots."

"Thank God." If she could trust anyone with Elliot, it was Ash, but she had to be sure.

"He wouldn't do that to her."

Olivia wanted to think that. She'd also wanted to believe that Ash would never bring in reality TV. It seemed so remote from that lovely city by the ocean, where she smelled sea-salt instead of swamp. "I'll pretend you didn't call," she told Henry.

"I know you will, or I wouldn't have called."

No one was on the veranda, but Olivia glanced around anyway. "I love you."

"I love you, too," Henry replied quietly. She hadn't expected him to answer and wondered where he was calling from. People bustled through Cypress Bend at odd times, especially since Ash opened it to tourists. Maybe he'd closed it off for the day. Olivia could picture Henry, seated in the library, laptop open on the desk, lean frame draped over a chair. His sandy hair would curl at those ends she could never play with in public; as he spoke, his blue eyes would scan the room, the doors, watching and watching until they settled on her and stayed. Olivia missed him so much tears almost rose.

"At least this means we'll see each other soon," she said. "Keep an eye on Elliot for me?"

"I always do, Livy. I'll see you soon." Henry clicked off. Olivia's fingers curled around the wrought-iron railing, warm in the summer sun. Scanning for sharks, she waited for Ash to call.

CHAPTER 4

RHYS

"Uncle Truluck passed," Rhys told his sister.

"I know," Olivia said. "Ash already told me."

Rhys almost laughed. Of course Ash had already called her. He liked her best, and only she still went home. She might have hated the cameras as much as him and Sullivan, but she loved Elliot.

"Did he say anything about Sullivan?" Rhys asked.

"Only that he's drunk." Olivia snorted, a somehow feminine sound. Everything about her was feline and languid as a hot day. Olivia carried herself like a perfect Southern lady; childhood had left her practiced in the art of pretense. They'd all come through it differently, Rhys decided, and not for the first time. Sullivan found solace in alcohol and art; Ash had faded into stage lighting. Rhys had emerged with genetic liver disease, with exhaustion and the looming terror of a transplant waiting ahead. His psychic damage remained untallied. If he dared ask, Sullivan could add it up. He was always best at that.

"When are you going down?" Olivia asked.

Rhys hesitated. He had research to do, and the funeral could soldier on without him. "I was thinking—"

"Don't you bitch out on me." Olivia could cuss better than any of them. "Ash says Sullivan's going up Wednesday. I know you want to see him, and you're not leaving me alone to watch those two snipe at each other."

Familiar misery clattered down. Rhys could delineate the Trenholm alliances and feuds better than anyone. Cypress Bend bent him into a flustered ambassador, always begging for a ceasefire. His uncle Truluck favored Sullivan with both his love and his fists; lingering childhood anguish set the brothers against one another. Left to themselves, Olivia and Sullivan would snark at each other like petulant children. Sullivan and Henry hadn't spoken in a dozen years.

Henry's tried, Rhys had told Sullivan over a French dinner in Richmond almost two years before, back when they spoke in more than memes and texts about the Murdaugh double murder trial.

I don't care, his cousin had snapped.

He's a phenomenal Black history scholar, Rhys had said. *He does his best to make up for it—*

Yeah, well, he can't, Sullivan had said. He'd swiped viciously at his mouth and shoved back a plate of steak frites. *He knows what he did.*

He does, Rhys had tried. *He knows—*

Then he knows that nothing he ever does can fix it, Sullivan had replied.

You know he was only a kid, Rhys had tried, stupidly, as if Sullivan might see reason on their childhood in general and Henry specifically.

Doesn't matter, Sullivan had said.

He was brainwashed, Rhys pressed, though he should have seen the warning signs in his cousin's tight expression, in his drawn-up mouth and outraged brow. *If you blame him for it, you have to blame us for the same thing. D'you remember getting drunk and singing "Dixie" on the barn roof with him? If you blame Henry for it, you have to blame us, too—*

His cousin had risen. Deliberately, he poured half a glass of expensive red down his throat; without a glance, he walked away. Ever since, they had spoken only in sporadic text messages. Though they might venture into friendliness, even jokes, they never touched anything real.

"You know the standard Trenholm will," Olivia continued. Rhys snapped back to his beloved antiques, his static-cracking call. "No funeral, no inheritance."

It hung between them, thick as smoke and just as noxious. Rhys hated to admit it: he needed that inheritance to pay for a liver transplant; a career as a PhD candidate and adjunct professor left him bereft of decent health insurance. With his uncle's money, he planned to buy good medical care, repay his student loans, then embark on a life of puttering academic research; he'd live out his days among history books and gracefully aged antiques. That inheritance would assure him a pain-free existence, then smooth life's sharp edges. After his childhood, he wanted peace, not flashing excess. "Look, it's not like I want to buy designer—"

"Yeah, but you still need the money." Olivia hesitated. "How are you feeling?"

Better to ignore the health inquiries then tell her the truth: meds cut the skin-itching common with his condition, but nothing could help his exhaustion and worry. The disease was progressing faster than his doctors had imagined. She knew that. Ash knew that, and Sullivan, too. There was no sense in discussing it. "You want the money as much as I do," Rhys said instead.

"I never said I didn't. You have to come—"

"I'm coming, I'm coming." Rhys flopped on his couch, a Victorian piece pillaged from a Richmond estate auction. All his pieces were pillaged, relics and histories that didn't belong to him. He haunted them like an uneasy ghost. "You wanna meet there Wednesday, too?"

"Call me when you hit the state line, and we'll get there at about the same time." Olivia paused, a silence that stretched too long. Rhys waited her out. "Are you scared?" she asked.

"No more than usual," he replied.

"Rhys." His sister's sharp laugh crackled through those long miles. "That isn't exactly encouraging."

He hung up and began packing in manageable stages, mindful of his energy. When his phone blipped about an hour later, he checked it. *Did Ash call you?* Sullivan asked.

Sullivan hadn't texted in two months. Rhys set it on the side table and dropped to his bed, a four-poster he'd scored for next to nothing from Virginia money gone to ruin. Dates often exclaimed over it. *I like your bed*, they'd coo as he took off their clothes. He met them in coffee shops and bars, where he drank non-alcoholic spirits slowly; he never called them back, and they never saw his beloved office, an anarchical kingdom of tattered books, file folders, and fountain pens.

Rhys stared at his cousin's name as if it might reveal some greater truth. They were best friends once. He could ignore the text. He could answer it.

Other than Ash and Olivia, he hadn't spoken to a soul in three days.

He dialed.

"Hey," Sullivan said, the first ring barely tolled. After so many benders, Rhys recognized that drawn-out, honeyed slur. Others might mistake it for a thick accent, but he knew better. In the morning, Sullivan wouldn't remember his call.

"You ready to go back?" Rhys asked. It was something to say—the only thing to say.

"Not really." His cousin drew a long, slow inhale. Either Sullivan had taken up cigarettes again, or he was smoking weed.

"Are you stoned?" Rhys couldn't help asking.

"Getting there. By the way, bring some of that legal Virginia weed down with you when you come, will you? I know you have a medical card. It's hard to get decent stuff down here."

Rhys glanced at his bubbler, smoothly modern, minimalist, designed by Snoop Dogg. He'd let his cousin provide the paraphernalia. "Henry will harass us for switching from bourbon to pot."

"Like I give a fuck what Henry thinks. If it pisses him off, all the better." Sullivan hit his joint again, then took a long swallow—alcohol, most likely.

"Give Henry a chance to—"

"Nope." There it was, that Trenholm stubbornness. Sometimes Rhys felt like he'd spent a lifetime battling it. But it was familiar, like a warm bath, nothing like Richmond's clamorous streets. *This is a real capital city*, he'd told Olivia when he moved. *I'm lost here.*

"At least keep the arguments where the rest of the clan can't see it, will you?" Rhys asked.

"I'm not going on camera. I swear to God I'm not." One more hit, one more pull. Sullivan would hit blackout territory soon.

"Now you're looking for things to snark over."

"I'll see you Wednesday," Sullivan said, and Rhys knew their conversation had ended. He'd hit too close, and his cousin had slammed the door.

Rhys tried one more sally. "You gonna see Talitha when you're home?"

"It was one night ten years ago," Sullivan said. "She doesn't wanna see me."

"But you talked to her for years, until you stopped calling—"

"I said she doesn't wanna talk to me." Sullivan spoke with the finality of a gloomy drunk, depressed and spiraling fast. "We hooked up the night I left. That's it. She felt bad for me. Look, I'll see you Wednesday, okay?" His cousin hung up and left Rhys to his packing.

Best cousins, everyone had called him and Sullivan when they were kids, as good as brothers: he had a picture of them at fifteen on his dresser, arms slung over each other's shoulders. Rhys stood an inch taller, with a slightly heavier build and straight hair instead of curls, but they still managed a family resemblance, something about their sharp features and dark eyes. Lately they'd only texted when Alex Murdaugh hit the news. Rhys never thought he'd be grateful for a double murder.

We should tell everyone we got drunk with Buster Murdaugh, Sullivan had messaged once. The murderer's surviving son was their age, or somewhere nearby; he'd gone to Wofford College in Spartanburg, and they'd never met him.

It's not true, Rhys had protested, but that never stopped his cousin. Sullivan spent at least an hour of his public debauches telling half-lies to anyone who would listen. People called him hilarious.

C'mon, Rhys, Sullivan had said. *We totally were at parties with Buster, even if we never talked. I'd recognize that red hair anywhere.*

You can't go around making up stuff.

Why not? Sullivan had asked. *All that matters is a good story. No one cares about the truth.*

There's a state motto, right there, Rhys had said. Sullivan sent back a row of laugh emojis. They reminded Rhys of his cousin on a good day, those crinkled eyes and scrunched nose. Rhys had a dissertation, a rising academic career, a string of one-night stands whose calls he never took again; he had a bum liver and a looming medical crisis. Rhys had no one. Maybe they could salvage something, him and Sullivan. It was a brittle chance, disintegrating as he seized on it.

Rhys clutched it tight.

CHAPTER 5

ASH

Ash moved the velvet rope, stepped beyond the plastic covering the rugs, then carefully replaced the barrier. Henry turned from the desk. "Your dad passed, then?" he asked.

"He passed." Ash dropped to a wingback chair. The dogs settled near his feet. As usual, the day's lethargy left Henry untouched. Ash would call someone to fix the air conditioner. During the calls to his brother and cousins, he'd neglected to mention its breakdown and felt only mildly guilty. It took no complex reckoning. They left. Ash employed every ragged scrap of blood relative and somehow broke even most years. He contented the tourists and kept archeologists from the door. It might have been morally indefensible—a plantation was a rich man's farm built with other people's blood; Ash ran one as a tourist attraction and wedding destination. But he was a Trenholm, and familial duty called. Ravening kin needed bread and board. When he was eleven, his father had seen Boone Hall down in Charleston and recognized a tattered family legacy as a windfall. They'd spent the rest of their childhood hiding from weddings and tourists, but their old people had decent nursing homes.

"Are the rest of them coming?" Henry asked.

"Yeah. Sullivan and Rhys, and Olivia too."

Henry finally shut his laptop, a clap too energetic for the drooping heat. "It's good of them to come. They don't have an ob—"

"They grew up here, same as me." Ash sat up straighter. "They have every obligation."

The sandy-haired man bit into an orange slice. He seemed to concentrate, as if the fruit demanded his whole attention. "Say what you want about your father," he said after he finished, "but it was good of him to take Rhys and Olivia when your uncle Simmons died. He didn't have to."

"What was he supposed to do, with his father and uncle and all the rest living here? Let them starve in the streets?" The house had echoed with relatives once. Only his Great-Aunt Alda and his uncle Wade's daughter remained. Like Ash, both disliked Truluck Trenholm, and they kept to their own rites. Dementia and inertia left Aunt Alda haunting her rooms, a delicate wisp of a ghost still living. Ash's first cousin Elliot spent most of her time on the patio with her father's parrots; though Uncle Wade died three years before, his squawking legacy persisted. That death had tumbled Ash into an uneasy parenthood. Mostly, he played big brother to the fifteen-year-old and hoped.

"Your daddy could've left Rhys and Olivia with their mama's people," Henry said. "A lesser man might've."

The Trenholms didn't do that, and the man next to him knew it better than anyone. While Ash could accuse his family of a multitude of sins, they never failed to take up bedraggled relatives. "I don't care what my father did or didn't do. He's dead." Ash shoved up from the chair, and an earthenware pot at his elbow rattled. There was no use talking to Henry. "I'll be in the office."

"You mean HQ?" Henry asked.

One day he would snap under the weight of familial obligation. One day, he would unleash a string of blistering invectives at Henry, every curse he'd ever learned. It wouldn't matter. Nothing could shock Henry, not since Ash had known him, and nothing ever would.

Dogs padding soundlessly behind, Ash passed through the stairwell and into a room of computers and screens, bookshelves and electronics. An enormous bulletin board stretched over one wall. Full of hand-scrawled notes, printouts, and blurry photos, it resembled something from a conspiracy theorist rathole. The motion-sensors had several hits, and Ash scrolled through them. Nothing—nothing—nothing. No reason to call his co-executive producer, though Ethan ought to know about his father. Ash fished out his phone.

"Hey, Ash," Ethan said. "You got something for me?"

"I wish." Ash lifted his damp shirt from his back. There was no easy way to say it. "My father died this afternoon."

Silence. He couldn't expect much. Californians were allergic to death. "Sorry to hear it," Ethan finally replied.

"Just thought you ought to know. Planning purposes, not that he was ever on the show, but—"

"It's the off-season, but I'll make the call—let's film it," Ethan said. "Family dynamics and all. That place always reacts to high emotion. Who knows what might happen?"

Gardens spread behind the house, all that Italianate statuary. The azaleas were wilting. He'd call the air conditioner guy next. "My brother and cousins will lose their minds. They won't agree to appear—"

"If they won't sign the waivers, we won't film them." Ash could almost hear the producer shrug. "Easy. We keep Elliot out of it, and God knows she'd slam ratings through the roof, I've told you over and over—"

Ash caught himself scanning the sky, an old habit, and turned his back to the window. It prickled his spine. "I told you, we're not putting Elliot on camera."

"Hey, hey, I was just saying." That old excuse again: Ethan would be holding his hands up like a victim in an old Western. He said what he meant, then backed off when his audience disapproved. Ash hated Californians. One day, an ocean would swallow the whole goddamn state, and they were too arrogant to build an ark.

"Yeah, well, you'll have to work around them—it would take something a whole lot stronger than your contracts to get them to consent to filming. I'll call when I have arrangements, but it should be a few days, give or take." Ash hung up. The motion sensors pinged at nothing again, and he stalked away. He would alert the rest of his personal bedlam. He would call the air conditioner guy, and he would tell Amelia, his first cousin once removed, to make up the bedrooms. The world soldiered onward. Ash would follow wherever it led.

CHAPTER 6

SULLIVAN

In the early hours of Wednesday morning, Sullivan dreamed of the three men.

The sun was going down over Cypress Bend's swamp, a whole sky shoaling into pinks and oranges behind a cobwebbing of clouds. Planted on the patio railing, Sullivan's hands slowly dissolved to nothing, and he was powerless to stop it. All of him disappeared, piece by piece, until he was nothing at all but awareness, then the three identical men walked through the rioting garden in lockstep unison, as if every gesture were choreographed and staged. They stretched too tall, too thin, monochrome against the sunset, and their old-fashioned clothes seemed to come from no era in particular. Slow grins spread across their faces.

We are time and we are always the same, they said, eerie voices echoing together. *Welcome home, Sullivan.*

He slammed awake, sweat soaked and biting back a scream. The dream was old, but the men's greeting—that was new, and it frightened him most of all.

Sullivan peeled himself out of bed, packed, and left at noon. As he drove inland, the sea breezes stopped. Aside from highway noise, I-95's corridor of loblolly pines seemed motionless, a world enervated into silence. His father was dead. Sullivan felt no grief for the man himself, but a wrenching sadness for the parent he never had. Other men talked about their dads as friends, confidantes, teachers. *I memorized Southern history,* Sullivan could have said. *I learned about the War of Northern Aggression and the grand Lost Cause. When my father wasn't lecturing us about history, he taught me that the world sees weakness and breaks it.* Exits passed, their names heavy with skirmishes fought, towns settled, blood shed. Too many carried history, ancestral or personal. Sullivan took the worst of them, the one that led him home.

His hangover rolled like a storm-tide. On a sheerly visceral level, Cypress Bend terrified him. It terrified most sane people, though Ash had armed some cousins to deal with trespassers and called them security detail. *Why do they try to break in?* he'd asked Olivia the last time they'd spoken.

They want to believe in something, she'd replied. Olivia had come down to Savannah to see some boyfriend or another. Sullivan had managed a single dinner at Husk, and the four-star food clumped his mouth like wet sand.

There's better things to believe in than that goddamn place, he replied.

Yeah. Well. Olivia dabbed her lips. *You say that, but we grew up with it. We never doubted there was something else out there.*

You mean we never had the luxury of disbelief, Sullivan told his cousin. *And I'd take that over any of the bullshit we lived with.*

Olivia went quiet. She pleaded social obligation—something she'd forgotten until that very moment—and fled.

Sullivan turned up his own front drive and stopped before a shiny steel barrier. He hadn't seen home since his twenty-first birthday. He'd resolved to run that night, but Talitha Merle cemented it. *It's not good for anyone there,* she'd told him, *least of all you.* Sullivan decided to call her. He'd welcome the sex, but he needed her plain acceptance.

He rolled down his window, and a pale man peered from the new brick gatehouse. Sullivan didn't recognize him, but inevitably, they were related. "What can I help you with today, sir?" the guy asked. "Just you? General admission to everything, including a guided antebellum house tour, our cultural history, hayride tours, and—"

Sullivan fished out his wallet. Rather than a credit card, he dropped his license on the narrow tray.

The man glanced at the license. "Sullivan? Jesus, you came home. I'm so sorry." He disappeared from the window. A side door opened, and the big man squeezed next to his Tesla. "I'm so sorry," he said again, scooping through the window, and Sullivan hugged him. Ten years swallowed memory, but he was a Trenholm, and the prodigal son had returned to the fold.

"Ash didn't tell us you were coming," the man said, drawing back. "Lord, you probably don't remember me. I half don't remember you. I'm Houston. My mama's Terrance's Grace."

"I remember now," Sullivan said, placing his second cousin, a chubby-cheeked boy with thick glasses. "How's your brother John?"

A smile bloomed on Houston's cheeks. "He's good. Graduated veterinary school last year. He's setting up a practice here in Lower Congaree. Got two little girls. I got a boy of my own." He reached for his wallet, then stopped. "You get on up to Ash. Stop back here when you get a chance though, y'hear?"

"I will." Sullivan clapped him on the shoulder. He meant it. Cypress Bend bred its own horrors, but cousins had never been one of them, no matter what he was asked to give for them. "Have a good day, Houston."

A quarter-mile up, Sullivan rounded a turn and nearly hit a vehicle stopped in the middle of his driveway. Sullivan rolled down his window again. "Can you move?" he called.

A wall-eyed woman in a flowered shirt lowered her phone. She and her husband were identically corn fed and unlovely; two kids sat in the back. Who the hell brought kids to Cypress Bend? But Ash had set up hayrides. The petting zoo hadn't lasted, but he heard kids loved the enormous swamp gators. "We're taking pictures. Wait your turn."

Of course they wanted shots of the Avenue of Oaks, once famed for its beauty, recently recognized from a lingering shot in a synth-laden theme song. "I live here!" Sullivan said. "Will you move so I can get up my own driveway?"

The woman threw him a glare etched with pity. "You're not Ash."

"No! I'm his brother!" As if to insist on his family resemblance, Sullivan leaned farther out the window, though he shared only his brother's dark hair, dark eyes, and medium height. His hair curled. His nose pointed. He seemed more likely to sulk through the woods with a bow than play the handsome prince. Men adored Sullivan; women played with his hair. His brother looked like a storybook hero, and women flung themselves at his feet. Ash was oblivious, or maybe he didn't care. Sullivan could never decide.

The man barely glanced at Sullivan. "Ash doesn't have a brother."

Hungover, sandy eyed, Sullivan fished his wallet from his back pocket and flipped it open. "You see the name on this license? T-R-E-N-H-O-L-M. Lemme in or get the hell off my property."

The man glared; slowly, he climbed in the car, turned it over, and pulled over just enough for Sullivan to squeak by. "You didn't need to be an asshole about it!"

This was all Ash's fault. His father had opened the farm to weddings and private tours. Ash had flung the doors wide and built a gift shop. Last time Sullivan looked, his brother charged twenty-nine fifty for admission, which included an antebellum house tour, a cultural history talk, tours of the Black History exhibits, hayrides, a gator trail, and a garden stroll. The petting zoo had gone under long ago. The cattle mutilations might have been supernatural, but they cost real money.

Sullivan gunned it up the drive. Afraid of what he'd see, he looked neither left nor right, ignoring the live oaks arched into a vaulted ceiling above. They hid rolling tobacco fields, an even six hundred acres of them. His daddy had been proud of that number. Beyond them, the dark-gray swamp brooded. Despite the heat roiling through his open window, Sullivan shivered. When Sherman's troops had marched on Columbia, his scouts had refused to walk through that dense, dark cypress-tangle. Determined, the general sent a contingent anyway. They never returned. People swore something lurked in that swamp, something old and dark and dangerous. Whatever it was, it had swallowed the Trenholm farm whole.

Cars clumped in front of the Barn, a redone cotton shed designed as party space. They were hanging Chinese lanterns. Sullivan hoped the bride's parents had shelled out for mobile air conditioners. The barn alone rented for six thousand dollars; a full wedding package could run as much as ten thousand—more with kickbacks to Columbia hotels and caterers. Between the Barn, the Gardens, and the Pavilion, Ash was likely throwing two events every Thursday, Friday, and Saturday night. It would slow when wedding season eased off, but for all its atrocious history, Cypress Bend was their goldmine. His brother was determined to strip it bare.

At least Ash had never opened the back field to tourists, though they snapped photos through its chain-link fence. Two hundred yards behind the house, four enormous cypresses grew so close that their trunks touched. A strange glyph marked each trunk of what the Trenholms had always called, for reasons lost to time, the Boundary Tree—to them, those trees were a single entity. When Sullivan researched those marks, back when he was determined to explain the farm's strangeness, he discovered that they matched the triple-spiral motif at Newgrange, Ireland's famous Neolithic passage tomb. Beneath those trees, strange blue orchids bloomed; in two centuries of searching, no Trenholm had yet pinpointed their genus or species. They seemed to be found nowhere else on planet Earth.

More bizarre than any flowers, however, the family regularly found earthenware pottery piled at the cypresses' base, as if someone had placed it during the night. They'd found worse there; Sullivan shoved that thought away. Ash had never discussed those findings on the show, and thank God for it. It was one of their father's original commandments, and he'd never broken it.

Nor had he discussed the Meeting Oak, a massive tree with limbs stretched like a creeping spider. Tucked behind what his father had dubbed the "slave cabins," it was over three hundred years old. The Trenholms had burnt a Union deserter beneath it. *Weren't they worried the tree would catch fire?* Sullivan had asked his father once.

If they were, they didn't much care, his father had said.

Sullivan rounded the mazy turn toward the house. A stand of cypress and live oak obscured the south field, torn up long ago for parking. After it came the Ivorybill Café and Gift Shop. An American flag drooped from its flagpole; Sullivan's father had insisted on it. At least his brother no longer flew the Stars and Bars.

Sullivan stopped at the front gardens. Let them try to tow him. For a moment, he gazed at the house, a four-story columned monstrosity, which the National Historic Registry called a "Federalist treasure." Sullivan could recite its history like a nursery rhyme. In 1790, Ashby Trenholm, the youngest son of a Virginia planter, had Cypress Bend's land cleared for tobacco cultivation. In 1820, his son St. George visited Richmond, where he attended a party at John Wickham's house. Designed by Alexander Parris, it was regarded as the day's best neoclassical architecture. "There's nothing Richmond does that we can't do better," Sullivan's father would say, drawing on his pipe. "So St. George hired Parris and demanded that he build another Wickham House."

But Lower Congaree's water table permitted no basement; the house was to lie in a maze of gardens, not a busy city street. Eventually, Parris shoved the whole thing above ground, reversed the front and back facades, stuck porches on the back, and washed his hands of what he called "the mad Trenholms." Nearly two hundred years later, the white plantation house still stood, impervious to the ravages of war, hurricanes, human bondage, and tourism. Sullivan stepped into the rose garden. He might as well get it over with.

At the porch's far end, a small, dark boy with a broom was sweeping, sweeping, his tattered tunic the same worn gray as a winter sky. *He's not real,* Sullivan reminded himself. *He isn't there. He's a memory.* Only the Trenholms seemed to see him and the others like him, or maybe only certain Trenholms—Sullivan could never be sure. Mentioning those silent shades was the surest way to summon his father's wrath.

Ash opened the front door as promptly as if he'd been peeping through the front windows. Maybe Houston had called up from the gate.

"Thank you for coming," he said. Four German Shepherds trailed his brother; after three seasons of *Paranormal Gone South,* Sullivan could have called them by name.

"Hi," Sullivan replied, like he'd planned. If his brother saw the small boy, he gave no sign. *Look at him,* Sullivan wanted to scream, but Cypress Bend's strongest rule held. What could Ash offer, anyway? *Don't you talk about them,* his father had snapped when Sullivan was small, his open palm a sharp crack against his son's cheek. *Don't you ever mention them. You give them power when you do, and I won't have it in my house, y'hear me?*

"Sullivan?" A teenager with elbow-length blonde hair drifted from the house, and Sullivan was startled to recognize his baby cousin Elliot. Freshwater pearl bracelets circled her wrists; necklaces dangled against her crocheted top. She looked like a refugee from 1969.

"Elliot?" Sullivan asked. "You grew up."

"People do that, I guess." Slow-blinking and dreamy, she studied him. The dogs left Ash and crowded at her side. Elliot had been a surprise. Uncle Wade had never married; Sullivan and Rhys had always presumed his bachelorhood was the euphemistic kind. But like his brothers, the old man had proven startlingly virile in his dotage. When he'd taken up with their ninth-grade history teacher, Sullivan and Rhys fought three kids for mouthing off about the family. When he came home with newborn Elliot a year later, everyone whispered that the teacher had delivered a secret baby, that the Trenholms had paid her an unholy sum of money for the child and even more cash to leave town. *If we punch them, they'll know it's true,* Rhys had said, so he and Sullivan ignored them.

But Elliot ginned up darker fears. *The ghost told us she'd come,* Sullivan had dared once. *She said—*

I don't wanna talk about the ghost, Rhys snapped, and Sullivan never mentioned it again. Instead he shoved those worries deeper, and when they bubbled up again, he knew better than to mention them.

Ash was saying something, and Sullivan jerked back to the porch, the heat, the thick-sweet scent of roses. He spared a glare for the slow-moving clot of people wandering from the parking lot. The small boy had not looked up, as if determined to spend an eternity sweeping. "Let's go inside?" Sullivan said. "We don't want your adoring fans to see too much. Anyway, it's sweltering out here."

Ash stood with his hands in his pockets, gazing over Cypress Bend. He reminded Sullivan of a prince on his balcony, royalty surveying the realm. "The guys are working on the air now."

"What?" Sullivan prayed his brother didn't mean what he suspected, but his shirt looked sweat-sticky.

"The air conditioning," Elliot said, as if it hardly mattered. "But it's still cooler in the house."

"Okay. I'm staying in Columbia." Willing himself not to flee immediately, Sullivan slid his phone from his back pocket and followed them inside. As they passed through the foyer, he caught himself, sweaty and rumpled, in the enormous mirror. Sullivan looked once, then looked away.

He'd last seen the house ten years before. Vegas-swirled carpet covered the spit-shined hardwoods he remembered, and the garishly wallpapered walls had been stripped and painted in pinks and peaches, then striped with pastel borders. The fireplace mantles, something like miniature Greek temples, were likely reconstructed and certainly hideous. Most clichéd of all, Ash had replaced the curtains; Scarlett O'Hara could have whipped them into a ball gown.

The heavy antebellum furniture hadn't changed. Neither had the Indian pottery. In the Trenholm house, priceless earthenware artifacts were common as paperweights. No one spoke of them, or how they appeared under those cypresses, perfect and intact, shiny as the day they'd been fired.

Don't you talk about that pottery, his father had said once. *If archeologists find out about it, the government will steal this farm and dig it up.*

Above every lintel, on the walls, atop the mantles, the swords also remained. Sullivan hated them, and hated their story more. When he was ten, the State Archives had junked ninety-eight rusted Confederate sabers. His father, head Civil War Archivist, had absconded with them all. After two years of shining, he'd slung them through every room in Cypress Bend—reminders, he'd said, of what the world wanted to forget. They lent the place a strangely martial air. *We'll be ready when the revolution comes*, Sullivan used to think. He'd never questioned which one.

"Why don't we sit on the patio?" Ash asked. "Amelia or McKayla could bring us sweet tea."

"As long as tours still skip it." Sullivan could watch Uncle Wade's parrots while he scrolled for hotels. "What'd you do with all those cypress hardwoods?"

"We laid down the replica of a carpet from the 1830s," Ash replied. "We got a historical preservation grant from the state."

Sullivan looked at the carpet. He looked at his brother. "You laid down the replica of a carpet from the fucking Luxor."

Ash cleared his throat loudly and obviously. "Sorry, Elliot," Sullivan said.

"Oh, I don't mind," she told him. "Boys say so much worse these days."

They passed through the central room, with its curving staircase, and into what used to be the den. He and his cousins had played Confederate Assassin there once, watched TV and lounged in a domain their father rarely entered. Ash had redone it as an undoubtedly historical ladies' parlor. Small signs ordered visitors to not sit on the furniture. Sullivan paused before the velvet-rope barrier. How did they keep people from digging through their drawers? "Do you let everyone use the bathrooms, too?" Sullivan asked.

"No, we built new ones where the storerooms used to be." Ash kept walking, straight as a soldier. "Before you start complaining, I'm happy to show you how much we make on tours."

"Nothing's worth Vegas rugs on the floor and tearing up your house," Sullivan replied. "Not to mention that you're making money off *plantation tours—*"

"Oh, we don't mind," Elliot said. Dogs padded at her sides. "People are mostly nice."

Ash whirled. For a moment, he seemed close to snatching Sullivan's shirt, but glanced at Elliot and drew back. "I keep upward of fifty people employed and insured." He spoke with their father's quietly dangerous tone. "Every single one is related to us, including some Black cousins Dad never acknowledged. I include as much Black history as I can while keeping profits high enough to maintain said employment. If I get too so-called 'woke,' I'll have protesters up and down the highway and our income will tank. I do every single thing I can to take care of this family, including this goddamn reality show, which lets me hire at least twenty more full-time people. *Twenty more,* Sullivan, and that doesn't count part time. So take your morality and shove it up your ass." Ash walked on as if he hadn't spoken.

Stunned to silence, Sullivan offered nothing; his father's voice shuttered rational thought. His heart beat in his fingers, and his body waited for a blow that wouldn't come. Ash was right. It didn't matter. Sullivan couldn't summon words.

"I know about Henry," Elliot said, half-turning as she passed through the patio doors. "You don't have to worry about that."

"How—" Why would Ash burden a child with that? They'd all sworn—

"Aunt Alda mentioned it to her," Ash said when she left. "She thought Elliot was Olivia."

"So who all knows now? You, me, Rhys, Olivia, Elliot, and Aunt Alda? Is that all?" Sullivan's therapist was also on that list, but he wouldn't admit it, and she probably didn't believe him anyway. "And Elliot knows not to say anything?" His feelings for Henry were complicated at best, but Trenholms didn't betray each other, no matter how distant.

Ash laughed, one short, sharp bark. "I trust her more than I trust the rest of you." He opened the patio doors. The arbor's Confederate jasmine had thickened, and its sweet scent clung to the damp air. His uncle's parrots clustered in potted lemon trees. Shooing a parrot from a clawed rattan chair, Sullivan sat. Henry nodded from across the table. They hadn't spoken more than a curt hello in a dozen years. Sullivan managed a nod back and angled his chair away from the table. He didn't dare turn his back to the gardens.

"Where's Aunt Alda?" Sullivan asked. "I thought she'd be back here."

Ash sunk a little deeper into his chair. "She's not well."

"How bad is she?" Sullivan said.

"She doesn't leave her room much," his brother replied, an unhelpful answer.

Sullivan sagged a bit. A tough old bird, his own grandmother had been prone to telling people that what didn't kill them made them stronger. Aunt Alda cooed instead. Always in a straw hat and gloves, she'd spent Sullivan's childhood puttering among the roses. Old age had reduced her to sweet confusion. He'd loved her best, but he never called her. She might have asked him to come home.

The world sunk into heat-soaked somnolence. Far away, some cousins, both Black and white, were stringing garden lanterns. One more time, Sullivan wondered how those Black cousins could stand to return—they worked at the site of their ancestors' enslavement, for and with the descendants of people who perpetrated those crimes. Plenty of Black cousins refused to speak to Trenholms who worked at Cypress Bend. *I understand*, Sullivan had always wanted to tell them. *I'd hate us too.*

Elliot chattered at a macaw. Henry ate fruit. Sullivan nodded in the right places and surfed for hotels. He would attend the funeral and run. He would never return. He didn't want to meet old ghosts, and maybe that lassitude was the farm holding its breath before it loosed something more suited to nightmare than daylight. Rhys and Olivia would come, and he would flee to a hotel. Maybe Rhys would go with him. He and Rhys and Henry had been best friends once; they drank on rooftops and sang "Dixie." He hated himself for it.

A howl went up, and the parrots screamed. Sullivan wrenched up from his phone as the dogs darted under the tables. "Excuse me," Ash said, as if it was normal for four German Shepherds to suddenly cower. Elliot baby-talked the dogs, and shakily, Sullivan stood, scanning the sky, the gardens, and the house behind. Nothing had changed, and he couldn't decide if that was worse or better. Animals always knew. At Cypress Bend, when dogs fled, something terrible had happened. It was a warning, a bellwether. Henry's face betrayed nothing.

Ash passed inside as if he were going to ask for more tea. Sullivan hurried after him. Like hell would he stand out there. He'd seen it too many times. Fumbling, he checked his phone. It had died with a full charge.

Ash strode through the redone den, up the stairs to their father's old office, familiar from each episode of *Paranormal Gone South*. It seemed strange to see the space, part of his childhood house, as if he'd stepped into a TV set. "My phone's dead," Sullivan told him, as if his brother would care.

"Lemme hit the motion sensors," Ash said, and clicked a few buttons. "What—there were no horses in that field. The groom knows to keep them out of it. What was it doing—"

Sullivan pushed close to the computer.

"We haven't had one in years," Ash told him. "I swear to God we haven't."

Sullivan glanced once, then immediately averted his eyes. A Thoroughbred lay on the summer-brown grass, neatly eviscerated.

CHAPTER 7

RHYS

Rhys rang the bell several times. No one answered. Finally, he called Ash. "I'm at your front door," he said.

"Who the hell is that?" Sullivan asked in the background.

"It's Rhys," Elliot replied. How she knew that from the patio, Rhys couldn't guess—that happened with Elliot sometimes. "He's here."

Ash sighed like a man of tattered patience. "I'll send someone to get you."

A few minutes later, the lock clicked, and Elliot opened the door. Rhys hadn't seen her since her father's funeral, just before the reality show began. "Hi, Rhys," she said, as if they'd parted at breakfast. "Ash and Sullivan are fighting on the patio." She wandered away, Ash's shepherds tagging behind.

Sullivan was shouting. If he didn't shut up, tourists would start recording, then posting and reposting, ginning up Trenholm family gossip. *I was at Cypress Bend the other day, and I heard. . .* On the back patio, Uncle Wade's parrots squawked in the trees; Henry watched Sullivan as if he were a mildly interesting film. All that angry gesticulation seemed to expend too much energy in the wet-damp heat. "What the hell is this?" Rhys asked his cousins.

"Talk to him." Sullivan jabbed a finger toward Ash, an accusation or denial. No gray laced his dark curls, and his eyes narrowed with something between rage and fear. He still looked somewhere around twenty-five.

"There was an—incident," Ash said.

"One of the horses was mutilated!" Sullivan gestured as if Ash had personally eviscerated the animal. "The dogs went nuts, then whatever motion-sensor setup he's got went off. Same as always—slit open, perfect incision, no blood. There wasn't a lightning strike beforehand, but other than that? Exactly the same as when we were kids. I dealt with it for twenty-one years, and I swear to God I won't deal with it again."

The back door opened. Rhys expected Elliot, but a man in coveralls appeared. "Mister Trenholm?" he said. "Fixed it. Blown capacitor." He paused, seemed to measure whatever family drama was playing out, then thought better of mentioning it. "If you could do us a favor and lock up your dogs next time? They're real big, and we can't deal with 'em."

"What d'you mean?" Ash asked. "The dogs have been with me or Elliot the whole time. We didn't want them bothering you."

"I don't mean those shepherds. I'm talking about the big black one of yours? Gotta be scaring all the people you got around here. He kept running by while we were working. Huge thing. What breed is he?"

"If you come inside, I'll grab my card." Ash spoke as if he didn't hear the question.

"There is no black dog, is there?" Rhys asked when they left.

"It's starting again," Sullivan said, dropping to a chair like a man felled by emotion too enormous to bear. Grateful, exhausted from the long drive down from Richmond, Rhys sagged next to him. Parrots settled in the lemon trees, and the world returned to cicada-filled laziness. "I knew it would if I came back, but I was stupid enough to do it anyway, and—"

"You had to come back," Rhys said. "You have to go to the funeral. You couldn't have—"

"I could have," Sullivan replied. Rhys had heard that defeat in his voice too many times. Far away, the gardeners set out folding chairs. Once again, Rhys wondered what insanities drove people to marry at Cypress Bend. They'd certainly seen Ash's show. Maybe they, like the tourists, were grasping at their possible fifteen minutes. The audience loved a bride whimpering that UFOs had ruined her wedding.

"You had to come back," Henry said, drawing Rhys back to their familial drama. "You couldn't do anything else."

"Don't," Sullivan replied. "You don't belong here. You're not helping."

"Lay off Henry," Rhys said. "He can't help being here. You think he doesn't want to go home?"

"I don't know!" Sullivan shot back, and the parrots flapped again. "Maybe he doesn't! It's better here! We have air conditioning, and—"

"Not last night," Henry said. Sullivan was right; Henry didn't belong, but no one could change it. One more time, Rhys wished they would all shut up and live in peace. Maybe then the farm would stop its sudden veers into the unearthly. He'd explained it over and over—the more they fought, the more unreality intruded. No one listened.

He and Sullivan and Henry had been inseparable once. One bleary July day when Rhys and Sullivan were sixteen, Henry somewhere around seventeen, depending how time counted, they'd hidden behind the barn with his Uncle Truluck's best cigars. Rhys had choked on the drowning smoke, but Henry puffed like an old man.

I'm leaving one day, Sullivan had said. *I'm going to college, and I'm never coming back to the fucking place.*

Henry blew a smoke ring. *If you both leave, what'll I do?*

Come with us, Sullivan told him.

Henry gazed over those long tobacco fields, maybe cursed and maybe something less, or more. *I can't do that,* he'd said finally. *It's not my world out there, Sullivan.*

Well, but— Sullivan started.

Henry drew a long puff on the cigar, held it, then let it go. *You ever seen the Milky Way?*

Huh? Rhys remembered feeling the oddness of that question, how it had seemed such a conversational veer that he didn't understand, at first, what Henry had said.

I said, you ever seen the Milky Way? Henry asked.

I mean, I don't know," Rhys said. *I guess?*

Then you never have, Henry told him. He leaned against the barn's old wood and stared into the sun going down over that cypress swamp. *You know I thought something terrible had happened when I first came, 'cause I looked up at the sky and all the stars had disappeared. The moon was too dull and the stars were all gone. And you don't know how loud it is. The world's so loud, y'all. Always some plane or car or hum or something going off. You can't hardly hear yourself think. Sometimes I want to clap my hands over my ears and cry. And the birds are gone. Where did all the birds go?*

Huh? Sullivan asked.

Used to be you couldn't sleep past dawn 'cause of the birdsong. He watched the far line of cypresses beyond the tobacco fields, and his eyes shone too bright. *Y'all have no idea what you lost, and you never will. This isn't my world. I could leave here, I guess. But I'd have to see how much worse it is out there, and I'm scared it'd break me.*

Sullivan had rested a hand on his shoulder. *I'm sorry,* he said, voice thick. *Were there really more birds?*

Henry pressed his lips together tight and didn't answer.

He'd never wavered. There he'd landed, by chance or otherwise, and years later, there he stayed. Henry reminded Sullivan of the conglomeration of weirdness surrounding the farm, whether familial, paranormal, or historical. Time had mired them into something like hate.

Years later, on that patio, Henry rested a hand on Sullivan's back. He didn't jerk away, and Henry's hand stayed, a frail, breakable connection. Maybe Sullivan couldn't bear to shrug him off.

CHAPTER 8

SULLIVAN

Skulking behind Rhys, Sullivan watched Olivia arrive with apologies about non-existent traffic. In tastefully expensive jewelry, Jackie O sunglasses holding back her streaked hair, she still looked like a Gamecock sorority sister. Elliot hugged her tight. With that poise she maintained even amid fantastic disaster, Olivia kissed Ash's cheek, then her brother's and Henry's. She studied Sullivan. "It's been a while," she said to him. "A year?"

"Something like that," he replied, avoiding once more his own reflection in that mammoth mirror, which Ash had flanked with tourist brochures and maps. Tacky.

Cousins carried in her luggage, far more than she ought to need for a few days, but Olivia always overpacked. When a knock struck the front door, everyone but Elliot jumped.

"Who else is coming?" Sullivan asked.

"No one," his brother replied. "The tour starts in fifteen minutes."

Sullivan bit back any snark that rose. They could argue about it later.

The house had cooled by dinner, fried chicken laid on Limoge. Candles flushed the dimming twilight to orange and yellows; somewhere, the air conditioner murmured. Silver scraped plates, and Elliot laughed about the parrots' dislike for their gardeners. Aunt Alda nodded along, though she likely didn't know what they were talking about. A tall, dark-skinned man in full velvet livery stood next to the mantle. Tray in hand, he gazed unseeing into the middle distance. He'd waited there ever since Sullivan could remember.

When people sat in the dining room long enough, a merciless but inexplicable ache settled into their arms and backs—the closer to the mantle, the worse the ache.

Worst of all, despite his dark skin, the man's features twinned Henry's. Sullivan hated to think about what those identical faces meant.

Who's the man in the corner of the dining room? Sullivan had asked Aunt Alda when he was small.

He's one of the people who lived here before, like the girl on the back porch or the woman in the kitchen sometimes, she'd told him.

Why won't he talk to me? Sullivan persisted. He'd spent half the morning making faces at the man, who ignored him.

They never speak, Aunt Alda said. *They're shadows of what was here once, not the people themselves. Those souls are long gone.*

But who were they? he'd asked.

She'd pressed her lips together. *Here, let's go look at the roses,* she'd told him.

"So tell us about that portal," Sullivan said to his brother eventually. "I mean, your 'disc-shaped phenomenon.'"

"I'd rather not talk about—"

"You talk about it enough on TV. And say 'disc-shaped phenomenon' enough." Mickie, their first cousin once removed, fried chicken that demolished the competition at Lower Congaree's annual Firefly Festival. Sullivan pushed his plate back anyway.

"Let's have a quiet dinner." Rhys, who begged him not to leave Henry, who argued that he shouldn't abandon his father, who pleaded for him to sacrifice his life for the greater family cause. Rhys, the perpetual peacemaker, always caught in the middle. Sullivan loved and hated him as purely as a brother, though he didn't know what to make of him since his return. Were they still best cousins? Or were they distant relatives again, doomed to speak only when familial tragedy forced them together? He'd take it as it came and hope Rhys forgave him for his distance. He'd tried to save himself. It hadn't worked.

"Let's talk about it later—" Ash started.

"No, let's talk about it now," Sullivan said.

"Sullivan, no one wants to discuss it." Olivia had somehow managed to cut her fried chicken. "Don't be a prick about this. Your father just died."

"What d'you do in Savannah, Sullivan?" Elliot raised her voice somewhat louder than she had to. "Ash never said."

He hadn't meant to upset his little cousin. Sullivan opened his mouth to apologize as footsteps crashed like gunfire, and a man in black dashed into the candlelight. For a gasped second, Sullivan suspected an apparition, possibly a deranged tourist, then he recognized the rangy, bland-faced man as Boo, Ash's head of security and their second cousin once removed. That semi-automatic rifle rode in his back holster during every episode of *Paranormal Gone South*.

"Ash," he said, "the wedding's setting off fireworks in the garden."

Ash dropped his napkin and dashed out, dogs behind. Curious, terrified, Sullivan followed. Ash and Boo raced out the patio door, startling the parrots to sleepy squawking, then pounded into the garden. Their feet crunched on pebbled paths, and dust puffed as fireworks popped behind the sprawling white pavilion.

"Quit it!" Ash shouted as they approached. His chest heaved; Sullivan thanked morning runs for his own wind. "For the love of God, stop it if you want to keep *any* of your deposit!"

"Why are you freaking out about some fireworks?" Sullivan asked, half-sick with it. He already knew. He should have stayed in the house, safe.

"That's how we summon the phenomena!" Boo said. "Don't you watch your own brother's show?"

If he hadn't been packing a gun, Sullivan might have decked him.

"Shit." Boo pointed. A purple light the size of a basketball skimmed the treetops, then fell from view. "That's not good."

"It's just an orb," Sullivan said, hating himself for it. Others goggled at orbs, torn between awe and terror; they bolted, shook, evaluated cosmologies. Sullivan was seven before he realized they were strange.

Music cut abruptly; confused chatter burbled. Behind the pavilion, Ash shouted plosive curses. Apologies rose. The night seemed far too quiet, and Sullivan took a moment to place it—the cicadas had stopped. No tree frogs sang. As a child, he'd have realized immediately, and he'd have run.

A high, pure scream cut the silence. Boo cursed quietly and bolted. Sullivan resisted the urge to look up. Somewhere in the sky, a light would be tracking too fast. It would lack a plane's red and green navigation lights, and its flight would trace patterns no satellite could manage. It would hover, reverse, swoop through impossible turns. It would make no sound. The wedding guests would point at it. They'd aim their phones and shout, and the UFO would have hardly winked out when they messaged Ash's tipline. If she was beautiful, the bride would make the show—*Paranormal Gone South* loved red-eyed brides in wedding dresses. The groom would pat her hand and nod while she told viewers that UFOs wrecked her special day.

He wouldn't look. He didn't need to. Sullivan ducked down a path, where lanterns threw the gardens into funhouse silhouettes, all distortion, dancing yellows and oranges. His heart skipped, caught—that corner by the azaleas was too dark, and the summer-sticky air went cold. *Paranormal Gone South* loved EVP recordings, but they didn't show the shadow people.

Sullivan didn't want to look at that corner any more than he wanted to look at the sky. That was the worst part of Cypress Bend: Even its worst terrors tugged hard, demanding to be seen and wondered at. But whatever lurked in that corner, if something did lurk, might snatch him up to horror Sullivan couldn't imagine and didn't want to. With a strength of will developed over years of living with that fear, he focused on the dance floor and ran, legs pumping, heart jamming his throat. He concentrated on the people, not the driving need to look, to *know*, to see if anything skulked in that corner. The bright light crowd chattered. Pebbles crackled underfoot. No sound rose from the corner and that soundlessness terrorized him. Two more steps, one—Sullivan burst into someone else's wedding between an ice swan and a heaped table of tastefully wrapped gifts.

"Who the hell are you?" snapped a bride.

"Sullivan Trenholm," he managed, somehow finding manners amid blank fear. "Congratulations, ma'am."

"Are you here to yell about the fireworks too?"

"Ash!" he called.

"How many of you are there?" an older woman in beige asked. "We can't feed your whole family."

"Sullivan!" Breathing hard, Rhys bobbed up behind a clump of wedding guests. "We can head back to the house. Ash says Boo will take care of the rest."

Sullivan yanked him past the cake, past the whirl of men in tuxedos and women in ball gowns. Their sandals made no sound on the parquet floor, which his brother's people must have carried in and taken down every night. Roaring static broke from the speakers; people shrieked as "The Final Countdown" kicked on mid-song.

"I'm not walking back through that dark," Sullivan shouted over European pop-rock. "You know how it is. You're too scared to see."

"Then we'll run," Rhys said.

"You can't run." Sullivan hated to say it. Rhys loathed attention given to his chronic liver problems, the exhaustion that came with them.

But catching Sullivan's hand, like he had so many times when they were kids, Rhys dragged Sullivan through the gardens' winding paths. Sullivan could have traced them in his dreams. He wondered how many times he and his cousin had run, eyes forward, looking neither left nor right, visceral terror of the unknown chosen over a choking certainty of knowledge—no one wanted to see what phantasms Cypress Bend could conjure. But suddenly everyone in America did, grasping desperately for evidence of something beyond their bounded, mechanized existence. *You don't want to know*, Sullivan could have told them. His heart pounded as he jogged, more from fear rather than exertion. *There's a price to knowing and the world asks for more than you're willing to pay. Ask me how I know. They asked me to pay more than anyone else.*

They were moving too slowly. Dark gathered in the gardens' corners, too black—

The patio lights drew closer as they rounded a fountain. Heat panted on his neck; Sullivan's breath came ragged and afraid. They thought they wanted to know, but they didn't, not really. *When I was fifteen, I found Henry washed up against the Boundary Tree. He was dressed in a stolen blue uniform and covered in bloody bandages. I thought he was a ghost but dust stuck to him. We helped him but he can never go home. What do you do with a Confederate soldier who can never go home? You pretend he's your agoraphobic cousin because there's nothing else to do.*

Parrots screamed in the lemon trees. Olivia waited at the door.

Ghosts clutter the corners. Only the family can see them, and almost all of them are Black, which means they were enslaved. They never speak, and they never acknowledge us. I've seen my father shoot at wolves too big to be wolves. I've seen horses cut open bloodlessly, surgically, on a clear summer day, with no one anywhere nearby. I've seen things in the sky I can only describe as things because there are no other words. I've seen three men walking together. I've seen three men walking together—

Sullivan flung himself up the patio steps and through the door, Rhys behind him, and didn't stop til he reached the living room. He could have thrown himself to the plastic sheeting and wept. He could have driven to a hotel in Columbia. Instead, he straightened and dusted off his jeans as if nothing had happened.

"What was that?" Olivia asked.

Sullivan strode to his father's liquor cabinet and pulled out a bottle of bourbon. He needed oblivion more than a change of venue. "You coming, Rhys?" he said.

"Where?" Rhys asked.

"Never mind." Sullivan stalked upstairs and collapsed on the library couch. Body and soul, he dedicated himself to that liquor. If he was lucky, when he reached peak drunkenness, Rhys would appear and shepherd him to bed. In college, he always had, and Sullivan loved him for it.

CHAPTER 9

OLIVIA

Sullivan refused to say what he'd seen in the garden, and Olivia's brother was no more help. "We went fast because we were freaked out," Rhys told her. "You know how it is at night sometimes."

Olivia knew exactly what he meant, though she wished she didn't. Cypress Bend could wreak terror with nothing more than shadows and dark corners, a prickling on the neck, silence fallen. She hated coming home. Friends usually cooed about it: *Cypress Bend looks so gorgeous*, they'd say, angling for a weekend trip. *I'd love to see it sometime.*

You won't see the ghosts, she'd imagine telling them, watching the shock and disbelief blanche their expressions. *They're strictly a family affair.* Olivia had realized, as that thought flashed—*a family affair*—exactly what horror those words could hold, what ugliness might bloom there, sick and bitter-bright. Those Black cousins Ash employed traced their beginnings to stomach-churning violation; their name itself, Trenholm, bore mute testimony to violence.

Olivia recalled that sickness one more time when she slunk upstairs to bed. A beautiful young woman passed in front of her. Loose, dark curls peeked from beneath the woman's white headscarf; her skin held the pale tan of a faded sepia photograph, and freckles dotted her nose. When she stopped before a door and lingered, her pained green eyes stared helplessly, hopelessly. Olivia had once imagined the girl to be cleaning or fetching something. She knew better now, and looked away before the girl stepped into the master bedroom, an inevitable misery. Olivia had seen her many times. That walk down the hallway had sunk into the mire of Cypress Bend: a moment unspooling over and over, time-bent, an amber-fly of emotional dread. Anticipation of certain agony clumped in Olivia's stomach. *It's not yours*, she reminded herself. *It's hers.*

It didn't help.

Olivia shut her bedroom door firmly and finally. Her first night home, and Henry would certainly come. She couldn't think of the girl, nameless now. Though the young woman was long gone, death-freed, her pain lingered. More than the orbs, the shadow people, the strange lights at night, Olivia hated Cypress Bend's mute ghosts. The farm could spiral anyone into terror, but those silent people left her gap-chested, raw-red with grief and guilt.

Olivia changed into pajamas and sat at her vanity. Makeup would help. Makeup always helped. When the world went twisted and bloody, she could fix her face and smile. Her uncle had taught her that.

She read until sometime after midnight, until Henry finally slipped through the house's night murmurings. "Sorry," he said, voice hardly above a whisper as he shut her bedroom door. "Sullivan's drunk in the library, and it took a while to get past him."

"Of course he is." Olivia set her novel on the nightstand. She'd picked fluffy escapism, something to spirit her away from Cypress Bend. Her brother and cousins would have ridiculed her for reading romance, but she needed some kind of happy ending in her life. "Sullivan came home, so Sullivan got drunk. Basic Trenholm mathematics."

Henry hung his robe on a peg behind the door; he wore the boxers beneath it as naturally as any man. Olivia had asked him about underwear once, what he'd worn before he came. *Stuff that didn't fit as well as what you have*, he'd told her, and left it there. "It's good to have you back," Henry said in that thick, slow drawl that tourists sometimes struggled with. "I missed you."

"I always miss you." Olivia tried not to think of Henry's loneliness. She tried not to think of the girl, too, but when Henry kissed her, she drew back. "Not tonight."

He propped on an elbow and watched her, those pale eyes searching. They had seen too much of life. "Something happened," he said. "Something's bothering you."

"It's not." Olivia rooted a pack of cigarettes from her drawer. He'd see the lie written on her face if he looked too long; all her skill at dissembling never fooled Henry. "I'm fine. Just not tonight."

"Did I do something wrong?" He spoke calmly, with no trace of the pleading many lovers might have handed her.

"No, of course not." She prayed he'd never—but Henry wouldn't have done that. He'd been too young when he left the farm. Maybe his father had, his grandfather, but not him. It was small comfort. She lit a Parliament; smoke filled her lungs. The sweet relief grounded her somehow, like stepping from sinking sand to solid ground.

When she offered Henry the pack, he waved it away. "I know you hate to come back," he told her. "I'm sorry."

Olivia gave him a half-shrug and a slight head shake, an upward-turned palm, gestures that added up *there's nothing we can do, but thank you for acknowledging it.* She couldn't be sure Henry saw the ghosts; her uncle forbade their mention, and even if she wanted to ask, the questions they stirred were too ugly. *Did you know them, Henry?* she might have said. *Did you see them every day? Do you still?*

"Can I stay for a while?" Henry asked. "Not to—you know—" He fumbled; certain words could fluster him into blushing. Long ago, he'd confessed that sex terrified him. *I used to think about it like breathing, Livy. No one's bad at breathing. But Rhys and Sullivan don't talk about it that way.* When she asked Henry to explain, he nearly cried, the boy who'd seen wounded men piled on Antietam's blood-slick roads. *Where I came from we didn't have words for certain things. Please don't make me say any more.*

"Yeah, of course you can stay." Too worried about getting caught, Henry wouldn't sleep. She would. Let everyone find them in bed; it would end the stupidity of sneaking around. On her first night back, she wouldn't touch that argument.

The sounds began as half-heard murmurs while she drifted close to sleep. Steadily, they rose to a desperate whisper; as she woke fully, Olivia parsed words, anger: Sullivan. She threw off her blankets and shoved her feet into slippers.

"He's just fighting with Rhys," Henry said. "Come back to bed."

"He's not," Olivia told him. "I heard enough of it. He's not fighting with Rhys. Just stay here." She stalked into the hall. Sullivan's voice drifted up from the second floor, too loud for something like one in the morning.

Her cousin knelt at the bottom of the stairs. "Why don't you talk to us?" he demanded. "We're sorry! We just want to tell you we're sorry! Look at me! *Look at me, dammit!*" A sob hitched his words, and a mostly empty bottle of bourbon dangled from his hand. Next to him stood a dark-skinned woman in a blue dress, a white apron, and a white kerchief—the uniform of the Trenholm house servants, Olivia guessed. The woman's dark eyes focused on the middle distance, on nothing Olivia could see.

"Sullivan." Olivia drew him up. "You can't do this."

"I just wanna tell them we're sorry." Her cousin's accent had thickened to a soft slur, half-Southern and half-drunk. "None of them will look at me. I've been walking through the house, and none of them will—"

"Sullivan. You know they don't talk," Olivia said. When he bent his curly head into her shoulder, tears wet her shirt. The scent of liquor could have slammed her backward, but Olivia patted his back. The woman in the blue dress said nothing, and she did not move. "They aren't real. They aren't here. This is just a memory."

But a memory more potent than most; inexplicable sorrow washed over her, and Olivia swallowed her own tears. Everything she loved could be snatched away. Everyone, taken with no warning, all the people she loved most. She fought not to sob along with Sullivan.

"They never look at us," her cousin said.

Would you acknowledge us, if you were them? she wanted to ask, but it would do no good. "C'mon to bed," she said.

"Why wouldn't you let me tell you we're sorry?" Whirling, Sullivan shouted at the woman. "My father's dead! You can go! We don't wanna keep this house! We don't wanna—"

"Sullivan." Henry touched his back. Olivia startled; she hadn't heard him come downstairs. He wore his bathrobe again, and pain etched his face. "Stop it. She doesn't deserve this."

"Of course you see them." Sullivan jerked away from him. "I hope you remember you fought to keep them right where they are. Well, look, Henry! They're still fucking there, like you won after all!" Canting sideways, bourbon in hand, Sullivan reeled upstairs.

The Black woman remained, her plain face lined with hard work, her mouth drawn with worry. A feather duster dangled from her hand. Silent, she seemed to wait for news of expected disaster.

"I wish he wouldn't do that," Henry said quietly. "I'm sorry, Juba. You don't deserve that."

"You can see them?" Olivia asked. "I thought only immediate family—"

"I think it's whoever lives in the house," Henry said. "I didn't see them at first. It took about three years." He started upstairs.

Olivia caught up. "You know her name."

Henry walked slowly, as if it pained him. "Please don't let's ever talk about it. It's bad enough to see them all the time. They can't hear me, I think. I've tried too many times to talk to them."

Shocked to silence, Olivia said nothing.

"Anyway." Henry stopped at the top of the stairs. "G'night, Livy." Sullivan had disappeared, perhaps to his bedroom, maybe to another escape. Briefly, Henry touched her hand, then strode down the hallway. Olivia could only watch him walk away, one more pained ghost in an echoing, haunted house.

CHAPTER 10

RHYS

Black suited, ready for the morning's disasters, Rhys waited in the guest bedroom until Sullivan's door opened—he hadn't wanted to presume they could share their childhood bedroom. When his cousin emerged, he strode from his own. "Oh, hey," Sullivan said. "Did you just finish up?"

"Yeah," Rhys lied. He wouldn't admit that he wanted to assuage a guilty conscience. *You shouldn't feel guilty*, he reminded himself. *Sullivan's choices are his own.* But he'd abandoned his cousin to drunkenness, to wake alone in the library on the morning of his father's funeral. Rhys tried not to imagine Sullivan opening his sandy eyes on a gray dawn. An empty bourbon bottle would have leaned next to the sofa; Sullivan's head would have pounded with regret. Worse would have been the night before, when his cousin might have watched the door and hoped: *Rhys will come soon. Rhys always comes.*

You aren't your cousin's keeper, he told himself.

"I can't believe Ash wants to film us," Sullivan said. "Is he insane? Bringing cameras to the funeral?"

"He said they won't air the footage if we say they can't," Rhys reminded him. "I've told you over and over. We just tell them that they can't show the footage, so they don't show it. It's not worth arguing over." He'd stopped an almighty blow-up with that reasoning. Sullivan had nearly stormed out when Ash brought up cameras, but Rhys had talked him down. *Let him do it. He says they won't show anything without our consent, so we just don't consent. Simple. Let them waste money filming if they want.*

"This is going to be a shitshow," Sullivan told him as he hit the button on the elevator, then stepped inside. *Inspected by the Department of Elevators and Amusement Park Rides, July 2022,* read the sign, with a signature from the inspector. When Rhys was younger, before the crippling exhaustion hit, every elevator in South Carolina had borne the signature of Floyd Padgett. Floyd had died, maybe retired; a new inspector had signed the form. Strange what you noticed, the small details that make up a life. "At least they won't have cameras in the church," he told his cousin.

Sullivan muttered something about a travesty as Rhys shut the door and the elevator grated into action. Rhys nodded sympathetically. He fell into his old role so easily, herding his cousin's temper like a trusted emotional collie. He loved Sullivan, and someone had to do it. Rhys wondered if his cousin's moods withered to banality with no one to witness them, or bloomed to a wilding tangle.

"Are you seeing anyone?" Rhys asked as they walked to the library. Mercifully, Ash had closed the house, picked up the plastic sheeting, and removed the velvet ropes.

Sullivan dropped into a silk chair. He would rumple his Brooks Brothers suit if he slouched like that. "Who the hell would want to see me?"

"I mean, you're not bad looking." It was an understatement. While they were in college, Sullivan had been infamous on both fraternity and sorority rows.

"You didn't ask who'd want to fuck me," Sullivan replied. "You asked who'd want to see me on a more permanent basis. I'm a functional alcoholic without a real job, unless you include working artist, which I do, and most don't. My money comes from adjuncting and dividends." He paused. "Admittedly, the dividends look attractive until they realize the functional alcoholic part. Men tend to stick it out longer than women, probably because they can keep up."

"Jesus Christ. D'you have to be so bleak?" Rhys asked.

Olivia swept in. "Is he being bleak again? This day is bleak enough, Sullivan. Don't add to it for once." Her black dress and heels were ostentatiously expensive in their simplicity; her plain black clutch probably cost more than Rhys's suit. Ash still bought her everything. He loved her with the guileless adoration of an oldest brother for his little sister.

"You seeing anyone?" Sullivan asked, likely for the excuse to ignore Olivia.

"Does he ever?" Olivia asked.

She didn't have to call him out. Rhys shifted, then rearranged, mindful of his suit. Lies tumbled before he could stop them. "Sort of. Maybe. I don't know."

Somehow, Sullivan managed to make slumping seem lordly. "You want to explain that?"

"Not really," Rhys said. "No."

"Now you have to tell us." Olivia perched neatly on the sofa, back straight, ankles crossed, like she was waiting her turn at Confederate Assassin. Her dart always spiked Lincoln's cragged nose.

"Is Henry coming to the burial?" Rhys asked, mostly for the sake of a subject change.

"Yeah," Sullivan said. "Do you still have him direct the cultural history tours? You know that's really—"

"Don't," Olivia snapped. "*He* decided that was really problematic. We know Henry's changed, and you'd know too if you ever bothered to come home."

"Y'all, please stop," Rhys said, hands extended, as if he could physically restrain their sniping. Dust motes swirled in the sunshine, and he could almost believe that nothing could touch them in that soft golden light. He knew better. Even the prettiest mornings at Cypress Bend could breed savagery.

Ash appeared, already rumpled into exhaustion. "Elliot's waiting on the porch," he told them. "The limo will be here any minute." He offered Olivia his hand, and she rose from the couch. "Y'all ready?"

"Guess so," Rhys replied. He could think of nothing else to say; people were never ready for a funeral, not really.

"Is Aunt Alda coming?" Sullivan asked.

Ash led them into the foyer, Olivia still on his arm. His cousin loved his Southern courtesies. They were beautiful in its mirror, black suited but dour. "At least three times, she'll ask who the funeral's for, and every time, it'll be like the first time she's heard. The nurses will bring her down for brunch afterward. She'll just think it's another family party."

"What about Henry?" Sullivan asked. "He could at least—"

"He won't ride in a car, and he won't leave the farm. You goddamn well know that, so why are you asking?" Olivia said, and he shut up.

The high church Episcopal service seemed the same as every other Trenholm funeral, but Sullivan helped them carry the casket. Rhys had first learned the hymns at his mother's service, when he was five; at nine, he recalled them as he stood dry eyed before his father's coffin. Sullivan's hand had crept into his. *You live with us now,* he'd whispered. *You're my brother.* Sullivan didn't understand that wrenching grief; his own mother had died not long after he was born, and no one ever spoke of her. But Rhys's cousin's words were a beacon against that long gray loneliness stretching into the unimaginable, a burden too enormous for a small boy to bear, and Rhys never forgot it.

A limo trundled them back to Cypress Bend. Though Ash hadn't shut down the farm, someone had cleared the drive of tourists, and his uncle's hearse reached the family cemetery without any ignominious pauses. The white cemetery, Rhys and Sullivan called it, to differentiate it from the other plot of graves near the enslaved people's cabins. Ash had cleaned it up, added all the information they could find about its occupants. It made no difference. *Cypress Bend, where even the cemeteries are still segregated,* Sullivan had once said at a fraternity party, which sent Ash blushing and stuttering. His embarrassment hadn't helped.

The grave was dug. The priest stood at its head, and mourners sweated quietly, waiting. Two cameras roved behind them. Rhys tried not to think about his relatives' certainly strong opinions. Drawn by familial obligation, few Black relatives scattered the mourners—Ash's co-host, their distant cousin Lewis; his sisters and parents. Rhys couldn't imagine they actually regretted his uncle's demise.

"Okay, easy does it," Ash told the pallbearers as they gathered around the casket.

"God, this thing is heavy," Sullivan whispered as they lifted it again. His curls had gone feral in the heat.

"Shut up," Ash hissed.

"Y'all don't argue over your daddy's body," said Lucky, their first cousin once removed, hefting the casket. "Truluck heard enough of that in life. He don't need to hear it when he's dead."

"Lay off," Rhys told him. His dress shirt clung to his back; a decade of silence hadn't wasted his uncle. Fatigue dragged at him. His doctor had warned him to stay out of the heat. "Face forward and carry the damn thing."

"Y'all ain't supposed to talk when you're carrying a casket," replied Maxcy, a second cousin. His shoulders hunched like a linebacker's in his black jacket; the sun was a hot, angry eye. "It's bad luck to talk when you're carrying a casket."

Rhys placed each foot carefully on the humped turf. They couldn't drop the coffin. Sweat beaded and stung his eyes. Cameras prowled closer as they approached the metal trucks, and mourners rustled like impatient starlings. "Okay, one more step, lower, lower—" Ash said. They wrangled the casket down and stood.

"Are they filming this?" Sullivan whispered as they settled among the other mourners.

"No, they're here for their health," Ash replied.

"They're not using this."

"Will you shut up?" Ash asked. "He's *dead*."

"For real?" Sullivan said. "I thought we were putting him in the ground to see if he'll sprout."

Boo did something between a snort and laugh. Ash smacked Sullivan's arm.

"OW!"

Glares peppered the crowd. Relatives glanced at them, glanced at one another, and Rhys read their faces: *Those boys are at it again, thirty-one and thirty-two years old, standing over their daddy's body and they still can't stop fighting. Those cameras in their faces, too. Truluck didn't raise 'em right.* "Will you two *stop it*?" he asked.

Olivia leaned past Rhys. "I will kill y'all dead, so help me God."

The minister, his bald head sweat-shiny, began to speak. His microphone screamed, and the crowd cringed. Reverend Winthrop adjusted it, and it shrieked again. "Everyone the Father gives to me will come to me; I will never turn away anyone who—"

A phone blared in the heat-stilled quiet. The minister plowed over it as everyone fumbled. Rhys checked his own and found it blank-eyed; Sullivan slapped at Ash. Red-faced, Ash punched his iPhone off and slid it back in his suit.

"—believes in me. He who raised Jesus Christ from the dead—"

Another phone sang as the microphone crested to a high, sharp whine. People pawed their pockets again, squinting to find the culprit. Rhys saw it etched on their faces, and thought it himself: *Who was stupid enough to leave theirs on after Ash's went off?* Snub nose wrinkled, Elliot drew a candy-pink iPhone from her rope purse. It stopped as she examined it. She shrugged and stuck it back in again.

"—will also give new life to our mortal bodies through his indwelling Spirit—"

A third tinkling ringtone broke over the crowd. The minister stopped. "Please silence your phones," he said. Funeral-goers craned to find the culprit. "Turn it off!" someone shouted, and the ringtone stopped.

"Thank you." The minister swiped his forehead with a wide, white handkerchief. "My heart, therefore, is glad, and my spirit rejoices—"

Lady Gaga's "Paparazzi" blared. "I swear I turned it off," Sullivan told the world at large as he pulled an Android from his jacket. "Seriously. I swear—"

"*Turn it off*!" the minister said.

"It's not me!" he protested. "It's this farm! You think I left that thing on? You think any of us did?"

"Sullivan." Rhys touched his arm.

"Oh no." Sullivan wrenched sideways, nearly falling onto Ash. "He's not gonna look at me like—"

The casket lowering device shrieked and shuddered once, hard. Women screamed; hands slammed over ears. In a mighty, clattering crash, the coffin fell sideways from the metal trucks and hit the dirt. Mourners rocketed backward. A casket handle snapped off, though the lid remained shut. Something inside thumped as momentum tumbled it sideways, then carried it wrong-side up. It rocked farther. Fleetingly, Rhys thought the coffin might crash and open. But it teetered, creaked, then was still. Other than the snapped handle, it appeared intact. For a long, shocked moment, nothing moved, and the macabre tableau held—the minister's open mouth, the frozen mourners, the coffin's white bottom, like a dead fish. Suddenly cameras darted closer. "What the *hell*?" Ash roared, turning on the pallbearers, his face an accusation. "Why did that thing malfunction? Did you put that coffin on straight? Did you hit a button?"

"You helped us put it there!" Sullivan shouted. "You know we put it on straight!"

"Stop it!" Rhys grabbed Sullivan's arm—he felt like his cousin's personal handler, as if no time had passed, as if they'd never left Cypress Bend. "You know what did that. It's the same thing that messed with the phones, and it wasn't us."

"It won't even leave his funeral alone." Sullivan's voice dragged down to misery; he gazed over the Spanish moss hanging limp in the slumped heat. "I went to the funeral. I'm going home, okay? I'm going home now, and I'm never coming back." Alone, he walked down the dusty dirt road, and Rhys watched him go.

CHAPTER 11

ASH

Cameras bustled through the internment's wreckage as Ash and Boo wrestled with the casket. Two morticians fluttered around them, all panicked apologies; arms folded, the minister stood silent, as if he personified God's judgment. After a moment, Rhys joined them, then the rest of the pallbearers. They levered the casket sideways, then upright; the body slithered inside. Sweating, they righted the coffin, everyone staggering as the corpse shifted. The pallbearers backed up and lowered the casket onto the bier. The mourners had disappeared, as if fleeing a disaster, natural or otherwise—like Ash needed one more misery. There were enough yet to come.

"Thank you for coming," he told the last scattered people, some Black cousins among them. About half of the white cousins welcomed them. Others ignored them. A few threw them angry glares, as if they didn't belong. *Why did you come?* he wanted to ask those distant relatives, his co-host Lewis most of all. *Why would you bother? I hope you're glad he's dead. I am.*

"Ash?" the co-executive producer said, waving him down as he trudged to the hearse. "Stay a minute."

"There's nothing to talk about." Ash walked on. "They said you can't use the footage."

"Give me a sec anyway. We'll drive you back."

Rhys glared like a man at the end of his patience—a feat for the family peacemaker. "Y'all go on ahead," Ash said. The funeral reception was clearly off, and it didn't matter.

Rhys would hate him soon enough. His cousin's expression sagged into resignation, and he left.

Dust puffed behind the hearse as it drove away. It hung in the air, and it didn't dissipate. At least the sweetgums and swamp oaks threw some meager shade, and sprinklers kept a sun-blasted, brown mat of grasses over the graves. Everything smelled dull and earthy, like the lingering, gritted dust. Ethan probably wanted to propose EVP conversations with his father's unquiet ghost.

"Look," the producer said in a low voice. "Your family's goddamn spectacular. We can sell the hell out of this. Can you convince them?"

"Excuse me?" Ash's father was dead, and the body somewhat desecrated. His will veered toward disastrous—

"*Gone South* has maybe one season left," Ethan said. "There's only so much more we can do with it. But we can make you people into the witchy Kardashians with a Southern drawl. Christ. You can make bank. What do you make now? Half a million a season? Double it."

Ash nearly choked there in that long, hot field among the familial dead. "*Excuse me?*"

"We'll give each of you two hundred and fifty K. Throw in Elliot and that good-looking cousin of yours always hanging around, too. Henry, is it?" Ethan asked. "You know that's the deal of a lifetime. We can get at least four seasons of it. The Kardashians got *twenty*, Ash. *Twenty seasons.* If we got five out of it, and I think it will, tell your family we'll jack them up to half a mill a season."

Ten million dollars—for ten million dollars, men shut up and did what they were told. It would solve that problem with his cousins. They would agree. He just had to convince Sullivan.

Ethan watched expectantly, almost smiling. Terrible taste to look so hungry in a cemetery.

"We'll do it," Ash told him.

CHAPTER 12

SULLIVAN

Sullivan and Rhys's childhood bedroom had been redecorated with anonymous family heirlooms. No trace of their boyhood remained, not that Sullivan lamented it. His walk home had stretched longer and hotter than he'd imagined, and after a cold shower, he balled clothes in his suitcase haphazardly, a man determined on a second hasty exit. Maybe his old things were squirreled in the attic with the rest of the Trenholm family detritus. Two centuries of it tilted in an anarchical kingdom of dust and black widows, Confederate bills on the floor and jewelry stashed in the rafters. When they were children, Ash had found an Enfield Pattern Rifle Musket behind a loose board under a window, a twist of minié ball paper cartridges shoved near its trigger. It could have been waiting since Sherman's March. When they'd carted it downstairs, their father had mounted it over the library's fireplace; he had to move up the portrait of Sullivan Hayes Trenholm, killed at Second Manassas. That portrait had frozen Henry to speechlessness once, with something like awe and dawning horror.

The door creaked. Sullivan wheeled and fell back on the bed, torn between shutting his eyes to the farm's terrors and the need to see whatever attack came. It was only Ash.

"I'm leaving," Sullivan said as he levered up. He didn't explain his panic, and no explanation was necessary; Ash should have known better than to walk in without announcing himself. Sullivan added it to his growing list of grievances. "Don't try to talk me out of going."

"Here's the thing." Ash leaned against the plain white wall. Posters had papered it once, mostly black-white-red renditions of pop-punk emo bands—Paramore, My Chemical Romance, All Time Low, Green Day. Rhys had some hot girls up, and Sullivan a teenager's clichéd Duchamp. "I had an offer—"

"No." Sullivan shoved in a pair of pajama pants.

"Hear me out."

"No." His suitcase zipped a final fuck-you.

"Two hundred and fifty thousand a season, and we can get at least four seasons."

Sullivan unbent and met his brother's eyes for once, dark as his own. They disturbed him in ways he couldn't describe. "I don't care how much it is. D'you understand that? Nothing you can pay me will be enough to stay in this house with you people. *Nothing*. My therapist would drive up here with a shotgun—"

"Here's the thing. You won't do it for yourself, and I'm not asking you to. But you have to do it for Rhys and Olivia. Elliot, too." Ash spoke not in that ringing older-brother tone, waiting for fault and probing to find it, but quietly. "You know Rhys needs a transplant sometime soon, right? And he doesn't have great health insurance?"

The suitcase handle was round and sure and real. "Don't start on a guilt trip. Rhys has enough to pay for that now, and don't you *dare* use Elliot to—"

"Dad only left him and Henry fifteen thousand dollars each. He left Olivia and Elliot twenty."

Sullivan's suitcase clattered over. It seemed a dim sound, unimportant. "Did you know? Tell me you didn't know."

Ash massaged his forehead, a tic familiar from their father. Were we the sum of others' gestures, or did they come down through our bones? "I only found out late last night. I was waiting until after the funeral. Sullivan, you know everyone's expecting he divided it equally. Hell, I thought he divided it equally. He didn't. More than that, he left very little liquid in assets—mostly the farm. I did the math already. We can't gift them anything without losing the land, and we can't lose the land. Don't tell me I have enough to give them, because I don't. I barely keep this place afloat with all these people to feed."

Felled one more time by his father's tyranny, Sullivan dropped to the bed again. He'd thought death had ended it. The old man could terrorize him from the grave.

"It's a miserable situation." Ash pinched his nose. Sullivan wanted to slap his hand away: *Stop looking like our father. He's dead and I hate him.* "But Ethan's offer is sort of a godsend."

Love trapped him. Rhys's paltry insurance covered very little, and he needed that money. Whenever Sullivan's father had left him bruised, bloody, Rhys had been the one sure thing left. *It's okay, Sullivan,* he'd say, a quiet voice in the dark. *It'll be over one day, I promise. We'll get out.*

And they had. But after that flight, Rhys was still there, always carrying Sullivan back to their dorm room, helping him with the final paper—the cousin who never left his side until he deserted. Sullivan had imagined distance would give him clarity, maybe, or something like safety. *I'm going to Savannah for grad school,* he'd said. *I'll call, I promise. I'll miss you.*

A day later, in his empty, echoing apartment, Sullivan realized he'd made a terrible mistake, but there was no changing it.

Almost worse, Sullivan had waved that license at the tourists. *T-R-E-N-H-O-L-M,* he'd shouted, a name he'd never change, no matter what battles and banners came with it. Whatever curses attached itself to that land were his curses. They would follow him. He would flee the land, but he could never abandon it to strangers. Sullivan owed it to Rhys. He owed it to Olivia, and Elliot. Help was needed, and he would give it. *If you need a transplant,* he'd always wanted to tell his cousin, *livers grow back. You can have some of mine.* But Trenholms didn't say those things, and before, a transplant had been years away, only Rhys had grown sicker since he'd moved—

"I'll do your stupid reality show," Sullivan said, hating it, hating himself. *It's what a man does,* his father would have said, and Sullivan hated him most of all.

"I'm sorry," Ash said.

"You're sorry you get to keep up your show?" Sullivan lifted his suitcase back to the bed and unzipped it. He would have to unpack. He would have to go back to Savannah and gather the rest of his clothes. He would have to do so many things, submit to so many indignities for the sake of those he loved. Ash had been doing it for years, but Ash had always been more afraid to leave than stay.

"I am sorry," his brother said. "I never wanted you to be part of it. I'm sorry that you have to be. I'm sorry about this morning. I'm just sorry, Sullivan. I didn't want it to be like this."

Sullivan drew a shirt out, lifted it, folded it. "When I walked into my therapist's office the first time, do you know what I said to her? I said, 'You know the show *Paranormal Gone South*? Ashby Trenholm is my brother.'" Another shirt joined the pile. Someone had taught him and Rhys to fold clothes in the laundry room of Preston College at the University of South Carolina. Dumbfounded, they'd suddenly realized that they didn't know how. "Just go. Get some people to rearrange the rooms again so Rhys is staying with me. If I have to be here for more than a few nights, I'm not sleeping alone."

Wordlessly, Ash left. He didn't shut the door.

Cursing silently, Sullivan unpacked his clothes.

CHAPTER 13

OLIVIA

Olivia kept her face a studied blank. A childhood at Cypress Bend had taught her that. Uncle Truluck drummed into her that ladies maintained their calm, no matter what calamities unfolded before them. Olivia wanted to be good, so she channeled emptiness instead of screaming. Sometimes she wanted to scream with rage, sometimes terror; sometimes she wanted to weep—for her mother, for her brother and cousins, for Elliot, for herself. The revelation that her uncle left her next to nothing would tally as one more indignity in a life that had brought many. Sullivan had to help her with her first period. Miserable with his kindness, she'd hated him for months.

"It's fine," Rhys was saying. "I can—"

"Sullivan already said yes." Ash's gaze settled on the portrait above the mantle—his brother's namesake, killed in battle for a cause long lost. Their uncle never could forget the indignity of that defeat. His pride sprung from that indignity, his history and destiny. He'd spun a whole life there.

"*What?!*" Rhys's word came half-gasped. Olivia imagined a camera zooming to his disbelief. Those dark-night eyes would break hearts. "Sullivan *agreed to it?*"

"Yeah." Ash's voice had gone tired and distant, as if he spoke from far away. "Elliot's doing it, too. She always said she would, and for that much—I mean, college fund, right? It'll set her up for life. At that point, I feel like I can't say no."

Once Olivia and Ash would have talked about it. They'd stolen Elliot from those nannies hired to brainwash her into that Southern belle nonsense that wrecked Olivia.

They sneaked her overalls and toy cars, and together, they'd assured her childhood's normal mud and dirt and tears. Ash should have asked her if he could show Elliot on TV.

"What d'you think, Rhys?" her cousin said.

"I mean, I can get off. I'm just an adjunct." Rhys probably hated to say those words. "I'd lose insurance, which barely covers anything anyway, then but it doesn't matter, not if I can pay for a better policy. Olivia? What do you think?"

"I don't care." Like so many things, she couldn't, not in the face of the alternative. Life had decided for her. People would say, *Oh Olivia, there's always a choice.* They were right. You could choose to make your life harder, stew in your own virtue. But living was hard enough, lonely enough. She'd been thirteen when her uncle brought Elliot home. He was an old man, and people mistook the baby for hers. Uncle Truluck made her perfect; the world called her a whore. Olivia had worn her sundresses, loved her cousin, and practiced silence.

"Can you put the business on hold?" Ash asked. She realized he was talking to her and wondered why he bothered. She owned an art gallery for Charleston tourists, the type who bought sweetgrass baskets from the downtown market. Someone else could run it for her. Second cousins bustled in with velvet ropes and that ugly plastic stuff Ash kept on the floors. She would have to live inside that circus—the tourists, the cameras, the orbs and far worse; Sullivan wouldn't tell her why he'd drunk himself stupid after the fireworks. Olivia wouldn't do it for herself, but she would do it for Rhys and Elliot.

"Why are we talking about this?" she asked. "You know we'll do it." Olivia threaded past the people busily laying plastic; Ash seemed to regard them as invisible, as if they could no more bear witness to a family drama than the lithe-legged end tables. Henry was reading in the sanctuary of the upstairs library. He stood when Olivia entered, a courtesy from another time she'd always adored.

"I overheard y'all before I came upstairs," he told her. "You don't have to do it."

She crossed the room and stepped into his arms. Henry smelled like Old Spice—she remembered when Sullivan, laughing, had given it to him long before. "I'm staying," Olivia said.

"You don't have to," Henry told her. She'd known he would say it. She loved him for it. Maybe he was thirty-two and maybe far older. It didn't matter in the end. You held tight to life's mercies, however strange.

"They can't do it without me," Olivia replied.

His lips brushed her hair. "I won't argue with you."

"There isn't a choice when there's that much money involved. Don't tell me there is because there isn't." She buried her face in Henry's black t-shirt. When he'd come, he'd said he was sorry to people in black. *Aren't they in mourning?* he'd asked. "We could tell them," she dared. "He's dead."

When Henry withdrew, the air conditioner chilled her bare arms. "No. I'm a guest in the house. I took advantage of you."

They'd slogged through the same argument for years; Henry had insisted on their secret even after her uncle's incapacitation, with the old man's furies settled to an impotent, silent glare. A decade and a half later, no new angles had emerged, no new solutions; their positions remained firmly, bloodily entrenched. *You were only sixteen when I kissed you, Livy,* he'd say. *I was nineteen.* She'd try to cut him off, but no argument would alleviate his guilt. *You're right,* he'd say. *It wouldn't have mattered where I came from. But it matters here, and I should've known. Sullivan and Rhys had left for school, then Sullivan came back, and he told me exactly what I'd fought for. You and I were so close anyway, and I made a terrible mistake.*

It was always the same argument. *Tell me you regret it,* she'd say.

I love you, Henry would tell her, the only answer he could manage.

"We don't even have to say it," Olivia told him. "I'll just move into your room. They won't care. They'd rather me be with you than—" She stopped. Of course she'd seen other people; she left Cypress Bend for the wider world. It hurt Henry every time. *If I don't see people, they'll wonder why,* she'd try to explain. *If you'd come with me, I wouldn't have to.*

"I don't want to take advantage of their hospitality," Henry said. Olivia could have recited his answer. She wondered why she bothered.

"Can't you—I don't know. Ask them for permission." She hated it. Treating women like children and insentient beasts in turns, his nineteenth century morals baffled her, though he'd done his best to trudge from their foggy maze.

"Asking's for getting married, Livy," Henry told her. "I don't think that's something you want."

"Please don't. You know why." They could argue in shorthand: *You won't leave and I won't stay, at least not forever.* "Can we just tell them?" Olivia asked. "It's Ash that matters now that my uncle's gone, no one else. And don't say anything about Sullivan and Rhys. They never come home, so they don't matter."

"But it's his father's house—"

"Maybe we can figure it out later," she told him. They'd been saying it for years, and she saw no reason to stop. At least they would be in the same house for a little while. She could snatch some happiness from disaster.

"I'll think about it," Henry said. When he hugged her, he smelled better than home. Henry's Old Spice reminded her, like nothing else on earth, of safety.

CHAPTER 14

ASH

All deep tans and bright-white smiles, the crew flew back from California. Ash introduced them to Sullivan when he returned from Savannah with a carful of clothes and a chip on his shoulder. His little brother smiled and laughed with men he'd never met. Was that Sullivan outside of Cypress Bend—witty and self-deprecating, those crinkled eyes and half-grin? It reminded Ash of opening the door on Rhys and Sullivan whispering at night. *What are y'all talking about?* he'd asked.

We weren't talking, Sullivan replied, sitting in the half-dark—even as teenagers, they kept a small light burning on Sullivan's dresser. He blinked hard, obvious in his pantomime. *We were sleeping.*

When Rhys and Sullivan came to the University of South Carolina, Ash was already there. Their SAE bids were sealed, for all purposes, before they set foot on campus, and he'd thought, *We'll be brothers for real now. It'll mean something, and we can leave Cypress Bend behind us.* But Rhys and Sullivan's icy politeness veered to rudeness, and they remained firmly in acquaintance territory, known mostly in rumor and reputation, Sullivan as a party boy and mild disaster, Rhys as the sidekick dragging him home.

Maybe Sullivan had changed. Ash hadn't, not that he could see. He'd departed college for the sucking quagmire of Cypress Bend, its predictable rhythms of wedding season and tobacco harvest, its unplumbed depths of strangeness. Thirty-two years old, Ash had no close friends; the wealthiest man in the county, he hadn't taken a woman to dinner in years. He was supposed to be good looking. It didn't help. In college, his few friends had teased him about going home too often. But the weirdness at Cypress Bend belonged to him. If he was strange there, he was a Trenholm, and people expected strangeness from a Trenholm. Unmoored, he became an oddity, unbelonging.

"Why did you bother introducing me to them?" Sullivan asked after the men left HQ. "I won't remember their names, and they'll have their faces shoved behind equipment anyway."

"You were different with them." Squatting on his heels, Ash petted Pandora and rubbed Q's belly at the same time. Both wore silly doggy grins. Ash kept the dogs for company as much as protection.

"What d'you mean?" Sullivan asked above.

"You were funny." Ash hesitated, but he had nothing to lose. Sullivan didn't like him anyway. "If I didn't know better I'd've thought you were flirting with them."

"Maybe I was." When Ash glanced up, his brother was watching the long, lonely sweep of garden. "You know I like guys, too."

"I mean, yeah." Ash had learned about his brother's bisexuality in college. Sullivan might have been their father's favorite once, aside from Henry, but he would have been disowned if the old man caught him.

"Why'd you even bother mentioning it?" Sullivan asked. "So what if I was flirting with them? You got a problem with seeing it—"

"I don't care who you hit on." Ash focused on his dogs, their smiles, Ganon nudging for attention. "I told you that for years. Why d'you always presume I hate you?"

"Maybe because you hate me." Sullivan's answer came as swift and predictable as the tides.

"I don't hate you," Ash had to say. *Dad might have loved you best, but I don't hate you. Maybe it only meant you got hit more, and you listened to more rants about battle strategy. Maybe I escaped, and you didn't.*

"You hate me," his brother replied, probably all he wanted—one more accusation, one more tally in a long list of wrongs. Sullivan still watched the garden, probably wondering what strange happenings Cypress Bend might conjure. Black objects sometimes flitted across a clear summer sky. The crew had caught some on camera, and the internet had picked them apart. No one could explain them.

Ash left his brother staring at the garden and settled on the patio with Elliot. She was mercifully uncomplicated, a lover of animals and nonsense pop culture. Little troubled her. She chattered nonsense at a green macaw; Ash asked McKayla, their second cousin once removed, to bring him a Stella Artois. Sunset gathered in pinks and oranges. Sullivan would learn to like him, maybe fake it for the cameras. Or maybe he wouldn't. Rhys and Olivia would return the next day. They would start filming the day after that. If nothing else, Ash would get paid.

CHAPTER 15

RHYS

The new TV blinked on like an angry eye. Since Rhys could remember, Sullivan had suffered from insomnia. Sometimes he'd chatter til he drifted off, then snapped up, disoriented. The cycle would continue until Rhys wanted to cry from exhaustion. They'd slept with a night-light on and the shade pulled tight, but nothing could stop sound from penetrating.

He was grateful Sullivan had asked him to share a room again. Rhys hadn't wanted to presume; he and Olivia were the cousins, the extra kids. His uncle always made sure they remembered that. Sullivan and Ash never treated them that way, but old habits died hard, especially at Cypress Bend.

Sullivan could have run. He hadn't. Onscreen, the Amazon Prime menu flashed, all superheroes and smiling starlets. It felt like those swallowing, desperate moments after his father's funeral. During the reception, Rhys and Sullivan had holed up in the bedroom and traded baseball cards. The world had shattered, but it went on nonetheless, both mercy and cruelty. You could sleepwalk through it if you tried.

But when Rhys felt around life's edges, he was startled to find lightness there. He spent his nights watching Richmond's traffic lights throw patterns on his bedroom walls; he woke to a hateful, unbothered quiet, to papers that never spoke his name. He should have wanted to flee Cypress Bend.

He didn't.

"I thought you said you were going to bed?" Rhys asked.

"I got addicted to streaming during the pandemic," Sullivan said as he scrolled the Prime offerings. "I mean, we were all addicted before, but I got *really* addicted, right? I think I watched *Game of Thrones* all the way through, like, three times. Anyway, that's how I get to sleep. I brought headphones. It won't bother you, will it?" As Sullivan settled, a long, slender lump shifted behind his pillow.

Rhys squinted in the TV glare. "Christ on a tricycle," he said. "Don't tell me that's the same baseball bat."

"This?" Sullivan drew the slim stick from his bedclothes. "Oh. No. I upgraded. This is a 29-inch Cold Steel Brooklyn Crusher. The Little League thing was for kids. That's in my bedroom in Savannah. I kept this one next to my front door." For a moment, he held it like his father had held those swords.

"What fucking neighborhood d'you live in?" Rhys asked.

"What d'you mean?" Sullivan's eyebrows drew together, too young in that strange, underwater light.

"Never mind." Rhys curled under his covers. "Why'd you agree to this?"

His cousin shoved the bat under his pillow again. Their shade was pulled. Everyone else had gone to bed; the house sighed its usual midnight condemnations. "You know why," Sullivan said.

"You didn't have to," Rhys told him.

"I know." Sullivan focused on the TV, not him.

Thank you, Rhys could have said. He'd passed a childhood of night-vigils with Sullivan, yawning when he wanted to sleep, talking blearily through the long dark when he wanted to lay his head on the pillow and close his eyes; he'd spent four years of college hauling his cousin from drunken escapades and rescuing him from his personal disasters. It was embarrassing to admit he'd assumed an inheritance would pay for his transplant, and he needed help. *I thought you always took me for granted, then you didn't*, Rhys could have told him. *You did the hardest thing. You came back, and you stayed.* But he couldn't find words to explain without embarrassing them both, so he pulled on an eye-mask as *The Wheel of Time* theme began.

CHAPTER 16

OLIVIA

I t was past midnight, and Henry's bedroom door didn't creak as Olivia stepped inside. Matching nightlights glowed on his bedside tables; the bed's four posters rose startlingly at the high ceiling, like spikes. Henry slept with his fists curled under his chin. *I dream about the war every night*, he'd told her once. *So I'd rather not talk about it while I'm awake, if you don't mind, Livy.*

Olivia touched his shoulder.

"What the *f*—what are you doing here?" Henry popped his jaw. "We didn't say you were coming tonight. It's better if I come to you."

"If they catch me, I'm twenty-nine and they can go to hell." Olivia untied her robe. She'd imagined a grand gesture. It would fall gracefully, and he would stare. They would tumble into bed. Henry yanked it shut.

"You can't be here." His fingers fumbled as he tied her sash. The patchwork quilt, hand-sewn by an ancient relative, slipped too low. He wore nothing.

"You were waiting for me," she said.

"It's hot." He pulled the knot tight.

She'd wanted it to be beautiful. Olivia had thought she'd appear, a miracle, and he would open his arms. After so long, she was staying, at least for a little while. Her uncle was gone, and she wanted to snatch something from his wreckage. She'd seen Sullivan's television flickering under his door and prayed he didn't notice her shadow. Henry should have kissed her, not bit back tight-lipped curses.

"Can't we stop hiding?" She was begging and she hated it.

"I told you I'd think about it. Thinking takes some time." Henry drew back. "Don't let them see you on the way back."

Sometimes Olivia hated his untroubled calm. "We need to tell them. This is ridiculous."

"Dammit." His hand passed in front of his eyes, and when he cussed, she knew he'd reached his limit. "How can I repay them this way?"

"How can you repay *me* this way?" she asked, not quite knowing what it meant, but that it meant something. He'd been timid with her for so long. *I don't know how,* he'd said. *When I did it before, I only did it for myself. We didn't think about it the same way and we didn't have the right words.*

Olivia had nuzzled closer in the hayloft's warm dark. *What d'you mean?* she'd asked.

Please leave it there, Livy, he'd said. *Please.*

A long time later, a women's studies professor mentioned that Victorians had few words to describe female anatomy. Olivia had excused herself. Locked in a plain bathroom stall, she'd cried for Henry, for herself, for their embarrassed fumbling.

I didn't know, she'd told him later. *Why didn't you tell me?*

Because I was scared enough, he'd replied.

Standing in his dark room, that old sadness cut her anger. Whatever forces swirled through Cypress Bend had marooned him there, and time always stood between them. The past would never stay behind.

"Is it a man or a woman right now?" Henry asked as if they were discussing her uncle's parrots. She wished he would shout loud enough for her cousins to kick down the door.

"It *was* a man." One word: *He and I are done.* "I saw him about once a week. It wasn't serious because it never is, and people always wonder why."

"One more reason—"

"Shut up." Olivia dropped to the foot of the bed, a hated stretch of distance between them. "It's like a script by now. Next, you're supposed to ask if he's better than you and that's why I slept with him. Then I say, 'No, Henry, of course not, no one's ever better because we love each other. Here, let me prove it.'"

"Livy."

"Can we skip to the proving part?"

"Livy."

"It was worth a shot." She stood, dropped her robe just to piss him off, and dug a pack of Parliaments from his bedside drawer. "Then I'm moving right along to the cigarette afterward. You want one?"

When she glanced back, Henry was simply watching her. "I know what you're doing."

"I'm not doing anything." Olivia pushed the window open, leaned out, and lit a cigarette. Its brittle, ashy taste seemed right. "You know why I came in here."

The quilt dropped as Henry got out of bed. She refused him the satisfaction of looking. "You're not yourself."

"I don't know what you're talking about." She knew exactly what he was talking about.

"Is this who you are with other people? They don't know the difference, but I do." Henry took something from a drawer. She wouldn't look.

"Is it that hard to—"

"It is, actually." He handed her an ashtray.

Olivia tapped her cigarette, glanced down, and fought a smile. "I'm angry at you," she said.

"If you laugh," he told her, "I promise not to forget you're mad."

She focused on the stars. Something streaked across them, too fast, too bright. A meteor, Olivia decided. If she refused to acknowledge it, it didn't exist. Her uncle had taught her that. "Dammit, we were having an argument. Like, several."

"I hate when you cuss." Familiar as heartbreak, he fit around her. "I love you."

"I love you, too. I'll leave, first thing. Set your alarm for four."

"Livy."

"I'm here already. We might as well." She dropped her cigarette in the ashtray. It smelled bitter-sick anyway. "It doesn't matter if they see us. I promise."

"Maybe they wouldn't care if I walked downstairs with you in the morning," Henry said eventually. His breath rose and fell against her. She could have closed her eyes and slept against its rhythm. "It feels like they would. It feels like—"

From the other side of the house, someone screamed.

CHAPTER 17

ASH

Ash sprinted from his room and threw open Elliot's door. The dogs swarmed her. Knees to her chest, she curled in the moonlight creeping through her window. That light etched the popstars on her walls to harsh cruelty; their baby faces and pouted lips seemed spectral, portentous. Ash had never heard Elliot scream—cry and shriek, but never scream. It frightened him, somehow, more than most things he'd seen at Cypress Bend. He dropped next to her and hugged her tight. "Honey, what happened?"

Shuddering with fear, she nearly rocked back and forth. Ash loved his baby cousin more than the rest of his exhausting clan. Elliot was easy; gracefully vague, content in herself, she asked for little and caused no trouble. "Why don't you talk back, like other kids?" he'd asked her once.

"Why would I?" she'd replied, pausing as she scratched a parrot's chin. Her pretty brow had puckered. "There's nothing to talk back about."

Arms drawn to her sides, Elliot looked desperately young in her tank and pajama pants. Her fear seemed blasphemous. She wasn't supposed to be frightened. Scared, maybe—Cypress Bend could scare anyone—but nothing like this, not crumpled, not curled up and crying. "Hey," Ash said, laying his hand over her tangled hair. "Talk to me, honey. What happened?"

"I don't know," she half-sobbed. "I don't know, I don't know."

Olivia appeared. Dimly, he registered Henry behind her. "Hey, baby doll," she said, immediately a mother. One scream, and they were jolted to premature parenthood again.

Ash could slip back into his old self, exchanging worried glances with Olivia, Elliot sandwiched between them; he didn't worry that stress would throw him into an asthma attack, but little else had changed.

Throwing on the lights, Rhys skidded in, Sullivan behind him. Christ, he'd brought that old baseball bat home. With Elliot curled on the floor, it didn't seem like a bad idea.

"Hey," Olivia said. "C'mon, baby. Can you talk to us? What happened?"

"I heard something outside," Elliot said. Q nudged at the girl's shoulder, then Pandora. "I got up to look, and there were three men? They were all dressed in these weird old-fashioned clothes and moving together, like they were *skipping*, like little kids, and they were getting closer—" Her voice rose into hysteria. "They *looked at me*, they *looked up*, then I blinked and Ash, I opened them, and it was all dark. It *wasn't dark* before. I hadn't even gone to bed yet. *I hadn't gone to bed*. All this time just passed, like hours and hours and hours—" Elliot's voice shattered to a sob, and the dogs glanced at Ash. *Do something about it*, they seemed to say. *Fix her*. "Where was I? What happened to all that time? Ash, time went away—I don't know where I was—"

"I don't—I mean, maybe you were dreaming on your feet—" he managed.

"She wasn't." Sullivan's face had plummeted to blank horror. Rhys looked little better. "Where did you go?" he asked.

Elliot huddled against him. Ash remembered her as a tiny, solemn-eyed toddler. *Ash*, she'd say, chubby arms outstretched. *Carry me*. He was her big brave cousin, and he could solve everything. "I don't know!" Elliot said. "I didn't seem to go anywhere! But maybe I went somewhere—"

"What did they tell you?" Sullivan asked. His questions seemed too specific. He'd seen the men too, whatever they were.

"They said—" Elliot stumbled, as if to correct herself. "I don't remember. Something about time." She spoke hurriedly, and Ash wondered if she remembered after all. "Ash, can I sleep with you? Even if we close the blinds, I don't want to—I mean—What if they come back, what if—*please, Ash*?"

"Let's grab something to go over that tank top, you're cold," he said as gently as he could. "If you really don't want to stay by yourself, just for tonight, okay?" He'd sleep on the floor with his dogs.

"Here." Holding her robe shut, Olivia unearthed another shirt from a drawer. She ought to have grabbed a shirt for herself; she and Henry really needed to own up to whatever they were doing. Purse-lipped, Rhys glanced at his sister, then at Henry, who watched not Elliot, but the far wall. Was Rhys just figuring it out? Ash had better things to worry about than Rhys and Sullivan throwing a tantrum. Brow furrowed, Olivia helped Elliot into that shirt gently, as if she were small again. His cousin might have hated the role they'd handed her, but she loved Elliot.

"D'you mind her staying with you?" she asked Ash.

"Of course not," Ash said. Reluctantly, she handed Elliot over. He led the shaking girl into his room and settled her under his down comforter. The dogs jumped up with her, a protective ring of shepherds, and though she still seemed frightened, neither did she protest when Ash camped out on the floor. He left a light on. "You okay?" he asked.

"No," she said quietly. "I don't know where time went."

Ash didn't know if she'd stayed rooted to one spot, or if something else had happened. He couldn't stand to say he didn't know, either.

"This place never really scared me before, you know?" she whispered. "I mean it did, but not like that. Ash?" Her voice tilted too high.

"Yeah?" he asked from his nest. The Persian rug scratched his back. No dog kept him warm; they all crowded Elliot. They loved her best, and always had. Just then, he was glad of it.

"Is that what happened to Henry?" Elliot asked.

"I don't know," he said honestly.

"'Cause if it did, how do I know you're still the you I knew before, and not some other Ash?"

"Oh, honey." The dogs shot Ash reproachful looks as he took their places on the bed. Elliot trembled as he rubbed her back, and her bracelets clinked softly. "I'm the same me. I promise."

"That's what every you would promise," she said.

He smoothed her hair onto the pillow. "The dogs wouldn't love you if you weren't their Elliot," Ash told her.

"No, they wouldn't." She settled a little. He'd known she would believe the dogs.

"You want me to stay here til you fall asleep?" he asked.

"Yeah." Her voice was a little girl's again.

Ash fell asleep sitting up, a hand on her back, dogs at his feet.

CHAPTER 18

SULLIVAN

Sullivan tossed through his suitcase and decided on his black Savannah College of Art and Design t-shirt. Confessionals started after breakfast.

"Don't you say anything," Rhys said as Sullivan examined his red-rimmed eyes in the mirror. He didn't need to ask what his cousin was talking about. They'd burst from their room just in time to glimpse Henry bolt from his, Olivia behind in nothing but a robe.

"Henry used to be our best friend!" Sullivan wanted to punch the mirror suddenly, watch his image shatter into pieces around his fist. "He could've told us. Would it be that hard to say, 'Hey, I'm in love with Olivia'? Does he think we'd *care*? I mean, it's like, '*Vaya con Dios*. Once we liked you better than her, and if this is what she wants, we'll live with it.'"

"Sullivan!"

"We did!"

"She's my *sister*! You can't say we liked the marooned Civil War soldier better than her!" Somewhat viciously, Rhys yanked on a black University of Richmond t-shirt.

Defeated once more by Cypress Bend's absurdities, Sullivan sank to the bed. He shouldn't have had a marooned Civil War soldier stuck at his family home. He was heir to a house of sabers, to silent ghosts in corners, a little cousin screaming about three men in the night, Thoroughbreds eviscerated under a blue-hazed sky. They snatched humor where they could, but what did it add up to? The three men had returned. *When three men come walking again, when the family walks with them*, he remembered, and shoved it back. He wanted to talk to Rhys about it, about the ghost that had come when they were twelve, but his cousin always went silent when he mentioned it. Sullivan couldn't stand to stretch the distance between them. Better to keep his mouth shut, despite the fear churning in his belly.

"C'mon." Rhys used his gentle voice, one that lifted Sullivan up and carried him home. He pulled his cousin to his feet. "Cousin Mickie probably has bacon ready. You love bacon."

"I'm not hungry," Sullivan muttered, but it didn't matter. He would always eat bacon.

Downstairs, his feet hit the plastic and life soured a little more. He should have worn shoes. In the kitchen, Sullivan found himself bowed by the weight of familiar objects—the Art Deco silverware and those mismatched Fiestaware plates, the rainbow-ringed glasses and tattered linen napkins. He recalled the Corningware platters from earliest childhood and might have teethed on the rubber serving spoons. Cypress Bend seemed trapped in time, and always had, down to the crossed sabers over the lintels.

An older woman in a kerchief bent over the stove, her dark hands braced against the metal. Deep, gathered lines etched her face; her hands gnarled with age and work. Sullivan tried to ignore her, but she had a kind of gravitational force, as if they took their accorded places in her orbit. His back began to ache; his face felt hot, as if he leaned over a hot stove himself. The household was already snarfing Mickie's heaped platter of bacon. If they noticed the ghost, they studiously ignored it, though Elliot seemed too pale. Glaring at everyone but Ash, the dogs piled close to her chair. A bleach-blond man sat next to Ash; his deep tan and whitened teeth marked him as too West Coast for South Carolina.

"This is Ethan, the co-executive producer," Ash said as Sullivan took his place next to Henry. "He flew in to talk contracts, and then go over what we're going to do this morning."

"You must be Sullivan and Rhys." Ethan smiled too brightly for the hour. He said hello, then outlined contract terms. Sullivan tuned out once he said, "Two hundred and fifty thousand a season" and "half a mill a season after five." Did it matter, really? He had enough. It was for Rhys more than any of them. Ethan couldn't see the ghost. He had no idea what strangeness lurked in Cypress Bend.

"Any questions?" the Californian finally asked.

"Questions about what, dear?" Aunt Alda asked.

Sullivan patted her hand. "Nothing important," he told her. She settled back to her scrambled eggs and oatmeal.

"I've got a question." Rhys leaned forward. Sullivan recognized those narrowed eyes and fixed gaze; he'd seen it the few times he'd pushed his cousin past endurance. Rhys had a long fuse and a high tolerance for life's absurdities. Sullivan envied him. When Rhys lost his temper, rooms stilled and men listened. "We get veto rights over any footage, or I'm not signing," his cousin said.

"Well, that's not—I mean—" Ethan stumbled. His Hollywood facade slipped, startling Sullivan nearly as much as Rhys's objection. They were supposed to sign their contracts and shut up.

"I don't care," Rhys said. "Veto rights, or we walk. You're not airing something that makes us look like idiots."

Olivia and Henry nodded. Ash gaped like a hooked fish. Sullivan stuffed down a grin. They had him. Ash knew better than to ask, but they could plead ignorance. And with Rhys asking, his brother couldn't guilt them into signing. They couldn't have ginned up a better plan.

The Trenholms waited. Ethan composed himself into sunniness again. "Sounds fine to me. We'll have to wait a day to sign the contracts, though, then we can't film, so maybe we can add something later—"

"I'm not signing anything til I read it," Rhys replied. "How about this? We'll agree to film confessionals anyway, but we don't sign the contracts til they're amended. And we send them to the lawyers to look over." He glanced at Ash. "Are you still using Lochlan Sutlais, or did one of the cousins graduate from law school yet?"

"Still using the Sutlais firm," Ash managed, at the same time Ethan said, "It's not the regular—"

"Or we don't film today." Rhys settled back in his chair. "Your choice."

Tension billowed like black smoke. Just when Sullivan thought he couldn't stand it, that he had to speak, or shout, perhaps storm out, anything to cut that oily, unbreathable air, Ethan cleared his throat. "I'll get the amended contracts to you tomorrow," he said. "We appreciate you guys filming today. Any more questions?"

Rhys settled back in his chair. Sullivan wanted to high-five him.

"Then onto confessionals," Ash said. "They're basically—"

"We've all seen reality TV," Sullivan told him, scooping up cheese hashbrowns. Mickie could cook.

"Are you gonna be like this when the cameras are here?" Ash asked.

"I hope not," Olivia said. Her plate was nearly empty. Maybe she'd already eaten.

"Am I gonna be like this? I don't know. Are you gonna ask ridiculous questions?" Sullivan was there for Rhys, the cousin who'd hauled him from a hundred drunken escapades, who'd comforted him through night terrors, who'd suffered through the same lectures on Confederate battle strategy. If he loved anyone, he loved Rhys.

"So we're going to ask you some questions to help guide the confessionals," Ethan said. "They'll be very basic. Don't hold back. Just pretend you're talking to your friend or therapist, you know? And we'll edit out whatever you'd like us to."

Thanks to Rhys, Sullivan could have muttered around his bacon, but his cousin might have kicked him under the table.

Breakfast dragged on. The ghost leaned on that stove, never moving. Sullivan's back throbbed. He tried to forget the night before; he hadn't slept til gray dawn seeped under the blinds. He never wanted to think about those three men again. *I saw them once,* he could have told Elliot. *On the night before my twenty-first birthday, they appeared behind the house. Ash will tell you I left because of the horse, but it wasn't the horse. I left because those three men are time, and their stories circle like a gristmill. I had to get out. The ghost-woman warned us that we'd see them.*

Ethan droned about confessionals. Sullivan ignored him. Olivia wasn't eating; Elliot pushed her hashbrowns around her plate. Sullivan wondered why she had bacon—Elliot was a vegetarian, which she wore more authentically than most teenage girls. He hid a grin when she sneaked that bacon to the dogs. Ash had to know. If Sullivan had tried it, his brother would have fussed. *Stop that or Dad will find out,* he'd have said, an adult's worry clouding his face. His stress might have bloomed into an asthma attack. Sullivan watched his brother and cousin, Elliot thinking Ash didn't see, and Ash carefully pretending he didn't. Did it happen every morning? Did Ash always turn his head, twisting his mouth to stop a blooming smile? It was sweet, and it ached. Sullivan's brother never loved him that much.

CHAPTER 19

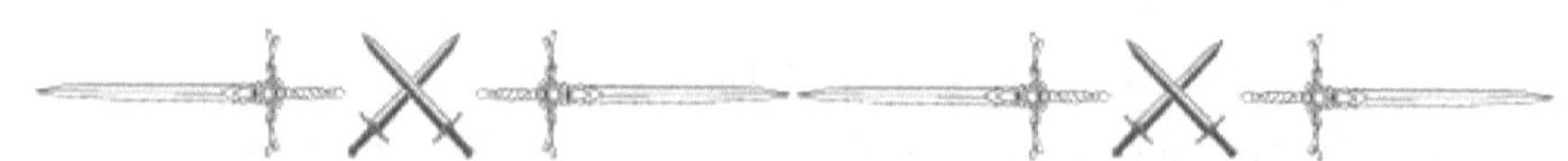

RHYS

"**R**hys, you first," Ethan said, snapping him from his wandering thoughts. Everyone was getting up, wandering to their personal hiding places. Tourists would invade the house soon. They'd track dust on Ash's plastic sheeting and exclaim over the sabers. Someone would try to sit on a couch, and the tour guide would tell them to get up. A small child would reel toward their furniture and slap it with sticky hands. Rhys had hardly noticed his breakfast. The ghost woman hovered over the stove, poised in her own grief; sometimes those spectral figures lurked in corners and sometimes they didn't. After so many years, Rhys thought he'd become accustomed to them, but some atrocities lingered, years exacerbating rather than dimming their horror.

I see people in the house, he'd finally told Sullivan when they were around thirteen. *Those people you mentioned that time—*

His cousin had whirled on him, eyes panicked and wide. *Don't,* he'd said. *Dad will kill us. You know that.*

Rhys never spoke of them again.

"Rhys." Ash touched his shoulder, and he twitched away. "You first."

"Me first what?" he asked, reminding himself that he'd won the argument over their contracts. He scraped together enough grace to smile.

"For your confessional." Ethan's grin never slipped. "We're set up in the second floor living room, like I said."

Rhys slogged upstairs. They'd positioned a single Queen Anne chair and a French end table in front of some bookshelves—very Old South, old money. Maybe Ash was used to strangers rearranging his house, but Rhys wasn't. He found it both annoying and unsettling, especially when they handed him a glass of water. He, the host, was supposed to fetch them water. Worse, though he'd met the crew, Rhys couldn't recall their names. It felt like a terrible omission, and he resented himself on their behalf.

"Okay, tell us about moving here," Ethan said after he was mic'd. "You were how old? Speak in complete sentences so we can cut my questions."

"My mama died when I was five," Rhys said. "My daddy died when I was nine, so my sister Olivia and I moved into Cypress Bend, mostly with our grandmother and uncle. But everyone lived here." Rhys had to tick them off on his fingers. "There was Sullivan and Ash; their dad, my Uncle Truluck; his brother, my uncle Wade; and their mother, my grandmother. Elliot was born when Sullivan and I were sophomores in high school. Then you had Cousin Valance, a first cousin once removed, plus Valance's wife Victoria Lee and our great-uncle Lucius. We also had our great-aunt Alda living here. The house feels really empty now, especially since Uncle Wade died two years ago."

It hurt to recall those kind old relatives, their patience and grace during his years of misery. Nearly as antique as those sabers and just as Southern, they'd adored his uncle's Confederate mania, though they'd hated his tendencies to strong drink and swift fists. *Don't you touch those kids again, Truluck,* his grandmother would say.

If I was a younger man, I'd make you quit that bottle and leave those boys alone, Cousin Valance would shout. *You leave off them, y'hear me? They didn't do nothing to you.*

"What about Henry?" Ethan asked.

He fed Ethan their old lie about Henry. "When Sullivan and I were fifteen, my uncle was doing genealogical research and found this distant cousin who'd been orphaned. You have to understand how we are." How did he explain it? The lie worked because it was true. "Family means everything to us. Doesn't matter how much we fight. Blood's everything. That's why this land's so important. It's all tied together, family and blood and land and soil. This farm is us, it's part of being a Trenholm, like blood's blood and you always take care of it. Family shows up at your door and you let 'em in. So Uncle Truluck found this orphaned kid in these terrible conditions and of course he brought him home, and that was the end of it. I think he's a fifth cousin." Only that rang false. Henry was a first cousin four times removed.

The questions continued, an interrogation in miniature. What was it like living with Ash and Sullivan? *They fought a lot.* Were there family alliances in place? *We all love Elliot. Ash likes Olivia best. Sullivan and I are best friends.* Time, distance, and argument had eroded their relationship; Rhys was unsure if it still counted. He prayed it did.

Who returned home the most? *Sullivan has been gone for a decade. Until the show started, I came back on Christmas, Easter, Elliot's birthday, Father's Day, the Fourth of July, and most Confederate Memorial Days. Olivia comes back all the time.*

"Now for the hard question. You've had some scary stuff happen around this farm. What's the scariest?" Ethan asked.

Rhys felt the cameras closing in. What did he tell them? There were so many worsts, different flavors of frightening. *I don't know, maybe that time Sullivan found a wounded Civil War soldier collapsed at the base of the Boundary Tree. Henry was too hurt to cry. Mud clung to him, and when we hauled him inside, blood seeped all over the rug. Cousin Valance's wife Victoria Lee cut his clothes off on the living room floor.*

Or maybe the worst thing happened when we were twelve. It was winter, and we'd built a fire in the library. We were settling down with books when a woman walked in. She wore old-fashioned clothes, but her pale hair spilled down her back like a girl. She could have been twenty or she could have been forty. We never figured out who she was, but we knew she was a ghost because we could see the bookshelves through her. Some of the ghosts here, they look as solid as you or me. She didn't, and that was terrifying. Oh, and she was white. As best as we can tell, the rest of the ghosts are all enslaved people, and we see them every day. Do you know what it feels like to choke on guilt, especially when you realize some of those enslaved people look like you? Of course you don't, Ethan. Hollywood feels no shame.

"Sullivan and Rhys," the woman said. A ghost knew our names, and my heart skipped sideways. *A ghost is bad enough. Do you know the terror that hits when one speaks? No, you don't, Ethan. I can tell by your smile that you don't believe in them.*

"I'll tell you three true things and give you a piece of advice," she said. "You'll listen to the advice because you see the truth."

"Who are you?" I asked. My tongue still worked, and that shocked me almost as much as the woman.

But she smiled. "I'm family," she told us. "The first true thing: a new first cousin will come to the house."

Sullivan and I glanced at one another. Even though we were looking at a ghost, I almost burst out laughing. My father had died almost three years before, and Uncle Wade was his only sibling. When you're twelve, sex between people over thirty is unthinkable.

"The second thing," she said. "You'll find a more distant cousin in the back field. He'll come from far away." I didn't know what she meant, but five years later, Henry came, and Sullivan didn't sleep for weeks.

Then she paused a second, flipped her hair behind her head. The gesture seemed too alive, and it scared me more than almost anything I've ever seen on this farm before or since. Sullivan was still, as silent as if his dad might start hitting. "The third true thing," the woman said. "When three men come walking, when the family walks with them, then it's time, if you want to stop it."

"Time for what?" I asked.

The woman smiled then. "Time for the house to fall."

Sullivan's hand crept into mine. We're still waiting for that, but Elliot came, and then Henry. It'll happen one day. I know it like I know my own name. And the three men came last night. Sullivan was terrified, but we didn't talk about it. Whenever he mentions them, I stonewall him. Trenholm men don't talk about things like that.

"The advice now," the woman told us. "Remember it, and listen. When the time comes, use the sabers."

"What?" I blurted, then remembered I was talking to a ghost and shut up again.

"You'll know," she said. Then she left as calmly as she'd come. I wondered vaguely why a ghost bothered with feet. Couldn't she just disappear? We never saw her again, and we never told anyone, because there was no one to tell. Ash and Olivia would have blown us off. Uncle Truluck would've called us liars and hit Sullivan for it, maybe me. You didn't talk about ghosts in this house, not ever. He didn't hit me and Ash much, but he beat the hell out of Sullivan. He never touched Olivia. She had to watch instead, and she learned to shut up and take whatever the world handed her. She learned to fake it. My uncle hurt her almost as much as he hurt Sullivan.

"Once, Sullivan and I were down by the horse barn right around dark," Rhys said, choosing something in the middle of Cypress Bend's possible horrors, a tale plausibly terrifying rather than cosmically bizarre. "We'd been riding, and we turned the horses loose in the pasture. They walked about—oh, I don't know, maybe ten yards—then both squealed and bucked, real high, not a play-buck, but like they were fighting something, and they ran. At first we didn't see anything behind us. Then Sullivan grabs my arm and he's like, 'Rhys, in the shadows over there.'

"So I'm squinting, and I don't see anything. We'd just finished riding, and I had my helmet on still. Sullivan actually takes the back of my head and yanks it up. 'On the roof,' he says." *On the motherfucking roof*, Sullivan had said in a high, desperate whisper. The moon had smeared high and white between blue clouds; heat had dragged low and heavy on Rhys's neck.

"I looked up and saw red eyes on the barn roof. They were too big to be a bat or something. Then—and I'm not kidding, I know what I saw—whatever it was stood up. It had to be six feet tall. I saw those eyes go from roof-level to six feet up, and they *stayed there*, attached to this black shape. Then another pair of red eyes lit up next to it, and another, and there were three in a row. They were all watching us."

What the fuck are we going to do? Sullivan had asked, staring, hoofbeats still receding. Twenty seconds had passed. A distinct malevolence radiated from the creatures, a heaviness, as if they sucked the air and returned it tainted. They seemed hazy shaped, and their red-round eyes did not blink. Rhys's hands trembled in the sick heat as if he were freezing. Behind the creatures, something streaked across the sky.

The hoofbeats receded. No cicadas whirred; no tree frogs sang. Even the manure-flies lay quiet. In the field's dipped hollows, fireflies should have blinked. Nothing moved in that long silence, and Rhys's heart beat in his fingers as those creatures brooded on the barn roof's sharp cant. He couldn't gather enough thoughts to wonder what they were or where they came from, only that they were there, and he shouldn't be.

"'Okay,' I said. 'We're gonna back away, and we're gonna keep our eyes on them, and we'll make it to the horses. They'll keep us safe, and we'll know if anything comes.' So Sullivan and I never stopped looking at those things. We went backward, one step at a time, God, maybe a quarter mile? Those fields are huge. I don't even know. We backed up til we couldn't see those things on the barn anymore, and we kept going til we found the horses grazing in the dark. Then we jumped on their backs and stayed til morning. That's the scariest thing I've ever seen at Cypress Bend."

It wasn't. But it was the scariest thing Rhys could say on TV.

CHAPTER 20

ASH

After lunch, the crew settled Ash's brother, cousins, and Civil War refugee in HQ. A standard lighting rig shone from its corners, and their sound guys rigged everyone with a mic, including Elliot. "I want to show y'all what we discovered in the back field," Ash said. "You know from growing up here that there's *something* going on with Cypress Bend. We've discovered what we call phenomena. Because of the frequency of lightning strikes back there, we focused our investigation on the back field, west of the Pavilion and southeast of the Boundary Tree. We shot some fireworks off there and threw up some dust. This is what we saw."

"Alright," Rhys said. Narrow eyed, suspicion writ large, Sullivan watched the screen. Olivia wore the face that won every poker game. Brandishing a remote, Ash pretended to hit a button.

"Okay, you might have seen the clip already," Ethan said after waiting a few beats. "Basically, we're going to show you the same thing you've seen on *Paranormal Gone South*, plus some stuff we can't air." He spoke as if the disturbing footage was simply cut for brevity's sake. "I'm going to run the whole thing so we can get authentic reaction shots." Ethan hit his own remote, the real one. "We filmed this footage last June. This was the season finale, so I flew in for it. At the point I'm starting, we've already set off several rounds of fireworks. They keep exploding somewhere right around fifty feet up."

First, the show rolled: fireworks burst in the night sky as their second cousins hollered gleefully. A row of computers glowed atop a table. "We got a signal of 1.6 gigahertz!" TV

Ash shouted. Ethan swore that his good looks reeled in viewers. Ash wasn't so sure. "Are we broadcasting that?"

"Nope!" The camera cut to their cousin Lewis, headphones on, ensconced in HQ. "Not broadcasting anything from here! You boys out there?"

"Nope!" their cousin Sinclair called.

Footage cut to a green-and-black radio frequency readout. "When we set off fireworks or otherwise irritate the farm," Lewis said in voiceover, "we often see a radio frequency of 1.6 gigahertz, sometimes 1.7. Those are radio frequencies used specifically for ground-to-space and space-to-ground communications. They see them all the time in connection with anomalous events, including those in Sedona and at Skinwalker Ranch in Utah." Lewis Trenholm's PhD in astronomy lent *Paranormal Gone South* credibility. His geek-boy hotness jacked their ratings. Ash's father had always ignored him: a Black cousin, unworthy of notice. He'd become something like the only friend Ash had. "Remember," Lewis continued, "the back field was once the largest cotton field on the plantation. We see concentrations of energy in places where this farm has seen a lot of suffering, which means anywhere associated with slavery—the cotton field, the cabins, the barn. So it's no shock that field is a hotbed of paranormal activity. No pun intended with the frequency of lightning strikes."

Their row of computers seemed a small bulwark against the night's long dark. "Hey, phones are out again!" TV Ethan called.

"Uh, that wasn't on TV," Rhys said.

"This is the footage we didn't show," Ash replied. "Keep watching."

"Set more off!" TV Ash shouted. Blue light drew him in eerie shadows against the dark. A spark flashed, then a firework hissed and flew. The Roman candle broke gold over the field; Sinclair and Parker, both second cousins once removed, high-fived and cheered. Those boys loved their explosions.

"Damn, that one went off around fifty feet, too," Sinclair said.

"We got orbs!" TV Ash yelled, pointing at the woods. Sickeningly, the camera swiveled; it caught several white globes threading casually between the branches. They hazed and flared as the lens zoomed. "I think they're about the size of basketballs, maybe?" Lewis was saying in the background.

"Fuck, I've never seen so many," Boo replied. They hadn't censored the omitted clips, but Ash still startled at the curse. "There has to be one, two, three, four, five, six, maybe? Okay, five, that one disappeared behind a tree. Four."

"Eyes on the sky, people!" Lewis shouted. "1.6 and orbs means we're likely to see UAPs!" The feed to cut to a take of him standing in HQ. "'UAP' is the technical term for 'unidentified aerial phenomenon.' We use that to differentiate our scientific work from less rigorous work." *Or from rank conspiracy theorists,* Ash could have added.

"Phone's are still out!" TV Ethan called on screen. It had irritated Ash then, and it bothered him once more. Ethan always stated the obvious. It marked him as an outsider, unfamiliar with Cypress Bend's strangeness. Of course the phones had died. They wouldn't turn on until that particular madness ended.

"Do we need to get outta here?" Parker asked.

"Fire off another set and then set off the dust bomb!" TV Ash told them. Footage cut, presumably for commercial, and rolled through a mini recap: some fireworks, then TV Ash standing in front of the bulletin board in HQ. He never watched his own show. The board's maps, scrawled-upon photos, and handwritten notes seemed to belong to someone else. But that room was his. Ash had become a conspiracy theorist, a Fox Mulder, a man determined to shout against science that something greater than the world was willing to acknowledge brooded in his own backyard. He might as well have donned a tinfoil hat and sworn that aliens murdered JFK.

"Like Lewis said, we've identified the back field as a locus of paranormal phenomena at Cypress Bend," TV Ash said. "We've noticed that no matter how high our Roman candles are supposed to go, they always seem to explode around fifty feet. Tonight, we're going to make sure the farm is paying attention, then set off a dust bomb to figure out if there's anything at that height that might be invisible to the naked eye. We're careful to keep the crew safe while we do this. At Cypress Bend, safety is paramount."

Ash hated his onscreen self. As usual, no one had warned him that his hair kicked out at odd angles or that he needed to shave his stubble. It always looked great in the mirror and awful on camera.

Roman candles splintered white and gold. Before anyone could exclaim, a deep *whoomph* boomed below them, and dust exploded in their wake. "Get the lights! Get the lights!" TV Ash yelled. Scrambling like ants, his cousins threw on a circle of spotlights. A dust cloud eddied above the field in lazy, hazed swirls. Ash remembered that moment—it had seemed, at first, like nothing special. *We got nothing*, he'd almost yelled.

Hands on his hips, TV Ash studied that cloud like a bemused foreman. His brow puckered, and he cocked his head like one of Wade's parrots. He'd thought, *Maybe we can't see anything in the middle.* "Turn them off again!" he called to his cousins. "Leave the one on the left, and move it down real slow."

Idly coiling, the dust's dense blur rolled and billowed. One by one, the spotlights winked off. Boo cranked downward the last. "Wait!" Lewis yelled. "There! Move it up again!"

"Holy—" the rest of the cameraman's words were bleeped.

"Yeah, and going around it!" TV Ash said. "Like on the sides, look!"

"Oh, there's something up there. Holy—" Parker's voice rang with fear, awe. Fifty feet above, the spotlight had snagged what Ash could only call a *something*, something that bent the beam around it and split it in two. Their light flickered with the dust, but the narrow disc held.

Ash couldn't explain it or rationalize it. What it was, it existed in that cloud of dust and light. In the field above his own farm, reality turned slant.

"There's something up there," TV Ash told them. "Y'all there's actually something up there."

"Oh my God," Lewis said, squinting through the dark. "That's not nothing."

"Yeah, what the hell is that?" TV Ethan asked.

No one answered him.

CHAPTER 21

OLIVIA

Olivia tapped a pen against her lips. If Ash meant his footage to shock her, it didn't work. But Henry pressed his lips together; he said he never watched the show. Nor had her cousin likely told him much about their pyrotechnic exploits. *Despite living in the same house, Ash and I seldom talk*, he'd written Olivia. *He has his show, and I have my research. I think of you often.* With their old-fashioned, slanted script, Henry's declarative sentences could accumulate to effortless devastation.

Ethan hit the remote. "Okay, this is where the video feed cuts," he said. "We have no footage of what happened next." He smiled a little. "You probably wonder why some of the show seems canned, but you know how the farm is. We have to reshoot a lot because our film gets lost. I'll let Ash take it from here. What we tell you next won't be included in *Keeping up with the Paranormal*."

Sullivan nearly spit out his sweet tea. For once, Olivia was grateful for his tantrum; he spared her the effort. "Is that seriously the title?"

Ash pinched his nose, a gesture so like his father's that Olivia might have laughed if she hadn't hated her uncle. *No, you won't be wearing those jeans, darling*, he'd often said. *Pretty girls like you wear dresses.* "We came up with some others," her cousin said, "but for liability reasons, we can't use anything that implies harm to visitors. *Home Sweet Horror* was out."

"Least that's not a *Kardashians* rip-off," Rhys muttered.

"I think it's okay," Elliot said, speaking for the first time. "But maybe a little overdone?"

"Can't you call it *Trenholm Confidential* or some shit?" Sullivan asked. "Some stupid pun on 'Southern Gothic' if you wanna go with that angle? I don't know about y'all, but I don't want Kanye West, or whatever he's called now, laughing while his wife stomps me with her designer heels."

"That got vivid." Olivia didn't let herself laugh; she seldom let herself in front of men like Ethan. "You keeping it together over there, Sullivan?"

"*Anyway.*" Ash had to herd them into consensus, and he'd never had the patience for diplomacy, except perhaps where Elliot was concerned. "Look, I'll just break it down for you. So we saw the thing in the dust cloud, right? We flew a heavy-duty drone up there to see what happened, and it disappeared. Sucked right up into the thing. Immediately, three UAPs showed up, and before you ask, there was no aircraft visible on the ADS-B monitor. Even if they weren't running transponders—which is illegal unless you're military, but we'll run with it—they were going at least two thousand miles an hour, calculated by approximate distance and how fast they passed known landmarks, which is *over Mach 1.*" As if daring them to argue, Ash crossed his arms and flumped backward.

From the table's far end, Henry scanned their faces, maybe deciding how to arrange his own. Once, Ash's speech would have been incomprehensible to him. But Henry had become unfortunately nimble at revising both cosmology and morality; by now, existence itself probably seemed open to dispute.

"The drone disappeared?" Sullivan said finally.

"Isn't that what I said?" Trust Ash to drop something beyond scientific understanding on the table, then seem irritated when they asked questions.

"It *disappeared*?" Rhys said. "Like, gone? Vanished? You flew a drone into some weird spot on the farm and managed to send it, like, somewhere else? Are you saying there really is a freaking portal?"

Sullivan leaned back and loosed an awed string of blistering but uncreative expletives.

"You're a conceptual artist," Olivia told him. "Do better."

"Excuse me?" Sullivan threw her an eyebrow quirk. He probably practiced it in the mirror, and a heavy exhaustion dragged at her. They would go on like that whether or not she needled them.

"Never mind," Olivia said.

"Wait a second." Sullivan smirked. Olivia couldn't decide if she wanted to smirk with him or slap him. She'd spent a childhood torn between the two. "That was the drone you always had on the show, right? The super heavy-duty, yellow-and-black one?"

"Yes." Ash glared, a child who'd lost his favorite toy.

"So somewhere, in some other timeline or dimension, your mega-expensive, custom drone dropped out of the clear blue sky?"

Eyes fastened to the tabletop, Henry fought a grin. If he met her eyes, Olivia would burst into shattering laughter. Something over their farm violated accepted laws of physics, and the Trenholms snickered around an antebellum table, busy baiting one another. Viewers would find that tendency amusing. They would never see Sullivan tense when his father walked into a room, or hear the old man rant about Reconstruction; they wouldn't see him dress the boys in Rebel uniforms or hand her a newborn baby to raise. The sum of sins committed for and against them, the Trenholms argued because it left no air for weeping.

"Can we please keep this discussion on track?" Ash asked as he slid from annoyance to anger. Captivated by his own cleverness, Sullivan might not notice. "You're the one who was so hellbent on discussing that portal."

"If you could bring it back to—" Ethan began, plastering on a shark-white smile.

"Bless your heart." Olivia smiled as falsely as he had. "If you could give us a moment, we'd appreciate it, darling."

Henry snorted, then coughed into his sleeve. Sullivan hid a snicker; Ash's expression turned murderous. She shouldn't have felt a small surge of satisfaction. Bless *his* fucking heart. They'd suffered enough. Her cousin never should have sold them into paranormal infamy.

Chipper facade never slipping, Ethan and the crew left. Ash rounded on the rest of them. Jaw clenched, face reddening, he looked so much like his father that Olivia grabbed Sullivan's hand under the table. He squeezed hers hard. Nearly thirty years old, and they still dropped into those lost children. "Y'all *stop it*," Ash hissed, that low voice her uncle used before his fists flew. The shaming would come next. She'd watched it happen so many times, always the witness, never the victim. "You want the world to see us act like that? You want that on the cover of grocery-store tabloids? Don't think they won't fucking do it. They will, and everyone'll laugh. You want them to laugh at us?"

"You could've told us." Rhys, the reasonable one, threw it right back. Olivia would have to thank him. "You think we don't deserve to know there's an interdimensional portal in our backyard?"

"You knew that," Ash snapped. "You think Henry wandered in off the goddamn street?"

"You sound like your father." Henry rose, and Olivia loved him one more time. "Don't you see their faces? You're better than that."

Ash blinked once, twice, as if rising from a dream. "Did I—oh God. I didn't mean to—I'm so sorry." Slumped into himself, he dropped to a chair. "I'm sorry, y'all. I didn't—I'm so sorry."

"Are you gonna lecture us on Chickamauga next?" Sullivan's thin voice wrecked his attempt at sarcasm. "I can tell you about it, if you want. It was the second bloodiest battle after Gettysburg. General Braxton Bragg crossed Chickamauga Creek, and the battle began just after dawn—"

"Stop it." Ash sounded close to tears. "Please don't."

"He wanted to wedge the Rebels between Chattanooga and—"

"Sullivan," Henry said quietly, and that was enough. Ash's conspiracy-theory bulletin board seemed a ridiculous relic of something that had never mattered. He'd discovered a portal in the back garden. He'd lost a drone there. He hadn't bothered with the house, where their own ghosts lingered, most unquiet of spirits.

CHAPTER 22

SULLIVAN

Sullivan tried to gather the shards of his composure. Ethan returned, and they manufactured thoughtful reactions to Ash's clips. It would always be that fake. Behind closed doors, they'd fall apart; cameras would capture smaller dramas. They would snatch their money and run—probably to therapy, certainly to pick up the pieces they'd torn from one another. He, at least, would run far, and he'd never go home again. Blood made a man, but it could also unmake him. No longer would he answer the family summons. Sullivan had stayed for Rhys; he would not do it again.

When they finished, he fled. Detouring through the downstairs living room, Sullivan snagged a bottle of bourbon, cursing that he'd have to drink it neat. He'd take his bender in the upstairs library. If they interrupted him, he'd refuse their shame. Ash bore the burden of their father's face, and he'd used it. He'd known they would freeze. They wouldn't argue, but they'd shut up, and he'd win. Almost as bad, the three men had returned. *When three men come walking again, when the family walks with them, then it's time, if you want to stop it*, the ghost-woman had told him and Rhys. *Time for the house to fall*, she'd said. Did he want to stop that? He'd have said, *No, let it fall*, but he loved his cousins. Maybe he hated the rest of it, but—it was a hopeless tangle, all those conflicting moralities of history and blood, of obligation and righteousness.

Slumped in a silk chair, Sullivan drank from the bottle. It was too hot to light a fire. Much later, cotton-mouthed and half-sick, he woke in his own bed. Maybe Rhys had dragged him there, or maybe he'd dragged himself. He wasn't sure if Rhys still loved him enough to bother. Certainly, he wasn't Rhys's responsibility, and never had been; he'd never taken Rhys's consideration for granted, though everyone presumed he had. Rhys knew he didn't. *Thank you*, Sullivan had said every time, no matter how slurred the words sounded. He'd say it once. Rhys would nod. They'd needed no more.

Dawn smudged gray under the blinds. He couldn't sleep any longer. His cousin snored on; the house muttered familiar recriminations. Shaky-handed, Sullivan showered and dressed, then walked downstairs, where that clammy plastic surprised him one more time. He needed slippers, coffee, possibly another shot. The kitchen's warmth seemed a hostility too early to bear as he filled the coffee pot, and its faucet's hiss loud enough to wake upstairs sleepers. One more time, an older woman stood at the stove, bent-backed, silent as always. Sullivan's own back ached at the sight, and an overwhelming hopelessness washed over him. Nothing would change. Nothing ever changed at Cypress Bend; stuck like bugs in amber, they were caught.

He slouched at the butcher block table to wait. Maybe he would drink his coffee on the upstairs porch and pray the sun brought no surprises.

"How was the sofa?" Henry asked, and Sullivan startled from his slumped daze.

"Sorry," he said, voice as unwelcoming as he could manage without outright rudeness. "I didn't hear you come in."

"I didn't expect you did." Henry wore his Levis like a birthright. Sullivan couldn't look at those jeans without remembering that Henry had once staggered out of Gettysburg, two Yankee bullets in his shoulder. *I'm lucky it was pistol shot*, he'd said. *A minié ball would've killed me.* "You're up early for a man who spent yesterday drinking himself half to death."

"I don't sleep well." He refused to blush. Sullivan opened the cabinet; Trenholms had likely kept mugs on the same shelf for more than a century. Ash had bought new ones, sinew-white and extra large, but their place hadn't changed. It seemed as sure as bedrock. The world would change, but Sullivan could always find the mugs. He poured coffee and set two on the table. The blue-dressed woman ignored them. Vaguely, he wondered if Henry could see her, and a forgotten moment rose: Sullivan shouting, the ghost at the bottom of the stairs, Henry. *I hope you remember you fought to keep them right where they are*, he'd said. *Well, look, Henry! They're still fucking there, like you won after all.* Heat crept up Sullivan's cheeks. Had Olivia stopped his yelling? Rhys? He couldn't remember.

Henry rose. One of the innumerable baby pictures fluttered from the refrigerator door; Henry replaced it amid engagement announcements, wedding magnets, and Christmas cards.

"Did you finally stop drinking your coffee black?" Sullivan asked.

"No," he replied. "But you drink it with cream and sugar."

"I don't," Sullivan said. His words seemed too loud for the early-morning kitchen.

Henry set out a carton of cream and a bowl of orange slices, then pulled a spoon from the drawer. "Why're you doing this?" he asked.

"Doing what?" Sullivan asked, trying to parse accusation from kindness.

"You got angry at Ash yesterday. I don't blame you, either. He deserved it." Henry took his seat again. Maybe coffee itself still seemed like an indulgence for him. During the Civil War, Union blockades had forced the South to chicory. Ash sold it in the gift shop. "But I've never seen your brother drink liquor."

"What're you trying to tell me?" Maybe he should have been angrier, but it was too damn early. Sullivan picked up the cream, then resettled in his chair, searching for an angle that eased his aching back.

"There's more than one way to behave badly," Henry replied, "and more than one way to act like your father. Don't do this, Sullivan. Rhys had to drag you to bed again last night. You're lucky he loves you."

At least he hadn't mentioned Sullivan shouting at ghosts. The woman still leaned over the stove; though lines knit her hands, her rolled sleeves revealed arms roped with the muscle born of hard work. Sullivan wished one more time that he could apologize, though he couldn't begin to imagine what he'd say.

"I know he loves me. I agreed to this stupid-ass show for him," Sullivan told Henry. It seemed treasonous to talk, in Cypress Bend, of life's bare bones.

"The show's a terrible idea," Henry said. "How d'you think I feel about it? I've tried to talk to Ash about bothering whatever's out there. What if it decides I shouldn't be here anymore?"

"D'you want to go back?" Sullivan asked. The question had always seemed ungentlemanly at best and naked cruelty at worst. Henry could never go home.

"It wouldn't send me back," Henry replied. "D'you think it could manage that? I wouldn't go home. God only knows where I'd end up, and I don't want that, Sullivan. At least here, I'm with family. My cousin's portrait is on the wall." Henry sipped his coffee.

"I never told your daddy, but I saw that Sullivan get shot at Second Manassas. We were exhausted, and we'd fallen back to a hillside. General Gregg cut some flowers with his old Revolutionary War scimitar. 'Let us die here, my men, let us die here,' he said, and Sully did."

Sullivan almost choked.

Once more, Henry's words robbed Sullivan of his own. How could he possibly answer? *I'm sorry you loved him. I'm not sorry he died. It's the same way I'm sorry you were in pain, but I'm not sorry at all you got shot.*

They finished their coffee without speaking.

After breakfast, Ash gathered everyone on the patio; Ethan had flown back to California, and he seemed to enjoy ordering his relatives around. In addition to mic'ing each of them, the crew had squirreled mics throughout the house—under tables, next to cabinets, and under the patio tables. "Ethan said that we seem to hang out here while the tours are going on," Ash told them. "We're going to ask you to mostly stick around here or in the upstairs library."

Sullivan nodded, as if he didn't mind being corralled like a steer. Perched on chair backs, red macaws with green wings shrieked for attention. Sullivan held out his hand to a bright blue one glaring from the middle of the table. Delicately, Varina stepped up. She'd always been his favorite, and they said birds never forgot.

"Don't encourage her," Ash said. "If you give them attention when they scream, you teach them to scream whenever you walk by. You know that—"

"I can pick up a bird once in a while." Varina puffed her feathers as he stroked her head. Sullivan counted himself a bird snob, and nothing would ever feel as decadent as feathers' silk.

"D'you want her to scream when—"

"Ash." Henry rested a hand on his shoulder. "Let them be today, huh? Sullivan just wants to hold the bird. Why don't you call everyone together and get the cameras going?"

"Good idea." Ash bustled toward the crew. Maybe, with their yessirs and smiles, they were easier to fuss at. Perhaps Ash surrounded himself with strangers because they were easier to wrangle.

"Thank you," Sullivan told Henry. Varina nibbled his finger. "You're good at—I don't know. Thank you."

"There was a captain in our regiment, Maitland." When Sullivan snapped up, Henry was gazing at the lemon trees, not him, not Ash marshaling the camera crew. He rarely spoke of his time before Cypress Bend, and even more seldom of the war. The morning's revelation had shocked him as much as Olivia running out of his room. "Captain Maitland had a terrible temper—God forgive me for speaking ill of the dead, but there are unkinder ways to say it. He was fine until he drank." A small smile played over Henry's face. "My father was like him, too. You just—you step up and use a quiet voice. Make them look somewhere else if you can."

Henry had never talked about his father. If he said little about the war, he spoke less still of his family. Once, and once only, he'd mentioned sisters. "Was your father—" Words deserted him. "Was he like mine?" Sullivan finally managed.

"Yes," Henry replied. Parrots shrieked into his silence.

After more than a dozen years, Henry was trying to forge something like peace. Sullivan had come home the summer after college and met his best friend's blue eyes. *You fought for the right to own Black people,* he'd said.

Henry had crumpled. *I fought for my home, not—*

You fought to keep slaves, and don't you tell me different. Sullivan had spit in his face. *You owned people.*

Henry had flown at him, fists swinging, as Rhys launched toward Sullivan and Ash threw himself at Henry. *You want me to forgive you?* Sullivan had asked. *Take that cultural history tour my daddy hates until you memorize it. Figure out what you really fought for, and figure out that you're sorry. Make sure you mean it, 'cause I'll know if you don't.*

Sullivan was gone when Henry finally did it, but Rhys told him about it later. *It broke him,* his cousin had said over dinner in Richmond. They'd picked Can-Can, one of the best restaurants in town, but Sullivan still couldn't eat. *Henry lasted about three months before he realized it was all true and he just—I think part of him broke 'cause he started to see what he'd done. He just stays in his room, and he hardly lets anyone in but Olivia. There's this terrible sadness to him.*

There should be, Sullivan had shot back. *He owned people.*

He was a child, Rhys had said. *You know that. If you blame him—*

Don't, Sullivan had snapped.

Varina whistled USC's fight song. Did you forgive someone their past, or were some things indelible? Sullivan wanted to walk away and punch something hard enough to break his knuckles, but he'd only look stupid on TV. The world was a muddy tangle—Henry, himself, the past and the plantation. Blood always seeped between them, familial and otherwise.

Ash clapped his hands. "Alright, y'all!" he shouted. "We're gonna walk through the garden, down to the Pavilion, and out to the back field. That's where we shot off the dust bomb and saw the disc-shaped phenomenon. Y'all ready?" He turned to Rhys. "You gonna be okay in the heat?"

Rhys's mouth tightened to a thin line. "I'll be fine," he said, nearly snapped. Maybe he would and maybe he wouldn't, but Ash should have asked beforehand, and one more time, Sullivan resented his brother's lack of concern. Rhys shouldn't exert himself in the heat, but his cousin would resent them for mentioning it. Regretful, Sullivan set Varina on a chair, where she squawked as if he'd betrayed her. "I'll be back soon," he said, and squaring his shoulders, plastered on a smirk, ready to play make-believe.

CHAPTER 23

RHYS

Trying to hide his crushing fatigue, Rhys marched through the garden. Cameras roved around them; the dogs orbited Elliot and Ash in turns. A gofer toted water bottles against the suffocating heat. Roses drooped. Bees droned in palm-sized azalea flowers, and Spanish moss hung motionless from live oaks. They stuck to the shade. Boo, Parker, and Lewis met them at the garden gate with backpacks full of equipment.

"Hey, y'all," Ash said, and family hugs went around. Cypress Bend was nothing if not cousins. One more time, Rhys wondered how Lewis could stand working there. *We're grateful you're here,* he wanted to say. *Please don't hate us.*

Tourists wandered near the Pavilion, and the cameras drew them like vultures to a carcass. "Ash! Are you shooting?" asked a rawboned woman in a bucket hat. She touched his cousin's hand as if they'd known each other for years. "Can I get an autograph?"

"Yes, ma'am," Ash replied. His cousin's smile seemed real, though Rhys wasn't sure which question he was answering.

Seemingly unbothered by the heat, the woman eyed them like she was sizing up discount chicken. "Who are all these people?"

"This is my brother, Sullivan, and these are my cousins." Ash's gesture covered them all in a grand sweep. While he resented inclusion in the generic Trenholm horde, Rhys was grateful to avoid Ash's fawning tourists. Sullivan edged behind him. One more time, Rhys should have wanted to return to Richmond. He was supposed to hate this.

The woman stopped digging through her purse for a moment; it looked large enough to function as a combat weapon. "Are y'all making guest appearances?"

"We're filming a new show with the whole family. It's called *Keeping Up with the Paranormal*." Ash scribbled his name on the back of a check. His smile never wavered. "Y'all make sure you watch, now."

"Oh, I will! Can I have y'all's autographs, too?"

"There's so many of them, and we have to get going." Ash tipped a wave toward her. "But you promise you'll watch?"

"I will! You have a good day, Ash!" A grin cracked her serious face, and she snapped his picture. Emboldened, more tourists approached. Sullivan's smirk wore thin.

"Can we get a pic with you?" a chubby kid with glasses asked. "I'm a huge fan. Do you really think you found a portal?"

"Maybe," Ash said. "And yeah, of course we can get a quick pic." He slung an arm over the boy's shoulder, and the kid's mom aimed her iPhone. Rhys remembered being that age. He and Sullivan wouldn't have spoken to strangers, no matter how famous.

"The reenactors are super-cool," the boy said. He shoved his glasses up. "They look ultra-real. I wish they'd talk to us, though."

"Ash, the dogs don't like them this close to Elliot," Henry said quietly.

Though his little cousin chatted happily with Lewis, the shepherds had arrayed themselves around her. They watched the tourists somewhat regretfully; those level stares said they wouldn't relish tearing holes in Ash's adoring fans, but they'd do any job they deemed necessary.

"We've gotta get going!" Ash called. "Thanks for all your support! Y'all have a good day, now!" He threw them that smile Rhys rarely saw: a grin like a kid in an ice cream shop, wide and unfeigned. Ash's smiles for Elliot and the dogs came gently, and sadness tinged the others. Maybe he faked it for the fans.

"You're really nice to them," Rhys said, pausing to snag a water bottle. At least he could stay hydrated.

Ash ducked from one patch of shade to another. "It's the least I can do."

"What d'you mean?" Rhys asked.

"I could tell them to go away." Ash pressed his cold water bottle to his neck. "I'd forget it in ten minutes, but they never would. If I take thirty seconds to be nice, it makes their week." Ash paused. Their feet grated on the gravel path. "It's not because I'm especially wonderful or important. But I'm on TV, so people get like that now. I try my best to be kind, even when I wish they'd leave me the hell alone."

"That's really cool of you," Rhys said. He wasn't sure if he should reappraise Ash's character or punch him in the face. *You never treat us that way,* he could have shouted. *You have never, not once, treated me and Sullivan and Henry with as much consideration as you treated that woman who you don't know from Adam's housecat.*

Narrow-eyed and suspicious, Sullivan watched him, but said nothing.

"How've you been?" Rhys asked Lewis as they walked.

"Y'know. Busy." Like the others, he held a water bottle against his neck. Rhys's doctor would murder him if she knew he was exerting himself in this fug.

"How do you manage this?" Sullivan asked suddenly.

"Hi, Lewis. How's your day? How's your mama? Haven't seen you in about, oh, a dozen years." Lewis glared, hefting his backpack higher. "Maybe at least pretend to engage in small talk before you delve into my motivations for working on the family plantation?"

Sullivan opened his mouth, shut it, reddening all the while. "Sorry," he finally stuttered, and dropped back, likely to stew in silent shame.

"Anyway," Lewis said, and told Rhys about his younger sisters working in the café. They wended through the mortifying are-you-seeing-anyone, likely just before an inevitable, *How are you feeling?* Rhys was holding a breezy answer ready when they reached the back field.

"So this is where you found the portal," Sullivan said as Boo unlocked the gate in the chain link fence, and they stopped at the weedy edge of the flat, ten-acre expanse of grass. Ash kept it mowed low, and heat had crisped it to a baked brown. The cameras fanned out, clearly looking for the best angles. Quietly, he added, "Sort of shocked you found it near the Boundary Tree, not right up in it."

"Yeah, the *disc-shaped phenomenon's* back here," Boo replied, his treasured shotgun bumping on his back. The tourists had snapped its picture with something like glee. "Y'all watch for horse manure, now."

"Imma pass out some monitoring equipment so we can keep an eye on things," Lewis said. Digging in his pack, he fished out shiny black tech, chunked with orange and yellow for a rugged, field-use look. It seemed too expensive to touch. "Holler if you see a reading between 1.6 and 1.7 gigahertz." Lewis handed Sullivan something called a spectrum analyzer. "Olivia, you get the thermal imaging camera."

"We're in the middle of a field in South Carolina in the summer," Olivia replied. "It's hot, Lewis."

"Yeah, and if it gets hotter, let us know." Ash scratched one of the shepherds, who rewarded him with a lolling doggy grin.

"Rhys, here's a Geiger counter," Lewis said, passing him a shockingly small device with yellow edging. "It'll go off when radiation levels increase from normal background levels."

"Oh God, do you *expect that* to happen?" Rhys asked.

Lewis shaded his eyes from the noon sun. They should have waited til dusk for their circus. "Normal background radiation for South Carolina is thirty to seventy CPM. Now, that's gonna run a little higher here, 'cause the Westinghouse Plant down on Bluff Road had a uranium leak through the floor."

"*What*?!" Rhys nearly dropped the Geiger counter in a pile of horseshit. Once he would have simply nodded.

"Yeah, they had a leak in a hydrofluoric spiking station that ate through the concrete," Lewis said. He held his palms skyward, a what-can-you-do gesture. Those things happened in South Carolina. You lived with it, like you lived with the palmetto bugs and hundred-degree heat, the institutional corruption and spotty postal service.

"So how will I know. . ." Rhys had seen the show, but usually with a joint for company. Reading its equipment reached beyond both his competence and inclination.

"It'll light up like a Christmas tree and start beeping," his cousin said. "The Amazon description says it 'sparkles,' but it's Chinese-made, so who the hell knows what that means."

"We bring the Geiger counter on investigations because many paranormal hotspots, including Skinwalker Ranch, have a history of gamma radiation spikes. Because this site has significant associations with the farm's violent history, we're taking extra precautions back here." One more time, Ash seemed to speak to the camera rather than the family. "We want the data, but we also want to make sure the crew stays safe. Here at Cypress Bend, safety is paramount." He faced the family once more. "Y'all ready?" he shouted. The shepherds perked up and galloped to his side.

"Sure," Sullivan replied, peering at his gadget. "Just don't let your dogs eat manure then breathe in my face, Ash."

"They don't do that!" His sunglasses probably hid a squinted glare.

"Uh-huh," Olivia said. "They best not. I just bought this Lululemon dress last week."

"Oh, it's not Ash's fault," Elliot told her. "They do it every time they come out here."

Ash led a parade of Trenholms toward the middle of the field. Grass crunched underfoot as cameramen danced around them; their shadows seemed too short in the punishing sun. "Okay, so if you remember from the footage, this is where we fired off the dust bomb," Ash told them. He seemed to speak for cameras more than them. "When we shined a spotlight on the area, it revealed a disc-shaped phenomenon about fifty feet up. That phenomenon split the spotlight beam. We're not sure what it was. I'm not *ready* to say it's a portal, but—"

"You're totally ready to say it's a portal," Sullivan said, barely looking up from the spectrometer. Olivia snorted.

"Will you stop it? I'm not."

"You are. *Anyway.*"

"I really wish you wouldn't call it that. It's a *disc-shaped phenomenon*. We don't know that it's a portal." Ash crossed his arms, already beginning to sunburn.

"You definitely think it's a portal," Sullivan said. Rhys couldn't hold back a grin. Sullivan did that; you'd want to smack him, but you laughed anyway. "Also, did you put on sunscreen? You're gonna end up with a wicked sunglasses tan."

"What am I supposed to be looking for on this thermal imaging?" Olivia asked. "It's all yellow and white, which basically indicates it's hot as hell. Henry, hold this." Lazily, she flipped the camera toward him; Henry caught it one-handed. Gasping, Ash lurched toward them as if she'd hurled a newborn. Olivia pulled a tie from her wrist and twisted her hair into a high bun.

"Don't throw the equipment!" Ash snapped.

"Oh, don't be such a tight-ass. Henry got it." She settled her Jackie O sunglasses. Standing in that empty field, pink dress tastefully fitted, Rhys's sister seemed as improbable as an errant flamingo.

"*Anyway*, so the disc-shaped phenomenon's approximately fifty feet in the air right about here." Ash stalked to the middle of the field and stood with his arms outstretched. Fifty yards behind him, the quadruple-trunked cypress, one tree or perhaps four, reared like a shadowy sentinel, the improbable orchids beneath it a cool blue smear. "Y'all want to get over here and look at it or stand there and fight?"

"C'mon," Rhys said. "It'll make him happy, okay?"

"We can't see shit. That's kinda the point. They had to fire a damn dust bomb *and* shine a spotlight to see anything. *There is nothing to see.*" Sullivan poked at the spectrometer. "And there's also nothing on this spectro-thingie, either."

"You know that's a damn spectrometer, you've seen the show." Rhys snagged his arm. "C'mon. We're going over there so we can check the instruments, make him happy, and go back to the damn air conditioning." The cameras were also recording every bit of Sullivan's ridiculous posturing. Rhys dragged. His cousin followed, and the rest of his family with him. Ears pinned, the dogs hung back.

"What're we supposed to be looking at?" Rhys asked when they'd gathered next to Ash, the sky above them clear enough to believe in. It was no guarantor of safety, and he held back a shudder. Pristine skies provided no bulwark against lightning strikes at Cypress Bend.

"I don't like what the dogs are doing," Sullivan said before he could answer. "Rule number one of Cypress Bend is if the dogs don't wanna be there, I don't wanna be there. Remember, Ash, here at Cypress Bend, safety is paramount."

"That's a good rule," Elliot said. Smiling vaguely, cowrie shell necklaces clacking, she hopped a manure pile and returned to the German Shepherds.

"Elliot, honey, it's fine," Ash said. "It's—"

The device in Rhys's hands shrilled, and one more time, he nearly dropped it. "Hey, Lewis?" he asked, blocking the sun so he could read the screen. "What's it mean when this hits 156 CPM?"

"Oh, shit! I got 1.6 gigahertz!" Sullivan said. "Ash! Check this out!"

"We gotta go," Lewis told them. "That's dangerous radiation."

"I lost power," said one of the cameramen. "Steven, you still—"

"Dead," said the other cameraman. "But you guys better tell that reenactor about the radiation spike before you haul ass."

Rhys glanced where he pointed just as a man in earthen-colored clothes ducked behind the Boundary Tree. An old-style rifle leaned against its base. "Shit," Ash said, and took off after him. Boo galloped behind. Fleetingly, Rhys realized that he'd never seen Ash run; his asthma had sent him into wheezing if he walked too far.

"Oh, damn!" Sullivan pointed at the sky, where a silver-shiny something caught the noonday sun. It tracked too fast to be a plane, at least any plane that Rhys knew. He turned away. If he watched, he'd have to think about it.

"Do y'all want kids with flippers?" Lewis asked. "Let's go!"

They fled.

Ash's dogs seemed to find their flight a grand game. Barking merrily, herding instinct stirred, they nearly tripped everyone as they darted on the group's fringes. Rhys leapt piles of shit, breath coming in ragged gasps; Olivia paused to ditch her Rainbows, then swore as she planted a foot on nettles. Elliot's jewelry rang merrily. Trailed by cameramen, the run seemed surreal, distanced, as if Rhys was playacting fear rather than actually afraid. Even the Geiger counter's alarm had felt artificial. He'd moved to Cypress Bend when he was nine, and spent half his time there before it; how many times had that same so-called dangerous radiation slammed him? Surely his siblings and cousins were thinking it. Had he spent a childhood bathed in gamma radiation? *Calm down,* he wanted to tell Lewis as they hurdled horse manure. *This can't be the first time.*

Sullivan reached the gate first and flung it open, cursing as he tangled up with a dog and nearly fell. Elliot hopped nimbly around them. The cameramen stood back, as if they had to let the Trenholms save themselves first. Rhys leapt onto the path, stepped out of the way, and sagged onto a convenient tree trunk. At least they'd finally reached the shade.

"No more 1.6," Sullivan said, barely out of breath. "Ah, hell." He slapped at the spectrometer. "It's dead." He glanced up. Eyes squinted, he scanned the sky. "UFO's gone, too."

"UAP," Lewis said. "We call them 'unidentified aerial phenomena' not 'UFOs.'"

Rhys slipped his Android from a pocket. An empty black screen glinted at him. "Phone's dead," he reported. "Geiger counter's only reading 27 CPM, though."

"This thing's dead, too," Henry said, shaking the thermal camera like a kid with an Etch A Sketch. Rhys hid a smile. That gesture, it seemed, spanned ages. Hands touched toddlers' heads as they darted by; kids snapped leaves off bushes. Confronted with broken technology, people shook it.

"Ash knew this would happen," Olivia said.

"I don't even care anymore." Sullivan handed Lewis the spectrometer and strode toward the house. Worn down, driven by herd instinct, the rest of the family followed. "Don't you wish you were back in Richmond now?" Sullivan muttered.

Rhys was a bad liar, and he didn't answer.

CHAPTER 24

ASH

Ash watched Sullivan and his cousins sulk back to the house. As usual, he had to tie up the day's dangerous remnants. "Hey," he said, catching Boo's shoulder as they trudged back to HQ. "I need you and Lewis to take the Geiger counter and drive around the farm—"

Boo nodded a single crisp up-and-down. "Lewis is already on it."

He thanked God for Lewis. If they hadn't been related and straight, Ash might have proposed. "Yeah, if radiation is spiking through this farm, we're screwed."

The dogs had left with Elliot. Occasionally, Ash thought about getting another puppy, but it would tag only behind the others, and he'd have five dogs shedding in the house instead of four. Amelia, McKayla, and her sister Madison complained enough about the dog hair, and they already posted warnings about possible reactions. *German Shepherds Live Here. Guests With Dog Allergies Should Be Cautious!*

When he reached the lower patio's relative safety, his phone worked again. Ash called Ethan. "Hey, do me a favor," Ash said. "Liability issues. I need you to cut the reenactor. If we show him after the radiation spike, we'll be in hardcore trouble." They probably shouldn't show the radiation spike, either, but Ethan would never have agreed to cut such a great investigation.

Ethan agreed fast. Those studio men would strangle their own mothers to avoid a lawsuit. Ash spent a tense hour sorting papers in HQ. Money was real. Insurance was real. People needed food and health care, roofs over their heads. Ash couldn't decipher cosmologies, but he could keep the rain off. Lewis finally reported back: no readings over 27 CPMs. Ash could have collapsed onto the floor and slept amongst the shepherds, dog hair tickling his nose. As usual, they'd disappeared with Elliot and a horde of other teenage Trenholms.

Ash's brother and cousins, of course, had abandoned the day's loose ends to him. To do otherwise hadn't occurred to them, or maybe the leftovers hadn't registered. Ash had become accustomed to seeing his house as more than itself, a museum, a cash cow, a zoo with him as the starring exhibit. A radiation spike was both an interesting anomaly and a dangerous liability. Somewhere around three hundred people were crawling over his farm.

Sullivan, Rhys, and Olivia didn't think about them. They imagined the tourists as an invading army, and Ash was William Tecumseh Sherman. *These people feed you*, Ash wanted to shout. *Who the hell d'you think bought that dress, Olivia?* It would do no good.

Even dinner couldn't be easy. Ash and Mickie stepped through their nightly ritual—he begged her, the cook, to eat in the dining room. She refused. Amelia, their first cousin once removed, laid the table for twelve, but also refused a seat, so McKayla filled out their number. Ash was exhausted before he sat down.

No ghost stood by the mantle, at least not that night. Boo's paws dwarfed the sterling silver, and he leaned his shotgun in the corner by the huntboard, away from the camera crew. Elliot sneaked shrimp to the dogs. Sinclair drank too much madeira. But Ash's family was beautiful in the candlelight, all cheekbones and wry smiles. Sullivan joked about the "disc-shaped phenomenon," but never too pointedly. Lewis teased McKayla about her boyfriend. Henry was quiet, but Henry was always quiet. No one talked about the back field, which would disappoint Ethan. Ash tried to forget it. It brooded on the horizon, a hurricane's yellow sky. They were saving it up.

Maybe Sullivan thought Ash didn't notice when he snagged a bottle of Pappy O'Daniel from the liquor cabinet. Rhys noticed. Olivia touched Henry's arm, as if to tell him, *Not now.* "So," Sullivan said as they climbed to the second floor. "Let's all five of us have a drink in the library, huh?"

"I don't want a drink," Ash replied automatically. He realized that he should have seen the ambush coming, from Sullivan or all of them.

"You just had madeira and two glasses of wine."

"Then go down and get the madeira if you're so hellbent on me drinking," Ash replied, "because I don't drink hard liquor."

As usual, the woman in blue waited by the stairs. She held an old-fashioned feather duster, and she neither noticed them nor spoke. "I'm sorry," Ash whispered as they passed, and that old wave of misery hit him: he'd lose everyone he loved, everyone he cared about—

Henry caught up with the madeira. It was coming, predictable as a nursery rhyme. Sullivan ensconced himself on a sofa next to Rhys. Olivia and Henry took the other one. Alone, Ash perched in a silk wingback chair. Nerves and slippery fabric kept him fidgeting. For once, Sullivan didn't fill the quiet with sarcasm; Olivia and Henry were practiced in the art of conversational silence. Ash stopped himself from shouting at them to get on with it. At least they hadn't brought Elliot. Ash thanked life for its small mercies.

"You wanna tell us about the reenactor?" Rhys finally asked. Only he wasn't drinking; Ash had nearly finished his madeira, and he didn't drink fast.

"You wanna not mention that in front of the cameras?" Ash asked. "I talked Ethan out of showing it."

"So that reenactor we saw in the fields," Sullivan said, a little bit louder, as if he wanted to assure that they couldn't use the footage, or that, at least they'd have to splice it. "Tell us about the reenactor."

"We don't have any," Ash replied, taking a small clay turtle from the end table. They'd found it under the Boundary Tree; it was pit-fire earthenware, unweathered. No one knew where it had come from. "Reenactors glorify all that Lost Cause crap we grew up with."

Henry sipped his bourbon as if Ash had commented on the weather.

"So who the hell was that in the field?" Sullivan refilled his bourbon. Henry held his glass out. It would be a long night, or perhaps a very short one.

Ash had known it was coming, but nothing could prepare him for the telling. "My hand went straight through him. When I told him to get out, he disappeared." *He wasn't like Henry*, he couldn't say. Ash threw down his madeira and poured another. He'd get drunk, but it would take longer. "That happens. People like that show up sometimes, but no one, uh, corporeal." He tilted his head, just a touch, toward the cameras.

"That just happens?" Sullivan asked after a pause that stretched far too long. Rhys and Olivia switched on lamps. Their yellow glow dallied on the delicate tables but left the room sunk in dim gloom. "So random ghosts just *show up*?"

The liquor, the library detour, the strategic lamps—had they arranged an elaborate *Scooby Doo* moment? *Let's take off this mask and see who the real villain is.* "Stuff just happens here. Y'all *know that*." Ash passed a weary hand before his eyes. "Why are y'all acting like something's changed? You know it hasn't. We just don't show it all."

They were getting dangerously close to mentioning those silent ghosts. *Don't make me talk about it in front of the cameras,* Ash wanted to hiss. *Don't you dare say the ghosts of enslaved people hang around the house.*

"Be real specific." The lamplight drew Sullivan's face in the icy dispassion of a runway model; he wanted blood and he would have it. "What do y'all see?"

The day's exhaustion dropped like a sodden banket. Ash would have to admit it all, and in front of the cameras. He'd stay as vague as possible and pray no one pressed for details. "What we always saw. Do I have to come up with a laundry list?"

"Have you seen the three men?" Sullivan asked.

"Like Elliot the other night?" Ash studied his brother. His question seemed too urgent, too sincere. "No. I've never heard of them before."

"So what else have you seen?" Sullivan said, passing over it too quickly, as if he'd never spoken. "I've been away a real long time. Refresh my memory."

The other three were watching like they'd elected Sullivan inquisitor. Damn them all. His brother had probably elected himself, and they were too chicken to argue. Ash sipped his madeira. He knew how it would happen. He'd recite a catalog of strange phenomena; they'd storm and shout at him. He'd protest that they'd seen everything he'd listed, so why were they yelling? *Don't shoot the messenger.* At least his father wasn't around to call them liars. "Did we see it as kids?" Ash asked. "Then we've been seeing it. We catch orbs on the motion sensors. There have been UAPs, noncorporeal materializations, corporeal artifacts, cold spots, hot spots, suspected corporeal time-slips—"

"Pause." Rhys held up a hand, the perpetual family traffic cop. When he lost his temper, the family frayed to bare emotional ravelings. "What's a 'suspected corporeal time-slip?'"

Ash had hoped to bury that obtuse syntax among familiar flavors of paranormal activity. "You know, things that don't belong," he hedged. "Like, uh, things from the past." The turtle's smooth warmth might have grounded him if it hadn't sprung from the farm's madness.

"You never said anything about that." Olivia crossed her ankles. She and Henry sat at least two feet apart. After all those years, Ash marveled that she still believed he didn't know. Henry looked for her first when he walked in the room. He knew when she was coming home; he winced when she mentioned a boyfriend. With his father dead, Ash wondered if Olivia would stop pretending.

"You know about the ivory-bill," Henry said to her.

Mid-swallow, Sullivan sputtered. Rhys pounded his back as he hacked, and they waited out his wheezing. "An *ivory-billed woodpecker*?"

"Oh, don't sound so shocked," Olivia said. "It's not a good look on you."

"Are you sure that's what it was?" Sullivan asked. "I mean, I've heard they're easily confused with—"

"It's the difference between a buffalo and a cow," Henry said.

Sullivan dropped his pointed chin and fixed a haughty glare on Ash, as if this were all his fault; Ash felt, sometimes, like his brother blamed him for everything. "Must be useful to have a live-in anachronism."

He'd come too close, but Ash could do nothing about it, and he'd learned, through their childhood, to ignore his brother's snark in favor of greater goals, most of them basic survival: *Don't get hit.* He focused on the towering shelves. Some of those leather-bound volumes had seen a century and a half of family squabbling. "What d'you want me to say?" he asked. "It's as weird as ever around here. That was the first horse mutilation we've had in years, and yeah, the casket falling was really bad, okay? It's gotten a lot worse recently. But it's not just the disc-shaped phenomenon—"

"The portal," Sullivan said. "Call it a portal, Ash."

He pinched his nose. "I'm doing my best over here," he told them. "I'm doing my absolute best, you get that, right? I have fifty people to feed—"

"You hide behind that excuse a lot." Olivia drained her bourbon again. Ash wondered when she'd learned to drink like that.

"Exactly how dangerous is it?" Sullivan asked. "I mean, brass tacks, Ash, if just for Elliot's sake, 'cause we all care about her. How dangerous—"

"I don't know!" he shouted.

The house seemed too quiet. They stared like he'd broken open something unspeakable.

"Look, I don't know, okay?" Ash said. "I started this show hoping I could hire more people and maybe understand what's going on here. Since we've been setting off fireworks, we've seen more UAPs. We've had more—" He hesitated, unable to say, *We see the ghosts in the house more often.* They would tear at him regardless of what he offered; the family needed a victim, and they'd picked him. "You've seen it. Electronics screw up. Stuff moves when no one's there—we catch it on motion sensors. All the horses froze that time, twelve hours without moving. We had two kids disappear and show up in the same place five hours later with no idea they'd gone, or that any time had passed—that was a shitshow, alright, we had the whole sheriff's department out here by then, and they were on the verge of calling SLED—"

"*How dangerous*, Ash?" Rhys asked. His expression was set; Olivia's and Henry's edged into anger. Ash didn't bother glancing at Sullivan. Vaguely, he wondered if they'd cut to Lewis in that footage. *SLED stands for South Carolina Law Enforcement Division,* he imagined his cousin explaining.

"It's getting worse and I don't know why." He threw down the rest of his madeira and wished fervently that it burned harder. "Why d'you think I started this? I wanted to figure out why it was getting worse. Safety—"

"Safety is paramount." Sullivan's tone was mocking. "So it was getting worse, and you didn't think it was important to tell us that?"

Ash focused on those books. "I thought you knew," he said.

"How would we know that when you don't show the worst things on TV?" Rhys leaned forward. "You expect us to sort that stuff from whining tourists, tech-y shit, aliens, and orbs? How were we supposed to know you're seeing 'non-corporeal phenomenon?'"

He had a point. "We've always seen that stuff, and I thought Olivia—"

"Don't pin this on me." Ankles crossed, gaze level, she eyed him over her glass. Olivia rarely turned that wintry freeze on him, and Ash almost wilted. "We made a deal—I'd keep coming home if we ignored your venture into media whoredom."

"Jesus Christ." Ash wished he drank stronger liquor. "You'd come home if we ignored it or not, Olivia. Don't do this."

"What are you talking about?" Calmly, she recrossed her ankles, and he wondered if she was trashed or baiting him.

"I think he means you and Henry." Sullivan said it, and Ash thanked any deity who bothered listening that he didn't have to. "Everyone knows. Y'all can stop faking it."

Henry froze and reddened, the pure fear of a boy caught at petty theft. Olivia smiled slightly. "Very good, Sullivan. Enjoy feeling clever while it lasts."

"You can't think of anything else to say?" Sullivan asked. "Like, nothing else?"

"You figured it out. D'you want a medal?" She leaned forward, tumbler out.

"And now you want me to pour you more liquor?"

"Hurry up. Family arguments make me thirsty."

"We're out," he said, shaking the empty bottle.

"Well, we've established that the farm's gone psycho and Ash should've told us, so we're done here, anyway." Olivia stood. If she was drunk, she hid it well. "Have Henry's things moved into my room tomorrow, would you, Ash? I'm going to sleep." Chin up, back straight as a soldier, she walked out.

Ash imagined the cameras panning their faces, gathering reaction shots. It would be mortifying, but more than anything, their fight would make great television. Ash would have to live with it. He'd take it all the way to the bank.

CHAPTER 25

OLIVIA

Finally free of the cameras, Olivia stretched on her bed and waited for Henry. Her ceiling tilted only slightly. She hoped he'd see reason. *I saved us the trouble of telling them,* she'd say. *I told you they wouldn't care.* His fuse burned long, but his temper was titanic, prone to hyperbole and cataclysm. The night was on her side—Henry wouldn't wake anyone—and even more than her deceased relatives, those old Southern belles, he loathed making a scene. Worried they'd hear him, he wouldn't shout, and he wouldn't leave her. In nearly fifteen years, he'd never set a toe off Cypress Bend.

I see those concrete cities on TV, he'd tell her. *When I can manage to watch it, that is. I think I'd cry to see it. I'd just stand there in the middle of all those people and feel so lost. How can you think, Livy? With all those people there, I mean. How can you think with all that noise and all those* things *happening all at once? There's no green anywhere.*

Olivia opened the window and lit a cigarette. Tree frogs sang in the live oaks, and night drowned twilight's blue shadows. A rich swamp-scent hung under the smoke. Beneath the fan's offbeat click, her old quilt held the air conditioner's chill. She remembered those hot nights with a sweaty toddler nestled against her arm. Olivia had hated it. She'd spent her teens torn between leaving Elliot with the nanny, ripe for brainwashing into beauty-queen perfection, or martyring herself into premature motherhood. Somehow, she and Ash had pulled it off. They'd screwed up a lot of things, but thank God Elliot wasn't one of them.

Twenty minutes after she left the library, Henry shut the door behind him. "You did that on purpose," he snapped. "And why are you lying here in the dark?"

She stubbed out her Parliament. "Took you a while. I didn't think you were coming."

"We need to have a conversation." He hung his robe on the peg behind her door. Enraged, he still defaulted to neatness.

"This is a new one. Say what you're going to say, and if you're still mad, stomp back to your own room. Don't think you're sleeping here angry." He flicked on a lamp, and she turned away. Her tone was easier to control than her face.

"No, Olivia. They'll hear me going back and know we argued. I'll sleep on the floor if you'd prefer."

Henry never used her full name. "If I hadn't said anything, you'd've waffled over it til the end of time," she said. It would shoot his rage into the stratosphere, but maybe he'd burn out faster.

"I looked like an ungrateful—"

"It's over." Hands above her head, Olivia stretched like a jungle-cat. Henry ignored her. "I'm the only one who cares what you look like. Come to bed."

"And then you left me there! How d'you think I felt—"

"You could've followed me." She lit another cigarette. It was pleasant to smoke while she was mildly buzzed, and she'd steal pleasure where she could, especially amid that moment's particular misery.

"I had to apologize," he said tightly, and that quiet voice stung far worse than shouting. "The cameras were rolling, Olivia."

One more time, she winced at her full name. "What'd you say?"

Back against the wall, Henry looked good in the moonlight, old-fashioned handsome. She wished he wasn't angry. "I said I was sorry for taking advantage of you. And when Sullivan fucking *laughed*, Ash had to stop me from punching him."

Olivia had heard Henry bite that curse back, but never pronounce it.

"Are you happy now? Did that turn out how you wanted?" He dropped to her vanity chair. Yellow light caught mirrored lipstick cases; her carelessly shed earrings and tennis bracelets glittered. Scattered face powder dulled gold. It seemed a life snapped in miniature. *Spoiled Brat,* she could have called it, or *Heedless.*

"You didn't have to do that," she said, though she knew he couldn't have lived with himself if he hadn't.

"He said it wasn't possible for me to take advantage of you." Leaning against her vanity, Henry sent a hundred dollars of Sephora clattering. "Of course I had to hit him! The cameras caught it, too. They caught everything."

She exhaled. Long, bitter rolls of smoke rose. "I don't know which of you I should be cheering on."

"This place is a travesty sometimes. At home, he'd've been within his rights to call me out. Instead, he *laughed*—"

"Did you apologize for hitting him, at least?"

"I didn't hit him," Henry said. "Ash stopped me, like I said. Rhys stopped Sullivan."

Her smoke sulked near the ceiling. If she squinted in bright sunlight, Olivia could see faint stains high on the walls, years of secret cigarettes written there. "Not the first time that's happened. Does he understand why you tried to hit him, at least?"

Henry's anger dragged down to fatigue; he was no longer the wide-eyed boy she'd kissed on the barn roof. "Livy, if he understood, he wouldn't've laughed in the first place."

"I'm on Sullivan's side," she said. "You can't hit people because you think you have to defend my fragile virtue. It's outdated. Let me hit him instead."

"You weren't there." A flame flared orange; in a short, hard huff, Henry lit a cigarette. The mattress sagged, another small defeat, as he sat next to her. "I'm sorry. You don't need me to rescue you, Livy. I should know that by now."

Across the distance between them, Olivia found his hand. "You can rescue me sometimes."

"You'll leave again when this is over." He spoke it not as a question, but sad fact. "I hate knowing you're with someone else. I always worry they won't be kind to you."

His concern was sincere, and it hurt worse than any recrimination. She didn't doubt that his worry overshadowed jealousy when she was gone. "I'm not myself with them," Olivia said. Henry's familiar hand in hers felt safe, known. "I have to pretend, you know? They expect things I won't give them."

"Stay this time."

When Olivia stubbed out her cigarette, she felt a sad pang for its cherry-red heat. "I'll think about it," she said. It was a lie, but that particular untruth would smooth the night's rough edges. Henry deserved something to hold onto.

Maybe she did, too.

CHAPTER 26

SULLIVAN

Life marched on. Tourists called the hotline; UAPs and orbs popped on the motion sensors. They filmed OTFs—on the fly interviews—and visited cousins. Nothing much happened, not even the odd lightning strike, but weeks often passed between strange happenings on the farm, and Sullivan knew that peace was no assurance of safety. Perhaps a week after everyone visited the back field, he spent the afternoon's bright-hot reaches hiding on the patio with Ash and Rhys, where they sipped sweet tea beneath twining Confederate jasmine. He was theoretically reading a *Star Wars* novel, but he'd long set it down to pet a blue hyacinth macaw. Ash poked at his phone, possibly playing a game; Rhys watched a third cousin bathe the parrots. The cameras were rolling. They were always rolling. Sullivan wondered if they could reuse the film that didn't capture anything interesting.

"It's not too bad, being back," Rhys ventured. "At least not when nothing weird is happening."

"Uh-huh," Sullivan replied. The macaw bobbed her head and took a piece of fruit from his fingers. "What would you be doing if you were in Richmond?"

"I don't know. Probably teaching summer school or holding office hours. What about you?"

"It's summer," Sullivan said. "No classes to teach. I'd like to say I'd be making art or talking to galleries? I'd probably be sitting on my couch with a joint and a bowl of Coco Puffs." He passed Varina another piece of pineapple. Delicately, she took it in her beak.

"It's three in the afternoon," Rhys replied.

"Oh, I know," he said.

The pause stretched. Varina squealed for more fruit.

"Is Henry speaking to you?" Sullivan asked.

"Not much," Rhys said.

"He hasn't acknowledged that I exist." Sullivan passed Varina another pineapple slice. "Neither has Olivia, really. I didn't mean—well, never mind." He stroked Varina's head. "It doesn't matter."

"It does matter," Rhys said. "You hurt their feelings and—"

The patio doors opened. Sullivan ducked under the table, assuming an unhinged tourist, which set the parrots shrieking and flapping with glee. "Fight! Win! Kick ass!" yelled Varina.

"Go Cocks," Boo told her solemnly, and she settled into a contented feathery fluff. The USC student body finished its fight song with those words, thirty thousand war-painted college kids packed into Williams-Brice Stadium and yelling cuss words during football games. Like so much of his childhood—the sabers, the history lessons, the orbs flitting beyond the treeline—Sullivan had never questioned it, and it seemed bizarre only when filtered through the wider world. *The downtown water sometimes tastes like moss*, he'd said once, and a Savannah acquaintance stared. *Are you kidding?* she asked. *Sullivan, that's not normal. Tap water shouldn't taste like moss.*

"Hey, Ash," Boo said, ignoring Sullivan's attempts to pretend he was searching for something under the table. "We got a client who wants to talk to you."

"I'm busy," he replied, barely glancing up, though he passed a macadamia nut to the macaw next to him.

"It's Whitney Braxton, the one marrying our second cousin, Judah? She's driving Uncle Oscar crazy and he sent me up to get you."

Ash slumped in his chair. "Tell him to bring the phone up here."

"Oh no, she's over in the office. Uncle Oscar says she showed up this morning and won't leave, and she's threatening to make a scene in front of the visitors if you don't get over there. If I throw her out. . ." Boo trailed off, palms held up.

Varina seemed to eye his shotgun, worn in a back holster that left its handle bobbing near his head. "Fight! Win! Kick ass!" she shouted.

Sullivan proffered another morsel of pineapple. She snatched it. "Varina thinks you should destroy Bridezilla."

"Destroy Bridezilla!" she crowed.

"I love this macaw," he said, squinting into the sun. "Are they putting up the lanterns again? Damn, it's a Wednesday. D'you really have a wedding on a Wednesday night, Ash?"

"Nah," he replied. The gardeners moved slowly over the rows of rioting azaleas, their palm-sized flowers lascivious against the dulled greens. "We do wine tasting and string quartet in the garden on fourth Thursdays. It's our biggest fundraiser for the postpartum nurse project."

"What's that?" Sullivan asked. His brother had never mentioned fundraisers or nurses or philanthropy.

"Legare County has one of the highest accidental infant mortality rates in the state. Postpartum nurses help lower it, but like hell will the General Assembly fund them. We raise enough money to subsidize two, but it takes a lot of legwork." Ash still watched the gardeners. "So what's Whitney want now?"

"I don't know," Boo told him. "Uncle Oscar just sent me up here to get you, is all."

"I didn't know you did the postpartum nurses thing," Sullivan said.

"There's a hell of a lot you don't know." Ash shoved his phone in his pocket. "Alright, let's deal with this so she doesn't make a scene. But we'll go out the back. I don't want to get caught up in the tour."

"Might as well come." Sullivan handed Varina a last piece of fruit, then showed her his empty hands. "We don't have anything else to do."

"There's no reason for you to—"

"Why not? Might show us something about the business." Far away, the cousins were ants moving over the gardens, industrious and anonymous. "And you said she's marrying Judah—you mean cousin Randolph's son Judah? I haven't seen him since I was fifteen. I fucking love Judah."

Ash heaved an enormous sigh and tilted his head at the camera. "You sound like an ass when they bleep you."

"Well, I wanna see Judah. I think Rhys and me gave him his first taste of bourbon when we were twelve."

"We did," Rhys said. "He got drunk and nearly fell off the barn roof."

"If you wanna come, I'm not stopping you." Ash stalked down the steps, and the parrots squealed protests as they followed.

"Hurrah! Hurrah! For Southern rights hurrah!" squawked a macaw from the lemon trees, and others joined in: "Hurrah for the Bonnie Blue Flag/That bears a single star!"

"Now I'll have that stuck in my head for the rest of the day," Rhys muttered as they passed down the patio steps to golf carts on the house's east side. "Y'know, we really shouldn't know every verse of that song."

"I know," Sullivan told him, inwardly cussing. Rhys had cemented the earworm, and he'd be stuck humming "The Bonnie Blue Flag" all afternoon. Once they'd passed stolen liquor on the barn roof, Henry between them, drunkenly slurring it between rounds of "Dixie." They were sixteen then, and no one had yet taught them better. Even then, it had a queasy edge of injustice. Sullivan hated to admit it: Transgression made the song sweeter.

He wanted to drive the golf cart, but running at it would have looked faintly ridiculous, and Ash got there first—always the older brother. The front seat would have hurt his pride, so he and Rhys ducked in the back. The cameraman took another cart.

"Who am I, freaking Morgan Freeman?" Ash asked, glaring in the rearview mirror.

"Call me Daisy," Sullivan replied. Rhys poked him. He waited for his brother to snark back, but he offered nothing else as they wound down the driveway, past clusters of slow-moving tourists, toward the office above the gift shop. His brother waved merrily to fans as they passed. Phones snapped pictures. Sullivan smiled and tipped his hand, but they ignored him. That would end soon enough. Ash would probably sulk about sharing the hot-guy spotlight with him and Rhys, not to mention Henry, who'd lost his mind the week before—Christ, those Victorian morals brooked no joking. Tabloids would figure out him and Olivia fast. *Cousins*, people would say. *South Carolina, what can you expect?* Never mind that they only had a fourth great-grandfather in common—mind-bogglingly distant, born around 1800.

His brother made excuses as they threaded through the gift shop: *So sorry, can't stop to chat, business in the office.* He seemed genuinely apologetic, and one more time, Sullivan marveled at Ash's patience with his adoring hordes. He'd always been a curt brother, doting on Olivia and Elliot but annoyed with him and Rhys. *Leave me alone. You can't be in my room. Dad will kill you if you do that, you know that, don't you?* For those swarming strangers, he found basic kindness. Maybe age had mellowed him, but Sullivan still resented it.

"Lemme handle this," Ash said as they climbed the stairs. "If Whitney's annoyed about something, and she always is, I'll deal with it, okay? *Please* don't make me regret this. And don't turn this into old family fun time with Judah, alright? No one wants to hear about twelve-year-olds getting wasted."

One more time, he and Rhys were bumbling children, and Ash the older, wiser one. It never worked that way, but his brother liked to pretend it did. Sullivan hated it, and either that cameraman knew or guessed it; he turned on Sullivan and caught that tight-jawed resentment. Dammit. He had to remember he was being filmed.

The stairs opened to the front office, a small room crammed with Native American and colonial artifacts. They were likely priceless. *These are amazing,* visitors always gawked. *Such a collection,* archeologists would say, suspicion creeping into their voices. *Why aren't these at the university? Did you find them here?*

Bought them, their father would lie. It would still piss off the archeologists, but it kept the government from digging up their property.

"Hey, Ash," said a worn-looking, forty-ish man—their second cousin Oscar, Boo's uncle, grown and spread into middle age. He looked like the type who followed Gamecock football, but only when they were winning. "Remember, Whitney and Judah have their wedding scheduled for next month. Huge one—they're fully paid up with the standard Trenholm family discount, the Barn rented, two hundred guests, massive package. She's the one who's bringing in the four food trucks? She wants to cancel."

"God." Ash pinched the bridge of his nose. "Did they break up? It's in the contract—"

"I think you need to hear this one," Oscar said.

Sullivan's brother swore softly. "Alright," he said. "And she's threatening to make a huge scene?"

"Yeah, and you know she'll do it, too. She already consented to filming, by the way."

A pouty-lipped, blue-eyed Southern belle waited for them in a blandly boring office, though a picture of Elliot and more pottery marked it as Ash's. Whitney wore pearl studs and Lilly Pulitzer; her hair was a tasteful shade of blended ash blonde. She probably played a fair game of tennis and enjoyed weekends on her boat at Lake Marion. "Ash?" she asked, rising from a leather business chair. "Hi, again. I'm sorry Judah couldn't make it today. I wanted to talk to you about the wedding? We've got sort of a problem going on."

"This is my brother Sullivan, ma'am," Ash said, "and my cousin Rhys. I don't believe you've met the two of them. Where's Judah today?"

Both said hellos and moved to shake her hand. Whitney ignored them, and offered another smile in lieu of a reply about their cousin.

"How can I help you?" Ash asked after an awkward pause, ensconcing himself behind the desk, a king in his country. Sullivan and Rhys had to lean against the wall. "I'll warn you that other than cases of severe illness, we generally don't refund wedding reservations."

"I know, but Judah and I have a terrible problem," she said. "I know y'all'll do your very best to fix it." When Whitney smiled, she showed very white, even teeth.

"Okay." Ash smiled too, his brave face before the storm broke.

The woman, hard not to think of as a girl, leaned forward. "Now, you know Judah and I just *love* Cypress Bend. Love it. As soon as I saw it, I knew I wanted to get married here. The history alone is just amazing!"

The history was appalling, but Sullivan was used to his father's ramblings. Maybe visitors imagined that enslaved people whistled as they marched to the tobacco fields at sunrise, and that the Trenholm family had been *good* masters, as if there was such a thing. More likely, they didn't think about slavery at all. He could never forget it.

"So we booked the Barn and the best wedding package," Whitney continued. "We were *so* excited—I can't tell you how excited. We really wanted Cypress Bend to be part of our special day. We did. But—well, it can't be. It simply can't. Judah couldn't even manage to be here with me today. I had to come alone."

"Okay." Hands folded, eyes meeting hers, Ash nodded. He was clearly practiced at the art of active listening. Maybe he'd read up on it.

"Ever since Judah visited Cypress Bend for the last walk through with the caterers," Whitney said, "we've been having, well—problems. Very bad problems." Her smile had turned slightly apologetic, like she hated to bother Ash, but hoped that perhaps he could help to resolve this difficulty.

"What kind of problems?" Ash asked.

"Well." She seemed to straighten, though her posture was already cotillion-perfect. "I hope we can be very honest with each other here. I know you have your show, so you have an open mind."

Sullivan glanced at Rhys. Busy watching Whitney, his cousin's face was unreadable. So was Ash's. Sullivan's stomach pitched sideways. He wished he could leave without looking weak, possibly over-dramatic. He wished he hadn't come at all.

"I try to keep an open mind," Ash said carefully. "But my degree's also in science."

"There's no easy way to say this," Whitney told him. That apologetic smile never slipped. "So imma just have to say it. Last time Judah was at Cypress Bend, he had an—an experience, and something followed him home."

Sullivan suppressed a shudder. It happened sometimes. People visited Cypress Bend, and part of Cypress Bend left with them. They experienced hauntings, primarily poltergeist-like activity, usually including shadow-men. A letter from his great-great-grandfather, dated 1890, mentioned someone complaining about "the ghost that won't leave him alone since he last stayed at the house."

"I don't know what you mean," Ash said. "Could you be a little more specific?"

Ash knew exactly what Whitney meant. Sullivan kept silent, though he wanted to call his brother a bastard.

"I had a hair appointment," Whitney said, "so Judah came to the last walkthrough himself. He was just meeting the caterers here, so we didn't think it would be a problem. Well, when he finished up, he walked behind the Barn. It was around noon, and as he rounded the corner, he saw three men in these old-fashioned clothes. They were identical, and they all moved at the same time. He doesn't remember anything else. But it was suddenly sunset. Judah was very confused—the gates were closed, and he had to call up to the main house to get Boo to open them. He drove home, very out of it, almost wrecked the car twice, he said. That's when the trouble started, Ash."

Sullivan almost choked. He'd never heard of those three men until the ghost mentioned them, when he was twelve: *When three men come walking, when the family walks with them, then it's time, if you want to stop it.* And he had never seen them, not once, until the night of his twenty-first birthday. He'd fled because of them. In a few slim weeks, Sullivan had encountered them twice, and it awakened a dry-mouthed, visceral terror. More than anything else he'd encountered at Cypress Bend, the three men seemed to slip reality sideways. They didn't belong. And he still didn't know what they heralded—what he might stop, if he wanted to. *Time for the house to fall.* He always wanted to ask Rhys about it.

Don't, he'd told Sullivan afterward. *I never wanna think about that again.*

When Elliot was born, Sullivan had tried again. *The ghost told us*— he started.

Don't, Rhys had said, swiftly and finally, and that was all.

Dread gnawed at Sullivan's stomach, and he wished he could sit down. But if hearing about those men frightened Ash, he didn't show it. Instead, his face remained impassive, and Whitney continued.

"That night," she said, "we heard knocking on our bedroom wall—we live in Columbia, near Shandon? We were laying in bed when this weird knocking woke us at exactly 3:33 a.m. It was really loud—it wasn't natural. It was clearly a person, like—" She rapped on Ash's desk three times. "The house was so quiet. It was the only thing we heard, just this terrible knocking, always in threes, over and over. Always every three minutes, too. You could time it. We called the police and waited in the bathroom until they came."

It was probably saner than looking on your own, and as ridiculous as cowering in the bathroom sounded, Sullivan would have huddled on the shower floor, too.

"The house was empty, of course," Whitney said. "They said they'd run patrols by, because we were insistent that we'd heard someone in there." She tucked her pale hair behind her ears, an oddly coquettish gesture. "The same thing happened the next night. It woke us up at 3:03 that night—the same knocking, the same eerie silence. Even the tree frogs were quiet. Like this." She hit the desk again, three more sharp knocks. "We called the police again. They heard it once, but they couldn't find anyone.

"When it happened the third night, we didn't bother calling anyone. It was louder, and it went on for an hour. Someone was knocking on our bedroom walls, over and over. We just held hands in the dark and prayed. Bang, bang, bang! Then this long pause. We'd hope it was over, then it would start again: bang, bang bang, sometimes closer and louder, sometimes a little softer and farther away. Endless. I don't think I have to tell you how terrifying it was to lay in the dark and listen to that, Ash."

Sullivan knew it too well: the sweat-sticky hands clenched; the tight, ragged breathing; the frantic hope it would stop and the dull knowledge that it wouldn't. He'd hidden in the barn, in the woods, and he'd listened with a dark certainty that something was out there, and it didn't belong.

"I'm sure it was very frightening," Ash said.

"Then it turned to footsteps," Whitney said. "Well, to make a long story short, the footsteps turned into shadow-people—"

"Shadow-people?" Sullivan couldn't help asking.

"I'm sorry," she said. "You're Ash's brother?"

"Yes ma'am," he replied, vaguely annoyed. The office seemed close and hot, and its ceiling fan clicked maddeningly. Sullivan swiped his palms on his shorts. "I'm Sullivan Trenholm."

"So you grew up here, too?" Her eyes narrowed a little bit, as if she'd decided he was worth her attention after all.

"Yes, ma'am," he said. "So did my cousin, Rhys." He gestured. Whitney ought to know all this if she was Judah's fiancée, and it bothered Sullivan as much as being ignored in the first place.

"So you're familiar with this kind of thing?"

"I'm sorry to say we are," Sullivan told her. Ash threw his favorite *shut up now* look, a furrowed brow and pursed lips, like an old maid. It could have come from Great-Aunt Alda.

"Then you understand how scared we were," Whitney said. "It's terrifying."

"Yes, ma'am," Sullivan replied. "I know it."

"We saw stretched-out people made of shadows," she told him matter-of-factly. "Have you seen them before?"

"We can't really say, ma'am." Ash spoke before Sullivan could.

"Yes," Rhys told her. He shoved off the wall and straightened up. "We have."

"One night, the footsteps didn't come," Whitney said. "Judah woke up and one was strangling him."

She was watching Ash for a reaction. He gave her none, and she pulled her phone from a quietly expensive designer purse. "Sometimes the thing pushes him down and scratches him. Do you know how frightening it is to watch a person go flying when there's nothing there to push him?" Whitney showed the phone to Ash. "See? It's always three marks. He had to get stitches that time. The shirt above it wasn't torn, either." She passed it to Sullivan. Ragged, bloody gouges ripped a man's shoulder. He looked as if he'd been clawed.

"I hope that's healing up for him," Ash said. "But other than severe illness—"

"Then the three men came again," Whitney continued, her tone business like, her posture a Victorian relic. Sullivan's nails bit into his hands. "They're identical, and black-and-white—I mean monochrome, like they've stepped out of a TV. They do everything in sync, and they wear these strange old-fashioned clothes. Sullivan," she said, "when I saw them, I was standing in my kitchen, and it was four in the afternoon. I just looked up from cutting bread and there they were, standing in the garden. They said something about time, and I don't remember what, but when they stopped talking I looked up and my oven clock read one in the morning. I don't know where time went. Judah couldn't find me for hours."

"I'm very sorry to hear—" Ash began.

"It keeps happening," she said. "It happens to Judah, too. There's something wrong with him. Watches go dead on his wrist. His phone won't keep a battery—he stopped carrying one. It just dies, all the time. Other people's do too, when they're around him for long enough. He can't sleep at night, and he passes out during the day. He got fired—I don't mind telling you that he showed up at his boss's door for a meeting that didn't exist after missing three that did. That, after sleeping in his office for hours at a time."

Ash cleared his throat, a startling rasp. "That's terrible to hear, but I don't see what it has to do with the wedding—"

"We can't do the wedding," Whitney told him. "Judah can hardly manage to get up in the morning. He sleeps all day. I dragged him to the doctor? They said his body temperature is too low, but their thermometers break. The digital ones won't work, so they tried to use an old-fashioned one, with the silvery stuff inside. It shattered. He says he sees these silent people that aren't there, always Black people in old clothes. He says they're dead—"

"We're glad to offer a full refund," Sullivan told her. Clearly, his brother was going to let the woman pay to suffer with whatever Cypress Bend had thrown at her. Ghosts were one thing, but the three men another. He didn't know what kind of mayhem Whitney and Judah were living with, but it was clearly terrible.

"Excuse me?!" Ash whipped up and actually spluttered.

"Thank you," Whitney said. "I'm deeply grateful, Sullivan." She stood up, nodded at Ash, and fled. Like any good Southern belle, Whitney knew a good thing when she heard one.

CHAPTER 27

ASH

A canceled wedding. Even with the Trenholm family discount, Sullivan had lost them three thousand dollars. After expenses were taken out, that was someone's rent—several people's rent—and Ash tried not to imagine a hungry relative. He drew a long, deep breath and tried to recall the techniques from one of his books on meditation. They escaped him. "You lost us three thousand dollars," he said instead.

"She and Judah deserve it." His little brother shrugged like money didn't matter, though his hands were shaking. "And we should get them some help—"

They had an empty venue—the farm's largest venue—on a Saturday, during the peak of wedding season. Even with a substantial discount, they probably couldn't re-book it. Possibly worse, Ethan would want to include Whitney in *Keeping up with the Paranormal*, assuring that anyone else who wanted to weasel out of a wedding would simply claim an entity had followed them home. Ash couldn't veto it. They had to get footage, and that footage had to be sufficiently dramatic, not like the nonsense fluff they'd been filming for the past week. He'd agreed to do it, for Rhys, for Olivia, and for Elliot, and he'd do it right. Ash had settled Whitney in that chair hoping to save the family business both money and face. Sullivan had lost both. He was right; they ought to help Judah, if not Whitney, but the economic and commercial fallout—Ash had to consider the *whole* family, all of them—

"You should put a paranormal rider on the contract," Rhys said. "Tell them—"

"There's no such thing as a paranormal rider!" Ash felt his pulse in his hands. At thirty-two years old, he probably needed medication for high blood pressure. He focused on his photo of Elliot. Hair dreaded with mud, soaked in creek-water, she grinned from Olivia's arms. Ash had snapped the picture, and it was his favorite. He tried to snatch back their remembered laughter. "You lost us three thousand dollars," he repeated.

"Let it go," Rhys said. "Some things are more important than money."

Elliot and Olivia smiled so wide. They were dirty and beautiful. "Like family."

"Jesus Christ." Sullivan flumped into the chair Whitney had vacated. "We *are* helping family. You're going to forget it, so just forget it now instead of later. Whitney and Judah need *help*, Ash, real help. Whatever she saw is the same thing that freaked out Elliot. I was thinking—"

"How much money do you think we have?" Ash asked.

"Ash. Focus. Something followed Judah home. Can we talk about that for a minute? You forget that I quote-unquote 'lost three thousand dollars' and I'll forget that you were willing to stiff a family member under paranormal attack, which you were pretending you'd never heard of." Sullivan hunched in the chair like he was the aggrieved one, and it only infuriated Ash more. How dare he?

"Yeah," Rhys said, like Sullivan's personal tough-guy.

"Seriously?" Ash asked his cousin. "He lost us all that money, and now—"

"You were acting like you'd never heard of shadow-people," Rhys said. "Sullivan saw them the day he got home. We *know* that sometimes things follow people home. Follow *family members* home. I mean, really, Ash? Do better."

He'd stolen that line from his sister, and Ash resisted pointing it out. The money's loss enraged him, and the betrayal ached. He should have sent Whitney packing. Instead, he'd still lost thousands of dollars, and looked like a jackass doing it. Yes, Judah was family, but what could Ash do to stop the farm's terrors?

"You're right," Ash said, because he could do nothing else with a camera trained on him. "I'm sorry, y'all."

"We need to figure out how to help them." Sullivan raked a hand through his curls, already wild with the heat. "There's something—this is bad, Ash. This is really bad."

Ash leaned back, laced his hands behind his neck, and cast his eyes to the ceiling, like men did when they thought hard. Maybe he should have let Rhys deal with his own medical bills, and simply kept supporting Olivia. But Rhys was family, and family did for its own. Legare County said that Trenholms would punch their own brother on a street corner, but come at one of them, and you came at them all. They took care of each other—

"—I'd call Talitha Merle," Sullivan was saying. "I still have her number."

Ash snapped back to his office. He'd been crushing on dark-haired, long-legged, don't-call-her-a-witch Talitha Merle since he was fifteen. They'd never spoken, though he occasionally saw her around town with her husband and kids. "Talitha?" he asked stupidly.

"Yeah." Sullivan snagged a small, earthenware dog from Ash's desk. *Don't touch that,* Ash nearly snapped. *Elliot found it at the Boundary Tree. She could have kept it, but she gave it to me instead.* "Talitha might could help. I think she mentioned dealing with something like that once."

"Mentioned it? What, like, to you?" Ash asked. Talitha had graduated from Lower Congaree High about ten years before they'd graduated from Maxcy Gregg Prep; she lived in a small house on the swamp's ragged edges. When the county's poor needed help, they went to her. His father had preferred healthcare to witchcraft. "When the hell did you talk to Talitha?"

"We were friends before I left, I guess." Sullivan turned the dog over and over in his hand, but he didn't look up. Whenever Ash spotted Talitha at the Gas N Go, he searched frantically for reasons to speak to her; by the time he ginned up something, usually a meteorological observation, she'd disappeared. She was beautiful. While he'd conquered his crippling shyness, that adolescent crush tripped him into stupidity—he couldn't manage to say hello. But Sullivan had her number.

"When did you get to be friends?" Ash asked as casually as he could manage. A cameraman still lurked in the corner. Ash could pretend for the camera.

"We've hung out a time or two," Sullivan said, but he flushed, and he didn't look up from the dog. Ash glanced at Rhys. Since he didn't drink til he blacked out, he probably knew more about Sullivan's sexcapades than Sullivan. Rhys was also blushing.

"When did you sleep with her?" Ash asked.

"Jesus Christ." Rhys dropped into the other chair. "Do you have to? We need to help this woman, and you're fixated on—"

"On my twenty-first birthday, I was an absolute mess," Sullivan said, and Ash almost groaned. Sometimes, he felt like his brother dragged everything to high theatrics. "I left that night, but I didn't wanna drive to Columbia, so I hit the Roadhouse. Talitha bought a round for the birthday boy, and when last call came, we were both smashed. But she was a little *less* smashed, so she offered me a ride home. We—"

"I get it," Ash told him, pained to hear more. This was the time for him to mention her marriage. An edged bit of malice kept him from it. Let Sullivan figure that out on his own.

"She makes really great chocolate-chip pancakes," his brother said. "She told me to call her again when I came back into town, but I never called because, well, I never came back. Might as well see if the offer still holds."

The hottest woman in Lower Congaree, and probably the most intimidating—Sullivan not only had her number, but a standing invitation. Ash would have liked to have a girlfriend. Rolling family crises left no time to find one, let alone one who would tolerate them.

"You really think Talitha can help?" Ash asked.

She probably could. People said a lot about Talitha. They talked about her cures, but they whispered that if people went missing, the sheriff called her for help. Rumors popped up like fairy-rings after a thunderstorm. People said Talitha spoke to ghosts, soothed uneasy spirits, maybe even sweet-talked the dead. If anyone in Lower Congaree could offer Whitney and Judah more than wafting sage and good intentions, Talitha could.

"She might help if we ask real nice," Sullivan said.

"Do whatever you want," Ash told his brother. "You two handle it." He pushed back from his desk. He could pretend something was waiting for him in HQ—surveillance footage, insurance paperwork, maybe a plea from some scruffy relative about overdue rent. He could become a momentary hero. It wasn't much. But they looked to Ash for rescue, and it was something.

CHAPTER 28

OLIVIA

"**A**sh?" someone was shouting. "Anyone know where Ash is?"

The tour had ended fifteen minutes ago. Olivia slipped down the stairs and into the central stairwell. "Boo?" she called.

"Olivia! D'you know where Ash is?" Boo poked his head into the central stairwell. "I can't get him on the phone."

"No idea," she replied. "He was on the patio with Sullivan and Rhys last I saw."

Her second cousin cussed a blue streak. "He was supposed to be going to the office, so I went out to check the farm. I thought he'd be back by now. Guess he's still in the office. Hell." Shotgun butt nearly banging the wall, Boo stumped upstairs.

Hopefully the firearm wasn't loaded, or at least the safety was on. Olivia squinted in the dim central room, where those sabers caught the wan light and gleamed. A younger Black woman in a blue dress passed into the room, solemn and silent. Eyes downcast, she held a feather duster. Sadness descended, thick and heavy as wet snowfall. Everyone Olivia loved would leave. They could be snatched away any time—

"You think Ash might be in HQ?" Boo asked. "I need to talk to him."

"Is it anything I can help with?" Olivia said.

"The quilt's gone." He shook his head like he couldn't believe people would be so awful, an elegant gesture blending both sorrow and rage. "Someone took the quilt."

What quilt was he talking about, and why would he stomp through the house about it? Long years of discipline kept any confusion from Olivia's face. "They couldn't've taken it far. I mean, it's a quilt. It's pretty bulky."

"Hey," Ash said, coming through the door from HQ. "I just finished up in the office. Mickie said you were looking for me."

"Someone took the quilt."

Ash's face twisted into sudden rage. "Jesus tapdancing Christ. Are you kidding me? That exhibit wasn't set to open for weeks!"

A camera appeared behind Ash, its light assuring they'd get decent footage. "What quilt is he talking about?" Olivia asked. "I mean, we have a lot of quilts around this house—"

Ash pinched the bridge of his nose. "You weren't supposed to find out before the exhibit opened. No one was."

"Did Boo say the quilt's missing?" Henry called from halfway down the curving staircase to the third floor. The cameraman swiveled to capture him. Olivia saw the footage they'd show, the transparent cuts. Everyone was already mic'd. They'd capture everything and call it entertainment.

"D'you remember when Henry found our fourth-great grandmother's diaries in the attic? Lucy Caldwell?" Ash asked. "It was right before *Gone South* started."

Olivia searched and came out blank. "Maybe?"

"Come along with us and I'll explain."

Ash led them outside. Henry would have known their fourth-great grandmother—his own grandmother. Olivia wondered at the fortitude required to read your own grandmother's diary more than 125 years after her death. The cosmic implications staggered her; perhaps after Henry's long years at Cypress Bend, they blended into background noise. She wished she could ask him about it, but cameras skulked behind them, hyenas circling a carcass.

After they crammed into the golf cart, Ash began. "So in 2022, Henry was digging through the attic when he found diaries that belonged to our fourth-great grandmother," he said. "It records about several years before the Civil War, from about 1856 to 1860. There are like, three books. I assume the paper shortages hit them after that."

"Paper shortages?" Olivia asked. Ash steered under the leaning live oaks and in front of the house; birds sang, a normal weekday afternoon at Cypress Bend.

"Yeah, there were massive paper shortages in both the North and South during the Civil War," Ash said. "It got so bad they were using old wallpaper for envelopes. Anyway, Henry read all three of the diaries, basically trying to get a bead on what was happening around the farm at the time? Turns out Grandma Lucy was real into describing domestic details—"

"Probably because that's all she had," Olivia said. Dust plumed from the pebbled drive, and she covered her mouth and nose. Trust men to be shocked that a woman focused on the real concerns in her life.

"Probably, yeah." Ash steered around a clot of tourists. "Anyway, those domestic details obviously included slavery. A lot about slavery, in fact. Those diaries gave us the names of several enslaved people, and a peek into their everyday life. She comments on a lot of domestic details—that's how we know that they gave out the yearly clothing allowance on Christmas, along with presents like liquor and cake or candy—Lucy only says 'sweets.' It's also how we know that like other planters, they generally sold or traded enslaved people on New Year's Day, when debts were due. They also occasionally gave them as presents." Ash grimaced, and Olivia winced. The naked traffic of human beings was a wound that never closed, not on Cypress Bend. Ghosts of it lingered, both metaphorical and literal.

"*But*, all that grimness aside, Lucy talks occasionally about crafts the enslaved people made. She mentions the enslaver cobbler who lived on the grounds, and their blacksmith, a man named George. Obviously, shoes are fairly impermanent artifacts, and we can't definitively trace any of the iron work. However, Lucy also talks about seamstresses. Apparently, they had an elderly woman who didn't do much more than sew. Lucy mentions, through the course of five years, three different quilts that quote-unquote 'Aunt Hera' made."

"The house is full of quilts," Olivia said, mentally cataloging the linen closets, the piles in the attic. She couldn't imagine the work necessary—

"And we don't get rid of quilts." Ash told her. "So we took descriptions of the quilts she talked about and started digging through the house. We were able to match two of them. One's fairly plain, but the other's an absolute work of art—applique chintz peacocks, all these tiny stitches, stunning. We crafted a whole display around it, and it's set to open in a few weeks. If we can't find it, it's an absolute disaster. Quilts made by enslaved people which can be definitively traced to a named individual—those are relatively rare, y'know?"

He stopped for a group of tourists crossing the road. They glared at the rising dust cloud as if they owned the place and resented their presence.

"They think we're custodial people and should get the hell outta the way," Olivia commented, almost amused.

"You can tell a lot about people by the way they treat the maids," Henry said.

Next to her, Ash shifted slightly. She knew he was thinking it, too—Henry's statement had the ring of an adage. It would have come from his childhood, and those maids he spoke of would have been enslaved. *There are no more slaves,* Sullivan had said when Henry asked why the household staff was white.

Okay, Henry had said, and that was all. When he'd used the n-word, Sullivan told him never to say it again. For years, they'd left it there; Henry's reckoning had come later. He'd long recognized his passive atrocities, though he'd never gotten over them, and Olivia wasn't sure if he should. Mostly, she forgot about them. That forgetting embarrassed her, but if she imagined the everydayness of that particular cruelty, she wouldn't love him. *He's sorry,* she always reminded herself, and remembered those long months he'd spent in cloistered agony. *I did this,* he'd say, holding a book. *I made this happen. They told us it was right, Livy, and I believed it. I was too stupid to recognize basic humanity. I know I was fourteen, but that's no excuse. I should've known better.*

Wordlessly, she'd held him.

The radio crackled as they rounded the turn between the house and the gift shop. "Y'all?" Boo's voice hummed, interference crisping it to frictives. "I had an idea. Don't get mad at me. But before we went wild trying to find that quilt, I opened the rooms to check? It's on Henry's bed."

Ash slammed the brakes, and Olivia's head jounced against the back of the seat. He hit the walkie-talkie. "*What?*" he asked.

"I didn't put it there," Henry said mildly, as if the quilt moving was no more miraculous than a tidal rise and ebb. "And honestly? I don't think anyone else did, either."

"That cabin was locked," Boo said, voice hemmed with static. "I checked this morning. You and I have the only keys."

"Well, how the hell did it get there?" Ash asked.

People moved around them, a crowd intent on nowhere in particular. They churned up powdery, age-worn dust from the drive. Olivia held back a sneeze. "Maybe a ghost did it," Henry replied.

Ash cursed quietly. Sometimes, in Cypress Bend, there were no other words.

CHAPTER 29

ASH

Ash had to plan dinner—a task which always devolved to him—check on progress with Talitha, coordinate with Whitney, and call Ethan; his co-executive producer had asked for one major investigation a week, and he had to gin up ideas. Sullivan had lost three thousand dollars. Sullivan and Henry weren't speaking, so Rhys and Henry weren't speaking. Elliot had wandered off with his dogs, and Uncle Wade's parrots were wet and squawking.

He collapsed in the upstairs living room. A camera hovered in the doorway, privy to his worst moments. He wished could toss his mic out the window.

"Want some company?" Still in her athleisure dress, sunglasses holding back her hair, Olivia appeared in the doorway. "I ran into Rhys downstairs. He told me about the wedding thing."

Ash gestured at a Victorian couch. Olivia sat, back straight and ankles crossed. He sipped his water and wished for something stronger.

"Sorry Sullivan is Sullivaning particularly hard. Is anything else bothering you? I mean, other than quilt-stealing ghosts." She recrossed her ankles. He wished she would unbend a bit—take a deep breath, slouch, maybe rest her feet on the coffee table. He'd seen her wear yoga pants and a tank top, but only in Charleston. Cypress Bend and reality TV dragged her back to childhood formalities. *Ladies always look put together*, his father would tell her.

"What's not bothering me?" he asked. "Christ. I don't know where to start. You can tell your boyfriend—"

"He's not my boyfriend," she snapped.

"Liv." He should have known better. Ash needed someone on his side. He only had Olivia, and it was a tenuous peace, fraught with childhood minefields. "I've known for years."

Her mouth a thin line, she watched the sky outside. Maybe she was waiting for something to appear.

"Seriously. Why didn't you—"

"I'm not ashamed of it, if that's what you're wondering." Olivia drew a long, deep breath and turned back to him. All traces of emotion had vanished. "He didn't want to tell you. He said he was a guest and he'd taken advantage of it."

"What d'you mean?" Ash asked.

Olivia gazed at some distant point on the bookshelves. "He always said that being with me was an insult to the hospitality you'd shown him. I think it's a Victorian thing. Anyway. I've tried to tell him to apologize to Sullivan. He says Sullivan should apologize to both of us."

"Sullivan should apologize to everyone." An alligator skull grinned toothily from a bookshelf across the room. His father had shot it in the swamp behind the house. They grew to monstrous size back there. The narrowed eye socket and crooked teeth lent the reptile an air of demonic knowing, as if the skull grinned at secrets it would never spill. Between those teeth and the sabers over the doorway, the soft parlor held too many sharp edges.

"Apologies were never Sullivan's strong suit," Olivia said.

"He slept with Talitha Merle." It came out before Ash could stop it. He shouldn't have whined about it, much less to Olivia; it said too much about what he wanted and what he couldn't manage. The cameras would capture it, too. He should have shut up.

Primly, Olivia recrossed her ankles. She seemed to search for words; clearly, she didn't want to hurt his feelings. Ash focused on that alligator skull. Even in bone-form, it seemed clever, stripped to bare wickedness. The alligator got what it wanted. "Of course Sullivan slept with Talitha Merle," she said eventually. "Why would that shock you? Sullivan's slept with everyone."

Ash wanted to sleep with a beautiful woman. He wanted to mention it casually, and find not approval, but indifference. It would descend from the miraculous into the everyday and obvious. But he had rules: no fans, no hit-and-runs. *You're such a girl*, a friend might say. He wished he had time for friends, too.

"I know Sullivan's slept with everyone," Ash replied. The alligator grinned at its own riddles; maybe it laughed at him, too. "Is that supposed to make me feel better?"

"It's not exactly a good look."

"But Sullivan always has someone," Ash pressed. He needed to shut up.

"Have you been in the heat too long?" Olivia popped the top of her Gamecocks water bottle. "He never has anyone. Why d'you think he sleeps around so much? He has Rhys, and I'd be shocked if they talk about anything other than where your dad kept the booze."

"At least he has Rhys." The alligator mocked him, like the sabers, like everything else in the house. He would never live up to it.

"You could have people, if you bothered to."

"You mean you?" he asked. "I know I have you. I mean, you're here."

"Not like you bother to talk to me very often." Olivia sipped at her water bottle. Even her flip-flops sported tiny blue palmettos and crescents, that state moon-spangled banner. She could have been South Carolina Barbie. They would sell her with tailgating accessories and a brunch playset. Ash hated himself for seeing it. His father had created her that way.

"Dad's gone," Ash said. "You don't have to keep it up."

"Keep what up?" Her posture never wavered. He remembered her tangle-haired and exhausted but uncomplaining, Elliot in her arms. *You should go to bed*, he'd say. *I'll take her.* He wondered if it was better or worse to see Olivia flawless but icily remote.

"I miss you," he said.

She lowered her water bottle. "I'm right here."

The alligator smirked. *I can't even find my dogs*, Ash wanted to say. He had to plan dinner. He had to do so many things. He stood. "Tell Henry to talk to Sullivan, will you?" he asked, then went downstairs to find Mickie. He would take care of everything. He was Ash, the oldest brother. The job fell to him, however little he liked it, however isolating it became. No one else would do it, so he might as well.

CHAPTER 30

RHYS

Dinner ran long, and cameras lurked in the corners. Rhys tried to ignore the ghost, a solemn, dark-skinned man in full livery. Back to the mantle, Rhys felt an ache settle quickly into his arms; his neck prickled. Maybe the man and others like him had been the real reason his uncle drank, the perverse force behind his Confederate mania. *Do the family ghosts refuse to show up on camera, or do you talk Ethan out of showing them?* he could have asked Ash. *Can we talk about them now that your dad's dead?*

But old habits died hard. Instead of bringing up the ghost, Rhys chewed Mickie's Virginia ham with pineapple glaze, tasteless with the knowledge of the man behind him. Aunt Alda smiled vaguely over her grits. Elliot fed her ham to the dogs; Sullivan pushed his food around the plate like a child trying to escape his vegetables. They should have brought Boo and Lewis in to keep the conversation moving. But it wasn't DoorDash, eaten with only his antiques for company. Despite the ghost, despite the weight of words unsaid, Rhys was ashamed to admit that for all its complications, he preferred Cypress Bend. At least he wasn't alone.

"Did Boo lock up the quilt?" Olivia asked when they'd exhausted a strained chat about Gamecock baseball.

"Yeah, he put it back in the cabin." Ash seemed no more bothered by the cameras than a passing cloud. "We still don't know how the hell someone got it out of there."

"What are y'all talking about?" Rhys asked.

"The latest weirdness," Ash said. "A quilt for the Black History exhibit walked away under suspicious circumstances."

Sullivan set down his fork. "What quilt?" he asked, suspicion lacing his voice.

"A quilt sewed by one of the enslaved people here. We were able to trace it—"

"I wish you didn't have to have an exhibit focusing on quilts," Sullivan said. "Doesn't exactly bring up the best memories, you know? But whatever. If we have something like that, I guess we should display it." Disconsolately, he stabbed at his ham.

"What d'you mean?" Ash asked.

"You don't remember?" Rhys said.

"Of course he doesn't remember." Sullivan pushed his plate back so hard it clinked against a platter. Rhys touched his arm, but his cousin shoved him away. "Either he doesn't care or he's fucking faking it. Which is worse?"

"Limoge and the f-word?" Olivia's tone and smile seemed more appropriate for a Charleston cocktail party than a family argument. "I thought you had better taste."

Ash closed his eyes for a moment and exhaled. Somehow, in that quiet gesture, he managed as much drama as Sullivan. "Please. Tell us all why I shouldn't have dared to display a quilt, one of the few artifacts on this farm that we can trace to a definitive person. One more time, tell us all why I'm the asshole. Please. The floor's yours."

"Y'all. Please," Rhys said. "I know, Sullivan. I know. But please, tell him without—" He read his own disbelief in Sullivan's wide eyes. Ash really didn't remember, and if he remembered, he didn't care. That callousness pussyfooted close to cruelty. Olivia had probably forgotten, but he couldn't blame her; she'd been seven years old and sick in bed with bronchitis. "You really don't know why?" Rhys asked.

"You too?" Ash asked. "Why am I not surprised?" A whole argument brooded in those words. *You always back him up. Why do you always have to take his side?* Maybe Ash wanted to plow past his own forgetting, willful or otherwise.

"Are you serious? One of the worst days of my life, and you act like it's nothing? I don't care what you display, Ash. But show some respect for what we went through." Silverware rattled as Sullivan shoved back from the table. "Thanks. Way to support your family." Cameras tracked him as he stalked out.

"There goes another bottle of bourbon." Olivia lifted her wine glass, and Rhys imagined the shot panning to her. "Try to keep him quiet when you drag him to bed tonight, will you?"

"Fuck you," Rhys said. "You don't remember."

"You know, Elliot's sitting across the table from you."

His little cousin glanced up. She'd been sneaking ham to the dogs while everyone argued. Rhys almost laughed. He wanted to hug her suddenly, the only sane Trenholm. "Ash, you don't remember either?" he asked.

"I don't know what you're talking about, and I'm really losing the patience to care at this point," Ash replied.

He would have to tell them, and he couldn't lose himself in that telling. Rhys rarely spoke of his childhood. He'd never spilled everything to a therapist; he never indulged in drunken confidences. He didn't talk about his uncle's sabers or fists or historical rants, or those moments of dry-mouthed terror wrought by both his uncle and the farm at large. Rhys kept both his literal and metaphorical ghosts close. "Dad died at the end of March," he said, trying not to think about those cameras panning to him, how they'd linger on his face. He focused on the far wall, somewhere above Olivia's head; he would recite the story, and it would spare Sullivan the telling. He could do it for his favorite cousin. "Sometime around the beginning of May, Sullivan and I came home from school with art projects. He was so excited, because he'd worked hard on his, and he wanted to show it to Aunt Alda.

"So he pulls this paper quilt outta his backpack. I watched him make it, and you don't know how much time he spent cutting those little pieces into perfect triangles and gluing them just right. But you know your dad hated Sullivan doing art.

"So just as he's showing it to Aunt Alda on the back patio, your dad stomps in. 'What've you got there, boy?' he asked. Well, even when we were nine, your dad had already started that bullshit about how art was for faggots, and we oughta spend our time playing baseball." Olivia cringed, but Rhys didn't stop. "So Sullivan says, 'It's nothing,' and tries to shove it into his backpack. But your dad, you know how he was when he got a bug up his ass about something. So he paws the thing out again, and he demands to know what it is.

"'During the Underground Railroad, slaves used quilts as a code to help them escape,' Sullivan told him. 'So we made quilts of our own.' And that's disputed now, but whatever—that's what they taught us. Well, you know how Uncle Truluck felt about us learning Black history. Anything like that was a waste of time. So now he's mad that not only did Sullivan make art, but it had to do with Black people.

"Uncle Truluck started going on and on about schools wasting our time and pandering to n-words. We had to stand there and listen. Cousin Valance was there. Sullivan and I weren't ten years old yet. Fourth grade, Ash. *Fourth grade.* That art project was made of kiddie construction paper."

Ash had fixed his gaze on the mirror at the dining room's far end, as if he were judging himself. Rhys hoped he was. His nails dug into his palm, and he felt the ghost looming behind him. He couldn't stop.

"So your dad finally pauses for a breath. The parrots were quiet—remember how your dad scared them? And Sullivan says, 'But Dad, if we don't do Black history, how will we know anything about the ghosts?' He had to have known it would set your dad off, but he wanted a real answer, and I think back then he still nurtured this misguided hope your dad could be reasonable.

"So your father slams to his feet and screams in Sullivan's face, 'There are no fucking ghosts! There's no ghosts on this place, y'hear me?' And Sullivan's terrified. He didn't answer, and that's when your dad hit him. He fell on his ass. I knew better than to cry. You just stood there, Ash—and that's not your fault. You probably figured you'd get hit too if you tried to stop him, and thank God you didn't have an asthma attack in the middle of it. 'Don't you ever mention those lies again!' your dad says, and God love Sullivan, he looks up at your dad and says, 'It's not a lie. I see ghosts every day. There's one in the dining room.'"

Rhys had shattered the sacred family code, and in front of cameras. It felt something like falling, something like freedom. He recalled his confusion, bafflement he was too frightened to mention to his cousin: Rhys had never seen the ghosts, and wouldn't for another two years. Now he couldn't forget them; the mirror reflected the man standing behind him. He looked too much like Henry; Rhys's chest felt hollowed out, as if he sucked air without oxygen. The Trenholms had enslaved their own children.

"So your dad hauls him up and hits him again," Rhys said. "'Don't you turn into a fucking liar,' he says, and he hit Sullivan a third time. I'd never seen y'all get hit. I knew he hit you, especially Sullivan, but I never saw it before. Then Cousin Valance says, 'Truluck, that's enough,' and he says, 'You gonna tell me how to raise my boys?' Your father hit Sullivan again. It just kept going, and we had to watch it. When he finished, your brother had two black eyes and bruises all over. Aunt Alda had to sit him in the kitchen with ice on his face, and he didn't go to school for a week. They said he fell off a horse." Rhys threw his napkin onto his plate. Half his dinner was left; he might never eat Virginia ham again. "So give Sullivan a break. You hate him 'cause your father liked him better? It only meant he got hit more."

Olivia's lazy cocktail-party smile had vanished. Elliot's lip trembled. Red-faced, Ash no longer met his own eyes in the mirror, and Henry held hands with Olivia under the table. When Rhys scanned the room, every camera pointed at him. Only the ghost remained impassive, unaffected. Rhys's arms ached as if he held that tray himself.

"Excuse me," he said. He should check on Sullivan—maybe his cousin didn't want him, but he would make sure. Angry all over again, shaking one more time, half with fear and half with rage—at his uncle, at Ash, at the misery of history that had brought them there—Rhys stood, and his chair scratched at the ornate carpet. He didn't look as the cameras swiveled. Certainly, they watched him stalk out. Rhys refused them the satisfaction of a glance.

CHAPTER 31

SULLIVAN

Sullivan's tumbler sweated a ring on the tablecloth. The sun pouted low over the cypress-swamp, and tattered clouds smeared the sky pink and orange. Maybe he shouldn't have given himself to that tide of blind rage, but he remembered every blow. He remembered his palms scraping the brick, his wind catching, his head whipping sideways as his father's palm burned his cheek. Why had he come to the patio? Its brooding jasmine-scent snatched him back surer than Ash's quilt.

"Hey." Rhys slumped outside, a bottle of water in hand. For once, no cameras had followed, and like Sullivan, he'd ditched his mic. "I told them so you didn't have to."

"Thank you," Sullivan said, gratitude thickening his voice. Rhys had covered for him. More than that, his cousin had found him afterward. "What'd they say?"

"They didn't say anything." Bourbon glugged drearily as Rhys refilled his glass. Uncle Wade's parrots rustled in their lemon trees. Long blue shadows marched from the west; a wedding gathered at the garden's far end, where an evening breeze caught long dresses and ruffled hair. "Elliot looked ready to cry. And I could tell by Ash's face—he remembered. He thought it didn't matter."

The bourbon didn't burn anymore. When it reached that fuzzy point, Sullivan knew he should stop. He rarely did. "Ash wasn't the one getting hit."

"I'll veto the dinner footage so you don't have to," Rhys told him.

"What'd they say when you mentioned the ghosts?" Sullivan asked, chest constricting. He almost felt that old taboo break, a brittle smash.

"They didn't say anything." Rhys focused on the long sweep of garden, all those nodding flowers and pruned bushes. "But they won't show it, even if Ash says it's okay. I won't let them."

"Thank you," Sullivan repeated—sometimes, he felt like he'd spent a life saying it. Like always, Rhys nodded. They wouldn't mention it again.

Rhys sat with him while he drank. They went to bed. In the morning, Sullivan vaguely regretted the concept of consciousness. His feet stuck to the plastic as he dragged down to the kitchen. When he reached the first floor, the rich, bitter promise of coffee hit him—Henry had woken first, but that first swallow would outweigh any awkwardness. The ghost would wait at the stove, but ghosts stood vigil in many of Cypress Bend's corners. He couldn't escape history. Sullivan hurried.

Ash waited at the table, cameras hovering behind.

Fuck the coffee. Sullivan turned.

"Please," his brother said. "I owe you an apology."

Sullivan stopped.

"I should've thought about it. I should've remembered." Ash stumbled, as if his words were spinning downhill. "I'm sorry I didn't. I just—I didn't think about it. Maybe I tried to block it out, I don't know. I didn't connect the dots, you know? I'm sorry for that." He stopped abruptly, and silence dropped too loud, too soon. It hung, ugly in the early-morning gray.

"Thank you." It seemed like the only thing Sullivan could say, though he didn't want to. One more time, the older woman bent over the stove. He tried not to look at her.

Ash's chair grated on the ancient tile. Taking a mug from their perpetual place, he filled it with coffee, added cream and sugar, and held it out to Sullivan. It was a fragile peace offering.

Sullivan had to take the coffee. It warmed his morning-cold hands.

When Ash sat again, Sullivan knew he should, too. It was supposed to be a pretty moment, the two of them sipping coffee before the day's heat broke, with Cypress Bend a solemn witness. It should have started something. *I'm sorry for the money*, he was supposed to say, though no remorse clouded his conscience, then *I'm sorry for laughing at Henry*. Ash would tell him, *It's okay, Sullivan*, and they would drink their coffee before the tourists' bustle began.

"Do they ever show up on camera?" Sullivan asked instead, hating himself, hating his brother and that house and maybe even the men and women stuck in its flytrap corners.

"Them?" Ash nodded at the woman. Age etched her face, cracked as baked earth. If Sullivan's words shocked him, he gave no sign. "No. Only Trenholms who live in the house can see them, I think. You oughta know that by now."

"How would I?" Sullivan asked. "We never talk about them. Don't you think that's fucked up, Ash? You're running a show about the paranormal, and you have ghosts in every goddamn corner—"

"Let it go." Ash's glare reminded him of their father: that narrowed squint, the angry brow. He bit off his words in single, snapped syllables.

"So one more time, I'm supposed to ignore the ghosts of sla—enslaved people standing around," Sullivan said. "Home sweet home."

"What else am I supposed to do?" Ash's voice rose to a shout. "They won't talk to us. We can't help them. And they aren't intelligent hauntings! We can't do a damn thing—"

"You could acknowledge their existence," Sullivan told him. "Maybe you could start there." Plastic squeaked underfoot as he strode upstairs. Sabers accused him from every lintel, from the hall's gray walls. He was supposed to broker a detente, and if not a detente, at least a ceasefire. He should have stayed quiet, taken the coffee and let Ash have his Hallmark moment. But his brother clutched money so tight he'd been willing to lie. He resented that Sullivan had slept with Talitha, and on a night when misery clawed him from the inside out. Worst of all, Ash didn't realize that their father's love meant worthiness for his fists. Sullivan had spent a childhood envying his brother's asthma. Coffee couldn't fix such brutal enormities.

Sullivan wondered if anything could fix them.

He took his coffee on the front patio, without cameras, where he could watch the sunrise without parrots squawking and ghosts hovering; no one would look for him there. The farm stretched and yawned. Cousins trundled by in golf carts, and the American flag rose over the gift shop, then hung limp in the damp-hot morning. Birds flitted through the live oaks. Afraid he'd spot an ivory-billed woodpecker, Sullivan refused to examine them too closely. He wondered what had happened with the quilt. Ash said it had "walked off," and Sullivan had shouted rather than asked him to explain. But he didn't need details, not really. The farm had heaped strangeness upon strangeness, and that was enough.

He'd promised to call Talitha. That had to be done; Ash would ask him about it later. Sullivan squinted. The sun smeared low over the cypresses, but Talitha, like him, slept little. Maybe she'd want to see him, and it would be a small, good thing against the world's larger tyrannies. When the sun topped the trees, he called her.

"Sullivan Trenholm." Talitha's voice popped and cracked; cell towers were few in Lower Congaree. "Heard you skipped town. Haven't talked to you in a minute."

"Hey, Talitha," Sullivan said, and a small smile curved his cheek. A woman's voice helped drag him back to himself; he reached beyond that boy lost in Cypress Bend and momentarily banished his father's ghost. "How're you doing this morning?"

"Married."

"Aw, dammit." It slipped out before Sullivan could stop himself, but Talitha's ringing laughter smoothed his embarrassment.

"So if that's why you called, you can hang up the phone," she said, half-breathless.

"Who's that?" a male voice asked; her husband must have heard her laughing.

"Tell him he's a lucky bastard," Sullivan said.

That laughter almost assuaged his disappointment. "I'm not saying that. Seriously, what d'you want, Sullivan? It's seven o'clock in the morning, and I've got three hungry bellies in front of me. Four, if you count me."

He hadn't thought farther beyond asking her out, and with that plan busted, Sullivan struggled. "I need a favor."

"Uh-huh." Wariness dropped into her tone, and he wished he'd threaded through some small talk. "What kinda favor?"

"Okay, so this woman showed up at Cypress Bend." It was better, perhaps, to get a running start and tell her in one blind leap. "My cousin Judah's fiancée. They were gonna get married here, but something followed him home. They need help. I thought—"

"No." Talitha spoke finally and firmly. "Your brother wants it for his goddamn show, doesn't he? Uh-huh. Hard no. I don't do reality TV."

Sullivan strode across the patio. He was a phone pacer, one of those who spoke better on his feet. "It doesn't have to be on camera. Maybe you could—"

"No. I'm not setting foot on that plantation."

From the high patio, Sullivan looked over the Trenholm farm, still sleepy, glazed with thin morning light. "Why not?"

"Because it's cursed as all hell," she said. "I don't know what's going on over there, but there's something wrong, and I don't wanna be involved."

"We need someone who knows what they're doing with this kind of thing." He added some pleading in his voice, but not too much, not so soon. "My cousin Judah's getting all clawed up, Talitha. Something's *clawing him*, in the middle of the night. It choked him once."

"No," she said.

"Please?"

"No."

"It gets so much worse. Those men, the three men? Remember? They see them. The ones I saw." He tried to stuff urgency into his voice. *Remember those men?* he wanted to ask. *They came back. It's time for the house to fall. I don't know what that means, but I'm terrified, and there's no one to tell, not even Rhys.*

"No."

"Talitha—"

"No."

"I'm serious. My little cousin saw them the other night, too." He reached the end of the patio and turned, paced back. "Something's happening here." All teasing drained from his voice. "I wouldn't call if I didn't mean it."

"You're not gonna give up til I agree to this, are you?"

"No," he said promptly.

"Goddammit. Fine. Call me when you figure out a time. But *no cameras*. Y'hear me? If there's a camera, I'm gone."

"You're the best, Talitha," he told her. "The absolute best in the world. For several reasons."

"If you don't behave, I'll walk out of there, Sullivan Trenholm," she said, but she was laughing again. Below him, the farm rose into wakefulness. He could still make her laugh. It was a small victory, but he couldn't count many anymore. Sullivan held it tight.

CHAPTER 32

RHYS

Rhys woke sweat-slick and tangled in the sheets. His dream ebbed, vision and broken narrative swallowed to coiling fear—clammy skin; a taste of pennies; a wild, thumping heartbeat. Shoving off the covers, he kicked upright. "You're awake," Sullivan said, setting a mug on his bedside table. "There's coffee downstairs. Maybe Ash too, fair warning. But also coffee, so the two balance out."

Rhys rubbed his sticky eyes. Morning glared like an accusation he wasn't ready to face. "I need a shower," he said, because the first belonged to Sullivan by right of waking. "D'you care if I go?"

"Sure," his cousin said, and the TV flipped on again. Rhys slept with its flickering every night. Sullivan never seemed to sleep.

When he stepped out of the shower and turned it off, Sullivan stripped shamelessly and turned it on again. Used to it, Rhys ignored him. "Wait for me before you go down to breakfast?" his cousin asked over the water's drumming. He pulled back the shower door, and the water's tattoo shifted, pelting skin instead of tile. "Ash's down there, and I don't wanna walk in alone."

"If you want me to." Rhys worked his soap into a lather, then smoothed it over his face. A snob about shaving, he hoarded clarifiers, oils, straight razors. He'd down his pills after he took care of his face. "Is this about last night?"

"He tried to apologize this morning and it was weird, okay?" Sullivan's voice echoed oddly from the marble. "He doesn't get it's so much, y'know?"

"Yeah," Rhys said, and that was all. His cousin didn't want to talk; he wanted to say it, and he wanted to leave it. Rhys knew him well enough to understand. If pressed, Sullivan would stiffen into silence. Trenholms held their feelings tight.

Downstairs, the family stepped through their normal breakfast rituals. Olivia pushed food around her plate. Elliot slipped bacon to the dogs while Ash pretended not to notice, and Henry ate a bowl of fruit. Aunt Alda slurped her grits. He and Sullivan nodded at everyone, helped themselves to coffee, and split the rest of the bacon. The ghost hovered by the stove. Just once, Rhys wished they could eat in that kitchen without the weight of history hanging over them.

"So, tomorrow," Ash said, as if he were gathering a strayed thread of conversation. "Ethan wants us to keep investigating the farm. So I have an idea. If y'all have any, I mean, feel free to make suggestions."

"What, like we should go hang out in the barn with a tape recorder and wait for nothing to answer us? That's your department," Sullivan said. Olivia stole a spoonful of Henry's kiwi. Lately she'd indulged in those small, possessive gestures. Henry didn't seem to mind.

Ash's face puckered like their cousin Valance's ancient wife, Victoria Lee. "It's called an EVP—"

"It's called talking to the air and playing the feedback on high volume," Sullivan shot back. Rhys couldn't help snorting even as he wished his cousin would shut up.

"So I'm assuming y'all have no ideas," Ash replied. "I guess we'll go with fireworks in the back field. We'll aim thermal imaging cameras at the phenomena area and see if there's any changes in the heat signature."

"Does this mean we have to go out there at night?" Sullivan asked. "I don't wanna step in horseshit."

Sullivan would snark at Ash til he shouted or stomped out. Rhys wondered if that sarcasm gave him some satisfaction for the night before, or if it sprung from a kind of reflex. "Y'all," he said, trying to marshal words that might both stop his cousin and diffuse blame. "Let Ash talk."

"Why?" Sullivan asked sharply, betrayal tainting his tone. "He'll make us do it anyway, and he'll have to say it again in front of the cameras. Might as well do it once and save us the time." He shifted as if pain had settled into his hip flexors. *Do any of you notice that we get terrible back pain when we sit in this kitchen?* Rhys resisted shouting. *Am I the crazy one here, or do you all see the woman standing next to the stove? Can we talk about her now?*

"For once, Bumble the Boy Wonder has a point." Olivia gestured with her spoon.

"Excuse me?" Sullivan's arch sarcasm dipped into annoyance.

"I know. It wasn't a great one," Olivia said, and Henry leaned back as she snagged more kiwi. "I'm tired this morning."

"I could always speculate about why," Sullivan replied.

"Oh, don't bother. Henry would only hit you again."

They would shove one another like children over a mud puddle. One of them would eventually fall in, then everyone would get dirty. But a small, vicious part of him enjoyed the pure bloodiness of it, and if they fought, no one had to look too closely about what they were fighting about.

"Henry never did hit me," Sullivan said. "And I apologize for anything that made him feel like he had to."

It was clever of his cousin—blurt an apology at the breakfast table, mid-argument, when social pressure would force Henry to accept it. And predictably, Henry nodded. Rhys could have laughed if he wasn't so close to despair.

"Are you two finished?" Ash asked.

"They are," Rhys said firmly. He could keep them from falling apart. He could gather up their frayed edges and weave them together again. A looming transplant only urged him on. What if he didn't make it? He couldn't let his family fight, not when he had power to stop them.

"Thank you," Ash said. "We're going out to the field tomorrow, get it? You're going to investigate. You're going to do it with a minimum of snark, because we fight enough on this show. Got it?"

"Don't talk to us like that," Sullivan snapped.

"Oh, stop arguing," Aunt Alda set down her spoon. Her voice quavered, but it carried like a drill sergeant's. "I don't know what this is about, but it's unbecoming, Truluck." She pointed not at Sullivan, but at Ash. "You leave him be now."

Ash huffed. Sullivan smirked. Olivia suppressed laughter. But they shut up.

It was as much as Rhys could hope for.

CHAPTER 33

OLIVIA

Olivia shoved her feet into her hiking boots. Before she could lean over, Henry knelt to tie them. "Are you serious?" she asked.

"You're really worried about that horse manure," he said. "I don't think I've ever seen you wear these before."

The Saturday night sky had gone down into darkness. Olivia missed Charleston's indigo twilights, those purplish nights that came only in southern cities by the ocean. Ash was taking them to tromp through the back field, set off fireworks, and observe his disc-shaped phenomenon through thermal imaging cameras. Olivia didn't care what they found. She slept next to a man who'd seen his cousin and uncles crushed in the maul of the Civil War; she'd watched her own uncle dig bullets from Henry's shoulder, then seen the antibiotics coax him to life. Ghosts cluttered Cypress Bend's dark reaches. Nothing that they found in that back field would surprise her.

"You didn't have to tie my shoes," she said.

Henry straightened. In a button-down and khaki shorts, hair trimmed into preppy curls, he looked like every other Southern boy she'd dated. "I wanted to," he replied. "We can finally get dressed together."

His smile hurt. Though Olivia had known Henry was lonely, his joy in those small details told her how deep that sadness cut, and she hated facing it. She could have stayed home. She could have bullied him into telling her uncle—he'd insisted on niceties even when the old man couldn't speak. Maybe that guilt would go away, or maybe it would always nag at her, like a scratched throat.

"We could get dressed together before." Olivia straightened some makeup on her vanity. It seemed important to keep her things neat. She hadn't shared a room since her sophomore year in college.

"I was always rushing to get out before sunrise. Now I get to watch you paint your face. I didn't know you did that naked." Henry smiled again, like she was brand-new, and Olivia remembered one more time that he'd never been with anyone else, not really. Never had Henry spent those first few weeks learning a person's mornings. He'd never attuned himself to someone's routines, or witnessed any number of small revelations that came from sharing space with a person. Wartime didn't count. That was necessity, and men did things differently from women.

Henry caught her hand as they walked downstairs, mics on their shirts. He wanted to hold her hand all the time, and she let him, though it seemed strange and almost frightening. Olivia didn't hold people's hands. She didn't sit close to them, and she seldom woke up next to them. *They aren't Henry*, she'd always told herself, or, *He says Uncle Truluck will kill him,* which he'd repeated even after a stroke had left the old man speechless and hardly mobile. Though she finally had Henry, long years of dissembling had branded those everyday gestures as treasonous, and it was hard to forget.

Ash waited in that room he called HQ, stacked full of computers and tech. Her cousin was a little boy playing a game; he might as well put a sign on the door: *No girls allowed.* Two cameras roved through the room, and Lewis sat at the head of the table. Sprawled on the floor, Elliot played tug-of-war with one of the dogs. "Two more calls on the hotline," Ash said in the brisk tones of a man describing his workday. "They say they saw UAPs flitting through the back field. There's phone footage. We'll likely use them. Oh, and Ethan says y'all are behind on your on-the-fly interviews, especially Rhys and Sullivan—"

"Where are they?" Olivia asked, taking a chair. Henry took one next to her. She loved that small gesture—life had finally broken open for them.

"Sullivan and Rhys? We're still waiting for them," Lewis said.

"Why am I not surprised?" Olivia asked. "Those two are joined at the hip, Christ. You never see one without the other."

"You'd think they were married." Henry said it straight faced. She'd never dared, but his Victorian sensibilities let him get away with it. Henry's comment had no shaded meaning. Olivia didn't dare look at Ash or Lewis—they would smirk, or worse, laugh.

"Hey, Lewis. What's Olivia all red about?" Sullivan asked. He and Rhys snagged chairs across from one another.

"You and Rhys being married," Elliot said from the floor.

"Life hands us tragedy. Rhys being straight and my cousin is one of them." Wearing Rhys's Sugarcult tee, Sullivan tipped his chair on two legs. He'd extended conceptual art to his life, one performance that never ended.

"Nice clothes," Olivia said. Ash had asked them to wear light colors, which would contrast sharply against the dark. "You only own black t-shirts, don't you?"

"Shut up," he told her.

"At least you didn't stoop to one of Ash's polos." Teasing him was a childhood habit, lazy but hard to break. "And do better than 'shut up.' You're making this too easy."

Rhys opened his mouth, but Ash slid into a chair and nodded at the cameras. "Okay," he said. "So, here's what we're going to do tonight." He seemed to speak more for an imaginary audience than for the family sitting around him. "We know there's a disc-shaped phenomenon—"

"Portal," Sullivan said.

"*Disc-shaped phenomenon*—" Ash continued.

"Just say it's a portal," Sullivan told him. "It's a portal, Ash. We *know* it's a portal."

"We can't say it's a portal," Lewis replied.

"We can."

"*Anyway*," Ash said. "We're going to set off fireworks so they pass through *whatever you wanna call the thing*, which in the name of science *I* am calling a 'disc-shaped phenomenon.' At the same time, we're going to watch that area through large-screen thermal imaging cameras from four sides. This will—"

"Wait a second." Rhys held up a hand as though it pained him to object. "Won't the fireworks just show heat on the thermal imaging cameras and obscure any data?"

"We're hoping to see more heat than the average explosions," Lewis replied. "And to do that, we're going to set off the same fireworks in another area and compare the thermal imaging results." His earnest look reminded Olivia of a child solemnly explaining dinosaur genuses.

"What d'you think we'll find?" Rhys asked.

"If we knew that, we wouldn't run the experiment," Ash replied. "Maybe nothing. I don't know. But even nothing is a data point."

Olivia almost rolled her eyes. Though they'd long left conventional science behind, Ash still insisted on its trappings—sop for his fans, who expected plenty of rambling analysis and shiny gadgets. "Be honest," she said. "We're going to set off fireworks until it pisses off the farm enough to send up some UFOs."

Ash's expression dropped into pitifulness. "UAPs. They're UAPs."

"It's okay, Ash," Elliot told him, still on the floor. "I'm sure the aliens will show up."

"We don't know if they're aliens," Ash said, anger almost breaking through. He wouldn't yell at Elliot, but his patience had tautened. A German Shepherd crowded its snout into his lap. Ash seemed to consider pushing it off, then petted it instead. "We're going to the back field," he said, words snipped snort, "and we're going to set off some fireworks. We're going to watch the area fifty feet above the field, where we've previously seen the disc-shaped phenomenon, with thermal imaging cameras. You're all coming."

"Can I set off the fireworks?" Sullivan asked.

Lewis shoved his glasses up his nose. "Uh, Parker was gonna do it. But I'm sure if you want—"

"Oh, I want," Sullivan said. "Fireworks are the fun part. I mean, fuck your disc-shaped phenomenon, Ash. I'm here for the explosions. Let's go, y'all. Time to blow some shit up."

"You know they'll have to beep that out and you'll sound like an idiot," Ash told him as they passed through the doors and onto the patio.

"Sorry we're not all G-rated all the time," Sullivan said.

Henry leaned close enough for her to smell his Old Spice. "I'll be upstairs, Livy," he said quietly. "I'm sorry. The fireworks will be bad enough from here. I was hoping Ash would change his mind. Would you tell him for me?"

She nodded once. He pressed her hand, then strode back into the house. They piled onto golf carts. "Where's Henry?" Ash asked.

Olivia tilted her head at the cameraman behind them, next to Elliot. Maybe her cousin would one day learn discretion. "War has a lot of explosions," she said blandly. "He's not a fan."

"Oh. I didn't think of that," Ash said. The underbrush rustled, and Olivia eyed it as they passed. Just beyond the parking lot, the darkness melted into velvet. It mingled with the wet-damp heat, the two seemingly indistinguishable; they seemed tangible enough to stain her face. When she glanced back at the house, Olivia caught a man glaring from the second-floor living room. Outrage colored her uncle Truluck's pale face; he stared with the fury of a man scorned, left behind. Stiffly, she turned, and his hate prickled her neck. Her uncle had returned.

The cameras were watching. If she told her cousins, they'd tumble into flustered panic. Swallowing her terror, Olivia kept her face blank and mouth shut.

"Well, I'm really excited about this investigation," Ash said. Olivia hated him speaking for the cameras in the guise of talking to her. "We ought to get some good data here, and like I said, no information is still—"

The dense weeds exploded. Four German Shepherds hurled onto the drive, and Olivia nearly fell from the golf cart as Ash wheeled sideways to avoid them. Close on their heels, a black-and-white creature erupted from the bushes, and Olivia screamed as an impossibly long, low-slung lizard flew after the dogs. The reptile moved like a predator, front limbs hardly touching the ground while it chased the dogs into the dark. Olivia caught spots, a beefy throat, a forked tongue, a whipping tail.

"What the *fuck* was that?" she shouted. The farm had thrown them something prehistoric, reached farther back than she had ever imagined—

"I don't know," Ash said. "I have no—"

"I didn't know we had tegus in Legare County," Elliot said. "Huh."

"You didn't know we had *what*?" Olivia asked, head cool on the plastic dash. Her neck hurt, two steps from whiplash; the dogs were still running. Someone should go get them. It wasn't going to be her. That thing had been close to the ground, but its vertical leap could have reached the soft parts of her belly.

"Jesus Christ, have tegus come this far north?" Sullivan called from the other cart.

"That was a *tegu*?" Ash glanced at Lewis for confirmation, as if their cousin's astronomy background granted him a leg up on lizard identification.

From the back of Sullivan's golf cart, Lewis nodded earnestly. "That was a tegu, yeah." He turned to the camera. "Tegus are pack-hunting lizards native to South America, but they've gained a foothold here. They popped up in the Lowcountry, probably after releases from the pet trade. They're highly intelligent and slightly venomous—and they're also partially warm-blooded. Pretty cool."

It struck Olivia as the farthest thing from cool, but she kept her mouth shut.

"Yeah, they found some tegus around Lexington Medical Center, and at the airport, too," Elliot said. Ash started the cart again. "I don't remember where I heard it. Maybe on WIS."

"So it's supposed to be here?" Olivia asked.

"I mean, not really, but yes?" Sullivan told them. "In the sense of it's an invasive species, but—"

"We get it," she said.

"What I mean is it didn't come out of the portal," he continued.

"You mean 'disc-shaped phenomenon,'" she replied, face as straight as she'd kept it in their teenage card games.

"Jesus Christ!" Ash banged the steering wheel, careening across the drive and nearly banging the other golf cart. "Will you two *quit it*?!"

They kept at it so they didn't have to think about the cameras, or the presumptive audience seething behind them, so they didn't have to look at the hollow dark and imagine what might wait beyond it. Sunk in their own cleverness, they could ignore present miseries. It had kept them coping that long.

Though it hadn't worked, not really—Sullivan had long spun into the fury of his own storms, or perhaps been abandoned to them; remote as a barn cat, just as detached, Rhys had disappeared, surfacing only to beg them to stop fighting. Ash had all but pulled on a cape and become the family superhero. Olivia refused to add up her own losses. At least Elliot had escaped. At least she had that, and it counted for something, however small.

Ash parked next to an elaborate field setup, all generator wires and huge screens. They could have walked from the house through the gardens; Ethan must have wanted footage of them driving, or maybe Ash had driven for Rhys's sake. She hated that cold reckoning, and she hated the exposed guts behind it. Ethan planned shots and laid out conversations. Ash knew what to say. He knew when and how to say it. A single sick detail, those golf carts reminded Olivia that she'd consigned her life to artifice.

The field operation teemed with people. Rather than use a plain canopy from *Paranormal Gone South*, someone had borrowed a small wedding pavilion; Ash had pirated antebellum dining room tables from the attic, and computers gleamed atop the polished mahogany. He'd poached the matching chairs, and as she came closer, she saw that her cousin was keeping water bottles in a barrister's bookshelf, and walkie-talkies on a piecrust table. Bundled cords snaked in every direction. Beyond the pavilion, darkness held its breath. Olivia tried to ignore it.

"Why didn't you throw down Oriental rugs?" she asked. A camera hovered behind her like an unwanted pet. She tried to ignore it.

"I didn't want to track horse manure on them," Ash replied. He and Lewis hunched over a computer monitor. Maybe Ash was serious. Maybe not.

"I can't decide if this is absolutely ridiculous or genius," Sullivan said. "So, where are the explosives?"

"Can you wait?" Ash replied. "We need to lay out this investigation and check everything. There's a lot more to this than blowing things up. And there's safety issues here, and safety—"

"Yeah, yeah. Safety is paramount." Dropping to a chair, Sullivan assumed a regal slouch that Olivia assumed he'd taken some time to perfect.

"We need to calibrate things," Ash snapped. "Rhys, can you handle him, please?"

"I don't need to be *handled*!" Sullivan said, but Rhys murmured something about checking fireworks and he left. A camera bobbed behind them.

Olivia waited. Eventually, Elliot came to sit with her. Ash wandered with Lewis and Sinclair; Sullivan and Rhys had gone away into the dark. She hadn't wanted this circus. Olivia remembered that dinner, a long time ago, when Sullivan had asked why people tried to break into the farm. *They want something to believe in,* she'd said. Back in the gardens, a bride and groom stepped through one of the biggest days of their lives; a tinny "Mr. Brightside" added yet another layer of weirdness. Elliot sang along softly.

"How long d'you think this'll take?" Olivia asked her little cousin.

"Oh, I don't know," she replied. "I never come to these things. Why does it matter if they find anything or not? We know what's up there."

"At least someone else is sane about this." One of Ash's dogs poked its long nose on her lap, and she messed with its silky ears. Her uncle had always kept shepherds. When he drank, the dogs had become wary; when he started yelling, they'd launch into a fury of barking, and he'd have to throw them outside. Olivia had always worried when the dogs were gone. *How will we know if something's wrong?* she'd fretted. *The dogs keep us safe.* Her uncle had always denied it, but he denied everything paranormal. Every Trenholm child knew: Look to the dogs.

Sullivan emerged from the dark, Rhys at his side, camera behind them. Both her brother and cousin wore looks of half-suppressed glee, like little boys on the edge of a water-balloon fight. Maybe that was what happened when children didn't grow up. They bought bigger toys, and with no windmills to tilt, took up ghost hunting. "Sinclair says the explosives are ready," her cousin said.

Though they seemed action-packed on *Paranormal Gone South*, her cousin's investigations seemed to require a lot of waiting around in the dark. Ash and Lewis didn't appear for another half hour, but they returned wearing those goofy grins Olivia had seen from Rhys and Sullivan.

"Okay," Ash said, and Olivia imagined one camera focused on him, the other zoomed on each of them in turn. "Sinclair's throwing on the thermal imaging cameras. We have enough people for two per side—"

"Rhys and I are together," Sullivan interrupted.

"Y'all somehow managed to live without each other for years," Olivia said. "Will an hour kill you?"

Sullivan's expression twisted. Something between anger and sadness, it hurt her, and she wished she hadn't spoken. Sullivan's pain seemed vaster than something tossed-off sarcasm should unearth. "I'll take Lewis, thanks," she told Ash quickly.

"You can't have Lewis. He stays back to monitor things. You can take Parker." Ash flung his hands into the air, palms up, patience waning. "Elliot and I will stay here. Sullivan, you and Rhys go to the west side—that's where the fuses are. Sinclair will tell you how to set them off. He and Boo will take the south side. Everyone take a walkie-talkie. We'll do an all-clear, then a countdown from ten before we set each one off. Several minutes in between each, so we have some time for observation. Eyes on the skies in between, people."

It was too canned. He'd probably planned it.

"Did you get that?" he asked. "Cameras still working?"

"All good over here," replied one of the operators. The other threw a thumbs-up.

"Hoping everything goes well out here tonight," Ash said. "Equipment has a way of failing here at Cypress Bend. Y'all watch the dogs, now." He tilted his head toward the shepherds roving at Elliot's feet. "If the dogs start acting strange, you know something's going down."

Eventually, Olivia grabbed a flashlight, a walk-talkie, and a water bottle, then followed Parker into the dark, a camera trailing behind them. Her light seemed too paltry for the swaddling black, and one more time, she missed Henry. "We've got the north side," Parker told her.

"Sounds good," she said. Parker threw a thin smile she barely made out. Olivia could feel the field unfurling around her, all the way to the fence, like stubbed teeth, then to the swamp's ragged edges. Far back in the dark, those inescapable cypresses loomed. She faced forward and walked fast, trying not to think about them.

CHAPTER 34

RHYS

As he and Sullivan strode to their position in the back field, Rhys began to understand why Ash loved his investigations. He pressed a slim, curved button on his walkie-talkie. "Check one-two-three," he said. "Approaching our position in the west, over."

"We got you, Rhys, this is Ash with base, over," his cousin replied, and Rhys's thrill felt delightfully, unabashedly child-like. Despite a static-y backsplash and the Android in his pocket, walkie-talkies hadn't lost their boyhood shine. Sullivan carried a long, deadly flashlight—the type Mulder and Scully used, Rhys had thought when his cousin grabbed it. If a coyote or tegu or red-eyed monster slipped from the dark, Sullivan could bludgeon it. Grass crackled underfoot; Rhys kicked at errant clots of dried manure. It was far too late and far too hot—his hair was already clumping up—but Ash's tech gave the investigation an air of grand adventure.

Their thermal imaging screen, at least 85 inches, gleamed like a television at the end of the world. Someone had mounted fuses on stands, and their big red buttons begged to be mashed, not pushed. Those fuses made up for the mosquitoes, already beginning to swarm. He should have sprayed himself down with Deet, but it didn't matter. They were going to set off fireworks, explosions they'd only dreamed of once, and no one would stop them. Maybe they'd scare monsters from the dark. Rhys understood it perfectly then: Their childhood, denied for so long, had finally arrived. It didn't have to be Confederate-haunted, relic-strewn. They had all the toys they wanted, and no uncle waited at home; if anything emerged from that night, they could fight it and win. Maybe something would come. But nothing could be worse, not really, than what had come before. They were grown, big, and it couldn't touch them. Whatever came would be easier than what had come before.

"It's different now," Rhys said as they took their positions. On thermal imaging, Sinclair became an orange-yellow blur as he checked the fireworks one last time. Behind the screen's bright light, the night became impossibly black, and even the camera next to them, a silent eye, used night vision.

"What d'you mean?" Sullivan asked. He hefted the flashlight. Rhys couldn't read his face.

"We don't have to be afraid," Rhys said. "We never have to be afraid again. It can't—"

"Ash to Sullivan, Boo, and Parker. Your screens working? You should be seeing Sinclair out there checking the fireworks, over."

"We got it, over," Rhys replied.

"Got it," Boo said. Static crackled; Rhys waited. "Over," Boo finally added.

"Why did you assume Parker has the walkie-talkie?" Olivia asked. "Over."

"You got the visual, Olivia, over?" Ash asked.

"Fine. Yes. Don't be a dick. Over."

"Okay, all set. Getting clear, over," Sinclair said, and the orange figure dashed offscreen. It had an air of unreality, like an elaborate videogame.

They waited. In dull greens, the screen showed that Ash had constructed a complex setup, four separate rigs of Roman candles set to go off when Sullivan hit buttons. "In position to the south," Sinclair told them. "I'm clear, over."

"Okay, y'all," Ash said. "Watch the screens. If what we've been seeing holds, those fireworks should fire off too low, somewhere around fifty feet. You'll see a white heat signature. We're looking to see what happens right before or afterward. Sullivan, you can start the countdown whenever you're ready, over."

Rhys didn't need to see: for the first time in days, his cousin was grinning like a kid. He imagined the camera zooming in on his face, capturing that handsome smile. "Ten, nine, eight," he chanted. "Seven, six, five, four, three, two, one!" He slammed the button. A firework hissed and sparked, then exploded in double, gold in the sky—about fifty feet up, like Ash predicted—and bright white on the screen. For a vanishingly brief moment, a thin yellow line flickered beyond the white. Rhys gaped. He'd seen nothing against the gold explosion.

"Did you see that?" he asked Sullivan. "That line, on the—"

"Wooooo!" Ash shouted, a victory crow that carried through the field. "Did you see it?" the walkie-talkie crackled. "Did you see it? That yellow stripe? Do it again, Sullivan! Hit another! Over!"

"What the hell was that?" Rhys asked. "Over," he added hastily.

"I don't know!" Ash said. "Do it again!"

"Clear, over?" Sullivan asked.

"Clear, over," Olivia replied.

"Clear, over," Sinclair said.

"Ten, nine, eight, seven, six, five, four, three two, one!" Sullivan hit the second fuse. Another firework fizzed, banged, and burst into a red flower. One more time, yellow flashed onscreen behind the white explosion. It didn't belong. A chill gathered at Rhys's spine. That thin yellow line shouldn't have existed. Something was above the field, and there was a sharp difference between hearing that and seeing it. A furious barking erupted near Ash's tent—something had set the dogs off.

"The spectrum analyzer just jumped to 1.6 gigahertz," Lewis's voice hissed over the walkie-talkie. "Look up, y'all!"

"We got aerial contact at two o'clock, over!" Sinclair said. Rhys snapped up. Twinned afterimages bloomed in the sky, but a small dot skimmed between the incurious stars. He resisted grabbing Sullivan's hand. The farm was reacting. They'd poked some sleeping beast, and it was coming for them. He whipped around. Rhys saw only darkness, stretching into the unimaginable. The dogs had not stopped barking.

"There's nothing on the ADS-B!" Lewis said. "That's a UAP, over!"

"What's an ADS-B again?" Rhys asked. Somehow, his voice still worked.

"That's the thing that tells him if there's any planes carrying a transponder anywhere in the sky," Sullivan replied. "Everything but the military has to carry a transponder, and even though we've got Fort Jackson and Shaw Air Force Base in Sumter . . ." He didn't have to tell Rhys that the tiny light moved far faster than most known human aircraft, and that their inability to place it, name it, unsettled them all.

The bright dot stopped, reversed, and streaked backward.

"Nothing moves in that pattern," Rhys said. He needn't have. They'd seen it many times.

"No more visual on the UAP." Sinclair's voice thickened with static. "Y'all got—" He fuzzed into unintelligible crackling. The dogs went suddenly, terrifyingly silent.

"Can't hear you, over," Rhys told him.

Feedback screeched, and Rhys dropped the walkie-talkie as the screen blew bright-white, then black again. Against the dark field, three tall figures stood hand in hand. Top-hatted, and dressed in identical, old-fashioned clothes, they grinned, and those grins spread too wide. They seemed to have too many teeth. Far away, Elliot screamed. When Rhys glanced at the field, the darkness revealed nothing.

"They're back," Sullivan whispered. "Oh fuck, Rhys, they're back. Don't look at them. Don't you fucking look—"

The screen popped and went black again as its power button blipped out.

"What the hell is that?" someone shouted.

"Lost power," said the cameraman. "Y'all got cell coverage?"

Sullivan dropped to the ground, head between his knees.

"Of-fucking-course not." Rhys's voice trembled, a little boy trying out cuss words. "We never do." He couldn't deny it anymore: The three men had returned. *Time for the house to fall*, the ghost had said. Whatever that meant, he hoped it was wrong.

He knew it wasn't.

CHAPTER 35

ASH

Ash paced the narrow gap between his conspiracy-theorist whiteboard and mahogany table in HQ. Elliot sat nearby, hugging herself; she'd refused to let him out of her sight. After the cameras died, Boo had rushed into the field; either the men had run away—if they'd been corporeal, which Ash doubted—or disappeared. They'd abandoned the investigation; Boo, Parker, and Sinclair would pack up in the morning. *Safety is paramount*, he'd reminded everyone. Sullivan, he could tell, had been too frightened to snark back.

On the phone, Ethan babbled a string of Hollywood nonsense. It was something like midnight in California. They said New York never slept, but neither did LA, and Ash felt no remorse for calling.

"We can't show it," Ash said when Ethan finally stopped talking. "People will think someone sneaked into the farm. They'll think *they* can sneak into the farm." It was an excuse. The three men were too strange, too disturbing. Worse, everyone would think they faked it.

"Hey, hey, calm down. I don't think you heard me right, Ash. I know how you think it looks—"

"No, I know how it looks." Ash imagined his co-producer in a room with floor-to-ceiling windows, a valley of shining houses spread below. Pools would glitter blue in the Hollywood night. He hoped not. He hoped Ethan was choking on wildfire smoke.

"It's scary, I get it, but the cameramen called me, and that yellow line, man, that's a great find. That's crazy! We have to keep it. And the scare factor just ups the drama! This is gold, Ash!"

Ethan kept repeating his name, an old trick to draw him in and gin up sympathy. Ash resented his transparent ploy. Ethan thought he was a useless Southern hick, his slower speech indicative of lesser intelligence. Maybe there was something to that; a smarter man might have fled South Carolina, might have left behind its purple politics and boiling racism. But you bloomed where you were planted, and that blood-soaked soil felt like home. "I don't think it's a great idea to show the men," he repeated, the third time. "I'd like to cut it." Elliot still sagged in her chair, the dogs pressed against her. They watched Ash. *Help*, they seemed to say. He continued pacing.

Ethan sighed, a rare break in his cool. "I'll do my best. I mean, we have outages all the time over there. We'll play it as an outage and say the equipment went dead. I'll figure it out when I get the raw cut over here."

"Yeah," Ash told him. "You do that."

"We need more footage, though," he said. "We can't keep ditching whatever your brother and cousins don't like. I'd have an easier time saying no if we had more footage to work with—"

"I understand," Ash said.

"I mean it, Ash. We can't do a show without footage, and we're not getting enough."

"I get it. I'll take care of it." He punched the phone off. Let Ethan stew. He'd deal with the producer later.

Elliot whimpered, and Ash waded through the worried bunch of dogs to his little cousin. "Hey," he said. "I know that was scary. You want to go sit on the patio with Olivia?"

Elliot nodded rather than reply. Ash helped her up, then shepherded her through the sleeping porch and outside. His guardianship, a sidestep from formal parenthood, still terrified him if he looked too close. *You are totally responsible for another human being*, he'd think sometimes, dread clenching his chest. *This is on you now—no one else.* It frightened him more than Cypress Bend ever had.

Thick, jasmine-scented air stuck in Ash's throat, and parrots murmured sleepily in the lemon trees. Beyond them, clutching dark enveloped the garden. Ash tried not to look.

A tumbler in front of her, Olivia sat at the bare table, her hair tangled and her face pale, Henry at her side. Despite the heat, his Gamecock sweatshirt puddled around her.

"Hey, baby." She stood and hugged Elliot, then herded her into a chair. The dogs followed. "I know that was scary," she said. "You want to talk about it?"

Shaking her head, Elliot seemed struck dumb. Ash had seen it before, when nannies shouted her into submission. He and Olivia had broken their lives apart to give her a normal childhood, and thank God it worked. Whenever Ash resented his family, whenever he despaired of their lingering fractures, he remembered Elliot. Alone, he'd wept with relief. They'd saved her.

Wearily, Ash dropped to a chair. The macaws complained a little louder. Already, the farm had sunk back into somnolence. No longer did his spine ice up; no more did he fight an urge to glance up and scan the sky. No enormous creature seemed to hold its breath, waiting. The moon had gone down, and low fog wisped the garden. The hour teetered between too late and too early. Ash would have to make a decision about that soon.

"You can stay with me tonight," Olivia told Elliot. "Henry will sleep in his old room, okay?"

"It's getting worse, isn't it?" Sullivan said as he came through the door. Ash bit back a groan. He thought his brother had gone to sleep, or at least retreated upstairs to lie awake with his baseball bat. A macaw shrieked, cringingly loud in the hushed dark, and leaves rustled as she fluttered from the trees. The parrots had never liked him as much as they liked Sullivan, and it felt like one more indignity, one more loss. "I said it's getting worse, isn't it?" Sullivan repeated, Varina hanging from his arm.

"I don't know. Worse than what, exactly? Do we need to repeat the other night's conversation?" They would tear at him again. Far away, that dim swamp was waiting. If Ash squinted, he could see it, darkness bleeding to darkness. Sometimes he wanted it to swallow him.

"It's even worse than it was when we got here, I mean," Sullivan said. "Those investigations have pissed something off. And maybe having all of us here, maybe that's pissed it off, too." Gently, he swung the macaw back and forth. She seemed to enjoy it.

"Where's Rhys?" Ash asked. "He's missing the action."

The patio's odd shadows furrowed his brother's face into wrinkles Ash had never seen. "Rhys can actually sleep. You were arguing with Ethan right below my bedroom."

"Well, I convinced him not to show it." Ash shoved up from the table. He would try to sleep, fail, and get up again when the sun rose. Sometimes there was nothing else to be done.

"You shouldn't have investigated it in the first place," Sullivan said. A wind kicked up. It carried that sweetish scent of swamp, like flowers gone rotten. The parrots stirred, and the lemon trees ruffled. Everything had happened before. It would happen again. "Whenever you do something, it gets angry."

Of course his brother was mad. So late at night, everything seemed inevitable, fated. Ash waited for Olivia to chime in.

"Let it go," Henry said. "We can't do anything about it now."

No one defended him. No one was supposed to. The familiar rules changed; Ash no longer knew the pieces, or even the board.

"It can stop, right now." Sullivan's voice rose.

"It can't." Henry seemed almost sorrowful. "We agreed to it. There's no way out now. Live with it, Sullivan. You signed a contract."

"I never agreed to—"

"Except you did." Olivia glanced at Henry as if she'd suddenly made up her mind to agree with him. "We all did."

"Do you want this to keep happening?" Sullivan asked. "Do you want it to—"

"It doesn't matter now," Henry told him. "Maybe it never should've started in the first place, but we can't change that. You let go of what you can't change."

Sullivan's anger clouded into something Ash recognized from their father, a predatory instinct intent on ripping at a man's softest parts, and he knew what his brother would say before he said it. "You let go of what you can't change. You know all about that, don't you?"

"I do." Without shame, Henry held his gaze. Maybe he'd made peace with it.

"Don't you dare," Olivia said.

Sullivan still held Varina. Olivia and Henry sat in wicker chairs clawed by parrot feet. A glass sweated on warm metal; jasmine-scent clotted Ash's nose. "Why do you put up with it?" Sullivan asked Olivia. "Maybe you're as bad as he is."

"Maybe I was once, because I condoned it," she replied. "Maybe you were, too."

"Please stop it," Elliot said softly, the first words she'd spoken since she screamed. "Please don't fight. It's bad enough right now."

Sullivan set a squawking Varina on the table and knelt in front of Elliot, the dogs between them. "Hey," he said quietly. "I know that scared you. I saw the men once, a long time ago. They took me away, like they took you, or at least I lost time."

"When?" Red-nosed, tear-streaked, Elliot lifted her face.

"On my twenty-first birthday, the night I left. They're why I left. I couldn't put up with this farm anymore. You're not the only one." Sullivan touched her shoulder, then stood. When Elliot was small, he was easy with her—he was the cousin who toted her on his back and made her squeal. If Ash and Olivia had been her parents, he was the mischievous older brother, one who sneaked her candy, who handed her extravagant Christmas presents, generally unwrapped. Since she'd grown up, he was awkward with her. Ash suspected fifteen-year-old girls were a foreign people to him, as remote as an Amazon tribe. But he was trying, and Ash was grateful. Elliot loved him.

"I'm going to head to bed," Sullivan said, though Ash had expected to say more about the men. "I hope you feel better, Elliot." The door rasped as he slid it open, then shut it behind him.

"Thank you," Ash told Henry. The family always painted Ash as a tyrant, a turncoat. For once, someone understood. "Thank you," he repeated, because he could hand Henry gratitude, and he had nothing else to give.

"Of course," Henry replied. "You don't have to thank me for it."

"No one takes my side." Ash closed his eyes on sudden tears, unmanly. Trenholm men never cried—his father's first commandment. He should never have spoken.

Olivia took some time to speak, as if weighing her words for their heft, gravity. "I'm sorry you feel that way," she said. "I don't want you to. I don't agree with your decision to do this in the first place. But I'm almost grateful we could do something for Elliot and Rhys, you know? He always counted on inheritance, even if he doesn't want to admit it. And he needs it now. He hates needing it, but he does. Thank you for taking care of him."

"Thank you, though," Ash said. "Whatever the reason." And he imagined it, for a brief moment: He'd sit under that twining jasmine until the sun rose gold over the cypresses, and Olivia and Henry would listen as his inner life broke open. He would tell them the loneliest things, and they would nod. They would say, *Me too.* They would say, *I understand.*

I wish you'd talk to me more, he could have said to Henry.

We did a good job with Elliot, he would have told Olivia.

Ash went inside before he said too much, or worse, cried.

CHAPTER 36

SULLIVAN

"I was glad when my aunt told him to shut up," Sullivan told Ethan three days later, trying to ignore the camera at his elbow. It loomed, a hulking stranger he'd never asked for. Ethan had flown in to direct on-the-flies—more sessions in the upstairs living room. The furniture's rearrangement seemed one more violation in weeks that had already brought many.

Sullivan hated on-the-fly sessions. Ethan poked at his ugliest moments, and Sullivan's dislike was settling into hostility. Forced to rehash arguments, he resented them all over again.

"How do you think your relationship with Ash is evolving?" Ethan asked.

"It's not," Sullivan said. He looked at the bookshelves, all those leatherbound volumes stretching back to before the Civil War. The Trenholms never got rid of books. "Ash dislikes me, and I dislike him, and there's not much more to say."

"Do you think his resentment goes back to your childhood?" Ethan held up a hand when Sullivan began to speak. "Answer in full sentences, including the question, so it seems like I'm not here."

Sullivan shifted on the couch's slippery silk. On-the-flies always felt artificial. "Ash and I have never gotten along. He resented that our dad ignored him, and I resented that—hell. I resented that Dad's attention meant getting hit. It's not my fault Dad focused on me. I didn't want it."

"We'll cut that part about abuse," Ethan smiled as if he'd asked about Sullivan's breakfast. "It won't play well with the viewers, and we'd have to slap on a content warning. Why do you think your dad paid more attention to you?"

These sessions were becoming more intrusive, more nakedly dramatic. Ethan wanted to stir up more tension. Wasn't there enough of it? Possibly worse, what was he asking Ash, and what terrible things was Ash saying about him in turn? "My brother had asthma," Sullivan said shortly. "Dad didn't want an oldest son who turned blue."

"What would you tell Ash if you could say anything?"

I'd tell him I miss him. I'd tell him I'm sorry for everything, even if it wasn't my fault. I'd say I loved him, and I wish he didn't dislike me so much. "If I could tell him anything," Sullivan said, with those full sentences Ethan loved, "I'd tell him to lay off. He can hate me as much as he wants, but he doesn't have to show it so often." He paused. "Are we done here?"

"We're done." Ethan's answer came like a verbal head-pat, chirpy and condescending. "I'll see you later."

Sullivan fled.

The next morning's breakfast moved in predictable directions. Silent, a ghost stood vigil over the stove. Sullivan pushed food around his plate while Ash babbled about recent calls on his hotline, all UFO sightings. Someone's pacemaker had malfunctioned near the Meeting Oak, maybe a coincidence, maybe not. Orbs had popped up on surveillance cameras. It was standard fare, boring in its repetition, though Sullivan had seen those events spiral people into existential crises. An endless barrage of the paranormal had reduced them to banality, and only the extraordinary could scare him anymore—shadow-people, the three men, particularly talkative ghosts. When he returned to Savannah, he'd have to discuss it with his therapist.

"—so that's about it," Ash said. "Any thoughts?"

The camera turned from Ash to the rest of the family. "I think it sounds great," Rhys said, clearly checked out while Ash spoke.

"I think you boys need to play outside more." Aunt Alda set down her spoon. "Now I know you're going to tell me about your asthma, Ashby, but that's no excuse. You boys stay inside too much. Go ride those horses your daddy pays for."

Ash nodded as solemnly as the child he'd been. "We will, Aunt Alda."

"I think it's getting worse on this farm," Sullivan said, anger from his on-the-fly spilling over. "I think we need to—"

Footsteps clattered on the stairs, and Boo burst into the kitchen. His red face and ragged breath said he'd been running, and Sullivan braced himself for fresh disaster. "Hey Ash," he said. "I'm real sorry to interrupt your breakfast, but—"

"Just say it." Ash sagged back in his chair. "What happened now?"

"It's the quilt," Boo told him. "It's gone again."

Ash pinched his nose. "Sullivan," he said, before his brother could speak. "I know. Just don't, okay? Just don't." He shoved back from the table. "C'mon," he told Boo. "Let's go look."

CHAPTER 37

ASH

Ash stomped upstairs to check the bedrooms. But the chintz applique quilt, covered in peacocks, hadn't appeared on any beds, and he could find no trace of it. At a loss, he returned downstairs. "Not there!" he called to Boo. "Let's head out and check the cabins." He avoided looking at the silent woman in the corner. Was she Hera? Had she sewn that quilt, or had her daughter, her niece? Ash hated not knowing. *I'm sorry*, he wanted to tell her. *We're doing our best.*

"Coming along right behind you," Boo said as Ash passed him in the mud room.

"I know you don't want me to come, but you don't have to let the door hit me in the face," Sullivan said, and Ash almost fell onto a pile of boots. When he mustered his dignity again, he saw that Olivia, Rhys, and Henry had all left their breakfast and followed his brother out. Elliot and the dogs peered around the corner.

"Is this a family excursion now?" Ash asked.

"I don't know," Sullivan said. "The cameras are coming, so I guess so."

"God knows you can't miss your fifteen minutes, Sullivan," Olivia replied. Ash rolled his eyes, and he caught those crossed sabers over the lintel; even the mudroom hadn't escaped his father's madness. Once he'd staggered into that doorway and begun a drunken lecture about Stonewall Jackson as they laced their riding boots. That monologue would have exploded into bare rage if they'd interrupted, and two hours later, Ash and Sullivan and Rhys were still sprawled on the floor, boots half-tied, listening to an in-depth explanation of the general's Sippy diet. When their father finally stumbled away, Sullivan had walked out the back door and vomited. Ash wondered if his brother remembered, or if the miseries had blurred, too many to count.

They piled into two golf carts; Ash drove one with Elliot next to him, Boo and the camera behind, shepherds chasing them. Sullivan drove the other cart. Ash had noticed that his brother loved them with the purity of a kid at the state fair. It was a small thing, but he hoarded details about Sullivan's brighter reaches: He made men laugh; he ate kids' cereal; he liked to drive the golf carts. Since Ash had last seen him, his clothes had veered from Southern boy button-downs and boat shoes to band tees and funky-colored Doc Martens. He sang in the shower, and he sang loud, unashamed. Sullivan usually wailed through Violent Femmes and Cake and what Ash thought might be The Velvet Underground. He wondered where his brother found that fearlessness, or if he simply assumed no one other than Rhys could hear him.

What do you sing, he sometimes wanted to ask. *Who does that song about Stephanie saying it's cold in Alaska?* But then Sullivan would stop, and it would be another morning moment gone, a moment almost as precious as Elliot sneaking bacon to the dogs.

As they passed in front of the house, Ash noticed a pale man glaring from the upstairs windows—his father, face red with rage. The golf cart veered; Ash struggled to right it as Boo cussed and Elliot grabbed for the strut. When he straightened it out and glanced up again, the ghost had disappeared.

"What was that?" Boo asked.

"Nothing," Ash said quickly—maybe he'd imagined it, a hallucination brought on by trauma. Not his father, not real. Not now. "I thought I saw a squirrel on the road. I guess we'll start at the cabins?"

"Might as well. Lock's not broke. The door was just hanging open. I don't think they touched anything but that quilt," Boo said, gravel grinding beneath the cart's wheels. "But you know better than me what's there, so we can check."

The day's heat had not yet stilled the birds, but neither had the front gates opened. Humming but uncrowded on a summer morning, the farm seemed like the Cypress Bend of Ash's childhood. That feeling dissipated when Sinclair and Lewis met them in the north parking lot, below the cabins. "I don't know what happened," Ash's second-in-command said without preamble. Lewis's black t-shirt, covered in binary code, looked as if he'd slept in it, and he wore sandals instead of his usual Doc Martens. His long toes seemed like creatures evolved to live in caves. "All I can figure is that with all the residual emotional energy around these cabins, it's causing some sort of disturbance."

"What d'you mean you don't know what happened? Something weird happened. Something weird always happens," Sullivan said, hopping from the other golf cart. Henry helped Olivia down. Those two were happy, at least.

They crunched across the road, down the path, and wended past what his father had called the "servants' cemetery." *Just call it the Black graveyard, Dad*, Ash had sometimes wanted to say, and never had. Ash had remodeled the closest cabin into an interpretive center, which included a guide to the known graves and all the information they had about their occupants. Henry had helped with the research, sifting through uncounted stacks of ledgers, family letters, papers, Bibles. Maybe he meant it as a kind of expiation.

They paused at the granite monument Ash had installed. Sullivan lingered, reading the names etched there: every enslaved person they could find named in the family records, even those mentioned only as "Dulcy's son," or "Leticia's two daughters."

"You have Henry and Lewis to thank for this," Ash said. He touched the granite lettering, Century Schoolbook—he and Henry had fretted for days over the font. *Cassie's son, stillborn*, read one inscription.

"I don't think it's Henry's place to speak for the people his relatives enslaved," Sullivan said.

It was foolish to imagine he'd escape it. Ash had hoped for a slivered moment of grace. Maybe Sullivan would say thank you, or at least nod in Henry's direction. But his brother probably wanted to make them both feel worse, and in Ash's case, he'd succeeded.

They walked on, up the pebbled path to the cabins. Grudgingly, his father had restored two and called them "slave cabins." Ash had gutted them, rebuilt the others, and redone them, two about the life of enslaved people on the plantation, the others as exhibits about Black history in South Carolina. He'd researched and chosen his subjects carefully: the Stono Rebellion, the Vesey Rebellion, the pottery of David Drake, the life of Robert Smalls, and the achievements of South Carolina's Reconstruction-era Black government. "We were supposed to open the last cabins in a few weeks," Ash told his entourage, hoping they might be listening. "It took a while to find craftsmen who could still build legitimate log cabins and get the right permits from the state."

"So what's in them?" Rhys asked. God bless Rhys. He held them all together.

"One's an exhibit on the Orangeburg Massacre." Ash kept his eyes forward. If he thought too hard about the National Guard opening fire on Black college students, he'd want to punch those brick walls. "The other is half about recent events, I guess you could say, and half about the quilt. We structured a whole exhibit around it."

"A survivor of the Orangeburg Massacre spoke to one of our honors college classes," Sullivan said. Like Ash, he looked neither left nor right, as if the horizon lent him strength. "The whole time he talked I kept thinking, 'You were a young Black kid, and you tried to desegregate a bowling alley. They called out the National Guard and shot you and your friends for it. They fucking *shot you*.'"

There was no way to answer that, and no one tried.

They walked to the last cabin. Beyond it loomed the Meeting Oak, an ancient tree with branches broad as park benches. Spread wide, those branches curled down, then up again, like nothing so much as an enormous spider. Unlike most trees, it never seemed friendly. Ash looked away.

"This was locked last night," Boo said, pointing at the cabin. "I showed up this morning, it was unlocked, and the quilt was gone." He stuck his head inside the building. "Still gone. Y'know, I was hoping. . ."

"Are there any signs of forced entry?" Rhys asked, as if they had stepped into a police procedural.

"You know there aren't," Sullivan said.

Rhys peered at the door frame. He and Sullivan had watched a lot of reruns of *The X-Files* as kids, probably too much *CSI*. Maybe he'd been waiting for that perfect moment to become a detective.

Sullivan shoved the door open. It banged impotently against the wooden wall, and its tin sign rattled: *Material inside may disturb some viewers. The depiction of recent events may not be suitable for children under the age of fourteen.* "C'mon, Rhys. You know this is ridiculous," he said, and ducked inside. The camera followed.

The velvet ropes that had once surrounded the quilt had been carefully replaced. Maybe they'd never moved in the first place, Ash thought, then tried to forget it. On its left, his grandmother Lucy's diary lay open to the correct page; they'd blown up facsimiles of the pages and hung them on the wall. *What Was Life Like For Hera?* another sign asked. Below it was a reconstruction of the maids' blue-dressed uniform; next to it, a collection of objects found during the cabin reconstruction: several dominos;

reconstructed pieces of coarse, unfired earthenware bowls; bone sewing implements, including a bobbin, a needle case, and a crochet hook. Old bottles of Dr. McLane's American Worm Specific anchored a display about illness, and a case of copper badges explained the plantation system of hiring out enslaved people. Ash was proud of what they'd managed to construct.

"That's quite a display you have there," Rhys said. "Looks like—"

"Jesus Christ, Ash," Sullivan said from across the room. "You—" He stopped abruptly, his words swallowed. His brother stood in front of a row of photographs. Six Black women and three Black men beamed radiant smiles above their names and a few sentences—they should be remembered, Ash hoped, as something more than victims. Next to them hung a photograph of a tonsure-headed white teenager posed with a Confederate flag. Photos of Midlands locales spiderwebbed outward: places the teenager had lived, high schools he'd attended, the gun store that sold him a Glock .45 caliber pistol. Ash wanted to tell visitors: *Look how close he was. He could have come to a church around here. He lived among you, and this hate brooded in your own backyard.*

On June 17, 2015, the display said, *Dylann Roof opened fire on a prayer meeting at Emanuel African Methodist Baptist Church in Charleston, South Carolina, killing nine Black parishioners. Roof was the first person sentenced to death on federal hate crimes charges.*

"That shooting was in Charleston," Olivia said. "I didn't know he was this local. I mean I sort of knew he was around, but I didn't know he lived here. God, he would've like, eaten at Lizard's Thicket and Rush's—"

"I don't—" Sullivan started, and stopped again. Rhys had a hand on his shoulder, whispering. Sullivan pushed him off. "You know, Dad bears some responsibility for this. It's messed up, but the way he thought of that flag, this farm, all of it—"

"I know," Ash said.

"Right there, with that flag?" Sullivan pointed at Dylann Roof. "How many pictures did Dad have with me standing under it? How many? He'd have thought that kid was a good influence on us. He's the same age as Olivia."

Ash offered no answer.

"I hate that kid. He goddamn deserves death row." Sullivan's fists clenched, and the cords on his neck raised into ropes. "Dad would've said well, it's terrible they were innocent people. You shouldn't hurt innocent people. Everything else, he would've brushed it aside. He'd've said it wasn't *his* fault, and had nothing to do with him, or us, and—"

"Sullivan." Rhys grabbed his arm and dragged. "Leave it go. No one's blaming you."

Sullivan brushed their cousin aside. Ash flinched back from his brother's dark eyes, which seemed to know too much. "We bear some responsibility," Sullivan said. "This display doesn't absolve you from it, Ash. Do you think you should be displaying this stuff here, on a fucking plantation? Do you think you have the right? These artifacts belong to the Black community, not your self-righteous history lesson."

"Better that they're displayed here than not displayed at all," Henry said.

Sullivan whirled on him, eyes narrowed, their father's rage simmering in his voice. "Don't think this makes everything okay for you, either. You're the last person who should be deciding who has the right to display this stuff. We're *still* making money off the suffering of enslaved people, you know that, right? Maybe their descendants deserve it more than we do."

Shock descended, a jagged silence. If those silent ghosts were unmentionable in Cypress Bend, the subject of reparations was even more taboo. No one ever acknowledged it: Their distant Black cousins deserved the money they spent every day. Ash couldn't look at Lewis.

"Y'all have your white apology party without me," Sullivan finally said. "Lewis, how do you stand it?"

Ash opened his mouth to speak, but his brother was already passing through the open door and into the morning. One more dramatic exit—his brother was fond of them. As usual, Rhys followed.

I don't think it absolves me, Ash wanted to say. But that display was an offering, however small, and he thought it might grant him a few drops of forgiveness. He hated himself for that. The offering meant something, but there was no redemption in it. "I'm sorry," Ash said to his Black cousin. "You didn't deserve that."

"He has a point, as stupid as he is at making it," Lewis told him, and Ash shut up again, misery settling like nausea in his belly. He was trying. Couldn't they see that he was trying?

When Ash thought he might suffocate with the sheer weight of silence, Olivia spoke up. "So what now?"

"I guess we're done here," Ash said. Suddenly, he hated looking at those displays. Sullivan was right: they were one more clumsy attempt at expiation, falling short. Whatever reconciliation meant, whatever it entailed, he'd never manage it. *I'm sorry*, he wanted to shout—to Lewis, to his family, to those unquiet ghosts. *Don't you understand that I'm sorry?*

They piled back into the golf carts, and dust puffed behind them as they crunched down the road. Thick, unbreathable, it hung in the air and made him cough. Ash half-hoped Elliot might say something, but it was unfair to ask that of a fifteen-year-old. More than that, he wished he had someone to talk to: Olivia, Henry, Lewis, a real friend. *I hate that I keep this place, but I have to*, he wanted to tell them. *It's a moral misery, and I do it so no one else has to. They can blame me, and maybe that's what I am more than anything else: someone to blame.*

Back at the house, Ash plodded up to the patio, an old man suddenly. Why had he been chosen to bear the weight of this history?

"I'll go check the rooms one more time," Henry told them. "Just in case."

Ash waved him on. Let him check. They'd find the quilt or they wouldn't. It would be a crushing loss, but the morning had sapped him empty. He was slumped at the table when Henry walked through the door with the bright, intricate quilt in his arms. "It was on my bed," he told them.

"Go*dammit!*" Boo swore, and the parrots rose into squawking. "It wasn't there. I swear it wasn't."

Ash asked Amelia, McKayla, Madison. No one had been upstairs. No one had seen who moved the quilt. "So how did it get there?" Boo asked.

No one answered. Ash didn't want to examine it too closely.

CHAPTER 38

SULLIVAN

"**R**emember Talitha's coming today," Sullivan announced at breakfast on Wednesday, the usual mishmash of hashbrowns, cereal, and coffee, Elliot slipping bacon under the table while Henry and Olivia yawned, the silent ghost standing at the stove—his back ached already. All around them, the farm seemed to stretch awake. It was a morning you could believe in, if you were a person who believed in mornings. Sullivan had long lost his faith.

"Where are we meeting her?" Ash said. Sullivan and his brother had spoken little since the quilt disappeared again. There was nothing to say; no one could deny that since Ash's so-called investigations began, the farm had spun out of control. Their days ground into more of the same. They toured the farm; they took turns manning the cameras in HQ. Cameras rolled. They snarked at one another, and nothing much happened. It had become a kind of routine, broken only by the quality of insults.

"Talitha's coming up to the house," Sullivan told Ash, because he had to answer.

"We're going to have to decide on another name for her," Ash said. "Since she won't go on camera, we'll have to shoot a reenactment."

Olivia's fork clinked into an awkward silence. "No, we won't," she said before Sullivan could answer. "We don't do that. Whitney can interview about it. We don't reshoot or I bail. I don't care what I signed. And if I can't get out of the contract, I'll talk to a tabloid."

"You signed an NDA," Ash reminded her. "They'll sue you into the ground."

"I'm sorry," Olivia said coolly, a Charleston girl to her fingertips. "You've mistaken me for someone who cares."

Coffee half-raised, Ash looked ready to choke into that settling silence. Even Elliot, a piece of bacon in her hand, went stiff and still. "Well, I guess that's settled," Rhys finally said.

"Thank you, Olivia," Sullivan told her. "Only you could manage to use tabloids as a threat and get away with it."

"I'm clever like that," she replied. Henry half-smiled and shook his head. He loved her, and Sullivan wished someone would smile like that for him. Maybe one day, when he herded his life into some kind of order, when he stopped drinking, when he shed that farm and left his demons far behind him. When he started making art again instead of simply keeping art books in his room, where they accused him from his bedside table. He'd already lived through the worst thing. Nothing could be as bad as childhood, and even if hope seemed thin, unbreathable, he could slog through the darkness.

"Talitha might not even want us to mention it on the show," Sullivan said. "I don't think she does. We need to respect that."

"But—" Ash began.

"We were stupid enough to sign our lives away," he replied. "She didn't."

"Ethan wasn't happy about the investigation the other night." Ash plowed on, as if determined to win, or at least have the last word. "He was able to splice some of the footage, but in general, he hasn't been able to grab as much quality footage as he thought he would. It's not looking good, y'all."

Sullivan wondered if they'd get paid anyway. It was probably covered in his contract's legal rambling.

"Just—we need to get some footage, okay?" Ash told them.

"We get it," Olivia told him.

Ash shot her a look, as if she'd betrayed him one more time. She ignored him, and the subject dropped.

At eleven o'clock, Talitha called. "Don't tell me I have to pay to get in," she said. "I'm waiting in line. I knew y'all were popular, but I didn't realize you were this cool."

"There's a pull-off right there before the gate," Sullivan told her. "I can come get you with the golf cart, or you can wait in line and tell them you're with us. Your call."

"Come get me," she said. "I don't wanna wrangle parking if I don't need to."

"Give me about fifteen," he replied.

Tourists eyed Sullivan suspiciously when he stopped the golf cart. "I'm picking up Talitha Merle," he told Houston. "We'll be coming back in the wrong way in a sec."

"I was wondering what she's doing here," Houston said. "She doesn't like us Trenholms much, and she's just standing there watching the cars like she wants to curse 'em."

"Jesus, Houston. She doesn't do that." Sullivan hoped she didn't, at least. Talitha collected rumors like a dowager collected furs.

"Uh-huh." He waved Sullivan through.

Talitha stood by the same orange Mazda LXI Sullivan remembered from the Roadhouse all those years ago. She was tall for a woman in Lower Congaree, maybe about five-eight, and as beautiful as Sullivan remembered, pale-skinned, long-legged, with a narrow waist that flared to real hips. At forty-something, a few strands of gray threaded her dark hair, but no real lines creased her face. Sullivan wished one more time that she hadn't married.

"Hey, Talitha," he called, grateful for every extra moment he'd spent on his hair.

"Sullivan Trenholm." Talitha strode to the cart with that unselfconscious, hip-swaying walk he loved. He'd have committed war crimes for her chocolate-chip pancakes then. "You grew up."

She'd always taken a vicious glee in pointing out Sullivan's age. It reminded him that he'd crushed on her since he was fourteen; he loved and hated it in equal turns. "It's good to see you."

"Shove your eyes back in our head. I'm here on business, and I'm married." But she smiled when she spoke. "What've you been up to?"

"Not much." He started the cart again. "Making art. Drinking too much. Cussing my brother for bringing in reality TV. It wasn't my idea. Before you ask, I only agreed to this bullshit because—"

Talitha held up a hand, and Sullivan shut up. "I don't need to hear it. People do things for all sorts of reasons, and I may not agree with them, but I'm not here to pass judgment."

"Thank you," Sullivan said, relieved, as he drove the wrong way through the gate. He wouldn't scramble with explanations, gauge her trust, and find himself wanting. One more time, Sullivan was grateful for her company, and one more time, he remembered the real reason he liked her so much: Talitha Merle never found him disappointing.

"That doesn't mean I'll be on your damn show, though," she continued. "I see cameras, I walk. I said that and I meant it."

"I know." Sullivan hit the gas, and she rewarded him with another smile. "I told Ash that. He wasn't happy."

Talitha seemed to watch the trees pass, all those live oaks lined in orderly rows, the tobacco fields stretched beyond. Tan pebbles crunched under the golf cart wheels. Ash must have had that drive serviced every two weeks, and the expenditure stunned Sullivan. "Your brother can't manage to say three straight words to me," she said.

"That's because he has a thing for you."

"Just because you have a thing for me doesn't mean the whole world does."

"I'm not allowed to have a thing for you anymore. You're married. And Ash does too have a thing for you. He was like, 'Why d'you have Talitha's number?' And then he figured out I slept with you. . ." Sullivan trailed off, glancing to gauge her reaction. Talitha kept watching those trees as if he'd spoken about the weather.

"What'd he do?" she asked.

"Got kinda pissed." Sullivan shot her that lopsided grin women generally loved.

"Poor Ash," Talitha said, and something in his midsection jerked. "He doesn't really have anyone, does he?"

The fun drained from it. "That's not true. Ash has. . ." He struggled and came up with no one; what seemed humorous before plummeted to sadness. Ash wished for what he had, Sullivan realized—something more than sleeping with Talitha. His brother drifted unmoored, the family savior but all the lonelier for it. "Ash's always been sort of—I don't know," he said. "He goes off on his own."

"Is it choice or necessity?" Talitha asked, and Sullivan remembered the other reason he liked her. They could drop into something real, and it never embarrassed him.

"I don't know," he replied honestly.

"Whenever I see him in town, he always seems like he wants to talk, but he can't figure out what words to use," she said. "I nod at him because I worry that if I do more, the poor man will run. Is he gonna be around today?"

Sullivan nodded, but said no more. Above the drive, the trees strained toward one another, battling for the sun, an unseen war. What looked like twining together was a fight for survival. Enough time passes, and those battles become the everyday, he decided. You live in this stifling heat and humidity long enough, you forget what it is. A few years before, he'd flown up North for a conference. It was January. His skin had cracked and dried; bundled into misery, he'd shivered through forty-degree weather in a coat and hat, boots and gloves. His colleagues had laughed. *I'm not made for these latitudes*, Sullivan had told them. He could only find comfort in that subtropical heat-sink, where his shirt stuck to his back and sweet tea drew life into bearable realms.

"So tell me about these people I'm talking to," Talitha said eventually.

"Whitney's high school was probably founded so little white boys and girls weren't subject to the indignities of public school desegregation," Sullivan replied, "and even though she's getting married, her daddy still buys her Lilly Pulitzer. Garnet and black dresses on gameday and matching high heels. Probably a Tri-Delt. You know what they say."

"What's that?" Talitha asked.

"Try Delt," he replied, a grin breaking through. "Everyone else has."

"Sullivan Trenholm!" She smacked at him, and it was good, a woman laughing while he ducked, her head shake half-annoyance, half-humor. He could have held that moment in his hands, snatched it and kept it. No one treated him like that anymore. He drank; he smoked weed; when he slept around, he kept it short. Sullivan would have liked someone to laugh with.

"Seriously, though," he said. "I told you the important part on the phone. She's my cousin Judah's fiancée, and something followed him home from the farm. We're hoping you can help, uh, detach it. It's those men, like I saw the night I left. You remember."

He said no more. Talitha would remember.

They neared a stopped car. A man and woman had spilled out to snap pictures of the long avenue. Talitha seemed to take them in as they passed—the man's Red Sox hat and sleeveless shirt, the woman's I Heart NY tee and flip-flops. They were stereotypical tourists of the worst kind, gauchely American. Sullivan caught the Trump 2024 bumper sticker as they passed. Ash had opened Cypress Bend to them.

"There's something wrong here," Talitha said. "Can't you feel it? That swamp's bad but at least I understand it. This is different."

"How d'you mean?" he asked. Sullivan wasn't sure if he wanted her to answer.

"I don't know," she said. "I hear some fucked-up stuff happens on your brother's show, and I've heard worse rumors. I know y'all get way too many lightning strikes around here—everyone does. But I also heard you had a dozen people with pacemakers malfunction last year, all in the same place around that big gnarled tree near your so-called slave cabins. Heard you had two develop some real weird cases of burns right there, too. Doctors couldn't figure out what the hell they were."

"Where'd you hear that?" Sullivan asked as he pulled around the house.

"Cash Briggs is the sheriff now," she said. "He stops by about once a week to drink beer on my porch."

"You drink that much with two kids?" he teased as he turned off the golf cart.

"Not much," Talitha said. "I mostly watch my oldest chase the toddler around the yard. My husband has about three beers with Cash, if he's not working."

Sullivan wished she hadn't mentioned her husband. "Don't know if Whitney's here yet," he told her. "C'mon around back and McKayla will grab you some sweet tea. We can sit on the patio, or if you'd rather air conditioning—"

"It's good to see you, Sullivan." Talitha said as they climbed out. Sullivan glanced at the sky. He saw nothing, but that meant nothing. Strangeness happened without anyone to see it. "I'm sorry you're lonely. I guess not much has changed for you, and I'm sorry for that, too."

"Thank you," he replied quickly, before it hurt too much, and led her toward his dead uncle's beloved parrots.

CHAPTER 39

RHYS

On the patio, cicadas droned endlessly, tunelessly; Rhys wondered if the ceaseless insect-buzz maddened outsiders. He'd grown up in it, and those cicadas could sing him to sleep. Mosquito bites barely bumped his skin, and they disappeared fast. Yankees swelled up like kitchen sponges. Bitten enough times, they'd land in bed, itchy and fevered. The body learned, Rhys decided, like he'd learned to deal with the farm's insanity. It had become part of the scenery. He'd thought, for that brief moment, that it could no longer hurt them. He'd been wrong—it could, but not like he'd imagined. When Rhys felt around his ragged edges, childhood's visceral terror had vanished; no longer did he dread something beyond comprehension. Naked shock supplanted panic. As a child, he'd accepted the farm's phenomenological violations. But the three men had shaken him, and deeply; he'd realized Ash's toys couldn't save them. Whatever lurked in that land would tear at them as surely as they tore at one another. *When three men come walking again, when the family walks with them, it's time, if you want to stop it*, the ghost had said. Rhys had no idea what she meant, but the men had certainly appeared more than once—and they'd appeared to Sullivan before. It likely terrified his cousin, who'd rather chew glass than mention it.

Perhaps it should have terrified him too, but Rhys could summon little energy for it. At least he wasn't in Richmond. At least he had his cousins. A transplant might loom; exhaustion might wear on him, but better to concentrate on the everyday than the cosmic.

Talitha and Sullivan chatted about people in Lower Congaree—who'd been married, divorced, jailed. It was small-town gossip, rich in drama but unimportant in its details. Sullivan seemed to enjoy it, probably because Talitha was the one talking. She'd always set Rhys on edge, like a lion pacing behind a gate. Talitha posed no immediate threat, but what-ifs spun around her. Lower Congaree said she healed people, or cursed them, or brought them back to life, or killed them. He'd heard that she could talk to crows and summon snakes. Rhys never knew whether to believe none of it or all of it. He'd seen his uncle shoot at wolves the size of ponies, and horses bloodlessly, cleanly eviscerated. A ghost had spoken his name. All those rumors could be true.

They drank sweet tea and sweated. Ash passed in and out, always saying a nervous hello, then disappearing again. Elliot played fetch with the shepherds. Eventually, Ash brought out Whitney and Judah. Their cousin was the good ol' boy Rhys remembered, with the ruddy good looks and rolled-sleeve button-down of a certain class of Southern man, one who spent summers drunk-driving a golf cart on Folly, possibly Edisto. He looked, however, nothing like a man on the edge of his wedding day. His dark-circled eyes seemed bruised, and his red face too pale; his clothes hung loosely, as if he'd lost too much weight too quickly. An odd scent of silted dirt clung to him. Rhys backed off their hug as quickly as possible.

Ash introduced Whitney and Judah to Talitha, then pulled up another table. It took some time to settle them—Whitney wanted tea, which Judah declined. The dogs clustered close to Elliot. When Judah leaned too close, Zelda growled, a low throat-sound that raised the hairs on Rhys's neck. Ganon whimpered.

"Can you tell me what happened?" Talitha asked, and Whitney opened her mouth. Talitha pointed to Judah. "No," she said. "If it's bothering him, he's the one who needs to tell me, please."

Judah drew the long, shuddering breath of a tired man. "When I try, it doesn't work."

"Maybe not," Talitha said, "but I need to see you do it anyway."

He shared a pointed glance with Whitney, a look Rhys recognized easily; they were sleeping together, and they had secrets. "I'll try, but please don't repeat anything I say," he said. "When I was six years old, my mother smacked me across the face for—" Wearily, he closed his eyes, shaking his head. "I mean, my father's a jackass. No! That's not it either. I hate my fraternity. I never wanted to pledge. I—this isn't—I mean, I'm trying to talk about—When Josh found those pics on my computer, he—" Judah finally stopped. "Please don't make me keep going."

Somewhere, tourists laughed. Rhys wondered one more time what madness drew them to Cypress Bend. Maybe, like Sullivan always said, they wanted to believe in something, or maybe they hoped to ride Ash's coattails into TV infamy. "So every time you try to talk about this, you find yourself babbling about something else?" Talitha asked.

"Something I don't want to tell people, yes," Judah replied. The parrots had fallen silent. They clustered in the lemon trees, still and quiet, as if sleeping. Uncle Wade's squawking horde never retreated during the day. That strange dirt-smell had become subtly stronger. It wasn't a good smell, but stunk like something once buried too long and burning in the sun.

"You've definitely got something attached to you." Talitha stood and began pacing, almost as if she wanted to put distance between herself and Judah. "I felt it as soon as you walked in, and it's getting worse the longer I talk to you."

"This morning was awful," Whitney said to Ash. "The shower wouldn't turn on. When it did, Judah says something made him slip and hit his head on the tub. His electric razor even cut him. They aren't supposed to be able to cut people. He kept pulling shirts out of his drawer, and every one was stained. I had to hand-wash one with Shout! so we could come. You don't want to know how many accidents we almost got in, just on the way from Columbia." Her hand passed over her eyes. They were spent; she was paler than Rhys had last seen her, her hair drier and her clothes slightly wrinkled. "I really hope you all can help us."

"Since Judah can't tell me what's happening, you do it," Talitha said. "Start from the beginning."

"I'm really sorry." Finally focused on Talitha, Whitney drew herself into debutante poise. Rhys realized that artificiality had been missing before. "Ash told us your name, but he didn't tell us why you could help us. We're not here to be gawked at, and before we keep going, I need to know why you think you can do something."

He hadn't noticed before, but he saw it then. Whitney wore a simple dress from one of those athleisure wear designers. Expensive sunglasses pinned back her highlighted hair; a gold pendant dangled at her throat. It was certainly real. Almost gaudily large, her engagement ring caught the sun when she tipped her hand. She could have been Olivia's sorority sister. Talitha wore jeans and a black tank top. Far smaller, her ring was set with black stone rather than diamond, and each wrist flashed tattoos when she gestured. She was Sullivan's type, gothier, interesting, with the look of a woman who'd learned independence from necessity, and too soon. At best, Whitney would regard her as beneath notice. The world poised them as natural enemies, Whitney a spoiled rich girl, Talitha a low-class whore—Rhys knew economics and dark hair would conspire into slut-shaming. He hated it, and he hated himself. To consider sleeping with a woman like Whitney, Sullivan would have to get blind-drunk. Sleeping with Talitha would never have occurred to Rhys.

"You wanna know how I can help you before you explain everything?" Rather than take offense, Talitha's mouth twisted into amusement, as if Whitney had offered a weak joke.

"Yes," Whitney replied.

Still as winter, Sullivan's fury seemed poised to spiral the situation to disaster. "Let her handle it," Rhys said quietly.

"What, you want credentials?" Talitha seemed close to laughter.

"If you want to put it that way," Whitney said, back almost painfully straight. Judah laid a hand on her shoulder, a small indignity she twitched off.

"Here's a credential," Talitha told her. "You don't have anyone else. I'm here as a favor to Sullivan. So start talking, 'cause I've got plenty of people who need help today." She took a chair on Sullivan's far side; only Whitney was left sitting near Judah.

For a drawn, tense moment, Rhys thought Whitney might object. She straightened her dress and tucked her hair behind her ears, as if stalling; just as Rhys was sure she'd walk out, she began speaking. Whitney told the same story they'd heard before. She and Judah loved Cypress Bend, something beyond Rhys's understanding; either they were snatching at notoriety or ignored its history for the pretty veneer. He suspected the latter. Something had followed them home, and that something began harassing Judah in increasingly distressing, dangerous ways. The three men kept appearing; Judah and Whitney were experiencing missing time. Judah was sleeping at odd times; watches, phones, and clocks malfunctioned around him—all electronics, in fact. Their electricity blipped out at odd intervals. Doctors could find nothing wrong with him.

"We think it might be demonic," Whitney said. "We're hoping someone can—I don't know. Make it go away. That's the only reason Judah agreed to come back here. It's making him sick. You see how pale he is. He can hardly eat. He throws up everything."

Talitha seemed to regard him more carefully. "What have the doctors done for him?"

"They can't do much of anything," Whitney said. "No digital thermometer would read his temperature, and when they bring out an analogue one, it bursts. Glass and mercury go everywhere. They try to x-ray him, it comes out blank. All their equipment fails, basically."

"That happens here," Ash said. "We have a lot of equipment failures at Cypress Bend."

Talitha hardly spared him a glance. "I know. I watched a few episodes before I came over here."

Rhys realized that the cicadas had stopped. Reflexively, he glanced up. Maybe a dot flitted against the blue sky, gone almost before he registered it. When he blinked, he saw nothing. The air hung limp, dull. He swiped at his forehead.

Talitha stood again. Crossing the short distance between the tables, she touched Judah's shoulder, then winced, but didn't cringe back. "I need you to relax as much as you can," she told him. "Think about sleeping—what it feels like to fall asleep. Can you do that?"

Judah wore the doubtful look of a man who'd lost hope. "I can try," he said, and closed his eyes.

Talitha gave him a few moments, and once he drew a long, deep breath, shifted her hand to his forehead. "Whatever's in Judah," she ordered, voice strong and sure, "speak to me. Who are you?"

Rhys genuinely didn't think it would work. He expected silence, stillness, but Judah's face twisted into the unearthly. His eyes opened, too dark, as if the irises bled into the pupils; his mouth gaped into something like a grin. It stretched too wide, and Judah suddenly seemed to have too many teeth. A low growl rose from all four dogs.

Talitha stepped back. "Who are you?" she demanded.

Sharded, brittle laughter cut the afternoon's silence. It rang with insanity; Rhys almost clapped his hands over his ears. If he listened to it long enough, if he heeded it, that shrapnelled sound would drag him down to madness. Too long, too shrill, it drew on and on—

"Speak!" Talitha snapped.

"Time is a mad ouroboros," Judah graveled, but it wasn't Judah speaking, not at all. "It curves back, endless and complete in itself. You cannot escape its shining clutch—"

Talitha slapped him across the face, a sharp, cracking sound. Hardly had her hand made contact when she leapt back. The lemon trees jumped as she crashed into them, and parrots screamed. Ash and Sullivan flew to their feet.

"What?" Judah blinked, confused. "I thought about sleeping. Did it work?"

"Uh-huh." Talitha raised her hands like a victim in an old Western. "We're done here."

"Look away!" a green macaw shrieked. Beating its wings, it flew from the trees and landed on Elliot. "Look away! Look away! Dixie Land!"

"What the *hell*?" Whitney clutched Judah's hand.

"Away away, away down south in Dixie! Away, away, away down south in Dixie!" shouted more parrots. They yowled and flapped, bursting from the greenery to alight on tables and chair-backs. Varina nearly slammed into Sullivan's arms. "Away! Away!" they called. "Dixie! Dixie Land!"

"Look, whatever's attached to you? It's nothing I've ever seen." Talitha pointed at Judah, and when her finger shook, a thick draught of that childhood fear choked at Rhys. Talitha wasn't supposed to be frightened. "Whatever that is? It isn't dead. It's not a spirit, and it's not earthbound. I don't know what the hell it is, but it's something. Call a Catholic priest." She snatched up her purse. "I'm done."

The parrots squawked snatches of "Dixie." Ash reached for Talitha, then drew back, as if he'd thought about grabbing her arm, but decided against it. "What? We were hoping—"

"Yeah, you were wrong. I'm done here. Sullivan, if you could drive me back to my car, I'd be real grateful." Talitha strode down the stairs. Sullivan mouthed something at Ash, maybe an apology, handed Varina to Elliot, then scurried after her. The cicadas tuned up again.

"What the hell was that?" Whitney asked.

"I don't know," Ash said. "I'm very sorry. We'll try to find someone else to help. I'll contact the other producer. We should be able to find someone for you—we'll start today. I can't express to you—"

"Then don't." Whitney hauled Judah to his feet. "Call us if you find someone." She dragged him out, Ash on her heels, murmuring apologies. He probably worried that she would contact the press, and Rhys loathed that oiliness, which Ash would excuse by saying that he worried about the family's reputation. *Just admit it,* Rhys wanted to say. *You're not worried about us. You're worried about yourself, and it shows.*

CHAPTER 40

SULLIVAN

Talitha climbed in the golf cart before Sullivan scrabbled the keys from his pocket. "Are you okay?" he asked. That felt like the first, most important thing. Whitney had tried to pull rank, class or otherwise, and he'd always hated that particular strain of cattiness. It was one more benefit of being a Trenholm—money and blood made those struggles irrelevant. Enforced by overarching tradition and incidental circumstance alike, Sullivan had never questioned it.

They pulled out of the carport and passed under a stand of live oaks. Birds chattered above. Idly, Sullivan wondered if they all belonged, or if some, like Henry's ivory-bill, had flown from another time entirely.

"I'll be okay once I get the hell out of here," Talitha finally replied. "You need to get out too, but you're too damn stubborn to do it. You all are."

"What d'you mean, I should get out?" Pea gravel crunched under them. Tourists stood back and photographed the house's front gardens, water-fat from Ash's irrigation system. The golf cart's small fan only worried the hot air.

"Your cousin's creepy ranting aside, I saw something when I slapped him," Talitha said. She looked neither left nor right, as if she wanted to ignore Cypress Bend and all its trappings.

Sullivan believed her without question. She'd believed him on the night of his birthday, when he'd needed her, and he was no stranger to sudden visions. "What'd you see?" he asked.

"Time," she replied.

He watched her, but sideways, still attentive to the driveway. The tourists moved like recalcitrant sheep. "What d'you mean, time?"

"I mean I saw time. I don't know how else to say it. You need to get out, Sullivan. You all need to get out, and you need to get all these people out, too." Talitha spoke as if dazed, as if she'd hit her head on those lemon trees. Sullivan knew she hadn't, and even if she had, she'd still tell the truth. "You won't leave. I know you won't. But you should."

"You saw time? How can you see time?" The flag hung like old laundry. People licked ice cream cones, and Marcus's little sister waved as he passed. Sullivan tipped his hand up.

"I saw—look, time repeats itself here, over and over. It's always the same, and it always will be unless someone does something about it. At least get these people out if y'all won't go. I mean it."

Ash would never listen. He'd gin up absurd excuses about blood and family; he'd brandish contracts. He'd spout ugly mouthings about Talitha, and Sullivan would have to hit him. Other than Rhys, Talitha was one of the few who'd ever listened to him—maybe the only one. He could rely on her more than his brother. The knowledge ached, an old wound. "You know my brother won't leave."

"And I know you wouldn't leave without him, no matter what you say. It's an admirable thing. It means you love him, you know that, right?" she said. Under the birdsong and the tourists and the gravel, silence brooded, the cold of a snowless winter. When Sullivan caught it, that nothing dissolved to chest-emptiness; his heart beat in a hollow of blood and bone.

"I don't understand," he said eventually. Live oaks arched above them into sunshine. A person could believe in their beauty. Plenty did. They brushed aside sin and death to hold that loveliness.

"You don't have to understand," Talitha told him. "You need to get the fuck out."

"I would leave." High and thin, Sullivan's voice betrayed him. It was a child's protest.

"You say you would, but you won't," she replied. "I don't think you'd do it again. I don't know why, but you wouldn't. Your father's dead, Sullivan. It's not a terrible thing to show loyalty to people who really love you. I understand."

"Ash and I, we're not—we're not close," he said stiffly. It was hard to admit even that much. He wondered how much she understood about his childhood. He'd never explained, but Lower Congaree talked, and Talitha read people like a meteorologist decoding clouds. She knew.

"You want to be close, though," she told him. "And your brother wants it, too. He's so lonely, Sullivan. You can do something about that."

Maybe Talitha was right. Sullivan wanted to believe her. Maybe that was faith—without a leap into the unknown, it meant nothing. Maybe he could try. Maybe he would fail, but he'd live with the knowledge of his trying. He could hold courageous heartbreak.

They didn't speak again until he'd passed through the gates and stopped next to Talitha's car. She seemed to gaze over those old, bent-limbs branches. The moment hung, still as the afternoon.

"My door's always open," she said. "You can sleep on my couch. There's always somewhere to go, Sullivan."

"Thank you." He wanted to hug her, but a misunderstanding might wreck them. "I'm grateful that you came, and I'm sorry Whitney was a bitch. You didn't deserve it."

That eye-rolling annoyance returned, her are-you-kidding-me face, and Sullivan might have laughed in another time and place. He wished, one more time, for her naked acceptance. "I'm used to it, trust me," Talitha said.

"See ya," Sullivan told her as she climbed into her orange Mazda.

"Hope I see you soon," Talitha said.

Sullivan watched until her car disappeared down the drive, and he was alone again.

Driving back to the house, he tried to take small pleasures as they came: the golf cart, the shady oaks, the cousins waving as he passed. He'd fight with Ash. He'd reach the end of patience or pain, then stomp out like a petulant child. In the morning, he'd smile for the cameras. Or maybe he would leave. He imagined his Tesla door slamming in the still, drooped heat; his suitcase handle slicked with palm-sweat; his cousins lining the porch. No— if he left, they'd hate him too much to say goodbye.

I thought he was different, Rhys might offer, but his shoulders would slump.

What can you expect? Ash would say. *You know how Sullivan is.*

His father had said Sullivan would be a great historian. He'd said, *It's time to stop fucking around, son. You're twenty-one. You're a Trenholm, and this will all be yours. Ash's weak. I see it. Stop this faggot art shit and come home. I'm not getting any younger, and I need you to help me.*

Sullivan had nodded once, as if he agreed. His father had clapped his shoulder and he hated himself still for loving that shine of parental approval. *You're a good boy*, he'd said. Sullivan hated himself for loving those words, too. Despite what he'd seen the night before, he'd wanted to stay for them.

This is time, the three men had told him. Skipping together in the hot-breathed night, they wore tattered clothes, the shade of sepia photograph, though Sullivan couldn't pinpoint them to a particular time. *Old*, he'd said to Talitha the next night. *They looked hazily old.*

We are what was, is, and will be, the men had said. Their voices were lilted, too high. *When you see us you see yourself. We are yours and you are ours.*

Rooted, mute, he'd stood on the patio as they jigged below him. Their smiles stretched too wide, with too many teeth, and their pupils bloomed too large under those brimmed hats. Nothing else moved. The cicada-song had disappeared. Sullivan no longer felt the heat, the bricks below him, the chair back smooth under his hand. He was gone, or had never existed.

You're a Trenholm, they'd said. *You belong to us, and we are always the same.*

Night had snapped to sudden dawn. The men were gone. Parrots rustled the lemon trees, and Sullivan had come back to something like himself. *It wasn't real*, he'd thought. *I hallucinated it.* But there was real and not-real, like the dead returning in dreams. You knew when you dreamed of a dead person, and you knew when the dead came to speak. He hadn't imagined the identical men.

I didn't know quite what it meant, he'd told Talitha. They were naked in her bed then; her house smelled like lavender, and an old woman had sewn the quilt that covered them. *I knew it meant nothing ever changed there, and it never would. When my dad told me I had to stay, I knew if I did—*

If you did, you belonged to them. Talitha flipped that dark hair behind her. She'd probably tired of him playing with it. *If you stayed, the whole place was yours, and you belonged to them. They never change, Sullivan.*

Have you seen them? He'd shoved up from the bed then. *Do you know what I'm talking about?*

I've never seen them. Talitha drew him back to the pillow. *But I know what they are. Like they told you, they're time, and they never change.*

How d'you know? Sullivan closed his eyes. Her fingers threaded through his curls.

I just do, she said. *Don't go back there.*

He'd shaken his head slightly, more of a pillow-rustle than a gesture. She'd let him sleep. Talitha fed him pancakes in the morning and smiled when he ate them in his boxer-briefs. *Thank you*, he told her when she drove him back to the Roadhouse for his car. *I don't know why you're sad, but I'd fix it if you let me.*

She stood on her toes and kissed his forehead. *I'd let you if you could. Go, Sullivan.*

Why'd you ask me to go home with you? he'd asked.

She'd laughed suddenly. It had broken like a wave in that muddy little parking lot, beautiful. *Because you heard all every goddamn rumor this town ginned up, and you wanted to go anyway.*

Will you come see me? he dared.

Her smile turned sad. *Probably not*, she said. *But I'll always pick up when you call.*

Talitha kept promises. She'd never come to see him, but she always picked up; after a few years, Sullivan stopped calling. Lower Congaree was so far. He hardly spoke to Rhys. *Talitha felt bad for you*, he told himself. *She doesn't really want to talk.* He missed her anyway.

When he glanced up at the house, a pale face watched him from the upstairs living room windows. Twisted, angry, it was too familiar. Sullivan blinked hard, and his father was gone.

He found his brother clicking through the day's surveillance footage. The monitor glared from Ash's wire-rimmed glasses, and its blue light carved age-furrows in his brow. "What was Talitha's problem?" he asked.

"She saw something when she slapped Judah. She said we need to get out." Sullivan slumped into a repurposed dining room chair. The sabers above each door frame shone like accusations.

"What d'you mean, we have to leave?" Ash said.

"Talitha told me we have to leave the farm." Sullivan tried to focus on the web of photographs, notes, news stories. It was easier than looking at his brother. "She said we wouldn't, but we should get the people out at least. She didn't think we'd do that, either. So I told you, okay? Let's not argue about it. I think she's right. You'll say I'm wrong. We can fight about it or just agree that I said it and shut up about it."

Ash didn't answer.

"What?" Sullivan asked.

"You okay over there?" his brother said. No sarcasm laced his voice.

"Not really." Sullivan wished for a glass of tea, a quiet room, a way out. "Does it matter? Will it change anything if I'm not? We're going to do this thing whether or not we're okay with it, so let's do it and just shut up. I said I'll stay and I'm staying." Talitha kept promises. He could keep promises. They thought he couldn't, but he could, if he wanted to.

The day seemed to settle around him. There was freedom in finality. Mist lifted; without choices, hazed edges sharpened. Sullivan would stay. He'd see it through, whatever it became, and he'd do it for someone else. They wouldn't say, *Well, you know how Sullivan is. He never cared about his family.* He couldn't have let himself care about his father, but he loved Rhys and even Olivia enough to do the show. He could love Ash enough to finish it. Maybe then he could build something. Talitha seemed to think he could.

"Sorry it didn't go well," Sullivan offered. "I hoped it would turn out different."

"Yeah, well." Ash focused on those sabers. With their father dead, the swords belonged to them. "Sometimes there's nothing you can do, y'know? Sorry Whitney was rude to Talitha."

It wasn't much. Sullivan hoped anyway.

CHAPTER 41

RHYS

Sunday's heat sunk Rhys into a lassitude that drowned thought, reason. He tried to concentrate on his book, but Stonewall wouldn't stop shrieking. Rhys passed him a piece of pineapple. The hyacinth macaw shrieked again; Rhys passed him another. That merely assured Stonewall would keep screaming, but macaws had strong beaks. A keeper at Columbia's Riverbanks Zoo had once told him that theirs bit off its owner's finger. Better, smarter, to give them what they wanted.

"What d'you want to do?" Sullivan asked. Perched on his shoulder, Varina nibbled his hair. He handed her a piece of cantaloupe.

"No idea," Rhys replied. "Read, I guess." Ash had dragged Olivia and Henry on a farm tour to visit cousins, cameras trailing behind. The other hovered behind him and Sullivan. The cameraman waited, film running, hoping something would happen—a fight, a UFO, anything to keep viewers watching, the bloodier the better. A fight about a UFO, Rhys decided, combining the paranormal with familial battles. They'd love that best.

"Wanna raid the kitchen?" Sullivan asked. At meals, he usually left his plate half-empty. Maybe he couldn't eat while the cameras rolled. More likely, dinner with the family killed his appetite, not to mention the ghost standing by the mantle. Worst of all, that ghost wore Henry's face, as if they'd been brothers. Maybe they were. Worst of Cypress Bend's violations, cosmic or otherwise, Rhys hated that knowledge most of all.

"Yeah, let's raid the kitchen." Rhys stuck a bookmark between his pages—Sullivan dogeared them, and Rhys cringed every time—then followed his cousin into HQ. After the patio's swelter, the air conditioning seemed two steps from frigid. As he passed the surveillance monitors, a small movement snagged him.

"Hey," Rhys said, squinting. "There's something here."

Sullivan hurried over, a camera bobbing behind him like an errant balloon. The screen showed the summer-crisped back field. A dark figure hunched there, clearly a person, moving slowly toward the Boundary Tree. "Goddammit," Sullivan swore. "Tourists aren't supposed to go back there! Ash said he put No Trespassing signs up."

"We should radio Boo," Rhys said as the figure crabbed closer to trees. "I don't think Ash would—"

"Nah, we'll handle it," Sullivan told him.

"But—" Rhys tipped his head at the camera. Ash had never let cameramen too close to the Boundary Tree. Tourists had never seen the strange marks on those trunks, the orchids beneath them, and the world only needed one leaked photo.

"Tell me you haven't been looking for the chance to tell someone off," Sullivan said. "Anyway, we'll catch them before they go too far. By the time Ash or Boo gets them, they'll have already reached it."

He was right. If they didn't want anyone pawing those cypress trunks, they had to hustle, and if they hustled, they might catch the tourist. "I'm driving on the way back," Rhys said as his cousin climbed in a golf cart, camera behind. Sullivan always hogged the carts. They could have been seventeen again, bickering about who would drive to school. It was a cozy argument, well trod. Despite years of talking in memes, he still had Sullivan, which was worth the cameras, the snarking, the strangeness. He should have regretted his dangling PhD. Instead, the farm's insanity felt as comfortable as a warm bath. It might have frightened him, but after years spent grappling with chronic illness, Rhys was used to being frightened. In Richmond, he spent his afternoons in library stacks. Life at Cypress Bend might have been terrifying and despairing in turns, but Rhys felt alive again.

"You always make me sit shotgun," Rhys said, more for the argument's ease than any rancor.

"That's because I'm a faster driver." Sullivan steered around a stand of live oaks. The cart bumped onto dirt, bouncing as they hit hummocks of grass. He jammed the gas anyway.

"You mean you're more reckless," Rhys replied. Its predictability soothed the ache of distance. They might have spent years apart, but they could still argue about driving.

"'Reckless' is just another word for 'carefree,'" Sullivan told him. He stopped, hopped out, and opened the gate. Rhys slid into the driver's seat.

"I call treason!" Sullivan said, clambering up again. Rhys snorted at the martial word called down from childhood, from years of his father's ranting. He scanned the field, looking, but didn't see the tourist.

Rhys stomped the gas. "I call fair play," he replied, their old call and response. When he glanced right, Sullivan was grinning. "I missed you," Rhys said.

Sullivan's laughter stopped. Rhys shouldn't have spoken; he meant it, and Trenholm men didn't touch those things. He tried to focus on driving, avoiding mole hills and manure.

"Thank you," Sullivan said eventually. "I missed you a lot."

"It sucked, not talking to you much," Rhys managed.

"Yeah," he said. When Rhys glanced again, he was watching the Boundary Tree; the person must have disappeared behind it. He cursed. They had misjudged the distance. "It sucked a lot."

The rubber wheel was hot, but Rhys clenched it tighter. "Why can't I just say I miss you, and you say you missed me too? Why does it have to be weird?" He knew the answer. He asked anyway. Maybe he wanted to see if his cousin would admit it.

"Because we got hit for crying." Sullivan spoke it as fact rather than tragedy. "When you get hit for crying, you learn to shut up."

"I really missed you, y'know?" Rhys said. "I missed you a hell of a lot, Sullivan."

"I know," he replied, still focused on that dark tree. It had an air of grim anticipation, like a sergeant before battle. Rhys tried to concentrate on driving. "I couldn't see you, though. I couldn't see any of you. I started to realize how bad it had been, and talking to you meant remembering it, and remembering it meant looking at it."

"You didn't have to do the show," Rhys told him. He had to. He wished the field was shorter.

"Of course I did," Sullivan said. His index finger scraped the red skin around his thumb. He'd started picking his cuticles again. Aunt Alda had always clucked and wrapped his thumbs in Band-Aids; Sullivan would peel them off when she wasn't looking.

"You really didn't have to stay," Rhys told him. "It doesn't matter if—"

"Except it does. How many times did you save me? This is the least I can do. You kept me sane." Sullivan grabbed the cart's strut as they hit a hard bump. "I just wish—never mind. Let's find the stupid tourist back here and forget it."

"No, what were you going to say?" Rhys asked. The field stretched around them, acres and acres, all dull summer grass. Heat hung dank, heavy; humidity clung, and the air seemed unbreathably thick. He wished they'd stayed on the patio.

"I knew it would be like this," Sullivan said.

"What?" Rhys asked. "Where'd that person go? Are they around the other side? I swear I saw them on surveillance." He stopped, and they got out. The Boundary Tree never failed to astonish Rhys. Ten feet in diameter, gnarled with age, each trunk was carved with triple spirals, the sections as wide as Rhys's palm. Trenholm family lore said the trees aligned with the cardinal directions. In their sprawled shade, hundreds of orchids bloomed. Knee-high, radiant blue, they had no name, and in decades of searching, no one had ever found any like them. A palpable strangeness hung over the area—not malevolence, but difference, as if reality had turned into the sun and gone wrong.

"I wish we were normal, y'know?" Sullivan replied. "Like we didn't all hate each other. Hello?" he called as they approached. "You're not supposed to be here!"

"We don't hate each other," Rhys said. They stepped into the orchids, and their scent reminded him of flowers left in a vase, that sick scent of rot. A wave of exhaustion hit, but he shoved it aside. "Hello?" he called. "You're not allowed here! You're trespassing!"

"Maybe we don't hate each other, but we sure act like it," Sullivan told him. Something rustled, then stilled—a squirrel, maybe. Hopefully not another tegu. When Rhys slapped at a sharp itch on his neck, his hand came away bloody. The mosquito swarm had arrived. Fleetingly, he felt bad for the cameraman, who had no free hands to swat bugs.

"I hate this place." Despite the heat, Sullivan walked with his arms tucked at his sides. "Talitha's right, it's not normal here—"

"I know. Let's not, okay? At least here?" Rhys would have rather talked about his uncle's fists. They rounded the far side of the tree, and Rhys bit back a gasp: a small figure splayed among the flowers. A straw hat lay beside it, as if knocked off, and long white hair caught on orchid petals. The person was so small, so delicate, that it took Rhys a moment to recognize their ancient great-aunt.

"Oh God!" Sullivan bolted. "Aunt Alda! Aunt Alda, hey!"

Their tiny aunt stirred. Leaves clung to her hair, and soil streaked her blue dress; when she blinked, her rheumed-over eyes seemed too confused. Rhys imagined the camera zooming on her, then panning back to take in Sullivan kneeling at her side.

"You shouldn't be out here," Sullivan said, cupping the back of their aunt's neck. "Why are you out here?"

"Sullivan?" Her high, raspy voice creaked, as if long years had dwindled it. For a few thudding seconds, Rhys had feared the worst. He crouched next to his aunt. Her sticky skin felt fevered, and he pressed his cool water bottle to her neck. Only then did Rhys realize that she'd recognized his cousin.

"What are you doing here?" Sullivan repeated. She tried to sit up. Hands heartbreakingly large against her wasted frame, he drew her from the flowers. Aunt Alda seemed shrunken into miniature, a broken doll.

"The men," she said. "The three men called me back here. Sullivan, they're so strange, and all they talk about is time. I don't like them." Tears filled her already-watery eyes. "Why do they keep talking to me?"

Despite the heat, a chill skittered down Rhys's spine. He snapped up and scanned the tree. Nothing moved in those stolid cypress branches. Almost judgmental in its austerity, the Boundary Tree reminded him of a Puritan preacher. The men—why had the men called Aunt Alda? And with her sprawled on the ground and babbling, they'd never keep that particular strangeness off the show.

"Shh," Sullivan told her. "Don't think about the men. We're gonna get you home, okay?" He opened his own water bottle and helped her drink. When she finished, he gave her a small, forced smile. He seemed too pale for the summer heat. "Rhys and I are gonna help you up, and I'll carry you out, okay? Are they still here?"

"I have to keep going." Weakly, she shoved Sullivan's water bottle away. "They told me to get to the Boundary Tree, and I'm almost there."

"You don't even have your cane," Sullivan replied. "And I don't want the men to come back. We're gonna get you outta here." Carefully, Rhys and his cousin lifted her to her feet, and Sullivan scooped her up. It hurt to see her so frail and small as she wrapped her arms around his neck. Rhys tried not to think of the men burning bright in the middle of a black field. If he thought of them, they would come. It worked like that sometimes—the more frightened you were, the more things happened, as if fear called them down, or the farm couldn't resist an easy target.

"What did the men tell you?" Sullivan asked, the same question he'd asked Elliot and Whitney. He'd seen the men. Rhys had suspected it, but the edged panic in his cousin's voice turned suspicion to certainty. The camera trailed behind them, as usual. He hated to think of his great-aunt subject to its glare. She'd never asked for reality TV.

Aunt Alda twitched back and glared as Rhys brushed a mosquito from her cheek. "I told you, all they talk about is time. They don't stop. They said I had to go out to the Boundary Tree, but I'm so tired. I was almost there, so I stopped to rest just for a second. I don't remember what happened after that."

"It's okay," Sullivan said as he carried her through the flowers. Crushed underfoot, they smelled damp, something like celery. "You don't have to remember. We'll be at the golf cart in a second. Rhys, can you call Ash or Olivia or someone to meet us at the house? She's gonna need a checkup at least. Imma kill that nurse for not keeping an eye on her."

"Don't you do that!" Annoyance crumpled Aunt Alda's wrinkles into crepe-paper. "That's your cousin Betty. Betty didn't have nothing to do with this. The men called me out here."

"Why did they call you out here, though?" Sullivan asked. "Can you remember?"

"Something's happening," she said.

Behind them, flowers rustled. Sullivan glanced over his shoulder and walked faster. Some deep, unknowable reach of consciousness told Rhys to run, run fast, get away from those trees before something snatched them. "What's happening?" Sullivan asked.

"Time is folding," Aunt Alda told them. "Keep them away, please, Sullivan? I don't like them. They dance and dance and I can't tell them apart. They all look the same."

They're skipping, and they're identical, Elliot had said, or something like it. Dancing on that thermal imaging screen, those men had smiled too wide, predators' smiles, toothy and grim. Rhys slid his Android from his pocket. It was black, dead. He'd never turned it off.

"Phone's dead." He spoke as if it didn't matter, but Sullivan would understand.

"Camera's still working," said the man behind them, as if they'd asked. Rhys ignored him, though he wondered how he could stand being there, a Black man asked to work on a plantation. Did they give him a choice, or simply send him?

If Sullivan was frightened, he hid it well. "Don't worry about it. The golf cart's just up there. You drive and I'll sit in the back with her." Sullivan hefted their aunt higher, then edged around a low-hanging branch. "You can stop filming," Sullivan said over his shoulder. "We're vetoing all the footage of Aunt Alda."

The cameraman shuffled behind, trying to both keep up and avoid tripping over hidden cypress knees. Rhys and Sullivan did their best to ignore him on principle. "Ethan will kill me if I quit, and so will Ash," he told them. Josh? Noah?

"You might as well not waste the film," Rhys said.

"I'll keep going and you guys can fight it out later." The cameraman stumbled and nearly fell. Rhys pulled him up. They could be rude to the other crew members, but a Black man on the farm was something else—it was bad enough for him already. No need to compound it.

When Rhys swiped more mosquitoes from his forehead, sweat and blood streaked his hand. "You drive," he told Sullivan. "You're faster."

Below his furrowed brow, Rhys's cousin smiled.

CHAPTER 42

SULLIVAN

Sullivan tried to balance speed and steadiness. But he couldn't help hitting mole hills, and the cart bounced, rattling as he hit the gas. Rhys held Aunt Alda upright and pressed cool water bottles to her neck while she fussed. "Rhys, you don't need to do that," she said, recognizing them both for the first time in years. She seemed far more lucid than usual—what had the three men done to her? Had the shock frightened her back to the present? Dementia didn't work like that. *We are the past, present, and future*, the men had told him. *We are all the same.*

They didn't need to film Aunt Alda. Sullivan tried not to resent the cameraman, whose name he couldn't remember. He was just doing his job. Sullivan tried not to wonder why a Black man had agreed to film a TV show on a plantation, tried not to imagine the man's secret hatred of every Trenholm on the place. He also tried not to look over his shoulder. If the men had visited anyone before his twenty-first birthday, he'd never heard of it; as best as he knew, they hadn't shown up again until Elliot saw them. Then they'd appeared to Whitney; they'd shown up vision-like, on their infrared camera. They'd exhorted Aunt Alda to walk into the woods. Nothing, then four dramatic sightings in the past few weeks. Did it mean something? Nothing? Had Ash's experiments churned up something awful? A sick feeling bubbled in Sullivan's chest. *Time for the house to fall.* What did it mean, *When the family walks with them?*

The words nagged at him: *It's time.* The men were time. What were they supposed to stop? The house falling, or perhaps some other passive atrocity? One time, the farm had handed them answers; those answers seemed like unsolvable riddles, maybe Zen koans with no real answer.

Sullivan checked his rearview again. Nothing followed them. His hands were growing hot on the rubber steering wheel, and he tried to concentrate on that. "Are the phones working yet?" he shouted over the cart's clatter.

"I can't check right now," Rhys said. "You saw those men before. You said it, the night they appeared in the field. You said it and then you refused to mention it again."

"Yeah, well, we can talk about it later," he snapped, focused on the ground, the way ahead. He refused to glance up at the sky.

When they reached the house, Aunt Alda was still complaining: *I have to go back. They told me to go to the Boundary Tree. Y'all need to let me go. I know I'm old, but this is ridiculous.* Ash met them at the carport with two cameramen tagging behind. "Jesus God, what the hell is this?" he asked. "Betty was looking for her, and Olivia saw you crossing the field. If you took her out—"

"She took herself out," Rhys said as Sullivan helped him ease her from the golf cart. "We saw her walking into the Boundary Tree on your monitors, and thank God for it."

Their aunt might have been in her nineties, but she had pride; the world shouldn't see her heat-sick and trundling from a golf cart.

"You always think it's Sullivan's fault." Aunt Alda shook her finger, a gesture so familiar that in another situation, Sullivan might have laughed. "He's a good boy. I always told you that! You know how your daddy treated him, so you have to be especially kind, Ashby."

Sullivan concentrated on helping his aunt so he didn't have to see his brother's face. Derision, horror, pity—which was worse? Aunt Alda shuffled forward, leaning on him, slow step by slow step.

If Ash startled to hear his name, he didn't show it, at least verbally. "Sorry, Sullivan," he said. "I didn't mean to assume."

"And pinch some color into your cheeks, Ashby," Aunt Alda told him. "You look dead."

"Yes ma'am," he told her.

Ash is lonely, Talitha had said. *You can do something about that.* He'd promised himself he would try. "Aunt Alda got too hot out there," Sullivan told his brother. "We might wanna send for Dr. Hayes or drive her to the hospital."

Rhys ducked out to find Betty. Ash took Aunt Alda's other side, and they bundled her into the house. Unable to fit in the small elevator, the cameras took the stairs.

"Can't you make them leave us alone?" Sullivan asked, fighting to keep his voice level as the gears began their slow grind. "They don't need to film this. We already told the cameraman along with us to stop filming—"

"Are they filming me?" Aunt Alda snapped up, her gentle expression narrowed into ferocity. "I don't have my hat on! I look awful! Ashby, you get those cameras away, y'hear me?"

"You look beautiful." Sullivan kissed her hand, and she rewarded him with a girlish spill of giggles. "But you don't need to be on camera if you don't want to be."

When the elevator clattered to a stop, Ash hopped out first. "Sorry, y'all," he said to the cameramen. "No filming."

"We've got to get something," one of them told him. Patrick? "Ethan's on our ass about not getting enough footage."

"Don't you cuss in this house!" Aunt Alda shouted as Sullivan escorted her from the elevator. Hair wild, lips pursed, she looked slightly unhinged. The cameraman fell into a bluster of apologies, and Sullivan couldn't help but laugh. Screw them, trying to film Aunt Alda. She'd never signed a contract.

Betty met them in his great-aunt's bedroom. "I'll get her into a cool bath," she said. "She oughta be fine. If she has any bruises, I'll call the doctor."

"Betty, you put on some lipstick," Aunt Alda told her. "You look dead, too. Sullivan, will you keep the three men away?" Her forehead crinkled like an old plum. "I don't like them."

"I'll do my best," Sullivan said, inwardly shuddering. He could do nothing to prevent the men from coming. "If they ask you to go outside again, though, don't do it, okay?"

"This is a lot of fuss," Aunt Alda replied, taking the cane Betty offered. "No, I don't need your help. Y'all keeping me prisoner in my own house?"

His aunt seemed more coherent than she had in years, as if the three men had jolted her back to herself. Sullivan let his aunt go, and Betty took over the hovering. "Glad to see you back to your usual piss and vinegar," he told her.

"I told those men not to cuss, baby boy. That goes for you too," she said, but paused to pat Sullivan's cheek. She was the aunt he remembered, the fussing woman who'd held bags of frozen peas to his face, who'd clucked over his father's rages. She couldn't stop them, but she'd let Sullivan cry afterward. "Rhys, you keep an eye on him, now," she said.

"I always do," Rhys assured.

They left Aunt Alda shuffling to the bathroom and regrouped in the hall. Her door had hardly shut when Ash whirled on them. "Ethan's flipping out about the footage," he snapped. "Y'all need to get with it."

"So we should let them film Aunt Alda?" Rhys stepped up to him, too close, too mad. "*You* need to get with it. You always say family comes first? Quit it."

Ash pinched his nose. Once, fury might have spiraled him into an asthma attack. "You always side with Sullivan. You realize this isn't about me versus him, right? This is about—"

"This is about you pacifying your Hollywood producer," Sullivan shot back. Despite his resolve to maintain a fragile peace, he matched his brother's anger. The converted oil lamps threw light in dim yellow pools; it could have been two in the afternoon or two in the morning. With its battered Persian rugs and antebellum tables, sabers hanging above, the upstairs hallway felt paralyzed, timeless.

"Yeah, and you both signed contracts," Ash said. "We have to pull enough footage—"

"Let's get outta here," Sullivan told Rhys. His brother's anger would simmer, then explode, and they would get slammed with the shrapnel. Sullivan wanted to build something, or at least start to. Ash wouldn't let him.

"We were having a conversation!" His brother reached for him, then dropped his hand. "I'm sorry," Ash said quietly. "I'm worried, that's all. This isn't turning out how I'd hoped."

"You had hopes?" Sullivan laughed, a brittle, cracking sound. "This is turning out *exactly* like I expected. We fight. We hurt each other. We're going to walk out bloody, you know that, right? All of us. We'll be lucky if we all speak when this is over."

Silence hung like stagnant air. Each of them was alone. They spoke, shouted, across a long, dim distance. "Is that what you think?" Ash asked.

"I said it, didn't I?" He shouldn't have. Sullivan had known it, and he'd said it anyway.

"I hoped—I thought it might bring us all together." Shadow swallowed Ash's face, unreadable. "I was hoping, y'know? Maybe I still am." Gathering himself up, he walked away. Sullivan watched him go.

"No sum of money is worth more than talking to you," Rhys said.

Water rushed through the pipes. Still sweaty from the day's heat, Sullivan rested a palm on the wall. It was smooth and cool, real. Rhys watched him, waiting. Trenholm men didn't talk like that. They shouted or stomped off. They sneered. They balled their fists and punched things. Sullivan had to hand his cousin something. "What I said to Ash—I meant that I thought it would happen," he said. "Not that I wanted it to."

"I don't want it to happen, either." Rhys stood with his arms crossed, drawn in, eyes on those old hardwoods, uncarpeted on the floor that tourists didn't see. "It won't if we say it won't. We could promise each other. I understand if you don't talk to Ash and Olivia, or if you never come home again. But we could promise to talk, y'know?"

He meant it. Sullivan shoved down the feeling that he ought to shut up, that men ignored comments like that. "I'd like that," he told his cousin, and between those walls, the words felt treasonous.

"Thank you," Rhys said.

Sullivan wrestled with himself. If he was going to say it, he had to look at his cousin. "Why d'you always rescue me?"

Rhys's expression tumbled to confusion. "Because you're my best cousin," he finally said, cheeks pinking in the yellow lamplight. His words came slowly and deliberately, as if he also struggled to speak.

*Best cousin*s, Aunt Alda always called them. Sullivan had never forgotten. He'd thought maybe Rhys had, or if he hadn't, he didn't care. "Thank you," Sullivan told him, and something broke open. He held out his pinkie. It was ridiculous. He refused to care. "Best cousins."

Rhys hooked a pinkie into his, a little boys' gesture and more consequential in its childishness. "Best cousins," he said, solemnly. And as if they were small once more, Sullivan believed him.

CHAPTER 43

OLIVIA

As she and Henry wandered down to an overdue dinner, Olivia snagged Ash in the third-floor hall. "Hey," she said. "Don't tell Elliot about Aunt Alda seeing the three men, okay? She might find out, but don't mention it. It'll scare the hell out of her."

Her cousin gave her a curt nod, a soldier's gesture. "I was going to ask you that, too. Good to know we're on the same page."

"I'm worried about her." Olivia didn't want to admit it, but it felt important to warn him. "She slept in my bed for three nights after that last investigation."

"I'm sorry," Ash said. "You've had enough of that for one lifetime."

"Yes" might have been cruel, and "no" would have been a lie. When she didn't answer, Ash touched her shoulder, then descended the stairs. She didn't have to agree with him. He already knew that she'd spent her teens with a small child stealing her covers, drooling on her pillow, and peeing on her sheets. Olivia had never complained, not even to Henry. You did what you had to, and she had to save Elliot. Even he'd once mistaken the girl for hers. *Ash is lucky to have a child so early,* Henry had said when they met. *I wish I had. It would have given my mother a lot of comfort while I was gone.*

She's not mine, Olivia told him. *She's not Ash's, either.*

She'd never forget that confused look drawing down Henry's features. That old resentment had roiled; she'd been fourteen years old, constantly mistaken for a mother. At least judgment hadn't followed, and for that minor kindness, she was grateful. *Then whose is she?* Henry had asked.

My uncle Wade's, she'd said. *He got a woman pregnant and paid her off.* Because we're Trenholms, she might have added. We keep blood close as those proverbial enemies. Sometimes they're the same.

Ash's footsteps receded, and Henry rounded the corner, as if he'd just left the library. "You're a good mom," he told Olivia.

"What d'you mean?" She faced him in that dim hall, shuddering to imagine how close and hot it would have been without air conditioning.

"I mean you're a good mom," Henry said. "You're good to Elliot."

"I heard that," she told him. "I mean what are you trying to say?" Was she picking a fight? Or did she want to head off something before its hints came? The yellow light caught on the sabers; between them, a portrait of William Hayes Trenholm regarded her with a mixture of judgment and pity.

"I only meant that you were great with Elliot." Henry spoke mildly, though he might have realized what she was thinking. After fifteen years, he read her well.

"If you're insinuating something," she said, though she knew he wasn't, "look around. You see how messed up this family is? You think I wanna make more of us?"

If Henry tried to keep the hurt from his face, he failed. Olivia realized he hadn't known what she was going to say, not at all. "Livy—"

"What are you gonna tell a kid, anyway?" she asked. "Daddy fought for the Confederacy and stepped through a time portal?"

"You don't have to say it like that." He spoke quietly. Olivia had never stated his circumstances so baldly, and they sounded patently ridiculous. The stupidity of her predicament, of his, infuriated her. She wished they were anywhere but the upstairs hallway. Arguments like this didn't happen in the sunshine.

"What am I supposed to say it like?" she asked. "Really. You try it."

The portrait still watched them. William Hayes Trenholm had been a fat man, overfed, content in his excess. "That was my grandfather," Henry said. "He loved us all, and he was kind. When he went away to Columbia for legislative sessions, he always came back with toys—"

That beady-eyed man looked like he'd use presents to lure children closer, then snatch them up. "How kind could he be?" Olivia asked. She'd already stuck the knife in, and it was too easy to twist. "He owned slaves."

"Dammit," Henry said. "Don't do this. I only meant you were good with Elliot, and while I hate that you don't want children, I love you—"

"Stop it," she replied. Hand in his jacket like his own personal Napoleon, William Trenholm seemed to smirk at her misery. She couldn't touch him, but he could laugh at her. "I don't want kids. I never wanted kids. Been there, done that. You've been on this farm too long. It's starting to affect your thinking."

"I'd go if I could," he said.

Henry had never insinuated that he wanted anything other than what he had. She'd begged for years. "Excuse me? Then why don't you?"

Henry hugged himself like a little boy. If she looked carefully, she could pick out his grandfather's features etched on his face, the sharp chin and wide eyes. "The golf carts are bad enough. I walk down to the highway sometimes, and I watch people drive by—these fragile people in enormous metal boxes, going so fast. No wonder cars kill so many people. And y'all get in them like it's nothing."

Olivia rested a hand on the hall table. Dust roughened the smooth mahogany; she'd have to tell Amelia to get more help. "It's just the cars?" It wasn't, but she said so anyway. Olivia was simply tearing at Henry to watch him bleed; she wanted to stop and couldn't.

"You know it's more than that." He focused on that portrait, the rich man, not her, not the sabers shining dully on the walls. "I see these things on TV, cities and highways and lights—you don't know how the sounds have changed. Where you'd hear people you hear machines. There were stars in the sky, Livy. You could see the stars." He shook his head as if lamenting a child gone to ruin. "You don't know how sad it makes me, and you never will. You grew up in this concrete hellscape. And there's some good here, I'll admit it—air conditioning, antibiotics, tolerance—God, the world has come so far, and it's so much better for everyone. It is, Livy, truly. But you brought so many bad things with you. Leaving this farm would break me. I know the land, and the trees, and there's something to that. This place never changed, not really."

Quiet, Olivia held his words. Though Henry might not agree with her, it was worth it, somehow, to hear him tell the truth. They were broken, but not in the ways that he thought. The world had moved on. Cypress Bend remained the same. Held by the twin prisons of blood and history, none of them had escaped. "You could find something other than this," she said. "You could try."

"Ask Ash about that." Henry laughed, short and sharp and frangible. "He can't leave any more than I can."

"He went to school—"

"And he came straight back, and he'll never leave," Henry said. "All of you. You're almost as bad as he is. Not quite, but almost. You drag it around with you."

"I left," Olivia reminded him. "I moved out. Sullivan, he ran as far and as fast as he could—"

"And landed right back here, Livy. Both of you. Right back where you started, because your uncle called you home. And what did you do while you were gone? Have you seen Sullivan's art? It grapples with history. You, from what I hear, you're down in Charleston selling the Old South in watercolors. You carry it with you." He sighed long and hard. It was a resigned sigh, both sadness and acceptance. *Here I am and here I'll remain*, he always told her. Olivia looked at her toes. Even her sandals were the same blue as the state flag, covered in palmettos. Better than Ash, better than anyone, Henry knew the Trenholm family. He saw through the madness to its red, beating heart.

"I'm sorry," Olivia said, marshaling all her self-control. She'd tried to forget her own wounds by going after Henry. As usual, he was right, and it infuriated her sometimes. "I shouldn't have. . ." She trailed off. Out of practice, she sucked at apologies.

"You shouldn't have," he told her. "But I understand why you did. C'mon, Livy. Let's go down to dinner."

One more time, she wondered what she'd done right. Henry never stopped trying, and he never failed to forgive her. "Why d'you still deal with me?" she asked. "After everything, why d'you bother?"

He picked up her hand as they descended the stairs. "Because I love you," he told her, and she fought not to burst into tears. "Just do me a favor. Be nicer to Ash? He doesn't have anyone, and you're the one he trusts the most."

She played with Henry's hand. Olivia liked those little gestures; she'd never indulged them before, not for more than snatched moments. "You think? But—"

"He's lonely," Henry said. "Trust me. No one understands that more than me."

That guilt crept back in, unwanted as a stray cat. She should have told Ash about them long ago, and she should have stayed. Her reasons to leave, her rationales for seeing other people—in the face of Henry's patience, they paled to excuses. Olivia should have stayed, and she'd never swallow that guilt.

They ate. They slept. They woke the next morning. Sleepy-eyed, hair kicking out at odd angles, Henry watched her put on makeup and dress. "I think this is my favorite part of the day," he said.

"Seeing me naked?" she asked from the vanity.

He smiled. "That's part of it. It's quiet. The farm's out there, and we're in here. It's good to finally have this, Livy. Don't leave again, please?"

She avoided his eyes in the mirror. "Henry—"

"I know." He finally climbed out of bed, and Olivia watched his image cross the room. He had a beautiful back, all long, strong planes of muscle. "I'm allowed to hope."

"Come with me," she couldn't help saying.

He didn't reply.

Ash, Elliot, Sullivan, and Rhys were already slouched at the breakfast table when they arrived, and two cameramen orbited them. Sunshine painted the kitchen in rich morning golds; the room smelled of coffee and second chances. In that pretty spill of light, Olivia almost thought she could start over. But the ghost still hunched over the stove, unspeaking and unspeakable. They were snagged, caught. Nothing changed at Cypress Bend. Olivia could have choked on the weight of history. *Do you hate us?* she wished she could ask the ghost. *Are we as bad as the people who came before us? We're trying.*

But the ghost would not answer. The ghosts never answered.

"So then the guy takes out his phone—" Ash was saying.

"What's going on?" she asked. Henry began filling her plate with pineapple and watermelon.

Next to her, Elliot was sneaking bacon to the dogs, and Ash studiously pretended not to notice. "We had an incident yesterday afternoon—they didn't call it into the hotline til last night. Apparently, a bunch of Apple Watches went off at the same time, all claiming people were having arrhythmias. They got it in on camera."

Her cousin looked remarkably unconcerned. "Well, were they?" Olivia asked.

Ash stabbed more scrambled eggs. They looked light and fluffy, perfect. "I have no idea. In the video someone sent, everyone seems utterly calm about it, so I assume their watches were malfunctioning. It happened over by the Meeting Oak."

"Isn't that where the pacemakers kept malfunctioning?" Henry asked. He filled his own plate with fruit. Sometimes Olivia thought he would happily eat nothing else.

"Yeah," Ash said. "No idea if there's any connection. Anyway, we got some calls about a UAP yesterday, too. Reconstructing it—you know how vague people can be—it looks like they might have occurred around the same time."

"When?" Sullivan asked. He and Rhys were devouring bacon like teenage boys.

"About a half an hour before you found Aunt Alda, why?" Ash said.

"That's probably when Aunt Alda, uh, left," Sullivan told him, glancing quickly at Elliot. Ash must have told him not to mention the men, and Olivia was grateful he'd thought of it, though her cousin tended toward the overly conscientious whenever Elliot was concerned.

"Sullivan's right," Rhys said. "It would've taken Aunt Alda a while to walk across the back field."

Ash's forehead furrowed. "I hadn't thought of that."

"That's why you have us," Sullivan said through a mouthful of bacon. They were children, really, boys with expensive toys, and snarked at one another like children sniping back and forth. A larger stage made them worse. They had an audience to watch and judge them clever.

"So the UFO appeared at the same time people's watches malfunctioned and Aunt Alda wandered off," Rhys noted, as if no one had figured it out.

"God, if this isn't interdimensional," Sullivan said. "Do y'all think it's coordinated by some higher intelligence? Or like, random?"

Confronted with such phenomenological violations, any other family would have shuddered; the Trenholms spoke as if it were a mildly interesting movie. A fair number of Ash's viewers probably assumed he was faking it. When you lived in madness, Olivia decided, you learned to accept it. They could have slapped that motto on the state flag.

"Anyway," Ash said, moving on as if they'd been discussing Gamecock football, "Ethan is harassing me for another investigation. Any ideas?"

"God, don't do your EVP shit again," Sullivan replied. "It's all holding up a mic and talking to—" He stopped, almost as if he was catching himself. "Never mind," he said. "We can do whatever you want. I know we need the footage." His last sentence dripped with resignation, and her cousin focused on his plate. Generally, Sullivan would rather chew glass than retract his attempts at sarcasm, however feeble; he lived to highlight his own wit. Or maybe it was deflection. If they focused on his snark, they wouldn't see the wounds underneath. *Sullivan's slept with everyone because he's lonely*, she'd told Ash, and her contempt evaporated. The snark was one more symptom of his sadness.

And bless him, he was finally trying. Helping him was the least she could do. "Why don't we investigate the Meeting Oak?" Olivia asked. "EVP, all your equipment—you know what I mean."

Happy, but clearly shocked at the support, Ash couldn't hide the dawning confusion. "Uh, yeah, that's a great idea," he said. "Why don't we do that tomorrow night?"

"Sounds good," Rhys said, one more voice of support, and she loved her brother for it. He was probably turning mental cartwheels at their sudden attempts at accord. It had always been rare for the Trenholms, before the show as much as after. They fought for her uncle's attention; they fought over his abuse. A battering childhood had turned them against one another, lines drawn, sides taken. Olivia had despaired of them ever fixing it. This sudden glimmer, however fleeting, lent her a modicum of hope.

"So we'll do the Meeting Oak?" Ash said, clearly waiting for objections. Olivia could have offered plenty: EVPs were wishful thinking; they'd never mentioned the Meeting Oak on *Paranormal Gone South*, and it was probably a bad look; you couldn't set off explosions under a tree. She kept quiet.

"Let's do it," Sullivan said, and Olivia's hope grew a little brighter.

CHAPTER 44

RHYS

Rhys drew a gray USC shirt from his drawer. Unlike his cousin, he kept his clothes folded; Sullivan generally pawed through his dresser, and Rhys wondered why he bothered folding anything in the first place. He tossed the shirt to his bare-chested cousin. "Here," he said. "This should work."

"Thanks." Sullivan yanked it over his head, then leaned down to tie his Doc Martens. Sullivan was the trendy, almost punk rock one, and it contrasted well against the others' polo shirts, button-downs, and khaki shorts. Maybe girls would fight pitched battles about which brand of Trenholm was hottest.

"You didn't even harass Ash when he asked you to wear a light shirt," Rhys said. "Don't think I didn't notice you've been nicer to him lately."

Sullivan grunted, a sure conversation ender, and Rhys let it pass. His cousin seemed to be biting back his snark, and while Rhys wondered why, Sullivan clearly wasn't telling. Privately, he didn't care much about the reason; the effort was enough. If Sullivan didn't want to talk about it, Rhys would appreciate it alone. Hopefully Ash was paying attention. Wrapped up in concerns both familial and occupational, he might not notice. Ash worried about Elliot; he worried that they weren't grabbing enough footage. He worried about a hundred little details of the extended family—who'd missed work, who'd fallen behind on rent, who needed rescue one more time. Ash remembered birthdays and anniversaries. He sent gifts for new babies, weddings, and baptisms. Someone had to do it. Or maybe they didn't, but it kept his cousin feeling needed. That's all anyone wanted, at least most of the time, Rhys had long ago decided. People needed to count themselves vital to the world's larger workings.

Ash had gathered everyone in HQ, and when Sullivan and Rhys appeared, two cameras already roved behind him. The prospect of another night investigation already exhausted Rhys, but he had no choice. *Best not to complain about what you can't change*, Aunt Alda had told him when he was first diagnosed with liver problems, when fatigue and itching drove him close to madness. *Do the best with what you have, and forget the rest.*

"Good to see y'all," Ash said, and it seemed like a genuine greeting rather than contempt, though Rhys and Sullivan were five minutes late. "We were talking about how we're going to conduct the investigation tonight. And yeah, we're doing EVPs."

Olivia caught Sullivan's eye, but neither offered anything.

"Okay," Ash said, as if the lack of sarcasm surprised him. "We're going to go down to the Meeting Oak with all the equipment. Lewis will come with us to monitor everything." He nodded at their cousin as if he doled out battle plans. "This is pretty straightforward, no fireworks—"

"No fireworks?" Sullivan spoke like a kid who'd realized Santa wasn't coming.

"We don't want to set the tree on fire," Lewis replied, "and there are too many buildings close by."

That was Olivia's cue to snark at Sullivan. *Don't worry, you can play with your toys another day*, Rhys imagined, or *Not today, pyro-boy*. Shockingly, she kept silent. Without any discussion, it seemed she and Sullivan had called a truce.

"So we're going to head down there with all the equipment," Ash said. "I'll take the digital voice recorder and ask questions—we can play the answers back after we investigate. We'll need something to excite the phenomenon, and we can't set off fireworks, so I have an idea. Sullivan, your shirt's appropriate."

"What? Why?" Sullivan glanced at his USC t-shirt as if to remind himself what he was wearing.

"You'll see." Ash seemed to repress a grin. "I have equipment down there. Boo and Sinclair are already waiting." He turned toward the camera. "Every Trenholm knows the story behind the Meeting Oak. After William Tecumseh Sherman took Savannah, he marched north through South Carolina. Union troops cut a swath of devastation sixty miles wide, terrorizing the only civilians left—old men, women, and children. He couldn't pass through the Congaree Swamp, but a few days before he took Columbia, a

Union soldier appeared at Cypress Bend. He was ragged, thirsty, and delirious from days lost in the swamp. The Trenholms should have taken him in and let him die quietly.

"But the women at Cypress Bend had lost too many men to the War—including my third great-grandfather, also named Ashby, his brother Lyons, and his nephews Sullivan and Henry." Ash avoided their eyes. Henry gave no start of recognition; his face stayed a studied blank. "There were more lost too, a lot more," Ash continued. "So when a soldier staggered onto the farm, they didn't hesitate, no matter what his condition. The gardener, the only man left on the farm, dragged the soldier to the base of the biggest live oak on the property. There they tied him to a stake and set it ablaze. It was horrible, merciless, and cruel. But it's part of the history of our land, and there's nothing we can do to change it."

The nameless soldier's death was an ugly story, another shard of Trenholm savagery, and Rhys hated anyone knowing of it. But they'd already thrown the family to the wolves. What was one more carcass? The camera lingered on Ash's face. Did the telling glorify it? Keep it alive? Atone for their ancestors' cruelty? Rhys wasn't sure. They'd thought of Henry when they burnt that man. Did that make him partially responsible? Maybe they were all complicit, and the telling made it worse.

Outside, everyone piled into golf carts; Elliot clambered into the back seat, a cameraman next to her. Rhys let Sullivan take the wheel. His cousin was trying; let him enjoy life's smaller pleasures. "You're not going to argue about who drives?" Sullivan asked.

"Nah. You do it." Rhys grabbed the strut as his cousin pulled out, dogs galumphing behind. Without fireworks, it would be a far quieter night. Ash would wave the voice recorder around. They would return to HQ and listen to it. His cousin would claim to hear voices speaking through the static. That static would sound like a voice if you were inclined to hear one, and Ash would be happy. But Rhys's calm brought a twin jolt of fear.

"Is it bad that I'm worried because I'm not worried?" Rhys asked.

"No, it's probably healthy." Sullivan pulled onto the main drive. "You should always be worried about this place. We've seen enough shit here."

"Olivia will lose her mind if she hears you talking like that in front of Elliot."

"Oh, it's okay," Elliot said. "You remember Walker and Colt, cousin Jane's boys? They can't say a sentence with the word 'fuck.'"

Sullivan stifled a snort. "It still counts if you're quoting it."

Someone lingered in the bright light of the house's second floor. Silhouetted into black, the figure canted sideways, tracking them, and Rhys recognized that straight nose, that square chin. He shuddered and turned away. Ghosts from the distant past were discomfiting reminders of a history he'd rather forget. His uncle's ghost—Rhys refused to think about it.

"So what d'you think Ash's surprise is?" he asked, mostly to distract himself from that shadowy figure.

"No idea," Sullivan replied.

The golf cart's lights barely cut the thick dark. Rhys hoped they didn't flush another tegu. The dogs sniffed in the underbrush; the night's hot breath wearied him to sagging exhaustion. After he left for Richmond, Rhys hated to admit that he missed the humidity. His skin dried; his lips parched. He'd despised that wet-damp air for so long, but he couldn't live without it.

"I hate coming out here at night," Elliot said.

"I think any sane person does," Sullivan replied.

"I used to think the orbs were normal," she told them. "Then Melinda, the fourth nanny I had? She said she couldn't take it, living here anymore, all the weird stuff. She said she could hardly look out her bedroom window without seeing an orb. I asked what they were and she told me. I was five and I thought that stuff just happened." She played with a bracelet, likely some kind of heirloom; Ash handed out jewelry recklessly and often. "I think I asked Uncle Truluck what the pretty lights were when I was four? He told me they were fairy lights."

Sullivan's jaw tightened, and he let out the long, slow breath of a man determined to prop up his frail patience. "Maybe fae lights. Like, drag-you-down-to-Fairy-and-never-let-you-out lights. I'm sorry, Elliot."

She seemed to watch the dogs snuffling in the brush, ducking in and out of the golf cart's wan light. "He said the orbs were our secret 'cause people would be jealous if they knew we had fairies, and I couldn't tell. He also said the fairies would go away if I ran to them, and I could only watch them from a distance. So I wasn't scared, not for a long time."

"Jesus," Rhys said. It didn't surprise him. His uncle's manipulations never did.

"I even said to Melinda, 'You're mad because we have real fairies, and if you leave you'll never see them again.' She sort of smiled and told me to hold onto that." Elliot ignored the camera next to her. Her sharp features looked night-hollowed and strange; her pale hair almost glowed. Primetime would swoon. Olivia and Ash liked to think Elliot had escaped unscathed, but the farm left its own wounds. They could save her from his uncle, or at least his lingering influence; they couldn't save her from the strangeness. "Oh well," Elliot said, still ignoring the camera trained on her face. "It doesn't matter. The dogs keep us safe, mostly, and I have y'all. It's worth it, I think. Most people have a mom and a dad and one brother or sister. They aren't lucky like me."

Rhys turned into the dark, embarrassed. Elliot was the best of them.

"We're lucky we have you," Sullivan said. He kept his eyes on the road, face away from the camera. It was hard to say those things to each other, but easy with Elliot. It always had been.

The golf cart bumped as Sullivan followed Ash off the road and onto a path winding between the cabins. They loomed like sentinels, low and hulking. Rhys looked once, then looked away. The path snaked past the graveyard and its monument, between the squat buildings, and goosebumps tautened his skin. Something was coming. He dreaded it. When they rounded a corner, Ash's mobile headquarters glowed ahead, and he was grateful.

"Remember, the farm's energy concentrates in areas associated with strong emotion," Lewis was telling the camera. "If energy is neither created nor destroyed, there's a hell of a lot of energy in this place, and it's angry. You don't have to stretch to imagine the violence here. The Meeting Oak was named, we think, because enslaved people on Cypress Bend used it as a gathering site. So aside from any immolations, we have a lot of pent-up suffering in this area. It'll be interesting, in light of that, to see what kind of reaction we might get from the plantation tonight."

Cousins had dragged out Ash's setup: mahogany table, dining room chairs, barrister's bookshelves loaded with water bottles. Glad to step into the light, Rhys couldn't roll his eyes at its excess. He tried to ignore the sprawling live oak. Wide, think-trunked, its branches scooped toward the ground, then arced up again. It reminded him of an insect, one ready to crunch a lesser creature in its yawning mandibles. He tried not to imagine the pain of burning alive. That soldier had been close to death, but it didn't matter.

"Okay." Lewis smiled, a strange gesture against the pressing dark. "Let's hand out y'all's equipment. Elliot, you're off the hook. Keep an eye on the sky for us." Like before, he handed Olivia the thermal camera, Rhys the Geiger counter, and Sullivan the radio spectrometer.

"Remember, we're looking for 1.6-1.7 gigahertz," Ash said, more to the camera than his relatives. "You holler if you see it. We're not broadcasting anything. Now, onto the surprise. We're going to summon the phenomenon with sound." He gestured, and Rhys noticed two speakers pointed toward the Meeting Tree. "Y'all got your devices on?"

"Nothing on the thermal imaging," Olivia said.

"No radio frequencies," Sullivan told them.

Rhys squinted at the Geiger counter. "I've got forty-five CPM. Normal, you said before, right, Lewis? I'm supposed to holler if it goes above like, eighty-five?"

Lewis nodded, grinning like Rhys was a third grader who'd won the school spelling bee.

"Okay. Keep them pointed at the tree. Remember, no data is still data. Sinclair!" Ash called. "Let it go." He threw them a barely suppressed grin, a little boy's. "This is gonna be loud, y'all."

The tree seemed too dark. Did ivory-billed woodpeckers hide in its branches? Speakers crackled as Sinclair turned them on. The world seemed poised, waiting. Four knocks sounded, then a drawn, high note. Rhys nearly dropped the Geiger counter as the night shattered with blaring synth. Ash had chosen to summon the phenomenon with "Sandstorm," the unofficial Gamecock football fight song.

Its notes grew closer, urgent, higher, tensed. Every Trenholm around that tree who'd attended college had matriculated at the University of South Carolina; in that other time, Henry would have, if he hadn't marched off to fight the Union, and Elliot would apply in two years' time. They'd worn USC swag from earliest infancy; Thanksgiving was a high holy day not only for its family dinner, but for the Carolina-Clemson game. *Trenholms bleed garnet and black*, Rhys's uncle always said, and though he'd rambled through a lot of bullshit, that was probably true. "Sandstorm" held, held through that strangling dark, then shattered to a tide of screaming techno, and every Trenholm leapt, shouting: "U-S-C! U-S-C!" All of them surrounding the tree, Lewis and Boo included, jumped and chanted like drunk undergrads. They bounced, yelling, probably absurd on camera, but did it matter, really? They were together. For once, every Trenholm was united in something, and maybe a university fight song was a start. They could build something from that wild dance, from their football chant, find that thread and weave it together again—

Sullivan broke first. His mouth moved, out of sync, speaking. Rhys couldn't understand until his cousin waved the spectrometer. "I got 1.6! I got 1.6!"

Elliot pointed, shouting herself, and something streaked across the sky, too fast, too irregular. They were still chanting and bouncing. What the hell would viewers think? Rhys didn't care, not nearly as much as he figured he should. Anything looking down from the clouds would imagine they'd gone mad. Something winked into view high in the branches of the Meeting Oak. Glowing purple, the basketball-sized globe bobbed like a lost balloon.

Then Sullivan shouted and ran toward the tree, Elliot behind. Henry and Olivia stilled.

"There's something here!" Olivia mouthed. "Something—"

She was pointing at the infrared camera. Rhys glanced, then stared.

On the screen, a fire blazed, and a man writhed inside it.

CHAPTER 45

SULLIVAN

The fire flashed to life suddenly, blindingly, man shaped. Agony wracked it; tied to a post, it screamed, mouth open, flames roiling. Oily smoke billowed into the live oak branches. Sullivan sprinted toward the burning man. Dimly, he registered that his cousins and brother weren't running, but urgency overwhelmed fleeting wonderment, and the sick scent of barbecue hit him. Drawing a deep breath, Sullivan plunged into the heat. For a quivered moment he thought he would burn along with the man, boil into smoke and grease and nothingness. That charred-flesh scent overwhelmed him. Three paces before the figure, heat bloomed to something unimaginable, and the flames drove him back. "Sandstorm" blared under the fire's roar; Elliot was screaming words he couldn't make out. Smoke stung his nose and teared his eyes. Sullivan tried again, another deep breath, a running start, a desperate plummet into the seething oven. Again, he was forced back.

"What are you doing?" he yelled to his family, hoping they heard. "Get over here and *help me!*"

Three men stepped around the fire. Rippling like a static-y television image, they stopped, bowed, and doffed their identical top hats. Identical orbs hovered above their heads. Sullivan stilled. In the back field, he'd seen those men on the infrared, but they'd been mediated, filtered through a screen. It took him a moment to realize that they were black and white, like an old film. *Do you see?* they chanted in terrible unison. *Time rolls back on itself, and you belong to us, Sullivan Trenholm, turning and turning, the world comes back without beginning or end—*

Eyes shut tight, he dropped. The music cut.

"Sullivan!" Elliot was shaking his shoulder. When he dared to look, the tree loomed above, unburnt. No smoke clotted the air; his face hurt, but the crackling blaze was gone. No scorch-marks charred the dirt. Sullivan flew to his feet and bolted to the tree trunk, hands out, waiting for the flames. His palms scraped on cool bark.

"What the *fuck*?" he shouted, and his face hurt worse. "There was a fire! The three men! I saw the three men! They were *right fucking here*!"

"We only saw it on the infrared screen. There was nothing there," Olivia said, Elliot already tucked under her arm.

"I saw them too," Elliot said quietly. "But I didn't feel anything."

"What just happened?" Olivia asked. She clenched Henry's hand. "We saw flames in the infrared, but they weren't there. Everything was black, but on the camera, you were running at a man—" She drew closer to Henry. "I'm going back. We're going back now."

"Were they talking, Sullivan?" Elliot asked. "I saw their mouths move. They were talking, weren't they?" Her voice rose too high, her words too fast, as Olivia led her away. "What did they say?"

"We're going," Olivia said. "We'll see you back at the house." She tugged Elliot and Henry toward the golf carts, away from that place. The tree reared like an enormous, grasping hand.

"Your face is burnt," Rhys told Sullivan, low voiced, as if he didn't want their little cousin to hear. "We need to get you back and—I don't know, put cool compresses and Aftersun on you. You'll be lucky if you don't blister."

"I saw it," Sullivan told his cousin as they stumbled back to the carts. The tree seemed too large, malevolent, and he was glad to leave it. "Those men were real. I can't—I've gotta get outta here."

"I know," Ash said. Sullivan startled when his brother rested a hand on his shoulder. "C'mon. Let's get you back to the house."

"Thanks," he said. His face stung. He had a feeling it would get much worse.

Boo, Lewis, and Sinclair came behind in another golf cart. "They'll grab everything tomorrow," Ash told Sullivan from the driver's seat. Neither Rhys nor Sullivan had stopped him from driving; the cameraman sat shotgun. "Safety is paramount at Cypress Bend."

Snark gone, Sullivan only nodded. He craved the house's friendly yellow light, something to chase away that choking dark. It brooded on every side, seething, barely cut by the thin headlights. He hugged himself, chilled by the men's desperate reality. Vision-like, it surpassed physicality; the men stretched into transcendence, and their horror lay beyond existence itself. They were more real than the seat he rested on, than the darkness pressing in. Sullivan shuddered. He didn't reach for his cousin's hand, but he wanted to, as if they were small again.

At home, Rhys marched Sullivan straight to the kitchen. "I'm sorry you got burnt," his brother said.

A camera still roved around them; at the stove, the ghost's shoulders rose and fell, as if she was crying. A wave of pain threatened to drag Sullivan under: he was stuck, buried in this house, and no one would ever help him—

"Here," Rhys said. "Look up at me. Ash, you wanna make some cold compresses?"

"Yeah." His brother began fussing. Gently, Rhys smeared Sullivan's face in Aftersun. It was good to be taken care of, good to have people hovering, even if he was still on edge.

"What did you see the first time you saw those men?" Rhys asked. "You never told me about it."

Sullivan hesitated. It seemed a private revelation, and he wished the camera would leave. Though it wouldn't pick up the ghost, it seemed blasphemous to allow them in her presence. "I was standing on the patio the day before our birthday party," Sullivan began, omitting that his father had come moments before, that he'd delivered that man-of-the-family speech. "I looked down and they were there. They said—it was weird. They said, 'We are what was, is, and will be.' They were dancing the whole time, like a jig, but all three in perfect sync, and they spoke in these weird, high voices. They were more like images of the same person than separate ones." It felt true, though he hadn't pieced it together before. "They told me, 'When you see us you see yourself. We are yours and you are ours.' Then it was dawn all of a sudden. I'd been standing there for eight hours like no time had passed." He gathered all his courage. They deserved to know, despite the camera. "That's the real reason I left, or at least one of them. And there's—there's something else."

He had to say it. Rhys might hate him for it, but they needed to know. "When Rhys and I were twelve, we saw this ghost," he began, "and it knew our names." He explained what she'd said about Henry and Elliot. "She told us that, 'When three men come walking again, when the family walks with them, it's time, if you want to stop it.'"

Ash asked the inevitable question. "Stop what?" he asked. "Time for what?"

"I don't—" Sullivan sagged. His face hurt. "I don't know. She said, 'Time for the house to fall,' but I think—those men *are time*. When she said 'It's time,' Rhys, I think she meant the men. I don't know what difference that makes. Or if it makes a difference at all." He wanted to shout, punch something, stomp away. Instead, his cheeks flushed redder, and he stewed in the shame of revealed emotion.

No one spoke for a moment. The camera skulked behind the table, a hungry predator. It would gobble them up and vomit them for the masses. Sullivan couldn't bring himself to care. "They said, 'You're a Trenholm. You belong to us, and we are always the same.' When I told Talitha about them, she said they were time, too. I kind of put it together, I think. I knew if I stayed I would never get free. I guess I'm still trapped."

"I guess we all are," Ash replied, and no malice laced his voice. "I need to talk to Lewis." He took some wet cloths from the freezer and handed them to Sullivan. If he noticed the ghost and its sucking pain, he gave no sign. "I hope you feel better."

"Thanks," Sullivan said. The cameraman hesitated, then followed, and he and Rhys were alone. Sullivan draped the cool cloth over his face. He likely looked ridiculous.

"Did the men say anything this time?" Rhys asked.

Sullivan searched for their exact words. "They told me that time rolls back on itself. And 'The world comes back without beginning or end.' They were time, like Talitha said. Nothing changes here. Nothing ever will." The camera was gone, and he slid the cloth from his cheeks. "Talitha had this vision, Rhys. She said she saw time? She said nothing ever changes here, and we should get out, but we never would."

His cousin focused on the cabinets. They seemed eternal. Dishes might break, but their places never changed, and the kitchen's glow seemed far from the farm's existential heresies. "We wouldn't leave. We can't."

"What if we did, though?" Sullivan pressed.

"Well, we can't. Put that compress back on your face. You might blister if you don't."

"Why can't we, though?" he asked. The compress smacked wetly on his cheeks. Its cool felt like God's own mercy, not that he deserved it. None of them did.

"We can't leave because we're Trenholms and it's ours." Rhys spoke as if it were a simple fact of addition. "And you can't, like, *see time*. That's not possible."

"Time personifies itself here," Sullivan snapped. "Don't say something isn't possible. After all these years, d'you really think anything's impossible here?"

"Fair point."

The woman hunched lower over the stove. Her hands, though dark, reminded him of Aunt Alda. "Can I ask you something?" he asked Rhys. "While we're talking about ghosts?"

"What?" Rhys's tone was guarded, and his eyes skirted to the stove. He knew.

"I see them all the time," Sullivan said. "They don't talk. But they don't leave, either."

The oven light hummed behind them, a reminder of the heartbreakingly everyday. He could lose himself in that, close his eyes and cling hard, then maybe nothing out there could touch him. The kitchen windows showed not the dark outside, but their own reflections. *Time for the house to fall*, the woman had told them. *Use the sabers.*

"I know," Rhys finally replied quietly. "I see them, too. It's not *them*, though. They're memories."

"They make my back hurt sometimes," Sullivan said. It felt like a confession, one too dark for daylight. "This one, in the kitchen—I always feel stuck around her? Like I'll never get out. And the one at the bottom of the stairs, I feel like everything I ever loved will leave—"

"I know," Rhys said again, even quieter. He slumped into a chair.

"What can we do about it?" Sullivan asked.

His cousin seemed to watch the woman at the stove. She wiped her eyes on her apron, and the sense of confinement rose to a crushing brutality; Sullivan resisted an urge to bolt, to sprint from the house and stand under the wide, swallowing sky. "We can't do anything," Rhys said finally. "We just have to live with them."

"But how do we do that without—I don't know, without breaking?" Sullivan asked.

"Have you broken yet?" Rhys asked.

Yes, Sullivan could have said. *I don't know what it feels like to exist unbroken.* But he said, "I guess not, no." Rhys had always been good at closing his eyes, at believing everything would be okay in the end.

Maybe hope was enough to see them through.

Sullivan didn't think so.

CHAPTER 46

ASH

The next night, HQ's windows turned to black-backed mirrors as Ash paced. Vaguely, he wondered what time it was in California, then decided he didn't much care. Ethan was probably at some fancy yogic retreat, breathing rehydrated oxygen and eating organic tree bark. "I saw the footage," the producer said flatly. "We can't use it. The Civil War names? Sullivan, Ashby, and Henry? Really? Don't you think that's a little overdone?"

"Those were their names," Ash replied weakly. Of course the names had been real, but appearances mattered more than truth. They sounded ridiculous, so they were ridiculous. After four seasons of *Gone South*, he ought to know that.

"And a man getting burned alive on infrared? Specifically, the Union soldier *your family* burnt? We can't show that. It's definitely MA, and we're trying our best to keep it PG." Ash imagined Ethan pushing himself out of a full lotus position and stretching. "Common Sense Media is already going to flag us for diversity. We'll get clobbered if we up the series to MA."

"I can't help what happened," Ash told him. "You think I plan what this place is going to do?" He regretted it immediately. Ethan probably thought he faked everything.

"I know," the producer said, and Ash couldn't tell if he agreed or not. He could see Ethan gazing out his window in the Hollywood hills, wildfire smoke rising in the distance. California always seemed a hellscape of flames and earthquakes, droughts and mudslides—maybe the mudslides were in San Francisco, a city he could never spell.

Maybe the wildfires were in Canada. Were those still burning? He could no longer parse the natural disasters. *Hell in a handbasket*, his father would have said. For once, Ash agreed with him. "That whole experiment is out," Ethan snapped, and Ash imagined a band of California health nuts staring at him in mild puzzlement, like baffled sheep. "Look, we're seriously short on footage. Your brother is vetoing everything with your aunt—he texted yesterday. Nothing's happening, Ash. We can't run a show about you visiting your cousins."

"We had an investigation last week—"

"Yeah, and you need more." Ash had rarely heard Ethan talk tough; the producer had always handed him the star treatment, sunny smiles and kid gloves. "I'm calling to tell you to *get me footage*, Ash. This isn't a discussion anymore. I'm telling you. You signed a fucking contract. Fulfill it or we'll sue."

"I'm doing my best!" he protested, trying not to tally the relatives he supported.

"I've given you people plenty of latitude and patience, but I'm running out of both," Ethan said. "You're lucky I have an out for you. I found another medium to work with. She's going over there Friday at noon, and you're going to meet her. My people contacted Whitney, and she'll be over with her fiancé at the same time. You're going to let them in, and you're going to film it. Got it?"

His brother and cousins stared from the bulletin board, all the photos unsmiling; even their images seemed to sit in judgment. *You're not good enough*, they said, and Ash tended to agree. "We can't do another medium," he said. "Bringing in Talitha was a disaster, I told you, and she's highly competent—"

"She's bullshit," Ethan replied, "I don't care if you get Jesus Christ out there. It doesn't matter if you don't fucking film him, and you didn't film her. I found someone who'll go on camera. Her name's Nova Shaw, and she'll be over there on Friday. You'll meet her and you'll fucking film her."

Ash dropped to a chair. Its embroidered cushion hurt his butt. He would lose, and he might as well do it with as much grace as possible. "Sounds good," he replied.

"Oh, and I want you to take a look at one of Sullivan's on-the-fly interviews," Ethan said. All animosity seemed forgotten; he had what he wanted. "I'm trying to decide how to cut it, and I want your opinion."

That was Hollywood: starstruck til they turned, then back to smiles when you groveled. Ash was used to mercurial misery; he'd grown up in it. Ethan was throwing him a bone, but meat was meat. "I'll take a look at it."

"Yeah, tell me what you think. Try to get some decent reels for me in the next few days, and we'll touch base Friday. I'll send you Nova's contact info."

"Sure," Ash said, but Ethan had already hung up.

He moved to the office chair and opened his email. He might as well look at Sullivan's clip and send a reply immediately; it would engender some goodwill, even if the request was bullshit. Ash clicked open the footage. It showed Sullivan sweeping out of dinner, a voiceover behind: "Ash dislikes me, and I dislike him, and there's not much more to say," his brother told the camera. The footage cut back to Sullivan seated in the upstairs library, a glass of water at his elbow. He wore a grimace, as if he found the task distasteful and wanted it over as soon as possible. Behind the couch, the alligator skull grinned. "If I could tell Ash anything, I'd tell him to lay off," Sullivan said. "He can hate me as much as he wants, but he doesn't have to show it so often."

The camera cut once more; they were fighting in the kitchen. "We never could stand each other," Sullivan was saying. "I think he's jealous. And he hates that I'm bi. He'll say it's fine, but it's—"

Somewhat viciously, Ash clicked it off. He'd really thought his brother was trying, and the clip hurt more than it should have. Sullivan was Sullivan, and he'd been stupid to expect differently. *This is turning out exactly like I expected*, he'd said. *We fight. We hurt each other. We'll be lucky if we all speak when this is over.* His brother's contempt was sure as sunshine and just as glaring. Why had he deluded himself? Ash had genuinely hoped that despite *Keeping Up*'s inauspicious beginning, despite everyone's contempt for *Gone South*, they could build something better than their contentious childhood. But Sullivan and Rhys—they'd grab the money and run. Maybe Olivia would stay for Henry, for Elliot. Ash hoped.

He couldn't talk to Lewis or Boo. Henry would humor him in a distant way, all sympathetic nods and pithy aphorism. *What did you expect?* Olivia would say, her head shake vaguely contemptuous. *Sullivan is Sullivan. He never changes.* The dogs had absconded with Elliot, denying him even canine sympathy. Ash glanced at the pile of insurance paperwork on the table, then picked up a pen. He would play doctor, quartermaster, benevolent dictator. Might as well make himself useful.

He managed to avoid his brother and cousin until the next evening, when Mickie called them for dinner. She'd whipped up mac and cheese, collard greens, and cornbread, then sent out for Little Pig's barbecue. The usual suspects crawled out of their hiding places, Rhys and Sullivan, Olivia and Henry, Elliot and Aunt Alda, everyone in neat pairs. Ash sat at the table's head, his father's place. Maybe solitude was the fount of his father's misery. Sullivan had been six months old, and him not quite two, when their mother fell from her horse. Everyone said their father had loved her to distraction, with an old man's adoration for his young bride. But his father never spoke of her. Ash suspected her loss had fueled his drinking, at least in the beginning. Did he keep drinking because the world seemed too empty? Ash understood that. Or did he keep drinking because he couldn't escape those lingering ghosts? Ash understood that, too. One more time, the dark-skinned man stood next to the mantle, tray in hand. His face looked too much like Henry's as he gazed into the middle distance, a testimony to violence stamped on his features. *I'm sorry*, Ash wanted to shout. *We're all sorry, and maybe me most of all.*

It would do nothing.

They laid napkins in their laps. A bottle of red breathed on the huntboard, but Olivia laughed and said it didn't go with barbecue. She fetched them beer. Stella for him and Henry, Yuengling for her and Sullivan; Western civilization could topple, and they'd still argue about which was better. Olivia let Henry butter her cornbread. Sullivan and Rhys had found their old BB guns in a closet and spent the afternoon behind the barn, playing target practice with old cans. Sullivan was a crackshot, his daddy's pride and joy, and he and Rhys were laughing that he still had it.

"It's irresponsible to shoot BB guns with all these tourists around," Ash snapped. "You want to deal with the lawsuit when you—"

"Shoot someone's eye out?" Sullivan wore a barely suppressed grin, and it enraged Ash, it really did. His brother assumed everyone else would chew and swallow the consequences. "You should've come with us."

"I'm too old to shoot a BB gun, and so are you." He stabbed a forkful of barbecue. Why did Sullivan bother? Ash couldn't hit the broadside of a barn with a BB gun. As a child, his glasses had complicated aiming; Sullivan and Rhys regularly trounced him at target practice. Their father had always slapped the winner's back and passed him a silver dollar. Ash pined for one silver dollar, just one. Sullivan kept them stacked on his dresser.

"Never too old to shoot a BB gun," Sullivan said. "Henry, you should've come, too. You'd've given us a run for our money."

Henry hated shooting. Didn't they know better? Sullivan probably said it to needle him.

"Olivia, you should've come at least," his brother said. "We know you can outshoot all of us." If Sullivan was a crackshot, Olivia could have competed. Their father had told her that girls didn't shoot guns and grounded her if he caught her at it.

"If I'd've known you were out there, I'd've showed up, kicked your ass, and come back inside where it's cool," she said, half-smiling, taking her cornbread from Henry. Ash wanted to butter a pretty woman's cornbread. He wanted to kiss her cheek as he got up to fetch her wine; he wanted to lead her upstairs, flushed and laughing. It didn't matter if they slept together. They could skip to the lazy, in-bed-afterward part. How long had it been? Calculations would ache.

"This is really good barbecue," Sullivan said. "I missed Little Pig's. Always liked it better than Jefferson's."

"Tastes the same, hand to God," Rhys said. "I hate to admit it, but it's true. Wish I could say Little Pig's was better, 'cause God knows I hate eating Jefferson's."

"Y'know, when I was a senior, we had this Irish poet visit USC," Sullivan said, and Ash almost groaned. A story was coming, one more chance for his reckless brother to bathe in the limelight. "So this woman was super-famous—won all kinds of awards, I don't know how they managed to snag her—and somehow, I finagled the right to pick her up at the airport. We're driving back to campus and you know Jefferson's BBQ is right on Charleston Highway. So she sees this enormous Confederate flag flying there and asks what the hell that's about. I had to explain Jefferson Sims, his flag, and his Biblical defense of slavery to an Irishwoman, 'He helped run George Wallace's presidential campaign and had to get a judgment from the Supreme Court to make him integrate his barbecue barn, which he said was against his religious beliefs,' I told her, and it was probably one of the most embarrassing moments of my life."

"That's not even in the top ten." Rhys smirked, and Sullivan clearly kicked him under the table, grinning the whole time.

Ash was thirty-two, and he'd never had a best friend he could kick under the table. Sullivan played his mischievous boy facade, then went upstairs and spit venom at the camera, his betrayal all the more bitter for his masquerade. "Are you two ten years old?"

Ash asked. "Do you have to act like bratty kids at dinner? You're ridiculous, both of you, grown men playing with BB guns and kicking each other. Fuck off, both of you. Take your act somewhere else because you're not fooling anyone." Vaguely, he realized he was shouting.

Everyone stared. Deliberately, Sullivan set down his fork. His chair scraped at the redone carpet, which he'd once said looked like the Luxor. "Rhys and I will be in the kitchen," he declared, as if he were onstage, because Sullivan always imagined himself onstage. He picked up his plate and walked out. His perpetual partner in crime followed.

Sullivan had deserved it. Maybe not for the BB guns—but he'd deserved it for that caustic erosion of trust. Resolutely, Ash focused on his plate. If glanced up, he might have seen the mirror, and he couldn't stand to meet his own eyes.

CHAPTER 47

OLIVIA

Olivia woke to a warm weight behind her. For a vague, dissolving moment, she snuggled in, then wrenched back as she remembered that Henry had decamped to his own room. One more time, she'd tumbled from sleep's vagaries to find Elliot curled against her. Scared of the three men, her little cousin had insisted on sleeping in her bed for the past three nights. She'd pretended not to mind, despite Elliot's propensity for throwing elbows and stealing covers. Even as a toddler, her little cousin was never a particularly agreeable bed-buddy; it didn't matter. Elliot needed her. *You don't have to,* Ash would always say.

I do, actually, she'd reply. *If I don't, no one will.*

Olivia checked the clock: five a.m. She slid from bed and sneaked down the hall to Henry's room. His austere bedroom, a monk's cell, still ached. It seemed one more symptom of his loneliness, and blame for that wrenching solitude belonged only to her. Her cowardice pained her. Olivia tried to be brave. She'd moved to Charleston with no job and spent a month sleeping on her old roommate's couch; she'd come back to Cypress Bend when she loathed doing it. But in the end, she'd failed at one of the most important parts of life, and Henry had suffered the consequences.

He asked for it, she sometimes thought darkly. Olivia hated that voice. His upbringing had left him few choices, and though he'd repudiated so much, those Victorian manners lingered. It had taken her two and a half years after he kissed her to finagle him into sleeping together; Olivia had finally resorted to begging. *I'm a sophomore in college*, she'd told him.

There are some things you don't do, Henry had said, still frightened of voices and morals long dead.

It's not like I can get pregnant—I told you about birth control. She'd been unable to suppress an eye-roll, and handed him her old argument. *If I can't get pregnant, what's the harm in it?*

They'd fought about it before, and she'd been sure they'd fight about it again. Henry had repeated a sentence she could have recited with him. *There are some things you don't do.*

Please, she'd said. *We love each other, and this is ridiculous. Were you lying when you said you didn't believe in Christianity anymore?*

No. Henry had maintained the steady calm that reassured and frustrated her in equal measures. *It doesn't matter. Everyone does it, and look how awful the world is? People take each other for granted. I never want to do that to you.*

On and on, circles in circles, one long, angsty slog. They'd settled it drunk in the hayloft one night; Olivia was naked when she asked. *Do you regret it?* she'd asked afterward.

How could I regret that? Are you asking if I feel guilty? In that thick-black dark, Olivia refused to let go of him for more than a heartbeat, and she couldn't see his face. It worried her. *I feel almost guiltier than I ever have in my life, Livy. But guilt and regret are too different animals.*

She never forgot those words.

An hour before dawn, Henry's bedroom was nearly as dark as that hayloft. "Hey," Olivia whispered, flipping back the covers and slipping into bed. One more time, Henry wore nothing. But when she touched him, he nearly leapt from bed, wild-eyed and panicked, biting back curses. Olivia flew backward, just as panicked, guilt burning once more. Henry so rarely lost himself. "Don't do that, Livy," he told her, half-relieved, half-stern. "You scared me."

"I missed you." It came more plaintive than she'd intended.

"We didn't say you'd come this morning." He settled next to her, and when she rested a hand on his chest, his heart beat too fast, too insistently. She really had frightened him.

"Sorry," she said, sitting up. "I'll go."

"That's not what I meant." He tugged her back down. "Just warn me."

Olivia curled around him. Henry's breath evened to a regular rhythm, and she closed her eyes. Maybe she could fall back to sleep, then stumble down to breakfast with him.

"If you'd stay, we could do this every night," Henry said, snapping her from the dream-like drifting that came before sleep.

"Don't start." Her words carried more exhaustion than anger. "You'll tell me to stay, and I'll say I don't know, then you'll ask again and we'll get quiet, because we're both sad. There, we don't have to talk about it now."

Henry's chest rose and fell in a tired sigh. "I guess we don't."

Did they argue in circles because they were stubborn, or because nothing ever changed? Stubbornness, she decided, was merely a desperate cling to the familiar—perhaps they argued because neither could bear anything different. They wheeled through the same dances and lost a little bit of themselves each time. Intimately acquainted with entropy, Olivia found a strange comfort in it. "So you're not going to make me go back to my room?" she asked. "Our room," she added quickly. He had to know it belonged to him, too.

"No. There's no point," Henry replied. "They know. Go to sleep, Livy. We'll wake up for breakfast."

"Or maybe not," she said into the pillow. It smelled like him, his mint shampoo.

"We have to get up for breakfast," he told her.

She'd won one skirmish. Better, kinder, to hand him a consolation prize. "Okay," she said, and promptly fell asleep.

Washed, dressed, and still yawning, they wandered downstairs at nine. A cameraman tucked in the corner, Sullivan and Rhys had started without them. Henry fetched coffee while Olivia piled two plates with fruit. The ghost woman still languished at the stove. *Only people who live here can see them,* Henry had said, which explained a lot. Olivia had never worked up enough courage to mention them.

"How'd you sleep?" Sullivan asked.

She glanced sideways, ready to ask if Henry needed to hit him again. But no smirk twitched up her cousin's mouth. "Uh, I slept fine," Olivia replied. "What about you?"

"As decently as I ever do, which is to say not much," he told her. "Also, Rhys snores."

Her brother snapped up. "I do not!"

"How d'you know?" Sullivan asked. "You're asleep."

"Because you'd've complained about it since we were nine," Rhys shot back. He was right, and Olivia laughed. Even Henry smiled, and the morning shone like a promise. Those small drops of goodwill could sustain them; the ceasefire held. No peace treaty had come, but maybe they could forget the skirmishes fought to bloody draws, those bitter family Shilohs. In that insular kitchen, the Fiestaware in its place, the smell of bacon lingering, it seemed possible. But the ghost wept silently, and grief flooded her. They could never leave it behind.

Then Ash stomped in. Each of them snapped up, and each looked away. Olivia caught those sabers over the doorway. She'd been foolish to hope.

Her cousin dropped to his usual chair, and no one greeted him. Ash somehow managed to infuse even his coffee-pouring with a sense of outraged hostility, and his spoon clinking against the cup seemed the first sortie of a wider battle.

"What's up this morning?" Rhys finally asked. Trust her brother to attempt talking down a storm tide.

"Oh, I'm about to piss y'all off," Ash said, spoon dropping with an audible clank. "I'll say what I'm going to say, and y'all will start harassing me, and sniping, and generally trying to outdo each other with stupid sarcasm. Sullivan will make a theatrical exit. That's how it always goes." He stabbed his eggs as if they needed killing.

Somewhat guiltily, they glanced at one another. Sullivan reddened.

"It doesn't have to be like that," Rhys said finally. "The past few days, we've been getting along."

"Except it always is. And where the hell is Elliot this morning? And Aunt Alda?"

"Elliot's up," Henry said. "I don't know where she got to."

"She went off with some of the cousins," Sullivan replied warily. "She took the dogs."

"Of-fucking-course she took my dogs. Not even the dogs stay around anymore. Well. No sense in beating around the bush, then." Sarcasm oozed from Ash's voice. "I talked to Ethan, and we have a major fucking issue, so listen up. Y'all can't argue, and y'all can't weasel out of it, so you might as well not bitch. We're not getting enough footage—"

"Old news," Sullivan said. "Ethan is only complaining since—"

"He's threatening to sue at this point," Ash snapped. "And he's got a decent case. He booked a medium to talk to Whitney and Judah. They're coming over Friday, and the medium's meeting us. We're filming all of it this time." He glared as if they were attempting a sabotage.

"Uh, that might not be such a good idea?" Sullivan said tentatively. "It went real bad last time, and Talitha is—"

"Ethan doesn't care and neither do I," Ash told him. "So you can let it ride. We'll all be there. Live with it."

"Ash." Rhys started up that stupidly reasonable voice, probably convinced he could fix everything if they'd only try. He'd fail. He always did. In the long game of Trenholm family relations, maybe her brother lost the most. "Sullivan has a point. Do we really want to piss off—"

"I told you, *live with it.*" Ash spoke firmly, finally, a drill sergeant to an impudent recruit. "You want to leave? There's the door. Sign an NDA on the way out and lawyer up, because that studio can wring blood from a stone."

"You can't talk to us like that," Sullivan said, but his faint voice undercut the words' bite.

"I already did," Ash told him. "Is it time for your dramatic exit? There's your cue."

Sullivan stood. He picked up his plate. Without a word, he passed under those sabers and was gone. Rhys shoved up and followed.

"Well, that's over," Ash said sourly. "You got anything to add, Olivia?"

"Sarcasm fails me," she replied, as if to cut a particularly parvenue Charlestonian. *Bless your heart*, she might have said. Olivia considered going after Sullivan, but Ash would have conjured it into one more injury. Composed, Henry continued eating. His father had been a twin to her uncle. Maybe it ran in the family.

Olivia wanted to try. The morning's glow had dimmed; a low misery hung over the kitchen, worse than usual residual sadness. She rested a palm on the table, oak hewn more than a century before. The same dance whirled around her, and it was up to her to stop. "What happened?" she asked as gently as possible. "We were doing so well."

"Ask Sullivan," he replied.

Her fruit seemed treacle-sweet and just as sickening. She set her fork down. "Did he say something to you? He's been making an effort—"

"Maybe to our faces." Ash threw his napkin down as if it had personally offended him.

"What d'you mean?" Henry asked carefully, the tone he'd use with an animal cornered and snarling. Olivia hated it. She wanted to go back to Charleston, to smell the sea breeze, to forget she knew a place called Cypress Bend.

"Ethan sent me one of Sullivan's on-the-fly interviews," Ash said. "You think he's trying? He's just trashing us behind our backs. Everything I do for this family—all of it—and he said he dislikes me, and I hate that he's bi."

Olivia focused on her fruit, its orderly assembly of melons and grapes, pineapple and mango. She'd heard it from her uncle too many times. *Look what I've given you. I brought you to this house and handed you everything, and you've given me nothing but grief.* He'd thought himself more sinned against than sinning, the relic of a bygone time when children were unquestioningly obedient, seen and not heard. *In my day, my daddy would've tanned your hide and don't you think different. Back then ladies were real ladies, not this bullshit women's lib stuff. No man wants a girl who thinks she's better than him.*

"Ethan sent you one of Sullivan's on-the-flies?" Henry asked.

"He wanted to see what I thought of the cuts," Ash told him.

Olivia gripped Henry's hand under the table. As a child, she'd never had an ally—her uncle's rages cowed them into silence, and silence had bled to complicity. "When was it filmed?" Olivia asked.

"I don't know." Ash glared at his breakfast; at least he wasn't glaring at her. "You think I keep track of this stuff?"

"I'm sure they didn't film it in the past few days," Olivia said. "He's been trying, he really has."

"D'you think Ethan sent it to stir the pot?" Henry asked.

Olivia knew its truth as soon as Henry spoke it. Ethan wanted them to fight—pitched battles made good TV, especially when they came with heavy casualties. Ethan was manipulating her cousin like a mother with a recalcitrant toddler. "I think Henry's right," she told him. Air conditioning chilled her arms. They should have stayed in bed.

"Does it matter?" Ash asked. "He said it."

"He said it a while ago," she pressed. "It doesn't mean—"

"Morning, Elliot," her cousin said. His steely expression snapped into sunniness for the first time that day. They had to fake it for Elliot. Don't fight in front of the kids—one more prod into premature parenthood. Olivia plastered on a smile. After a childhood with her uncle, her facade was immaculate.

Conversation spun into banal gossip. The Trenholms were good at that. They could fake it, and they could pivot their misery to someone else as easily as one another, chew them up, spit them out. Reality TV worked like that, too. It was no wonder they were so good at it.

CHAPTER 48

SULLIVAN

Styling Nova Shaw's blonde hair, the type of arrangement properly called a coif, likely required at least an hour and several different heating tools. She wore too much gold jewelry, and her white pantsuit, ill-suited for the Carolina heat, probably came from Anne Taylor. Sullivan imagined her as a woman prone to summoning managers and haranguing school principals. Nova was almost certainly not her real name. "Oh no, like I told you on the phone, I can't work outside," she said to Ash, hand up, head shaking slightly. "You'll have to bring everyone in from the patio, please."

"Of course," Ash told her. Sullivan hated the obsequiousness padding his brother's voice—he seemed intent on fawning over this woman, whom Sullivan could guiltlessly call a total Karen. Nova had already insisted that she had to conduct "the work" at midnight; she required a lit fireplace, a bowl of water, and a bowl of dirt. As she settled on the salon's sofa, a Victorian piece carved with an eagle head, Sullivan wondered what outrageous demand would come next.

"You must be Olivia!" Nova said, leaning toward his cousin. "I've heard *so* much about you, darling. You went to USC, I hear? Which sorority did you pledge again?"

"ADPi," she replied, and Sullivan bit back a laugh; Olivia's cool tone said she found Nova offensive, probably trashy, and unworthy of notice. "Sullivan, my brother Rhys, and Ash are SAEs."

Nova swiveled to him. Her eyes narrowed, as if she were searching for a Carolina frat boy beneath his Doc Martens and red jeans. "My father insisted," Sullivan explained. "It was my compromise for majoring in art. They'd've kicked me out if they could."

"They almost did," Olivia said. "Twice."

"Three times." Sullivan pretended to study his nails. "The last time, they caught me *in flagrante delicto* with a Sigma Ep. The fraternity bothered them more than his gender."

Face flat, Nova regarded them as if waiting for a punchline. She had no idea what he was talking about.

"We were banging," Sullivan clarified. The camera regarded him with a steady blank eye. They'd almost certainly keep that exchange for the show.

Ash chose that moment to bring in Judah, Whitney, Henry, and Rhys. Judah appeared worse than before, grayer and somehow wispier, vaguer. The dogs avoided him; they threw Nova suspicious glances, as if they knew she couldn't be trusted, but reserved immediate judgment. The dogs always knew. They piled in front of Olivia; with Ash insisting that Elliot stay upstairs in bed, Sullivan supposed they regarded her as the most vulnerable.

Ash introduced everyone around, and Nova seized Whitney's hand. "It's *so* lovely to meet you," she said—Whitney's dainty gold jewelry and Lilly Pulitzer dress must have met her approval. Nova patted the sofa next to her. "Why don't you two sit down and tell me everything that's happened, back to front?"

Rank distaste distracted him, and Sullivan watched the ceiling fan click-click-click lazy circles as Whitney drew their story to an epic length, rambling about knocks on the wall, footsteps in the hallway, shadowy figures lurking in her peripheral vision, missing time punctuated by the three men appearing. When she'd spoken to Ash, she'd seemed almost apologetic; for Nova, Whitney played the story as high drama. She brandished photos. She gestured. When she reached into her purse for medical records, Sullivan almost groaned.

". . . and we almost didn't make it today, because Judah had one of his sleeping spells. They come more and more these days." Whitney passed a weary hand over her eyes, but it seemed studied, as if she'd practiced that particular gesture to death. "We're just looking for some kind of relief, ma'am. We need help, and that so-called psychic that came earlier didn't help at all."

Sullivan opened his mouth, but Rhys smacked at him. Classism annoyed him more than most personality flaws—money bought neither virtue nor sense. A childhood at Cypress Bend had taught him that.

"Well, I'm here to give you some help, child," Nova told her. "Now, we'll all need to sit on the floor in a circle, and you'll have to turn off the lights. Nothing but the fire. Maybe someone could bring us pillows? Those dogs will have to leave, please."

Olivia snapped up. She must have zoned out, too. "The dogs stay."

"I'm so sorry." A bless-your-heart lurked behind Nova's simpered smile. "I can't work with dogs in my face."

"The dogs tell us when something's wrong," Olivia said. "The dogs stay."

"Oh, honey." Nova's expression veered into pure condescension, probably the same face she used on her local Whole Foods manager. "You don't need the dogs when you have a medium here. I'll stay between y'all and any dark forces."

Her necklace certainly came from Kendra Scott, and her purse from Vera Bradley. Sheerly on brand loyalty, she wasn't a person Sullivan would trust to hold back anything. "The dogs stay," he said.

Nova huffed. "I can't work like this."

"We'll put the dogs out." Ash whistled, and gestured to the door. Unmoving, his dogs regarded him steadily, as if to say, *You've got to be kidding me.* "Ganon! Zelda! Q! Pandora! Let's go!"

The dogs stayed put. Ash crossed the room and pointed again. "Out."

One lay down. Sullivan had never seen them disobey.

"Dammit! Out!" Ash grabbed a collar. The dog gave a deep, guttural growl, and he jerked back. "Sorry," he said, straightening up, perhaps thinking that if they wanted to stay so badly, they likely had good reason. "The dogs won't go, I guess."

Nova side-eyed the shepherds. "Those are big dogs. You shouldn't let them get away with that."

"I generally don't. I'm very sorry, but you'll have to work around them." Ash took his seat again.

Nova seemed to think about arguing, then pursed her lips instead. "Well, I'm not sitting on the floor with them. We'll have to move everything so we can all hold hands."

Rhys sighed heavily, stood, and dragged his chair over the supposedly authentic carpet. After plenty of furniture tugging—the dogs stood when Olivia did—they arranged the chairs in a tight semi-circle around the sofa, with Judah between Nova and Whitney. Reluctantly, the dogs remained outside it. Ash turned off the lights.

"Now, please join hands." Nova flicked her wrist, a needlessly dismissive gesture. "We'll prepare to cross the veil. I can tell just from being near you, Judah honey, that you have a departed soul attached to your spirit."

"Talitha said it wasn't a person," Sullivan reported, suspicion rising. Maybe Ethan had found someone whose vagaries fooled live studio audiences, not an actual psychic. "She said it was nothing she'd ever seen before."

"I don't know who this Talitha person is, but I can only assure you that I do this for a living," Nova snapped.

"Maybe that's the problem," Olivia muttered.

"Do we really have to hold hands?" Sullivan asked. But no one answered; when Rhys and Olivia poked him, he grudgingly laced his fingers into theirs. The cameras tracked around them, as if looking for angles. Behind him, the fireplace snapped and hissed. Outside, low, brooding clouds hid the sky, like a dirty ceiling. At least Elliot was in bed, a slender mercy.

Nova closed her eyes. Whitney and Judah closed theirs. He and Olivia glanced at one another; she shrugged and closed hers. Rhys wore a look of intense concentration, as if he were straining to see a pattern behind his lids. Sighing heavily, Sullivan shut his eyes. Might as well play the game.

"Empty your minds," Nova said. "Listen to the fire crackling."

Sullivan wished this farce would end. Talitha hadn't needed them to hold hands and listen to a fire. Behind him, a shepherd growled. He cracked an eye. Nova looked perfectly composed. Henry threw Sullivan a small smile. *What can we do about it?* he seemed to say.

"We're attempting to pierce the veil between the world you know and the world of the dead," Nova told them. "Focus on my voice, on the fire."

Well, which is it? Sullivan wanted to snark. Rhys gripped his hand tighter. How could he find the patience for this charade? Talitha had told them to get out.

"I feel us nearing the threshold," Nova intoned. "We are close."

Wind gusted, then died. It might have been spooky if Sullivan believed Nova was the real deal. Heads bowed, as if in prayer, they looked like a circle of fundamentalists at prayer meeting. If Nova was psychic, wouldn't she have sensed the ghosts in the house? They'd have walked past the little boy on the porch.

"You!" Nova's eyes snapped open, and she pointed at Sullivan.

"Me?" he asked.

"Your doubt in the paranormal is impeding this seance!" As if to emphasize her words, Nova jabbed in his direction again. "You'll have to leave, sir!"

"I can only assure you I believe in the paranormal," Sullivan replied. It felt drearily typical, and he couldn't decide if her accusation demanded laughter or fury.

"Get it together," Ash told him.

"I have it together!" Sullivan might have tolerated Nova's idiocy, but his brother knew better. "You think I don't believe in the paranormal? Lemme tell you—"

"Spare us," Ash said. "Sit your ass down and close your eyes."

"Okay, okay." Rhys held up his hands as if facing a gunslinger. "We *know* he believes in the paranormal. Sullivan, why don't you just—"

"I won't 'just' do anything! Why am I getting blamed for this?" He crossed his arms over his chest, hands tucked at his sides, like he was daring his cousins to grab them. "Talitha didn't complain about people harshing her vibe!"

Olivia covered her giggle—poorly—with a huffing snort. Rhys threw him a pleading look. Whitney and Judah regarded him with a mix of contempt and pity; Ash's glare never changed. If pushed, he'd babble about Ethan and money and lawsuits. Sullivan shut his eyes and held out his hands. He wasn't going to win, and he hardly knew what winning looked like, anyway. No one won at those things, not really. He could only hope for a bloody stalemate.

"Listen to the fire," Nova said again. "Become one with its primal energy. We are seeking to pierce the veil between worlds." She said more, mostly New Age psychobabble about reaching beyond. Sullivan drifted. Dread brooded low in his belly. *You need to get out*, Talitha had said. *We wouldn't leave*, Rhys had told him. *We can't. We're Trenholms.*

The house shuddered and seemed to hunch as wind gusted again. Windows rattled like shrapnel-fire, and everyone jumped—those low clouds had broken into a furious storm, the first rain in weeks. "It's just the weather," Nova said, and when Sullivan cracked his eyes, hers were still closed. "You'd be surprised how often that happens. Focus, people, please. We're nearly there."

Sullivan breathed in smoke and ozone. Neither scent boded well, especially since the farm was far overdue for a lightning strike. He'd promised to stay, and there he remained, against his better judgment. Rain battered the windows, walls, roofs in a numbing tattoo;

like a drawn bowstring, the farm seemed to wait, tensed. Olivia's hand clutched his, and a dog growled, a low, curdled sound.

"I sense the presence." Nova's voice turned graveled. Head thrown back, she slumped against the couch, and only the whites of her eyes showed. "The dead are with us," she intoned.

Olivia's grip tightened. Something wasn't right. The air had become gaspingly thick.

"Speak to me," Nova said.

This struck Sullivan as a very bad idea, and he sensed that whatever brooded there agreed. Rain surged to a deafening pound, as if something beyond reason beat time upon the house. When he tried to draw a deep breath, the atmosphere seemed strangely airless. The fire burned too low, and orange shadows danced evilly, like inkblots.

"Speak!" Nova ordered, almost shrieked, and Olivia nearly cut off his circulation. Sullivan might have complained if he wasn't cutting off hers, and Rhys's too.

Judah wrenched backward. Marionette-like, he jerked once. For a long, falling moment, he was still, and the room with him. Even the shadows seemed motionless, as if the farm crouched, waiting.

"I told you to speak!" Nova ordered.

Judah's mouth contorted into that ugly grin, the toothy one. It reminded Sullivan of an angry gorilla, all fang. "Time twists like mating snakes," Judah said, and his jagged, hoarse voice chilled Sullivan's spine. Whatever was in him had actually come through. "It coils around and spirals. Here, the future is the past is the future."

Olivia had the look of a panicked deer, half a breath from bolting; Rhys managed to gape and wince at the same time. Whitney plastered herself to the back of the couch. Clearly, this had veered into something far more frightening than she'd hoped.

"Come out of him." Nova's words rang with command, and Judah stiffened. His back arched; a thick black vapor stretched from his throat, a substance like smoke that seemed to have heft, weight. Olivia stifled a scream. At the same moment, the dogs wailed, and a frenzied scrambling went up behind the couch. Bolting from the circle, they cowered against the far wall, howling, as the stream grew thicker, blacker. When it forked into three pieces, Sullivan knew. He wanted to flee, but his cousins clung to his hands. The smoke-shadow poured from Judah like water, like blood, gouts of it hemorrhaging, congealing. Judah convulsed again. He hacked as if he was choking on black shadow, then the last of it spewed from him, and he lay still.

Sullivan was dry-mouthed, and his heart beat like a small, trapped bird. Rhys's hand shook in his; Nova's eyes were wide, terrified. He'd been right about her, but there was no satisfaction in it.

The three forms split, then solidified into three identical men in old-fashioned top hats. Black, they were made of shadows, as if light fell on them and disappeared there. As one, the men lifted their right arms and touched their hat brims.

"Was, were, am, are, will be," they said. "Be, been, being."

Sullivan shut his eyes tight. He wouldn't look at the men. If he looked, they might snatch him away—

"The end is the beginning," the men chanted. "In the beginning, you find the end."

"Don't look at them!" Sullivan managed to shout. "Don't you fucking look!" But a need to see tugged at him, the raw panic of a terrified animal. Fear warred with sanity. They couldn't take him as long as he held onto Rhys—

"You are this place and this place is you," the men said.

Unable to stand it, Sullivan flew up, to run, to at least hit the wall and put distance between him and the men. His feet touched the floor. The fire was suddenly, viciously snuffed; lightning struck, and a thunderclap staggered the house. Sullivan felt it in his teeth. Reflexively, he grabbed the couch. The dogs leapt up, barking; Olivia screamed. Rhys fell on him. There was a lot of confusion and cursing then, a lot of scrambling and grabbing, his back slapping the cushions and his cousin's hand in his, the one sure thing. They froze. The scrambling stopped, and they stayed like that, breathing hard. Someone said, "Are you okay?"

"Power's off." Ash word's seemed snatched, as if his childhood asthma had returned.

"Here." Some scraping; a match struck.

The men were gone. Whitney looked stricken. Judah was sitting up, pale and shaking, and the dogs piled around Olivia. Light wavered as Henry relit the fire.

"Where's Nova?" Sullivan asked.

"I don't—I don't know?" Rhys said.

Ash scrambled up. Nova Shaw's car was in the drive, but when they searched the house, top to bottom, no one could find her.

CHAPTER 49

RHYS

By two a.m., the power returned, and Legare County's finest arrived. Sheriff Cash Briggs was a rangy man, over six feet, with wavy blond hair and stubble that showed off his chiseled jaw. A plug of tobacco snugged in his cheek, a handgun riding at his hip, he moseyed into the downstairs library with the lazy, rolling stride of a jungle cat. Rhys liked him immediately and instinctively. Ash walked beside him, phone jammed in his ear. He appeared to be on hold.

"Hello, small-town sheriff," Sullivan said under his breath.

Rhys smacked his cousin's shoulder. "Behave. Nova's missing."

Sullivan stood, hand out. "You must be Sheriff Briggs. Sullivan Trenholm. This is my cousin, Rhys."

The sheriff had a working man's grip and calluses. "Cash Briggs. I hear y'all had a woman disappear on you tonight? Mind if I sit?"

"Please." Sullivan gestured at the sofa next to him, but the sheriff took the chair. The camera swooped closer, and Ash disappeared again. God forbid they didn't film their interrogation.

"So, Nova Shaw." The sheriff flipped open his pad and snagged a pen tucked improbably behind his ear. "Your brother said on the phone earlier that she disappeared during one of your investigations earlier tonight? 'Bout what time was that?"

What helpful information could they possibly hand him? Nova had vanished along with the three men; they couldn't find her anywhere. Ash had only called the sheriff because it seemed remiss not to, at least to the cameramen. Nova would reappear or not; Sheriff Briggs and his deputies could do nothing about it. Lewis had said as much, half under his breath, when Ash summoned him and Boo and Sinclair from their beds in the guest house. Ash had simply glared.

"Uh, Nova disappeared about two hours ago?" Sullivan told the sheriff. "The fire went out. When Henry lit it again, she was gone. We have no idea what happened to her."

"I assume there were cameras?" the sheriff asked.

"The cameramen say the equipment cut when, uh. . ." He glanced at Rhys, who shrugged. One of them had to say it eventually.

"When?" The sheriff straightened, as if this was the hint he'd waited for.

"Our second cousin Judah had some kind of entity attached to him?" Sullivan spoke as if he was in pain. "I know you've heard rumors. And before you ask, I had Talitha out here, and it went bad, and this was *not* my idea—"

The sheriff held up his hand. "What happened here tonight, Mister Trenholm?"

"I'm getting there!" Sullivan protested, defensiveness snapping in his tone. "So Talitha wouldn't let Ash film her—*not that I blame her*—and it went bad, so Ash's executive producer sent out this woman, Nova Shaw? He said she was a psychic, but that's a big fat maybe. So she orders whatever's in Judah to come out, which she says is a dead person when Talitha *swore* it was something that was never alive and not even from this *plane of existence*—"

"So am I to understand this was some sort of demonic possession-type situation?" The sheriff shoved his hat back slightly. It might have been funny, those words in the mouth of a small-town Southern sheriff, but it was happening in Rhys's house, and it was real, and it wasn't funny, not at all.

"No." Sullivan slumped backward. He looked frayed suddenly, tattered. "It wasn't demonic possession. Talitha said not. It was time."

"Excuse me?" The sheriff glanced up from his pad. "Time for what?"

"Whatever came out of Judah was time." Sullivan swiped his face, as if he was sweaty, or tired, or had finally given up. "He was possessed by time."

The sheriff seemed to take him in. "You can't get possessed by time, son," he said finally. "I think you need to lie down." He turned to Rhys. "Were any drugs or alcohol consumed at the house tonight?"

"What? No!" Rhys spluttered, though he knew he shouldn't have; there was no other rational response to his cousin. Of course they must be drunk. Rational men didn't think these things, let alone say them to a sheriff. "I mean, some beer at dinner, but not like you're implying."

"Could you tell me approximately how much beer you consumed at dinner?" the sheriff asked.

"One beer each." Sullivan stared at the ceiling. "Two for me. Then after Nova told whatever was in Judah to come out, this black stuff poured out of him, and it became three men. They tipped their hats and chanted, then the fire went out. When Henry lit again, they were gone and so was she, and that's what happened. Believe us or don't. Whatever. You can't find her. Nova will only come back if it wants to let her go."

Maybe, when Elliot had seen the men, and Sullivan before her, they had gone somewhere else during the missing time they experienced. Nova might reappear on the farm in eight hours, confused but whole. Hadn't two children disappeared, only to show up hours later in the same place? Rhys opened his mouth to ask, but the sheriff spoke instead. "She'll only come back if *what* wants to let her go?"

"Time," Sullivan said, again toward the ceiling.

The sheriff stood. Narrow-eyed, he looked at Sullivan like he might have regarded an undersized bass, too small to keep, then strode out. Rhys caught up to him. "Sullivan's not drunk or deluded," he told Sheriff Briggs. "This stuff happens out here. Like he said, you've heard the rumors. Didn't Ash have you to investigate some kids disappearing?"

The sheriff neither stopped nor turned as he walked down the curving stairs. "I'm just trying to find a missing woman. Why don't you go back to your cousin, son? I think he could use some help."

Someone else expected Rhys to wrangle Sullivan, and it should have annoyed him. Instead, he was grateful. There was need, and he could help. Rhys found comfort in that simplicity, and it humbled him. "Yeah, I probably ought to get back to him," he replied. Leaving the sheriff on the stairs, he went back to the library. Sullivan still stared at the ceiling.

"He was hot," his cousin said, unmoving.

"You're fucking ridiculous." Rhys collapsed next to him. The Victorians had constructed their couches with dramatics in mind.

"It's that or think about the men," Sullivan told him. "I'd rather think about the sheriff."

Rhys knew better than to suggest bed. Ash would kill them—sleep seemed a kind of treason when he'd summoned Lewis, Boo, and Sinclair. Olivia and Henry were upstairs; the deputies had woken Elliot, and she was terrified. Whitney and Judah were huddled in the living room; their second cousin seemed no better or worse than before. There was nothing for them to do. Rhys stared at the ceiling too. And silently, he and Sullivan waited for whatever came next.

CHAPTER 50

ASH

Ash paced back and forth, back and forth through HQ. For nearly an hour, he'd been calling Ethan, and the producer wasn't picking up. Ash was being ignored, a punishment and not-so-subtle fuck-you. *Here's your place in the pecking order,* Ethan was telling him. *You're expendable, and you're going to wait.* Ash kept calling. He imagined Ethan lotused amid tinkling spa music and natural wood, perhaps in a yurt. Or maybe he was wrong: maybe Ethan was dancing between throbbing bass and blonde starlets, cocaine on a mirrored tabletop. Ash had only seen cocaine in movies. He'd avoided it in college, when certain members of his fraternity regarded it as a weekend partying staple. "Dad'll kill you," he'd said to Sullivan once, as his brother slipped off to the bathroom again. Sullivan had rewarded him with a flat-eyed stare, as if he were focused not at his eyes but the inside of his skull. Maybe it was the cocaine.

"God-*dammit!*" Ash kicked at the mahogany table leg, but he didn't hurl his phone. He needed his phone. The dogs watched from a heap beneath the whiteboard, recrimination in their mild eyes. Henry had herded Olivia to bed, and Ash had abandoned law enforcement to the space cadets. That was a mistake. Jamming his phone in his back pocket, he started toward the library. He got as far as the doorway before nearly colliding with the sheriff.

"Now that you're off the phone, you wanna tell me what happened here tonight?" Cash Briggs asked.

"Oh, Christ. Didn't Sullivan and Rhys take care of that?" Ash had provided a description of Nova and fled.

The sheriff pulled out a chair and planted himself like he planned on taking up residence. "Your brother told me some cocked-up story about your second cousin getting possessed by time. I don't guess you want me to pull a warrant and search his room for drugs."

"Sullivan doesn't have—" Except he probably did. Damn his brother to hell, and his cousin, too. "Sullivan's not intoxicated," Ash said instead.

"Uh-huh." Sheriff Briggs seemed to take in the bulletin board, its UAP photos and hand-scrawled notes. One more time, Ash felt like a basement-dwelling conspiracy theorist. "So maybe you could tell me what happened here tonight."

"Let me guess. Sullivan told you there was some kind of seance with Judah?" Ash asked. "The fire went out, and Nova disappeared. Didn't take her purse with her. It's right here, and you saw her car on the way in." He elided the supernatural details. Best to keep it simple.

The sheriff made no move toward the purse, a paisley bag heavy enough, and patterned enough, to make a fair murder weapon. "Your brother said some kind of spirit came out of that guy?"

"Maybe," Ash hedged. "It was dark." Sure as the day was long something had come out of Judah, but he wouldn't be the one to say it. "He and his fiancée Whitney are down in the living room."

"I'll need to talk to them, please, and anyone else who was there. You said you searched the house?" The sheriff wrote something on his notepad, but Ash could make no sense of his chicken-scratch. He might as well have drawn hieroglyphics.

"We searched the house," Ash replied. "We have Boo and Sinclair and Lewis searching it again, not that it'll do any good." *This is useless,* Lewis had said, pissed-off and rumple-shirted. *You know the farm took her.*

"Here's what I'm gonna do." The sheriff set a radio on the table; it looked brown and old next to Ash's slick tech. "I'm gonna call for backup and have deputies search this farm while Vick Finley and I take statements from whoever saw this woman last. I'll level with you. I know things turn screwy at this place. I'm hoping she shows up again, like those kids—"

Ash's phone rang. He slid it from his pocket.

"Excuse me," he said to the sheriff. "I have to take this."

Ash slipped into the sleeping porch, then out the door to the patio. It seemed strangely empty without parrots, spirited inside during the storm. Rain dripped from the eaves, and humidity clung like the breath of some primordial beast. "You're not gonna like this," he said to Ethan.

"You're sure as shit I don't like it!" Inside Ash's chest, something slithered, unmoored. "The crew called me. You fucking *lost her?* You lost Nova Shaw? You want to tell me how the fuck that happened?"

He didn't, not really. Darkness brooded in the lemon trees, too close. Flowers littered the ground; their scent hung in the still, steaming air. After that storm the night had a washed-up, shipwrecked feel, and Ash wanted to sleep, to forget. "She just vanished," he told the producer. "I had nothing to do with it."

"You need to find her," Ethan said.

"We called the sheriff—"

"I don't fucking care what clown-ass local law enforcement you called. You *find her,* but I hope you film every single piece of this, because I hear the crew got a whole fucking lot of nothing. They got sound with blank film? They're fired as soon as my guys find their replacements, because I need more footage *right now.* You find her, but you film every second in the meantime, do you hear me? I want you to wring every inch of dramatic tension from that goddamn search, do you hear me? *Every goddamn inch.*"

To Ash, dramatic tension seemed measured by weight, not length, but it felt imprudent to mention. Something flashed in the garden, a light that shouldn't be there—maybe his cousins searching for Nova, maybe something else. Unable to stand the darkness any longer, Ash returned to the sleeping porch. "I'll make sure they're filming," he replied.

"You sure as shit will," Ethan told him. "And you'll find Nova, too. The casting agency will be on us like white on rice."

"Casting agency?" Ash passed inside and picked up a carved earthenware crane. Mud-colored, it fit snug in his fist.

Ethan laughed, one sharp bark. "Do you know how long it would take to find a psychic?"

Ash dropped hard onto an ancient wicker settee; its wood crackled worryingly. Wide windows showed his own rumpled reflection. "She wasn't a real psychic?"

"Oh my God." That laugh again, more suited to Ash's shepherds than a man. "You really thought we called a real one."

Ash hung up. Really, he hit the "off" button, and wished vaguely for the fuck-you physicality of banging down a landline. Of course Nova wasn't a psychic, and so of course that seance, or exorcism, or perhaps visitation had ended in total disaster. If a cosmic intelligence did control the farm, a contingency Ash neither believed nor discounted, it had licked its chops and tied on a dinner napkin when Nova Shaw sashayed over the threshold. People handed Ash disasters from the custodial to familial to cosmic, then expected him to clean them up.

Ash dropped his head in his hands. He couldn't decide if he should weep, laugh, or punch a hole in the wall. He stayed that way, motionless, maybe trying to decide, or maybe waiting for someone to decide for him, and he was still sitting with his head in his hands when Olivia spoke.

"Henry says the sheriff wants us," she said.

Ash looked up. Olivia wore yoga pants and a t-shirt that certainly belonged to her boyfriend. Ash could have been sitting that way for two minutes or twenty. "Who told Henry the sheriff wanted you?" he asked.

"Rhys." She dropped next to him.

"Who has Elliot?" Ash lifted his head. He could care about Elliot.

"Calm down. Henry has Elliot."

Better Henry than Rhys and Sullivan. "Ethan said Nova wasn't a real psychic." He probably shouldn't have told her.

"Is this news to you?" Olivia crossed her ankles, back straight, a debutante posture incongruous with her athleisure.

Ash struggled. How had his cousin known? "We have to find her," he said, unable to bear an admission of his own gullibility.

"The sheriff called in some deputies," Olivia replied.

They lapsed into silence. The dogs flopped at Olivia's feet. They were good dogs, devoted, serious about their jobs. If no women were around, they'd follow Ash, and they'd hold their ground to any living threat. Only paranormal ones sent them running, and thank God for it. Ash could live with losing a drone, but he'd never forgive himself if the farm snatched one of his dogs. He dug his bare toes into Q's fur. It helped, somehow, brought him back to earth. The dog's tail thumped on the carpet. Sullivan was right; it did look like something from the Luxor. You sacrificed yourself for history. You gave and gave until you bled, and what did you get, really? An ugly carpet. Guilt that kept you up at night. A brother who hated you, talked behind your back, and a lifetime of cleaning up everyone else's messes—

"We ought to make coffee for those deputies." Ash stood, and the settee crackled again, as if its wicker might splinter.

"Guess we should." When Olivia rose, so did the dogs.

"Can we talk about what came out of Judah?" she asked as they dragged out the massive coffee pot, scaled and scarred from years of Trenholm parties.

"No," Ash replied.

They didn't mention it again. Cars arrived. "I'll finish this up if you want to go meet them," Olivia said.

One more mess he had to take care of. Ash dragged himself to the front door, out to the porch. The sheriff was barking directions to a clot of deputies. Despite their MagLites and pressed uniforms, they had bleary eyes and tousled hair, an air of little boys caught night-wandering. "There's coffee in the kitchen," Ash said.

"Oh sweet baby Jesus." Congaree High's former champion defensive lineman, Denver McAllister, shifted his weight onto both legs. Even Ash knew he'd blown his knee senior year and never played another game. "Let us get some coffee 'fore we go running across this place, boss."

"Five minutes," the sheriff said. "We got a woman missing, boys."

"It's this way, y'all," Ash told them, and the men clomped into the house behind him. They'd certainly track mud in; he wished he'd kept the plastic on the carpet, however ugly. Amelia would ask McKayla and Madison to help clean it up. Madison would make a very pointed joke, something like, *Next time a woman goes missing, put the plastic down*, or *Tell those deputies to wipe their damn feet*. Teasing but serious, and blaming Ash for it.

In the kitchen, Olivia was all demure smiles. She poured coffee and murmured appropriate pleasantries. *How's your mama? Your sister? She was always so sweet. How's her boy? How's your daddy?* Ash couldn't tell if she genuinely remembered or if Olivia knew Southern passcodes well enough to fake it. It didn't matter. When she mentioned their families, those deputies stopped staring at her and spoke in low, quiet tones. She set out a tray of cookies and another of sliced fruit, which Ash recognized as Henry's breakfast. No one noticed the woman at the stove. She stared at the wall; she did not move. Unconsciously, the company seemed to avoid her, as if she was as solid as Ash.

Maybe she was. Ash had never tried reaching for those Black men and women who peopled his home. He didn't have the heart to inflict that indignity.

The sheriff set his hat on the counter. He spoke to Olivia; she smiled, though the expression didn't reach her eyes. He asked her about Charleston, about what brought her back to Cypress Bend. How long was she there, and how long did she plan on staying? Briggs was perfectly polite, but transparent about his interest in her.

Henry appeared in the doorway, Elliot pale at his side. She crossed the kitchen to Ash, and the dogs galloped to her.

Eyes on the floor, Olivia was telling the sheriff that she didn't know how long she'd be home. He leaned on the counter next to her, a posture somehow offensive in its mildness. Henry squared his shoulders and strode to Olivia; she startled as he wrapped a proprietary arm around her waist. Henry spoke into her ear, and the sheriff shoved off the counter.

"Time's up, y'all!" he called.

Ash turned away.

The cameras were rolling as Briggs gathered his deputies on the front porch again. A few had hound dogs at their sides. The shepherds arrayed themselves in front of Ash and Elliot, as if they sensed trickery. As the men milled around, finishing their coffee, Ash tried not to look at the dark drawn taut a finger-length beyond the potted jasmine. He tried not to think of three men. They had Nova. He'd managed to shove back thoughts of her, of that smoke bleeding from Judah. He should have listened to Sullivan. The house dripped sullenly, steadily; men and dogs steamed in the night-heat. Ash swiped at his forehead. Leaning against the brick, Boo and Lewis had the air of petty officers, inclined to distrust the regular military rabble.

"I need you in pairs!" Briggs shouted. "It's dark as the devil's basement out here, and stay together, y'hear me? I'm not stopping the search to look for one of y'all. All y'all got a map?"

The men nodded and brandished papers at him. Someone must have lifted them from the piles by the front door.

"Carroll! McGregor! You two go west, into the gardens and the back field. Forest, you and Baker are gonna take the barns and the Pavilion to the south. Mac and Hewitt, y'all are gonna look north, to the cabins and the cemetery. Henley and Garcia, y'all go east, you got the gift shop all the way on down to the gate house. Anyone see anything, y'all got radios. Priority goes to buildings, check them before you go haring off into the brush. I sent her pic to y'all's phones, so look at it good before y'all go out. Any questions?"

"Do I call the tipline if I see a UFO?" one guy asked. The deputies laughed.

Ash made himself smile. "You sure do," he told them. "Y'all see anything strange, make sure you radio, and we'll get a crew on out there to you."

"Don't you fucking do that," the sheriff said. "This is an active investigation."

"Y'all's radios look real outdated," Ash replied, hating himself, hating Ethan, hating the tangle of history and blood, land and family that drove him to this particular madness. "It'd be nice if you had some new ones. Maybe some to go in your cruisers, too. Did y'all like the ones you saw in the house?"

"Let us know if y'all see anything strange," the sheriff said, and Ash knew he'd won.

The deputies broke off, lights bobbing forlornly as they walked into the dark. Worried an orb might pop up between them, Ash tracked each one as it left. When he finally turned away, he noticed Sullivan and Rhys next to Boo. Ash braced for his brother's ugliness—Sullivan would offer something pithy and withering about the radios, a cutting bit of sarcasm that would leave him wincing.

Sullivan and Rhys passed through the door. His brother said nothing.

Briggs and his head deputy, another Hollywood cop type, interviewed Henry and Olivia, then Whitney and Judah. "I got the same damn story from all of them," the sheriff said. "That room she disappeared from, does it have doors that close?"

"Yeah," Ash said.

"I need to see it," he replied.

Ash sent Elliot upstairs with Olivia, then showed Briggs and his deputies to the salon. Under the ridiculous Grecian mantle, the fire had dwindled to scrimmed embers. Ash flicked on a lamp. Furniture still clustered near the room's center, and the sofa lay on its back, legs in the air. It looked oddly obscene. "There's nothing here," Sullivan said from the doorway. "I told you, she's gone, and she won't come back til they decide to let her go."

The sheriff barely glanced up. He squatted next to the sofa, where he seemed to be examining the floor. Was he looking for fibers? Scorch marks? Did he even know what he was looking for? "I need you to leave, please. I'd like to talk to your brother alone, and you're not helping this investigation."

"You're not helping this investigation," Sullivan replied. "Ash, why did you bother calling them? You know those men took her. She's not coming back til they're done with—whatever they're done with. Boo and Lewis and Sinclair know it. So do you."

Dawn would come soon, and Ash had been awake for nearly twenty-four hours. "Go to bed," he told his brother. "Rhys, take him to bed."

"You treat him like he needs a handler." Rhys leaned in the doorway next to Sullivan. Those sabers glinted above them, inescapable. Ash hated them. His father should have left them to rust, like everything else in that house.

"I treat him like he needs a handler because he needs a handler," Ash said, unable to stop himself. The deputy whistled low, but he didn't look up from the floor, either. Ash hated him, too. Without glancing to his left, where the camera's blank black eye hovered, he knew it was focused on him.

"This is insane." Sullivan flipped the couch onto its legs, a sudden thump that startled everyone. "The three men leak out of Judah's fucking mouth and you just call the cops about it? We're going to stand around and pretend Nova just wandered off? Am I taking crazy pills over here?"

"You're sure as hell acting like it, son." The sheriff straightened, a slow and conscious gesture. It carried something of the spaghetti western, those serious men with ready guns, intent on their own brand of law and order. "But you can stay. Shut that door behind you, though. I don't want anyone out there to hear what I'm about to say. You probably want that camera to leave, though."

"The camera stays," Ash said—Ethan would kill him if he banished it. Rhys closed the door. The dogs barked. He opened it again, and they dashed in to pile at Ash's feet, offering something of a bulwark against whatever misery would come. After the high strangeness of Judah's exorcism, the room seemed mundane, or as mundane as rooms in Cypress Bend ever seemed, all grand plantation drapes and Greek revivalism.

"You people keep mentioning these men," the sheriff said. "I'd ask you to describe them, but I already got descriptions. You're gonna level with me." The sheriff stepped closer. Ash topped out at five eleven, but Cash Briggs was at least six two, all lean muscle, like he spent whatever spare time he had in contemplative sweating with his weight bench. The dogs stood, but none growled. "You think I've been Legare County Sheriff for five years without seeing my fair share of weird? I thought you called me to deal with something I could get my hands around, and your brother was spouting bullshit. But I got the same story from every person who saw that fire go out. Don't tell me I got my boys over here to mess with something above my goddamn pay grade. And before you ask, someone possessed by time, like your brother says? That's way the fuck above my pay grade."

"I, uh, didn't call you about the possession," Ash managed.

"You gonna tell me they're not related?" the sheriff asked. His deputy leaned against the couch, a silent audience. "'Cause they seem real goddamn related."

"I told you to leave it alone." Sullivan wouldn't let it go, and Ash wished his brother would shut up. "I told you, Talitha said—"

"You really did have Talitha out here, didn't you?" Briggs said. "We're done here. If the woman's missing for twenty-four hours, y'all can call us back, and we'll talk about it then." He strode from the room, his deputy behind him. The camera followed.

Ash sank to the sofa. Victorian, carved with an eagle, it had probably been purchased new by Trenholms long-dead. His father could have told him who bought it, and who died on it; someone almost certainly had. Ethan would sue him to pauperhood, and the tabloids would laugh him into the grave. "I told you," Sullivan said, three words only, and he and Rhys turned to go. They were shutting the door behind them when the dogs sprang into a fury of barking.

Ash jerked up.

Eyes lifted like a dime-store Madonna, Nova Shaw stood in front of him. Her arms wrapped her chest, and her red-painted toes, once hidden in heels, were streaked with dirt. Nova's lips moved, then pursed. She tried again, words a graveled whisper he couldn't quite catch, then a third time.

"Time is a crow with two beaks."

The dogs went suddenly, eerily silent when she spoke. Sullivan blew through a string of curses; Ash sprang up and grabbed Nova's shoulder. It felt frail in his hand, a thin twig. "Are you okay?" he asked. "Where'd you go? You were gone for—God, hours."

Slowly, as if looking away from eternity, her gaze dropped. "I went to the swords."

"Jesus fucking Christ," Rhys intoned behind him, something like a prayer.

"Why don't we, uh—let's get you sitting down." Ash guided her into a chair. Nova's eyes stayed glazed, fixed ahead, as if an invisible figure hung before her. Sullivan went for water, Rhys to tell the sheriff they'd found her. "You're fucking joking," the sheriff was saying as he strode in. Then he saw Nova. "Hey, Vick," Briggs said into his radio. "They really did find her. Get EMS over here."

It went quickly after that. The sheriff called for a blanket. Whitney appeared with Judah. He seemed grayer, dimmer than before, and Ash's hopes sagged. "How you doing, man?" he asked his cousin.

Judah ignored him.

When EMS appeared, Nova's semi-religious vagueness seemed to clear. "I don't need help!" she snapped. "I saw *time*. Get your hands off me!"

After EMTS called her emergency contact, a sister in Lexington, they bundled her off to Lower Richland anyway. Whitney herded Judah back to the car. Boo, Sinclair, and Lewis grumbled back to bed. The family stood on the porch as early fog clung under the live oaks; mold had bloomed in the night's storm, and a strangely old smell hung over the morning. It was the first rain for several long weeks, and the ground was sopped with it.

The ambulance pulled away, and they watched it go.

CHAPTER 51

SULLIVAN

Nova didn't seem sick enough for sirens, but emergency lights blued the morning mist as the ambulance trundled away. No birds sang in the storm-wrecked morning. Branches littered the front garden; roses petals shone startlingly red on the paths, like blood. Sullivan cracked his back. Last night had stretched into the unimaginable, then interminable. For once, he could trust sleep's vagaries, though something huge seemed to brood over the Cypress Bend, as if a giant held his breath, poised to snatch them up. Lightning had finally come, almost a relief. He didn't dare think about the men.

"She was an actress," Ash said. Palm against the wooden rocker, he stared after the ambulance. Exhaustion sagged his face into lines.

Of course Nova was an actress, but Sullivan had hoped his brother didn't know for sure. The terrific betrayal snatched his breath. "You lied to us," he managed.

The statement settled in the dawn quiet. Ash watched the ambulance lights disappear. "I didn't lie to you," he said. "Ethan lied to me. He told me when I called to say she was missing. It doesn't matter, though." His brother kept looking over that sweep of land, like it could show him something that might yet save them all. "We'd've done it anyway, whether she was an actress or a psychic or the Man in the Moon."

Sullivan clenched his fist. Elliot stood next to Ash. "No, we wouldn't have. We shouldn't have done it in the first place, I told you Talitha said—"

"It doesn't matter what she said," his brother replied. "We signed contracts."

"Fuck the contracts!" The debacle felt emblematic, a sum of grievances rather than the thing itself. Sullivan had promised to salvage something, but that vow seemed unreachable in the storm's grim wreckage. "Do you care what happened to Judah last night? Have you thought about what he might have opened in the house? Let's do a brief recap, Ash—"

"Let's not," Olivia snapped, head tilted at Elliot.

"Your problem is that you don't understand what a contract means," Ash said, eyes still on that driveway. His words were quiet, unruffled. "It's a promise, Sullivan. Have you heard of those? I know you have trouble with commitment."

Sullivan could have choked on his own inchoate anger. Rhys touched his shoulder. So many times, it calmed him down, brought him back. He resisted ducking away. "Ash didn't mean that," his cousin told him. "He's real tired. I'm sure Ash is upset about Ethan lying to him. Aren't you, Ash?"

"Even Sullivan will see through that," Ash said. He straightened; the rocking chair creaked backward. "You're gonna have to try harder."

"C'mon." Olivia wrapped an arm around Elliot's shoulders. "We need to go up to bed."

Elliot hunched up miserably. Barefoot, she still wore a robe.

"C'mon." Olivia tried to draw her away. Elliot murmured something and inched closer to Ash.

Olivia made her face serious, like a mother's. "Elliot. You need to go up to bed."

"If I leave, y'all'll fight for real!" Elliot shouted. Her words hung like the fog in that early-morning quiet. She was right. Sullivan loved her for it, because he couldn't hate her, not Elliot.

"We already were, honey," Ash told her. He rounded on Sullivan. "When are you going to understand," he said, voice poisonous, "what we have to do here? This farm depends on you now. Do I have to spell it out? We fill this contract, or we lose it. Keep Ethan happy, or all these people are unemployed. There's nowhere else to work in this town but the chicken plant. They'll lose their houses and their health insurance, every last one of them. They'll leave or they'll pluck chickens. So we shut up, Sullivan, and we do our fucking job."

His words bloomed and grew, choking in the rising dawn. They echoed from the porch's wet brick, and no one spoke. Rhys's hand lay heavy on his shoulder; the sun etched age-lines on his brother's forehead, around his mouth.

"Talitha told us to leave," Sullivan finally replied, struggling to keep his voice level, calm. "Maybe it's better if they lose their jobs and get out. You want them to end up like Judah?"

"They know where the door is," Ash told him. "Do you really want to go through this? Again? Don't you get tired of it?"

There was no help for it. Sullivan went inside while his brother said something about exits and dramatics. He and Rhys climbed the stairs in silence. The three men had appeared in the house, and it felt invaded, haunted. Something had opened there; Sullivan wasn't sure if Judah carried it with him, or if it remained. He'd seen so many horrors unfold at the farm, but seldom any so vivid. He stripped to boxer-briefs. For a precious few moments, he'd believed in sleep again. After that near-fight with Ash, it wouldn't happen.

"He's tired," Rhys said, finally breaking their silence. "He didn't mean it."

"He meant every word." When Sullivan flopped down, his back banged his steel baseball bat. "He has to be right."

His cousin didn't reply. Sullivan lay awake in the TV's aquarium glow. Images flickered, and day crept below the blinds. The images meant something. He ought to concentrate on them but he kept thinking about the men made of smoke. *Time is a crow with two beaks.*

Eventually, exhausted beyond reason, his eyes closed. Fighting sleep, he slept anyway.

Rhys was still out when Sullivan woke, tangled in his sheets, heart pounding. He couldn't remember the dream that terrified him—something about the vastness of time, how it lapped like an endless tide, repetitive, wearing. Stale with sweat, he showered and contemplated his next move, complicated by tourists. Cypress Bend had killed his running habit. Rhys complained he was gaining weight from Mickie's cooking; Sullivan spent meals pushing food around his plate, and he'd gone down two belt holes. *You should take better care of yourself,* he wished someone would say. *Eat more, Sullivan. Drink some water.* His therapist would tell him that adulthood meant taking responsibility for yourself. But was it so bad to want someone else to care? *You're getting thin,* they'd fuss at him. *Stop this nonsense. You'll waste away.*

He'd eat if he smoked some weed. He'd forget about that bad dream, too. He'd chase away thoughts of the three men, who were time.

Sullivan opened his underwear drawer and rummaged. At the back, instead of the joint he'd hidden, his fingers hit an edged piece of paper. An old photograph, folded up—Cypress Bend was full of them, tucked in odd places. He uncreased it. In the distilled yellow light of summer, three teenage boys grinned toothily at the camera, arms slung over each other's shoulders. They slouched together on Cypress Bend's front porch, each dressed in a t-shirt and cargo shorts. *Best friends*, read the back. *Sullivan, Henry, and Rhys, 2008.*

For more than a decade, Sullivan hadn't seen a photo of himself at that age, much less Henry and Rhys. Henry, something like seventeen, smiled as goofily as the distant cousins flanking him. The three of them were hardly older than Elliot. But Henry had already seen his relatives mowed down by Yankee bullets, had slogged through something like two years of war—he was a child. He'd seemed so old then, world-weary and self-possessed. Sullivan had looked up to him. It had seemed unimaginable that Henry was too young to make his own decisions.

That grin, that slung arm, the baby face—did Henry even shave regularly?—they told him otherwise. Henry had been a child-soldier. What had Rhys said, when Sullivan stalked out of that restaurant? *He was only a kid*, Rhys had told him. *If you blame him for it, you have to blame us for the same thing.*

We were terrorized into believing in the Lost Cause, Sullivan had once told his therapist. *We thought it was right because the alternative was too awful to contemplate.*

Rhys had hit his growth spurt before Sullivan; in the photo, his shoulders slanted higher than Henry's. Their relatives had handed a child a gun, had marched him north to fight for the right to own human beings.

And Sullivan had blamed the child himself for their crimes.

The photo trembled in his hands. He was close to tears when snuffling told him Rhys had awakened. "What are you doing?" his cousin asked.

Sullivan shoved the photo among his boxer shorts. "Looking for weed," he said. "You want to smoke up?"

"I just *woke up*." Rhys pawed the sleep from his eyes. "Jesus, Sullivan. Have some breakfast first."

"I don't want breakfast. Weed is supposed to fix that." It was a logical solution, but his cousin frowned and scrambled from bed, overly motivated for a man who'd just blinked himself awake.

"Come on," Rhys said, checking the time. "Mickie's probably taking a nap before dinner, but I know where she keeps the bacon."

"I haven't smoked yet." Sullivan edged the photograph farther into the drawer.

"I'll make you bacon," Rhys said.

"You can't cook," Sullivan told him. "You don't even know where the frying pan is, and tourists—"

"You think I live by myself and I can't fry bacon?" Rhys grabbed his arm and dragged. Halfway down the stairs, he asked, "You can fry bacon, can't you? Tell me you can fry bacon."

"Of course I can," Sullivan said, affronted. "If I have to impress someone the morning after."

Rhys's belly laugh echoed from the curved stairwell. It was odd for Cypress Bend, especially after the night they'd had, but good. They passed a tour group on their way to the kitchen, and the sunburned people gaped as they walked by, shirtless, barefoot, residents and clearly unashamed of it. Rhys sat Sullivan at the table, rummaged for a while—he didn't know where the frying pan was, and Sullivan teased him about it—then cooked a whole package of bacon. He even set out a platter of fruit. No one ever cooked for Sullivan, not like that. They sat across the table from one another.

"It's adequate," Rhys said.

"Thank you," Sullivan replied. He looked at the fruit, the bacon, anything but the cousin who always saved him. The ghost stood motionless, its sucking sadness for once at bay.

"You were hungry," Rhys said. "Eat it before it gets cold."

Sullivan could have cried. Instead, he ate.

Drawn by habit, they found Olivia and Elliot on the patio with the parrots. Cameras tracked them. It was inevitable, Sullivan supposed, regular as rain. A mid-afternoon torpor stretched over the farm; tourists babbled somewhere, intent and insistent. When Varina screeched, he picked her up. Elliot played tug-o-war with a shepherd, and glasses of sweet tea sweated rings on the tablecloth. It had happened before. It would happen again. Henry was there too, eating pineapple slices. Sullivan wanted to say something. *I found a photograph*, he could begin. *Henry, I saw you. You were so young.*

It sounded too small for the enormities that stretched between them, that history too large to hold, and so Sullivan kept silent, wondering what to say and how to say it, until his brother slammed onto the patio. That had happened before, too.

"I finally talked to Ethan." Ash collapsed into a parrot-clawed chair. Raindrops shook from the jasmine. "He talked to Whitney and Judah. Well, Whitney."

Sullivan wanted to ask why Ash was letting Ethan speak to their cousin, or his fiancée, instead of doing it himself, especially after last night's singular disaster, but they were all thinking it, and he didn't bother. It would only start another fight. *Ash doesn't really have anyone*, Talitha had said, and she was right; Sullivan didn't have much, but Rhys had cooked him bacon. *Best cousins*, they'd pinkie-sworn. Ash cared for every last ragged Trenholm, but counted none of them as his. In so many ways, he was as lonely as their father.

"What did Ethan tell you?" Sullivan made himself say. Ash wanted someone to ask, and it cost him nothing. He couldn't look at his brother. The sum of his parts was too hard to bear—too much of their father, their childhood, that tangle of brutality and history and pain. But if love stacked into gestures small and large, lived moment by moment, Sullivan could manage it.

"You're just going to bitch," Ash replied. "All of you. But there's nothing we can do about it."

"There never is, is there?" Sullivan asked.

"No," Ash said. "Not really."

Time stretched into the interminable pause of an August afternoon, endless, the stillness possible only in the enervating depths of those long, dull dog days. "Just tell us," Henry finally said.

"The footage we were supposed to get with Nova? It was all blank." Ash stared into the gardens, maybe scanned the cloud-wisped sky. Sullivan tried not to look. "So Ethan talked to Whitney. And he must've talked fast, because they're still getting married at Cypress Bend next week. The wedding's back on. And Cedric Johnson, the guy who does *Psychic 911*? He's officiating. They're making the whole thing into a giant investigation and filming it, and we're going to be there."

"I thought Judah wasn't well enough—" Olivia started.

"I think Judah got a lot better real quick," Ash said to the treeline. "And I don't think it had much to do with what happened last night, either."

Ethan had paid them off. Whitney had ignored Judah's health, along with her parents' good opinion, unless she came from the type of family who smelled money and snatched it. Sullivan tried not to imagine those negotiations. Had she accepted Ethan's first offer, or demurred until the sum climbed and its lure became too strong? Sullivan didn't want to know. He hoped Elliot didn't understand, or wasn't listening.

"*Away down South in Dixie!*" Varina shrieked, suddenly flapping her blue wings.

"Quit that," Sullivan said, then undercut his words by passing her a piece of Henry's pineapple. "I only brought a black suit."

"We'll order you a seersucker one," Ash told him, mildly irritated. "Rhys, too. Is that your only objection?"

He had many objections, but none he could offer. In that thick August heat, the sun so slow, time so long, there was nothing Sullivan could do to stop the inevitable. What would happen would happen. He should have seen that coming. Fate would find him. It always had, and maybe that was the great secret: giving in to it. "That wasn't an objection," Sullivan said. "It was an observation."

"Good," Ash said, and they lapsed into silence once more.

CHAPTER 52

ASH

The bride's mother fell into hysterics. It happened every time. Maybe the meltdown happened over food, or hair, or a last-minute wardrobe malfunction, but it was inevitable, and Ash was used to it. "Right according to schedule," murmured Cousin Oscar, their business manager, hanging up his phone as they left the wedding office, a camera behind them. Oscar's daughter Anita would handle it. Anita's natural tone was a soothing coo; she could work miracles with clear nail polish, bobby pins, and an improbable dab of Silly Putty. Ash strode through the dying evening in a seersucker suit; silently, he thanked whoever had decided against black tie, though comfort had nothing to do with it. Ethan wanted a grotesquely Southern wedding, all sweetgrass baskets and mint juleps. Ash had heard rumors that guests had been issued a dress code. For the sake of his sanity, he'd chosen not to investigate.

They were locked in, locked up. Ethan had them by the balls. Those contracts kept them stuck on the farm as surely as a judge's sentence. A week after the seance, Nova was still in Lower Richland Hospital. Ash had heard that she slept and ate at odd hours, that she spent her days babbling, mostly about time. There were rumors of a lawsuit, but against him or Ethan, the farm or the studio, Ash wasn't sure, so he tried not to think about it. More immediate than any lawsuit, the land bristled, like a dog with its hackles raised, all edged agitation. Something was coming. He felt it in his marrow.

At least the past week had provided plenty of wedding-prep footage. His cousins and brother barely had to appear, which was lucky, because other than Elliot, they'd seemed to ignore him since Ethan had forced down what he called The Wedding Solution. Ash tried not to care. It stung anyway. They'd fallen apart. *Ethan lied about Nova, not me*, he wanted to tell them. It would do no good. They feigned anger over Nova, over the three men, but he knew the real indignity. Ash whitewashed their bloody history and sold it to a rapacious public, tied up neat. He deserved their fury, even if his compromises kept the lights on, kept the rain off. *If I knew a way out, I'd take it*, he'd have told them. They wouldn't listen. Worse, they might listen and laugh.

You don't care, Sullivan would have said. *You're too busy playing superhero.*

Ash could have told his brother that he'd taken the role because no one else would, that it had fallen to him, maybe devolved on him. Running that farm—*plantation*, call it a plantation, three blood-slicked, sweat-soaked syllables—had certainly eroded his conscience, and sometimes he wondered how. What poisonous moralities had swollen in that darkness, hidden, fat as grubs? Privilege blinded him, but he'd done little to lift those scales. As purely as he loathed his father, Ash hated himself.

And in an hour or so, he'd have Ethan to contend with in person—his co-executive producer was bringing Cedric Johnson, of *Psychic 911* fame. Ethan wouldn't harass him about footage while they were actively filming. But Ash would have to prevent his family from haranguing the Californian, possibly worse. Exhaustion was already dropping, heavy as the wringing humidity, and the day's work had hardly begun.

When Ash passed the Ivory-Bill Cafe, Chloe and Rosie were wiping tables under a single yellow light. Without tourists, the restaurant seemed too empty, like the world had ended and he'd missed the news. "Y'all about finished?" Ash asked.

Chloe's piercings glinted in the sunset. Ash had always liked Lewis's sisters, some of the few Black cousins who consented to work on the farm. "Yeah, 'bout to head home. We had a toddler spill juice all over just before closing."

"You going to the wedding?" he asked, uncomfortably aware of his suit against her elf-like smock and jeans. Ash was always different from his cousins, the boy who lived in the big house, and he hated wearing that difference on the outside.

"You think Whitney wants us at that thing?" Chloe asked. "We're lucky she let Lewis go."

Ash sagged, wincing at the truth. Chloe had said the quiet part out loud. "You're a Trenholm," Ash said weakly. "It shouldn't matter if you're Black." But it did, and horribly.

"Yeah, well." Chloe ducked down to wipe the floor. "Have fun."

You too, he almost said. Instead, he told her, "Have a good night."

As he and Oscar climbed into the golf cart, their cameraman behind, the radio crackled. "We got another food truck here," Boo said. "We're parking 'em behind the Barn."

Ash wished for the dogs' friendly galumphing. As usual, they were with Elliot. "Which food truck?" he asked as Oscar started down the drive.

"The BBQ one," Boo replied.

"You can park that one close in," Ash said. "Those trucks don't explode." He had to consider those contingencies—which trucks were warming food, which trucks were frying it. All caterers submitted menus beforehand. Though Oscar usually handled those details, Ash had taken over most of them for Whitney and Judah's wedding. In the span of a week, Ethan had ginned it into a four-hundred-guest monstrosity, the biggest bash Cypress Bend had ever thrown. They'd hauled in folding chairs and spare Port-A-Johns; extra trolleys shuttled guests from satellite parking. Cousins had spent the week manicuring the grounds, and the night before, contractors had poured new pebbles on the driveway. Ash cringed to think of the expense.

"When's Cedric Johnson supposed to be here?" Oscar asked.

"Any time now." Ash settled into the white-pleather seat and watched the live oaks pass. He'd spent some time googling Cedric, a psychic investigator famed for haunted house investigations. The cowboy-handsome, stubble-jawed star of *Psychic 911* was supposed to have special expertise in exorcisms and poltergeists; allegedly, he worked as a police consultant on missing persons cases, and a hysterical Redditor claimed he'd predicted the Russian invasion of Ukraine. No matter how hard Ash searched, he couldn't find the man's credentials to officiate a wedding. "What kind of minister is this guy again?" he asked.

"I don't know," Oscar replied. "Church of What's Happening Now, I guess. One of them online things."

Tires ground on the pebbles, and twilight purpled as the sun sulked into the swamp-cypresses. Oscar parked in front of the Barn. It glowed with hanging lanterns, and citronella torches burned smoky-sweet along the flagstone path, a scent familiar from a hundred summer weddings. Lewis bustled over. His seersucker suit rode up his arms; grass cuttings stuck to his white bucks. "Hey, Ash," he said, shoving his glasses up his nose. "We're getting the cameras aimed at the sky, but these lanterns are throwing off a lot of light pollution."

"Move 'em farther to the edges." Ash knew camera setups. He'd planned weddings, planned investigations. He'd done this before. He'd do it again.

"The trees get in the way." Lewis shoved his glasses again.

"Put 'em on the roof," Ash told him. He sounded dismissive, armed with a solution for every problem and ready to pronounce it obvious. Tension did that; he hated himself for it. "Sorry," he said.

"It's okay," Lewis replied. "C'mon, y'all," he hollered to Sinclair and Parker. "We gotta get these on the roof. Let's get that done so I can head back to HQ." He turned back to Ash. "I can't believe you let that barbecue truck in, by the way. I hope you didn't know about it. If you did—fuck you, Ash. You know better." Before Ash could answer, Lewis strode away.

Boo appeared at his side. A seersucker suit hadn't dissuaded him from strapping on his shotgun. "Hey boss," he said. "You wanna check out the food trucks in back?"

"What's Lewis talking about?" Ash asked. But he made himself smile. It was Whitney and Judah's wedding day, and Trenholms smiled on wedding days. They smiled for food trucks, and seersucker suits, and mint juleps; they smiled for cousins and ministers, even those from The Church of What's Happening Now. Boo led him down the flagstone path, past the Barn's yawning entrance and rustic-looking cypress logs to the wide clearing out back. Ash had supervised the accumulation of supplies, but silver glimmered under the festooned Christmas lights; bouquets of gardenia and magnolia leafed the long wooden tables. Whitney had booked BBQ, seafood, donut, and biscuit trucks; everything but the seafood had arrived.

"Good, you got that donut truck in the back," Ash said. "We can't have them near the Barn."

"Yeah, I figured that," Boo told him.

He squinted. The BBQ truck had something above it, a scrap of cloth silhouetted against the purple sky. Ash squinted harder. "Tell me that's not a Confederate flag," he said. "I thought they had Little Pig's coming! No wonder Lewis is—"

"Oscar told me Whitney canceled on them once," Boo told him. "When she rebooked, she couldn't get all the same vendors. She wanted a BBQ truck, and this was the one available."

"Jefferson's BBQ isn't on the approved vendor list." It was the only argument Ash could manage.

"I guess Oscar okayed it," Boo said. "You want I should tell 'em to leave?"

Whitney, or more likely her mother, would raise Cain if he ejected half the main course. The owners would show their asses on social media if he told them to take the flag down—they'd call him woke, and he'd have protesters lining the highway from Columbia to Gaston. Profits would drop. He'd have to lay off staff—not *staff*, but relatives. "Ignore it," Ash told Boo. "It's dark. No one will notice the damn thing, but make sure you tell Lewis I didn't know, will you? Anyway, if we throw them out, they'll still get their money."

But with Lewis heading back to HQ, there would be no Black people at the wedding to see. Ash knew that. He cringed to know it, but what could he do? Henry said things had changed at Cypress Bend, but nothing had, not really. Maybe they never would.

He'd change them, if he could. If he had the courage. If he knew how. There were always *if*s. There were always excuses. The flag hung still in the limp evening air.

If only he could think of that *how*.

Then he remembered that cameraman behind him. "You can stop filming that flag," he said over his shoulder. "You won't be showing it."

CHAPTER 53

OLIVIA

Olivia stepped into her dress. It was pink, tea-length; she preferred black, but Ethan wanted women in pastels. Henry zipped her up and kissed her shoulder. "You look stunning," he said.

"You say that every morning." Hiding a smile, she turned to her vanity. Old habit to hide it, old habit to pretend she didn't care when she did. It was hard to shed those pretensions she'd lived by for so long.

"I need to put on my suit," he told her. "You'll be okay over here?"

"I always am," she said, which wasn't quite true, but he'd trust her. Henry was generous with his belief. He kissed her shoulder again, and the door snicked shut behind him. He was quiet with doors, children, disagreements; Henry passed gently through the world. Olivia wondered often why he stayed with her. *Here I am, and here I'll remain,* he said of the farm. Maybe that was just as true for their relationship.

Olivia hated weddings. They reminded her that she would never have one, not with Henry. *I won't stay and you won't go,* she'd tell him. *There, we had the argument, and we don't have to have it again today.* But she would go to Whitney and Judah's wedding; she would smile like a good girl. She would murmur pleasantries at her second cousins, third cousins, fourth cousins. She would try to avoid Ash, who had sold them into this madness.

But for once, Olivia wouldn't have to hide Henry, a strange thing around Cypress Bend; they'd decided to tell everyone it happened when she came home. *I'm not seeing anyone and neither is he and—well, it just worked out*, she'd say. They'd fend off further questions with smiles and deflection.

Everyone would throw them knowing grins. *I always knew you two would end up together*, they'd say, though no one had, and Olivia had made sure of it. They'd make obnoxious comments about how Olivia and Henry would be next.

We'll see, she'd say, thinking, *That'll never happen.*

Olivia slipped a robe over her dress, then applied face creams: Vitamin C, toner, hyaluronic acid. She let them dry and set her hair into long curls. It should have been their wedding, but she and Henry would never have a happy ending. There were no happy endings. There were no endings at all, only a long slog into an ever-stretching distance. Olivia suspected death only upended the hourglass. She primered her face and slathered on foundation. Had this happened before—this room, this wedding, uncurling her hair from this iron, awaiting the expected guests? Olivia hated it. She wanted to smash the mirror, maybe the window, hear that satisfying glass-shatter, shards flying, glittering, slashing her half-done face. Henry would come running. *Oh, Olivia, what have you done*, he would cry, and she would fall into his arms, weeping. Blood would stain his suit. He'd kneel in the jewel-like pieces and hold her as she cried. They'd skip the wedding.

Olivia dabbed bronzer across her nose, then contoured her cheeks. The farm had felt drum-tight since Nova disappeared, poised for disaster. She hated it. Nothing changed at Cypress Bend. It never had. She believed that. Why else could the three men come? Why else *would* they come? Olivia was ready to believe in something else. As she set down her bronzer and picked up her eyeshadow, she wondered what that might be.

CHAPTER 54

RHYS

"**S**tand still," Rhys told Sullivan. He stepped behind his cousin and retied his pink bow tie, hopelessly askew. In the mirror, Sullivan bloomed into a smile. Little gestures like that made him happy—loaning him a t-shirt, giving him the first shower, tying his bow tie. Those smiles said that away from Cypress Bend, Sullivan lived unnoticed, his comings and goings unheeded. No one looked up when he walked into a room. Worse, he knew it, and it hurt him. Rhys tried not to think about his own life in Richmond. *We're the same, you and me,* he could have told Sullivan. *People call me more responsible because I cover my problems with work. At least you hide it more honestly, and who's to say which is worse? You said you'd help me when no one else would.*

"It looks good," Sullivan said, examining himself in the mirror. "Thanks."

"'Course," Rhys told him. He tied his peach bow tie, rhyming but not matching. They threaded on belts, pulled on jackets and straightened lapels.

"We look good," Sullivan said. "I think we're ready for this thing. It won't be too bad. Weddings never are, y'know? You dread them, but then you always go and have a good time. At least I do. C'mon. Let's get downstairs."

His cousin could have left after Nova disappeared. A sane person would have, but one more time, he'd stayed. He stayed despite the growing sense of fatality sizzling in the air. Everything had happened before. Sullivan lingered in the doorway, almost smiling. "C'mon, Rhys," he said again.

"Thank you," Rhys said.

"For ordering the suit? Ash said you needed one. C'mon."

"No. For—" Rhys snatched a glance at the window. Twilight purpled the sky; uncertain stars bloomed to regular constellations. "Look, when we got here, you asked if I was seeing anyone." Trenholm men didn't say these things. *Act like a man*, his uncle roared in his ears. *Men don't talk like that.* For once, between those walls hewn from swamp-cypress, Rhys refused to listen. "And I said no, not really. I said that 'cause I see them once and I never call them again."

Sullivan reddened. "Yeah." His white bucks shuffled on the hardwood, kept on the third floor when Ash dragged in that hideous carpeting. "Why do we do that?"

"Because it's easier," he replied. "If we kept someone around there's so much we'd have to look at, and so much we'd have to explain, and it's easier if we just don't, y'know? But I'm glad I came back. It's fucked-up here, but at least it's not lonely." Rhys braced for his cousin's recriminations. Sullivan would hate him for it.

Instead, his cousin raked a hand through his curls, wild with humidity. "Yeah. Coming back here—I hate it, but you're here. That's worth something, I guess. I mean, that's worth all of it." Sullivan studied his shoes as he spoke, as if those white bucks could alleviate his mortification. Without asking, Rhys knew those furious words echoed in his ears. *Don't be such a pussy. Boys don't cry.* "I missed you so much."

"It's over now," Rhys said. He cleared his throat and spoke those words he'd never dared, despite the past's drowning denunciations. "I love you. I mean, it's stupid. Not like that. But I love you, man." He hated himself. Habit, force—he couldn't say it without qualifications. Nevertheless, it seemed enormous, as if he'd flung a wrench into a well-oiled factory and thrown the whole machinery off-line. The world seemed to grind and turn. In that house of sharpened sabers, something pivoted. Rhys felt like he'd changed the world.

When he looked up, when he managed it, face flaming, Sullivan was smiling. "I love you too," his favorite cousin replied.

Together, they clattered down to meet whatever strangeness came next.

CHAPTER 55

SULLIVAN

Sullivan and Rhys ran into Henry on the second-floor landing. He had to say something. Sullivan had held knowledge of that photograph for a week, and that image of a teenage Henry haunted him, a smiling ghost and worse for it. "Meet you down there," Sullivan told Rhys. "Can I—can I talk to you for a second?" he asked Henry.

Henry nodded once. They waited as Rhys's footsteps receded; Henry regarded Sullivan with a mixture of curiosity and something else—suspicion, maybe? He deserved it. Somewhere, air conditioning hummed; the hall had gone gray and dreary with twilight. If Rhys could say he loved him, Sullivan could also break those deep-running taboos that coded manhood in Cypress Bend: *Trenholm men don't act like pussies.* He owed it to the boys in that photograph, if not to Henry and himself in the here-and-now, and the best way was to take a deep breath and begin. "I found a photo," Sullivan said. "Of you and me and Rhys, when we were teenagers? We were—we were really young. How old were you? When you left home, I mean?"

"Fourteen." Henry's blue-eyed gaze never wavered, and if the question startled him, he didn't show it.

"And how old were you—" He focused not on Henry—he couldn't stand to look at Henry—but a piece of tan earthenware pottery on a nearby table. Sullivan wanted to cradle its smooth roundness in his own two hands. "How old were you when you saw my cousin Sullivan get killed?"

"Fifteen," Henry said. The answer came with no hysteria, only fact, as if Sullivan had asked the name of the current president.

"You were brainwashed," Sullivan told him, words tumbling faster than he could gather them, "as brainwashed as us. It wasn't your fault. And I'm sorry I blamed you—I'm sorry I acted like—"

"I bear some responsibility," Henry said.

The bowl on the table looked silken, as if worked for long hours by patient hands. Perhaps Elliot had found it, or maybe Ash. Like Henry, it had come from another time entirely.

"But not the responsibility I thought you did," Sullivan said.

Henry said nothing for a long time. Sunk into the gray gloom of that hall, the only light pooled around small table lamps, the silence stretched unbearably. Sullivan thought that perhaps he shouldn't have spoken at all. Just when he could stand it no longer, when he began gathering himself to nod and walk down the stairs, defeated, Henry spoke again. "I owe you thanks," he said. "You're the one who made me examine what I believed. And I hated you for it afterward—I did—but I hated more that you'd never forgive me for it. I finally gave up. I wouldn't chase forgiveness that was never yours to give in the first place."

"That's fair," Sullivan told him. He couldn't ask for much, but he had one more thing to say, and it was the hardest of all. But if Rhys could speak up, he could shatter that last taboo, the worst. "I hated in you what I saw in me. It was easier than looking in the mirror."

It seemed unfair that spoken words could leave him feeling flayed open, chest-empty. Why did those old strictures still hold? Sullivan tried again. "It was easier to be angry at you than at myself."

Henry reached across that long, grim distance, and a hand touched Sullivan's shoulder. It was a small gesture, but solid and sure. "I know," he said. "You were living as best you could. That's what happens, most of the time. We do the best we can with what we have. The past is over, if you let go of it. What matters is what you do now."

"I'm sorry," Sullivan said again, lamely, stupidly. Those two words could never bear the burden of that simmering rage he'd carried—at Henry, but really at himself.

"What does Olivia always say? There's only one thing left." Henry smiled then, as if conjuring her made the world bright again. "Do better." Henry's hand left Sullivan's shoulder, and he nodded once, then descended the stairs. As he passed the dark woman standing silent on the second floor, he paused.

"I'm sorry, Juba," Henry said to her quietly.

Maybe he thought Sullivan couldn't see. Maybe he didn't care. The woman stood motionless, feather duster in her hand, as if frozen in the realization of disaster. Henry nodded once and walked on. He'd spoken her name—he'd known her. That half-recalled memory rose again: Sullivan shouting, first at the woman, then Henry. He'd been so angry.

He couldn't blame Henry for it. He'd been a child, and known no better.

Dizzy with forgiveness, Sullivan met Rhys in the library. The room glowed golden with antique lamplight; dust motes swirled near the upper shelves. It was a soft room, and a friendly one. He refused to be fooled.

"This won't be terrible," he told Rhys, more for something to say than the words themselves. "Weddings, you know. We've been to plenty of weddings. They're like funerals, only less depressing."

An odd sense of déjà-vu nagged at him. He'd seen this before. He would see this again.

Olivia strode in. She wore a pink dress; her shoes and clutch dripped with expensive minimalism, which valued designer labels only if they were invisible. She alighted on the sofa like a bird, and her posture was noticeably perfect. It pained him. His uncle had hurt her in so many ways.

"Weddings are nothing like funerals," she told Sullivan. "Must you? It's bad enough Ash is turning this into an investigation. Try not to make it worse."

Sullivan opened his mouth, ready to snark back. His gaze slid to Rhys, who hated when they picked at one another. Rhys loved him. Henry seemed to forgive him. He shut it again. It was a small thing, but the world turned on small gestures. He almost believed they could chip away that tense sense of anticipation hanging over the farm.

"I thought so," Olivia said.

"Oh, good." Ash appeared, his seersucker wrinkled, bags etched under his eyes. A cameraman trailed him. "You're ready. Lewis is all set up in HQ. Elliot and Henry are waiting on the porch, and Cedric Johnson's here with Ethan. We're supposed to meet them at the Barn."

He offered Olivia his arm, and she stood. Wordlessly, Sullivan and Rhys followed them to the front door. As they passed before that enormous mirror, Sullivan saw it again: this had happened before. It differed in the details, small colors against a larger pattern. *We are time, and we are always the same*, the men had said. He hoped they were wrong.

"I shouldn't have to remind y'all to behave," Ash said as they stacked the golf carts in familiar configurations—Sullivan drove one, with Rhys beside him, the cameraman in the back; Ash drove the other, with Henry and Olivia behind, Elliot riding shotgun. "Ethan's a guest. Don't fly off the handle at him."

Sullivan could think of several answers to his brother, then remembered his promise. He was trying. By sending them Nova, Ethan had put them all at risk with his stupidity. *He doesn't understand*, he imagined Talitha saying. *He's an idiot, and he doesn't matter. He's not worth fighting with Ash over.*

Sullivan kept silent as they pulled away. Twilight had dropped to full dark, and he hated leaving the house's familiar light. The farm felt edged, restless with trolleys trundling from the north parking lot every ten minutes. It only ramped up the sense of brooding—reality was turning on its head. He felt it tilting, shifting, like the air before a storm. Maybe another lightning strike was coming, or maybe something far worse. He never knew.

"I don't like this," Sullivan told Rhys. He glanced back at the house. That figure stood in the second-floor windows again—that silhouette he knew too well. "Rhys?" he said. "Look at the house."

Rhys glanced once, then turned away. "Nope," he told Sullivan. "He can stand silent in that house all he wants, but I'll never acknowledge him. Never. And neither should you. He's dead, and he can stay that way."

Ash's radio screamed into a high, staticed whine. "This is Sinclair down by the Barn," the device shrilled. "We got something in the sky at ten o'clock."

Sullivan had to remind himself that the hour hand always pointed north, then decided he didn't want to look, anyway. "I got nothing on the ADS-B," Lewis replied from HQ.

"Oh shit! Oh shit! It's going, going, oh hell, that puppy's fast—gone over the horizon," Sinclair said. "That wasn't a plane."

"Y'all check in with me," Lewis said. "Ash, where—"

The rest of the transmission garbled as something burst from the underbrush. A black-and-white creature, all subtropical otherness, darted in front of the golf cart, and tires crunched as Sullivan swerved. It ran on two legs, tail whipping; visceral terror gripped him for a moment before he remembered that pack-hunting, venomous Argentinian lizards existed. Even this had happened before. He let the cart spin out. "You okay?" Rhys asked.

"Fine," he said. "Christ, that tegu scared me."

"—door's open," Lewis was saying over the radio. "I can send someone over there again, but I'm pretty sure it's gonna be gone."

Ahead of him in the dark, Ash was cussing a blue streak. "Yeah, it's gonna be. Sinclair, you get on over there and check anyway."

"What is it?" Sullivan called, starting the cart again.

"The quilt went walking again!" Ash shouted. "And we don't have time to deal with it right now, so keep driving!"

Sullivan focused on the dark ahead, thick-black, barely cut with those thin golf cart lights. "Do you ever feel like—" he started.

"We've been here before?" Rhys asked. "Like these patterns keep repeating, and there's nothing we can do to stop them? Why d'you think I said what I said?"

Sullivan remembered that moment, bright-shining in the dark. "I love you too," he told his cousin, and that was one little light.

CHAPTER 56

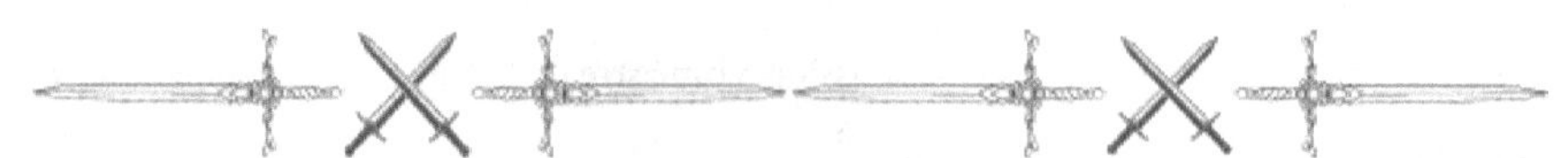

OLIVIA

Ethan, Cedric, and another cameraman met them in an occasional room at the back of the Barn, an anonymous space something like a posh waiting room stuffed with bridal favors. The executive producer took his time standing when they entered, which would annoy Henry on her behalf. She kept her face blank as Ethan introduced Cedric Johnson. Olivia disliked him immediately. Ministers, even casual ones, did not wear Nehru collars. When he shook her cousins' hands, he eyed them as if they might expect to fight; he eyed her as if they might sleep together, despite Henry's arm around her waist. Cedric spoke loudly, quickly, and enunciated his consonants. Something about him seemed to loom, though he didn't stand particularly close to her, and he didn't appear particularly tall. Two silent female assistants flanked him, both slim, blonde, and dressed in black; their presence was ignored. At least Elliot had gone off with the other Trenholm teenagers, and Cedric couldn't stare at her, too.

"I spoke to Whitney on the phone," he told Ash, who he'd honed in on as the only Trenholm who mattered, likely because he already had a TV show. "We talked on the flight over. She's got a real problem going on, with Judah, I mean. Those three men, I've never heard anything like it. Missing time. I think it might be tied into all the UAP phenomena you see at the farm here."

"We don't know," Ash replied. Hands clasped behind his back, he spoke politely, remotely. Cedric was an unwanted stranger recently come to town, and they were locals who wished him gone.

Ethan watched them, eyes slightly narrowed, as if they were children whose behavior had been found wanting.

"I'd like to meet her fiancé," Cedric said. "Your cousin, what's his name—"

"Judah," Sullivan interrupted. He stood in the center of the room; no one had yet taken a seat in the leather chairs. Olivia doubted, with the heavy tension, that anyone would. "He's the possessed one? And before you make the same mistake the other psychic did, he's possessed by time. It's not a dead person. It's time."

Cedric turned to Sullivan slowly. "Time, you said? And you're Sullivan, right?"

"I'm Ash's brother, yes," he replied.

"I've never heard of anything like that," he said. "In my experience, simple possession cases like this can be compounded by UAP interference—"

"He's possessed by time," Sullivan repeated.

"Yeah, I don't recommend repeating Nova's mistakes." Rhys spoke from the center of the Trenholm gang. There were more of them, and Olivia took heart in their numbers. "Last I heard, she was still holed up in Lower Richland Hospital telling the nurses that time is a crow with two beaks."

If he meant it to sound intentionally off-putting, he succeeded, and Olivia stifled a giggle.

"Excuse me?" Ethan asked.

"Yeah, when we asked where she'd been, she said she went to the swords," Sullivan told him. "If you can figure out what that means, be my guest. Doesn't sound like any abduction experience I've heard of. And in all my time at this farm, I can honestly say that while I've seen some bizarre shit, I've never been abducted by aliens."

Cedric blinked his oddly light eyes once, twice, a strange gesture of studied surprise. "Maybe none of you are genetically prone to abduction."

Olivia turned on her best smile. "Bless your heart," she said. "If this was alien abduction, in over two hundred years, *someone* on this farm would've been abducted. We just don't have any records of it happening."

Cedric's teeth gleamed, something of a predator in his grin. "My mama was from Mobile," he told her.

It was a polite way of saying, *I know what 'Bless your heart' means, bitch.* Olivia's smile didn't move. "Then you understand completely," she replied. Those clipped consonants had let her underestimate him. She wouldn't do it again. His assistants watched her with something like sympathy, though their faces remained expressionless. Olivia wondered what indignities had melded into their everyday.

"Well, let's take you to meet Judah," Ash said, after a pause that stretched too long in that small, close space. The back rooms were air-conditioned, but the main hall was not; the Barn was notoriously drafty. At least Whitney—or the studio—had shelled out for mobile air conditioners, and they wouldn't sweat through the ceremony.

"Lead on, MacDuff," Cedric told him.

"It's 'Lay on, MacDuff,'" Henry said into her ear as they filed from the room. "And it's bad luck to invoke the Scottish play before a theatrical production, so I can't help but think that holds true for a wedding."

Olivia squeezed his hand. Her uncle had held it bad luck to invoke *MacBeth* at all. *Don't mention that thing!* he'd shout. *I won't have witchcraft on this place, y'hear me?*

Why do you care if you don't believe in it, she'd wonder, but no one contradicted Truluck Trenholm, not in his own house. His relatives knew better.

Their footsteps sounded on the reclaimed cypress boards. Like the Barn's yawning main gallery, its back hall was lit with faux-rustic lanterns, which were not lanterns at all, but whose warm electric light gave only the appearance of primitivism. If the house clutched the past close, the Barn play-acted it. Olivia had always hated that. She preferred honesty in architecture.

The groomsmen waited in a room designed for them, all leather couches and taxidermied boars. Her uncle had shot them; they grew to startling size in the tucked back corners of the swamp. Those staring, glassy eyes seemed to watch her as she entered, and Olivia tried not to look. Too many groomsmen packed the room, all of them in seersucker, most of them cousins, and their faces tightened with worry, more appropriate to a contentious funeral than a young man's wedding.

Judah slouched in a plush chair, already rumpled; his face was sagged and winter-gray. A tumbler of something dark dangled unnoticed in his hand. It puddled on the boards below his wrist, and the glass dripped. When he raised his eyes, they looked no better than those boars'. Her cousin Randolph, his father, half-crouched next to him. "Straighten up!" he hollered as Ash came in. "Goddammit, Judah! We talked about this!"

"He can't help it and you know it," Ash snapped, and Olivia cut her eyes at him; her uncle would have backhanded him for mouthing off to Randolph. Mandates to respect their elders had always cowed them to silence, and no matter how much they'd grown, her cousin's casual dismissal shocked her.

But Ash had taken over the Big House, taken it over a decade ago in name if not fact, and Cousin Randolph nodded to him. He stood. "Hey, Ash," he said. "Trying to get Judah here to stand up and do his part today." He ran a hand through his curls, dark ones that matched Sullivan's. "This might've been a mistake, son. It was Whitney's and his mother's idea. You know Judah hasn't been well."

"I know," Ash said. "This is Cedric Johnson and my co-executive producer, Ethan. Cedric's performing the ceremony today. We're hoping he might be able to help with how Judah's been feeling. Cedric, this is my cousin Randolph and his son, Judah, the groom. Randolph is my father's—"

"Hey." Cedric moved forward, hand out, teeth showing. It seemed more aggressive than friendly, an ape-display of dominance. He shook hands with Randolph. Judah hardly lifted those dead-boar eyes. Cedric paused for a moment, as if sizing him up, then flicked his hand as if shooing flies. "I need some people to leave," he said. "There are too many of you in here, and I have to talk to Judah."

Groomsmen glanced at one another. The Trenholms hadn't greeted each other in more than nods. Olivia's second and third cousins filed out, throwing glances at Sullivan and Rhys as they passed, touching her hand. Question lurked behind those looks, but she kept her face expressionless. Cousins or not, she couldn't betray Ash to them. She might hate what he was doing, but he had her loyalty.

Randolph hesitated. Cedric motioned to him to leave, too, and with a last glance at Ash, who nodded back, he filed out. An accident of birth and residence had crowned her first cousin head of the family, and so Randolph trusted him blindly, totally; Olivia hated that. *You don't know these men he's with*, she wanted to shout. *Don't leave Judah with them.* But she could say nothing as Randolph, like the others, pressed her hand and left.

Cedric strode in front of Judah. When he didn't look up, the psychic grabbed his chin and jerked it upward. Judah started back. His face was strange, washed out, with the bemused expression of an old man lost in dementia. Something tugged at the pit of Olivia's stomach. Her cousin wasn't well. "Cedric," Judah said, a measured tone, as if they'd met on the street.

"There's something wrong with you," Cedric told him. "I can feel it under your skin. It's in your eyes, too."

"I'm tired," Judah told him. He drew away, drooping back as if wedding preparations or life itself had wearied him. "I'm trapped in this."

"What, you mean getting married?" Rhys shoved up next to Cedric and squatted next to him. Olivia loved her brother, who tried to fix everything but himself. "You don't have to do this, y'know. You can always call it off—"

"No." Judah turned those old, dead eyes on Rhys. "The wedding? No. The circling. We're Trenholms, and we're all trapped. Blood-pinned, every one of us. Ever since I came for that walk-through and I saw the men, it's so clear that I can't imagine why no one else sees it. The sword has endless edges and we turn it on each other."

Olivia edged closer to Henry. She didn't quite know what Judah meant, but it was true, and she hated it.

"Uh-huh," Cedric said.

"We deserve it," Judah said. "All of us do. It's soaked into the soil here. This is our fault, and it keeps being our fault, over and over and over. I'm so damn tired."

Whip-quick, Cedric laid a palm on his forehead. It stayed only a moment until the psychic's face twisted into horror, those oddly pale eyes widening and his mouth gaping. Cedric twitched back as if to rip away, but Judah snatched his hand and held it. Writhing, the psychic screwed his eyes shut, as if with pain, and his head snapped from side to side. He strained backward. Slighter, thinner, and certainly ill, Judah seemed to hold him with no effort at all. A soft grunt slipped the psychic's lips, something between a sigh and a gasp.

"*Help him!*" Ethan shouted.

No one moved. Henry held her tight, tight.

Cedric wrenched back and fell on his ass. Eyes bugging, he clutched his chest. He looked as if he might vomit. "All rivers run to the sea," Cedric said, voice low and horrified, "and the sea is never full. It's hungry, and it goes back to the beginning." The psychic scrambled to his feet. "I'll do the wedding. But I don't know how to deal with whatever's in there." Cedric faced the camera. "Part of being a responsible psychic is knowing when to step away," he recited, appearing to regain his composure. "You have to realize when something is too much for you to handle. Whatever this is, it requires more than I have on my own, and we're going to have to bring a full team down here after the ceremony."

He strode out of the room. Ethan followed, and they were alone with Judah.

"I'm sorry," Ash told him. Olivia was grateful. It seemed the only right thing to say.

"You're not sorry enough," Judah said. "This is nothing. You can stop it, but you don't."

"I don't know how!" Ash cried. His face fell into his hands. Henry's arm around her tightened.

"Yes, you do," Judah told him. "But you're too pussy to do it." He turned his face to the wall. "Send my father back in," he said. "I'm tired of y'all and your circus."

There was nothing else to be done, and they did what he asked.

CHAPTER 57

RHYS

Groomsmen in seersucker escorted bridesmaids up the aisle in slow, measured steps. Rhys sat in the front row amongst his sister and first cousins, their group abutting some of Whitney's close relations. Mobile air conditioners whirred tunelessly, endlessly, and heat gobbled their chilled currents; as fans worried the air, Olivia's stray hairs lifted and tickled his cheek. Rhys batted them down.

Somewhere behind them, a phone rang. Relatives cussed and pawed for it. "I swear I turned that off," someone said.

"Lord, don't play that game again," someone else replied.

Dread fluttered in Rhys's chest.

Another phone rang across the room. If his cousins or sister noticed, they gave no sign; the marching groomsman and bridesmaid didn't falter. The wedding party filled in the dais, where Cedric wore a frozen smile, Judah a rictus grin. Something brooded there, squatted low and vast as the tropical fever-heat. "Hey," Rhys hissed in Sullivan's general direction, unable to bear the tension any longer. "Something's happening."

Abruptly, the organist switched to Pachbel's "Canon in D." Chairs scraped as four hundred people stood and turned.

Rhys startled at a vicious crackle. "—see something back behind the Barn. There's several orbs floating—"

Ash swore quietly, radio in hand, and ducked down the side aisle. Sullivan followed. Rhys went after him. No one seemed to notice, including the cameras, as they hurried down past the rows and out the side door, where the blast of cooler night air felt something like mercy.

"What's going on?" Rhys asked, as Olivia, Henry, and Elliot ducked out the side door behind them.

"I thought I turned this thing off," Ash said, fiddling with his radio. "No, I *did* turn this thing off. I *know* I turned this thing off. *Fuck*!" He seemed ready to toss it.

"We might as well go check," Sullivan told him. Citronella candles threw his dark eyes into a wicked gleam. "I hate sitting through ceremonies, anyway. Boring. Lots of words."

"What, you'd rather tear around in the dark out here?" Olivia drew a shawl over her shoulders, more for protection, it seemed, than any chill.

"Six in one hand, half dozen in the other, barring any tegus," Sullivan replied.

Wordlessly, Ash tramped down the torch-lined path. It seemed one more symptom of an indomitable anger he held against them, or the farm, or maybe even himself.

With the investigation concentrated out front, the reception area seemed eerily still. Fairy lights glowed over tabletops strewn with bunched greenery, and the food trucks' lights looked vaguely, oddly industrial, out of time and place. They paused. "There's nothing here," Ash said.

Rhys started through the tables, and Sullivan followed. He was searching, peering, when a flicker caught his attention, a movement against the night sky. Rhys shaded his eyes. "Hey!" he called, pointing, then he saw it: the truck was flying a Confederate flag.

"What the hell is that?" Sullivan shouted. "Ash! Are you telling me you let in—"

A light beyond reason and thought flashed, brighter than anything Rhys had known, and a simultaneous thunderclap boomed that seemed to shake his brain. He tasted that lightning as it hit, sharp and metallic. Rhys curled, ducked, and his knees hit the turf; the force seemed mental rather than physical. Purple afterimages bloomed, the fire bright behind them, Ash shouting, Sullivan groaning. Fire burned hot and bright: that lightning had struck the barbecue truck's flagpole. Those flames snagged, blazed as the Confederate flag went up, red and white and blue snarling among the orange before they charred. The barbecue banner melted to the fire like a lover, sinking and vanishing down to the metal, bubbling, burning with a sick scorched-plastic scent that stung Rhys's nose.

"What the hell was that?" Sullivan shouted.

"Tell everyone to get out of the Barn!" Ash was yelling. "That fire'll spread—get them across the driveway!"

Rhys kicked up, ran, spitting dirt, Sullivan at his heels. Ash was right. A nearly rainless summer had left the farm crisped dry, and the Barn would catch fast. They had to get those people out. "You okay?" his cousin asked.

"Yeah," Rhys managed, tiring quickly. "Fine. Mostly. You?"

"Yeah. I landed good," he said. Rhys threw open the Barn's back door, and they slowed as they entered the pitch-dark hallway. He tried to ignore a crawling sense of unease as he fumbled for his phone flashlight. The Barn seemed too quiet to hold four hundred people. "Hey!" Sullivan shouted. "There's a—"

Rhys smacked him. "Don't fucking yell 'fire!'" he said as they kicked into a run again. "They'll trample each other." They burst through the door and into the main hall.

"Hey!" Sullivan shouted. "Sorry to interrupt, but—"

He stopped. They stared.

Every seat was empty.

They were not overturned; there were no signs of a hasty exit. Women's purses hunched under the chairs, and a few jackets draped the chair-backs. As Rhys shined his phone into the corners, he saw both cameras placed neatly on the floor; they appeared to be off. All four hundred people were gone.

"It's like they disappeared," Rhys said. "They must have gone out the front door—" He started forward. Sullivan yanked his arm.

"Judah." His cousin spoke in a low, strangling voice. "I knew this was a mistake. I *fucking knew it*. Judah. It was Judah, Rhys. He did it again. When that lightning struck, whatever's in him took the whole damn wedding, just like it took Nova."

Rhys stared at the empty hall. The thunderclap. He felt that truth in his bones.

"The family—" his cousin's voice echoed in the empty hall. "*When the three men come walking again, when the family walks with them, it's time, if you want to stop it.* The family left with the men. It *is* time. And we can stop it from circling."

"If the house falls." Rhys saw it clearly then: They had misunderstood. The men were time, like Sullivan had said, and they could stop this endless repetition, the misery of blood that kept them chained. "The house has to fall, and we can stop it."

"Damn right the house has to fall." Sullivan said. He spoke, stronger, surer, and most of all, angrier. "That's how we end it. Fuck the show, fuck everything. We can end this."

Sullivan was right. Rhys turned to the cousin he loved best. "Let's do it," he said.

CHAPTER 58

SULLIVAN

"**W**hat d'you mean, they're *gone*?" Sullivan's brother shouted. They stood in among citronella torches in front of the Barn, and a thicker, sharper smoke cut their summer-night scent. Olivia's curls were falling flat; Elliot's pale hair crimped into waves. Both had ditched their heels. Henry had a sooty face and soaking seersucker; maybe he'd slowed the fire's spread, but he hadn't stopped it.

"They disappeared," Sullivan said, shortly, trying one more time not to loose that towering rage—Ash never listened, never paid attention; when he did, he greeted each fresh revelation with disbelief, as if Sullivan was histrionic and perhaps delusional. But it wasn't time to lose his temper at Ash, not now, with a fire burning out back and the wedding guests vanished. "They're not out here, and they're not in there," Sullivan told his brother. "Cedric, Ethan, everyone. Judah did it. We've gotta get out of here."

"The phones all went off, and I can't get any service," Ash said, punching at his iPhone. "I've tried over and over, and—"

Sinclair, Parker, and Boo appeared, that shotgun still strapped above his cousin's seersucker. "What the hell was that?" Boo asked. "We tried calling everyone on the radios, but they're down—everything's down—"

"Everyone in the wedding just disappeared," Sullivan told him. "Gone, like Nova. Look, I need you three to go back to the house. Get Aunt Alda and Lewis and get out. Leave the property. Go past the front gates and get out. Something's happening."

Frantically, Ash checked his phone, Elliot's phone, Olivia's. He held out his hand to Sullivan, who passed over his Android.

"Sure as shit something's happening after those things we saw hovering over the Barn." Sinclair shoved his sweaty curls off his forehead. "We saw a whole fleet of orbs above it and behind. A UAP, too. Tracking right across the sky, then it stopped like it was watching us—"

"You said the wedding disappeared?" Boo asked. "Vanished?"

"Goddammit, I'm not getting any service," Ash said. Rhys passed over his phone.

"Yeah, they disappeared just like Nova," Sullivan told Boo. He appeared ready to bolt for the Barn, as if to check himself, and Sullivan stopped him. "There's nothing you can do for them! Get Aunt Alda out of the house, and Lewis. I need them out of the house, y'hear me?"

"What are you talking about?" Ash asked. "Boo, they don't need to—"

"Get them out," Sullivan told him. "It's not safe here." That was it, the watchword of all those stupid reality shows—didn't Ash always remind them that safety was paramount? "We've gotta get out of here ourselves. The Barn's going to catch."

That was enough, and they bolted for the golf carts. Rhys slammed in next to him, and behind them, shockingly, Elliot. "What are you two gonna do?" she asked, leaning forward as Sullivan pulled out.

"Burn it," Sullivan said. "We're gonna burn the house down. We have to stop this, and that's the only way to—"

"The house? Thank God." Elliot glanced back. "Sullivan?" Her voice tilted into the upper registers. "There's something on top of the Barn. *Drive.*"

He spared a look over his shoulder and regretted it. Three identical, monochrome shapes stood on top of the barn, too high, too unstable on that pitched roof. Their grins stretched too wide, too white, and light snagged and caught in them like shards of stained glass. Malevolence radiated from them like a fever, hot and winter-bright. Sullivan mashed the gas pedal. His tires spun, ground and flung pebbles, but the golf cart leapt like a fresh horse. Elliot clung to the struts, and Rhys frantically buckled his seatbelt as they flew up the drive. Orbs flitted through the treetops, those bright balls of light that did not belong, a mockery of common sense, of the rational world of edges and planes and Newtonian physics. Sullivan focused on the driveway and the pale-yellow glow that hardly cut the dark. The night was unbreathable, smoke-tinged, and he prayed that the men lurking atop the Barn stayed put.

"Are they following us?" he called.

"No!" Rhys said. "But they're watching us, and Ash and Boo too. Just *drive*."

More pebbles sprayed as he rounded the long corner at the gift shop. It was dark, empty as an eyeless face. Orbs glowed above it; he looked once and did not look again. They would reach the house soon. Their father had always stockpiled gasoline in the shed, several cans of it. With it, they could end this madness. The property was on fire anyway; no one would question that flying sparks caught the house. Sullivan tried to ignore the orbs. He refused to glance at the sky. The ghost-woman's predictions had all come true, and they could stop this madness.

"Are they coming?" he shouted.

"Not that I can see!" Rhys said.

The house loomed ahead of them. It shouldered up from the gardens as if to insist upon itself, one proud beacon aglow in the darkness. That house would save them if he let it. This time, he refused. Ash would kill him. It didn't matter anymore—the studio, the horde of relatives, the family and the land. Only bloodshed mattered anymore, that endless hemorrhage, one long span of people ripping and tearing what did not belong to them and never had. They could end it.

Sullivan wheeled up to the rose garden and stopped at the front door—they needed a quick getaway. The little dark-skinned boy on the edge of the porch was no longer sweeping. He held his broom instead. Staring into the middle distance, shoulders hunched in sadness, he was a sad wisp of a child. Pain slammed Sullivan, as strong as an errant wave. He missed his mother suddenly, brutally, with the pain of a neglected orphan.

He couldn't think about that right now.

"Get in and go back to the shed," Sullivan barked. "The gas is back there. Elliot, stay with—"

"I'm helping you," she said, jumping out behind them. "This is the only way to stop whatever's been happening here. Those men told me time is a carnival ride and the end never comes until we stop it."

Sullivan paused, one slivered moment in that dream-run into the house. "You said they didn't speak to you."

"I lied." Elliot shoved a straggled hank of hair behind her bare shoulder. Her pale dress was ruined, flecked with mud—fleetingly, Sullivan remembered a nanny swaddling her in ribbons and white. Elliot had grown up better than they deserved, more beautiful muddy than pinioned. "I had to think about it before I told anyone. C'mon."

"Don't light it until we're sure Boo has Lewis and Aunt Alda out," Sullivan reminded them as they dashed through the house, out the door, across the patio and into the shed. Rhys grabbed the smallest gas can and passed it to Elliot; he took two himself. Sullivan grabbed the others. Ash, Henry, and Olivia met them on the patio. Artificial torches lent the scene a surreal, indoor glow, as if they were finally safe. Sullivan knew better.

"What the hell is this?" Ash demanded. Dirty-kneed, angry, he no longer looked like a gentleman.

"Get out of the way," Sullivan told his brother. "Didn't you see those men on top of the Barn? This is going to keep going until we end it."

Olivia's pale face, and her grip on Henry's hand, told him she'd seen them, and she wished she hadn't. "Elliot, gimme that," she said.

"No, this has to happen," Elliot told her.

"Yeah, and I can carry it easier than you," Olivia said, taking the gas can. "Where do we start with this, Sullivan?"

"I think we need to—" he started, then stopped. A macaw shrieked "Dixie" in the potted lemon trees. Ear-splitting and wildly off-key, another joined it. *"Old times there are not forgotten! Look away! Look away! Look away! Dixie Land!"* they cried, repeating it like a looped recording. Fear clogged Sullivan's throat. They were snagged in some terrible spiral, a match struck, a fire lit, then the wedding gone, and something worse unspooling around them. Together, as if they'd decided it, the parrots stopped their repetition and screamed the chorus:

O, I wish I was in Dixie! Hooray! Hooray!
In Dixie Land I'll take my stand
To live and die in Dixie
Away, away, away down south in Dixie!

As if their throats were suddenly slit, silence dropped.

Sullivan caught the sound of faraway water. For a snatched moment, he thought of the Congaree River, seven miles off. But the susurration rose; its murmur grew to a rustle, then a rush. "What's that?" Henry asked, a dangerous question at Cypress Bend. Sullivan snapped up—something about it seemed skyward—and the rush coalesced into a wingbeats. It was a flock of birds. Sullivan had never seen so many at once, at least a thousand, never seen birds like them. Flowing low over the patio, they were brightly colored, green-bodied and orange-headed, something like lovebirds. One by one, the parrots took wing and joined them. Each was lost as quickly as it flew, swallowed in the carnivalesque mass. Henry gaped. "Carolina parakeets," he said, voice breaking. "They're Carolina parakeets. They went extinct a century ago—"

They whirled as the flock did. Crow-sized, the birds seemed too tropical, too vivid to perch among the cypresses. Their green bellies gleamed, and tears pricked Sullivan's eyes. For once, the farm had handed them beauty.

"*Away down South in Dixie!*" a macaw screamed. It exploded from the lemon tree closest to them, swooping low over their heads—Varina, Sullivan's favorite. She dive-bombed them, pulled up at the last minute, and disappeared into the flock.

"They were rare when I was coming up." Henry's voice thickened with tears. "I never saw so many. I—" He sniffled and stopped, dropping his head. Sullivan had never seen him cry, not even when his father had dressed those infected wounds.

"I saw a stuffed one once." Rhys watched the sky, as if another miracle might come. "I was in Dublin, in this museum, the Dead Zoo. It's full of stuffed animals. They even have a thylacine, one of the extinct Tasmanian tigers. I saw that little bird behind glass, and I stared at it for so long. I just imagined those flocks, you know? I stood there and just imagined them—"

"Stop it," Sullivan snapped. "Y'all. You know what this is, right? We're standing here holding gas cans—"

"I've never seen the macaws try to fly away," Elliot said. "My whole life, you know? Never, not once."

"Yeah, well, it saves us from evacuating them," Sullivan said. "Focus. This is Cypress Bend trying to save itself with some pretty parrots. Remember that wedding? Four hundred people? We don't know where the hell they went and if they'll come back? Olivia, take the south wing, I'll take the middle, Rhys, hit the north. We'll make sure the gas meets and light it up."

"Livy." Henry laid a hand on her arm. His eyes were still wide, like a child's. "Don't. I can't leave—"

She ducked away. "You know this has to happen. Don't."

"They'll kill us, y'all." Ash was pleading. He must have known they wouldn't listen to anger. "They'll sue us. Think of the rest of the family—"

"That's exactly who I'm thinking about. They need to get the hell out of this spiral as much as we do." Sullivan began pouring gasoline at the house's edge, and its keen, deep scent both frightened and elated him.

"They don't have anything else!" Ash's voice rasped, like he had when they were children, when an asthma attack threatened. "You can't do this. You seriously—all y'all, you can't—"

"Ash." Elliot caught his hand. Ash looked at her as if surprised she'd grown up. "You need to breathe. We'll be fine, as long as we take care of this. Please. I don't want to live like this anymore."

It seemed to draw him back to himself, and Ash stilled. "You mean it?" he asked.

"Yes." Elliot shoved her pale hair back. She was as steely as Olivia, but no one had broken her. They had made sure of it, Ash and Olivia both. Sullivan's vision blurred, and he couldn't look at his little cousin anymore.

"Burn it," Ash said. "Burn the house to the fucking ground." Their gazes met, brother to brother, and Sullivan felt as if he were seeing Ash for the first time—a man of complex sorrows, tangled morals, one doing the best he could and often failing, but rising each morning to try one more time. It might have broken him. Sullivan glanced away and slopped gas at the foundation.

Rhys and Olivia ducked into the house. They left the doors open, and it seemed strange; his father had been forever shouting at them to shut the door—*Shut the damn door, you'll let all the air out. How many times have I goddamn told you to close the door? Is your head made of rocks, boy? Shut the door!*

He almost shuddered, remembering his father's face, ruddy with alcohol and anger and diabetes and the red raw heart of the South, the South, always the goddamn South, was there anything it didn't touch? His father's rage, that unholy pile of a house, the tugging tides of family, blood—it haunted him, a ghost large enough to call history and hungry besides. Sullivan splashed gas on the doorframe. He'd burn it down. He'd burn it all down in a cleansing fire as righteous and holy as the wrath of God.

The dogs bolted from the house. Left for the wedding, they beelined to Elliot and shoved close. The gas-smell was becoming overpowering, rising from both ends of the house. Sullivan ducked through the doorframe and splashed the parlor curtains; inside, the gas-smell was even stronger, richer. Ash trailed in, half-dazed, as if he didn't know his place among the wanton destruction. Rhys appeared in the doorway, gas cans dangling from each hand. "Everyone's out," he said. "The guys got Aunt Alda and Betty and Lewis clear. I watched them go. They're gone."

Sullivan didn't ask if those cousins knew what they were doing. It didn't matter. They were Trenholms, and they would never tell. *Come at one of them, and you come at them all,* people in town said. He soaked the couch and trailed a line of gas toward the central staircase. They could cross the lines of gas there—

A thunderclap as loud and close as the first struck, and a blinding flash. It rattled the house, shook Sullivan's teeth, and bent him double. Gas spilled over his feet; the dogs flew into frenzied barking. Trebled laughter echoed through the house, and he knew without seeing the three men that it belonged to them, or it. *It's time, if you want to stop it.*

"Everyone okay?" Sullivan shouted. His voice seemed strange, doubled. When he opened his eyes, his vision blurred—objects seemed to overlap. Familiar furniture shared space with tables and sofas he'd never seen before, obvious antiques that looked as solid as the others. Sullivan dropped the gas and reached for a strange armchair. His hand passed through it, though it hit the solid mahogany table underlying it.

A commotion sounded above him, from the salon upstairs—angry voices, and Rhys had said Boo got everyone out. "Olivia? Henry!" he called. "Rhys?" Ash and Elliot stood in the sitting room. Barking dogs pressed close to them; his brother and cousin clearly stared at the same overlaid visions, old furnishings and new, as if two times were occupying the same space at once.

"Something's wrong!" Rhys yelled, skidding in from the dining room. "I'm seeing—"

"Who's up there if we're all down here, and you saw Boo leave?" Sullivan asked.

"Boo and Lewis and Aunt Alda and Betty left!" Rhys shouted. "It's the house screwing with us again! We have to get out!"

Then Sullivan remembered, sudden as those lightning strikes: the quilt had gone missing. It always appeared in Henry's bedroom.

He charged up the twisting stairs.

"What's wrong with the house?" someone asked, a thick-accent voice he didn't recognize. "I can't see right."

"Why's it smell like that?" another said. "What's that stink?"

Were they the wedding party? For a soaring moment, Sullivan thought the mystery was over; the guests had reappeared. The blue-dressed woman kept her post, impassive, staring but unseeing. "Juba," Sullivan said.

If she heard him, she gave no sign. Sullivan ran past her, up to the third floor. That strange doubling effect continued through the house, but he couldn't stop to marvel at it. Sullivan snatched the quilt from Henry's bed and bolted downstairs again. But when he reached the second floor, Rhys was pointing, fear written on his face. "There are people in there," he said. "They're not from—not from our time—"

He should have run. Instead, Sullivan stepped through the front living room and into the salon, where they'd held the seance. The people there—three men, and three women—were dressed in long, old-fashioned coats and bustled dresses, as if they'd stepped from a period film. The same furniture seemed blurred—Sullivan realized he was seeing overlaid images, the same pieces in two times at once, end tables with different knickknacks atop them, the eagle-backed sofa doubled but reupholstered. A mirror above it showed no twinning; when he glanced again he realized it did not include his reflection. It was as if something had opened there, in the place the three men had come before, and the past itself had streamed through it.

In the corner, a young woman watched them from a wingback chair. She nodded once at him, and he knew her. Somewhere between twenty and forty, she was beautiful, with hair trailing down her back—but she was substantial, fleshed, and when he had last seen her she had been wisped and transparent. That slight smile never moving, she pointed at something above his head.

"Who the devil are you?" one man shouted. About Sullivan's age, he looked vaguely familiar, dark haired, with something in his sharp nose and chin that suggested a Trenholm.

"Sullivan," he managed, his arms full of the quilt. "Who are you?"

"Someone whose house you're in," the man replied. His companions looked angry, as if he'd stepped into a meeting clandestine and possibly dangerous.

"This is—it's my house," Sullivan said.

"The hell it is." The man seemed to take in his clothes, his hair, and make a decision. "Get out, thief, and leave our things! Lucas! Come up here and get this man out! Lucas! Where'd that boy get to? I swear, that boy—"

"Wait a second," Sullivan said. "We can talk—"

"More of you!" He jabbed with his cane. Someone was shouting for Lucas, for Baxter, for men to come and take them. The man unsheathed his cane into a sword.

"Sullivan!" Rhys shouted. He half-turned; his cousin held not a can of gas, but a saber. He must have taken it from the front living room. Silver-shined, bright in the light that seemed half-electric, half-candled, it gleamed as if it had never been used. *I will give you a piece of advice,* the ghost had told them, when she had come as a ghost. *Use the sabers.*

Two other men unsheathed their own canes. It was a nightmarish thing, almost too slow, as if he dreamed it. Sullivan dropped the quilt, darted back, and yanked a saber from its place above the oddly twinned mantle. He tossed the sheath and held it like he knew what he was doing. His father had dressed them in Rebel uniforms, handed them guns, but never taught him how to use a sword.

"What's going on?" Henry called from the stairwell. "I hear—that's not—"

"Relatives!" Sullivan shouted.

Henry barreled in. His expression bloomed into something between horror and wonder as he saw the people across the room, their old clothes, those faces clearly known from so many years before. Hardly pausing, he threw himself at the oldest woman, a wordless cry of love and despair on his lips. The woman rushed at him, and something like a grief-keen rose high and pure and desperate from her.

"Henry!" she said. "Where in God's name have you been, baby? And what are you wearing? You've been gone for twenty years—"

"They're our cousins," he managed. "Owen, put up the sword."

"They're thieves!" he shouted. "This is our house! You kept Henry from us!"

"No, Owen!" Henry said, but the men rushed them, and as Olivia appeared, Elliot and Ash behind her, they were driven into the front living room. Like the other rooms, it was oddly doubled, the furnishings from their time blended with whatever had come before. In their time, the alligator skull grinned from shelves once covered with books; a TV lined shelves once full of china.

"Henry!" Olivia tried to push past them, but Rhys yanked her back just before their sabers met the cousins' sword-canes with a shattering clash of metal, steel on steel, a clamorous battle-sound both terrifying and exhilarating. The shock of that meeting rattled Sullivan's arms and shoulders, but those old sabers held. A third sword was next to his—Ash; his brother had grabbed a saber and fought beside them, keeping Elliot behind, the dogs arrayed in front of her and barking madly.

"They're our cousins!" Henry was calling from the salon over the noise of steel-on-steel, of furious dogs. "Don't touch them! Don't—"

"*Henry!*" Olivia was yelling, trying to get past them, past the three cousins, who crowded Rhys and Sullivan and Ash, slashing with their swords. Somehow, they barely held the relatives back. Sullivan's arm ached already.

"Get out!" ordered the dark-haired Victorian cousin, Owen. "How dare you invade our home?"

"Sullivan, Rhys, don't touch them!" Henry shouted. "I can't see our time! Our furniture disappeared when I hugged my mother!" He popped up behind the cousins. "Get out now!"

"No!" Olivia shouted. "Henry!"

"Get out, Livy!" he yelled. "I love you!"

"I won't leave you here!" She shoved past Rhys, face determined. "I'm coming, Henry!"

"*No!*" Henry cried, and Olivia launched herself at a Victorian cousin. Shocked to see a woman flying at him, he lowered his cane, and she fell in his arms. The men stepped back for a moment, and the cousin lifted her. Her expression was fierce; she pushed him back. "What the devil—" he spluttered. "Henry! Who's this harridan?"

"It's done," Olivia said. "I can't see our time anymore. I love y'all. Get Elliot out."

Before he had time to despair, to regret Henry or shout for Olivia, the cousins rushed them again, and the sabers sang, holding with another martial clatter. One dog flashed forward. Its teeth nearly sank into Owen's leg, and he almost dropped his sword as the dog flew back again. Sullivan and Rhys pressed the cousins a step back.

"Elliot," Sullivan said between his teeth, meeting another sword-thrust. A shepherd ducked under his arm and feinted again, throwing another cousin off balance. "Get her out, Ash. Get her out and light it up."

"What about you?" his brother asked. "You can't go with them—"

"Get her out and light it up and run," Sullivan told him. "We'll cover you and come behind." He thrust, parried. They couldn't last long against these men. But they could save Elliot and Ash, and that was worth something. It was worth everything, in the end.

Sullivan spoke the words he knew would let his brother go. "I love you," he told Ash. "Run. Save Elliot."

And Ash did.

CHAPTER 59

ASH

Elliot ran with Ash when he ducked back, grabbed her, and bolted, out the side door and into the central stairway. All four dogs clattered behind them. Feather duster in hand, the woman in blue hugged herself. She did not watch them; she seemed unaware of the battle behind them. Gratitude flashed through Ash's terror; if the ghosts had suddenly become aware and thinking, he might have lost it. But they'd remained the same through this madness: trapped reflections, nothing more.

Ash was thankful that Elliot had enough sense not to scream about Olivia and Henry left behind, about Sullivan and Rhys left to fight. Steel met steel, and cousins fought cousins as he and Elliot pounded downstairs, the family turned against itself. Ash was left to end it. They'd done their work well; the foyer was covered in gasoline. He grabbed a book of matches from a drawer. The dogs stuck close to Elliot, nearly tripping her. They were good dogs, and Ash was glad of them.

"Out," he told his little cousin. "Out and get clear of the house."

Ash looked one last time. The foyer was enormous, too big for a house, really, and Sullivan was right—the carpet was hideous. He might have laughed if a sob didn't threaten to shake him. The saber clattered to the floor. Above him, his brother and cousin shouted nonsense. Those Scarlett O'Hara curtains were soaked in gas, and they'd go up like one of his fireworks.

A man stepped from the dining room. Rage seethed him, a fury caught in those angry dark eyes. "Don't you dare burn my house, boy," Truluck Trenholm growled.

"It's not yours anymore," Ash managed, dry-mouthed at the sight of his father's ghost. "You're dead."

"It's my house until I leave it!" his father shouted. White-crowned, ruddy-faced, he personified Ash's nightmares. "Drop those matches, boy! You were never worth half your brother. Prove you're better than him. Keep this house standing."

But the dogs had left Elliot's side. They formed up around Ash, growls clotted thick and angry. They stared at his father, and they hated him. Ash caught his reflection in the foyer mirror. He almost startled to see a man there instead of a child.

"This house no longer belongs to you," he told his father, a little kid no more. "It's ours, and everything in it. And we see the ghosts in corners, Dad. They're there." His voice rose to a shout. "We see them! They're here, and they're part of this, too!"

His father's expression settled into pure hatred. "Don't you dare."

Tears rose, and shame tugged at Ash. But those tears were a sign of strength, not weakness: his father never cried. Could a sane person look on Cypress Bend without weeping, see its muddle of blood and history, its silent ghosts, and remain dry-eyed? The man before him believed in a cause long-lost, best lost. "You're dead," Ash repeated. "And this house is going with you."

"Do it, Ash!" Sullivan's yell sounded over the din, as if he felt his brother's hesitation. Footsteps crashed on the stairs, but brother or distant cousins, he wasn't sure. "I told you to light it up, dammit! Don't pussy out now!"

Ash met his father's furious gaze. Truluck Trenholm had been a man of complex hatreds, perhaps visceral sorrows. None of that mattered now. Ash struck the match.

"No!" His father lurched toward him. But the dogs were there, those shepherds who generally fled the supernatural, and they met his fury with their own.

Praying he didn't condemn Sullivan and Rhys, Ash dropped the match and pelted through the front door. He shouted as he ran: "Ganon! Pandora! Q! Zelda! *COME!*"

And the dogs clattered out behind him. His father's howls rose to a rage unearthly.

Ash launched himself from the porch as the fire caught like the force of some long-brooding, titanic vengeance. He bolted through the rose garden; Elliot stood next to the golf carts. Only then did he realize that the world no longer twinned with something from another time. They were free of it.

On the corner of the porch, the young boy dropped his broom. He flickered like the image on an old tube television. Then he winked out, and was gone. At the same moment, his father's howls stopped as suddenly as a snuffed candle.

Fire burst into full flower. Behind those tall plantation windows, flames bloomed like hell's own garden. As they caught, something boomed, a sound he might have called thunder if it didn't feel seismic, earth-shuddering. Ash threw himself over Elliot, a tussle of fur and cold noses around them, protecting his little cousin from whatever blows might come. She was the best of them, and he would save her even as everything else fell around them. The dogs pressed close as something enormous shifted, caught, then stilled. Fire still roared, but at Ash's hip, something crackled, and he startled to recall the radio.

"—back!" Lewis was shouting. "If you can hear me, Ash, the guests just—they're back! We're moving them away from the fire!"

Ash staggered upright. "You okay?" he called to Elliot, voice stolen by that raging inferno, heat already beginning to slap his face. Flame slithered up those once-white columns.

"I didn't know if you'd do it," Elliot shouted over the growing inferno.

"Olivia's gone," he managed. "And Henry. Sullivan and Rhys—" He couldn't say it. Henry had returned after all. Gone with him to that other time, Olivia had made her choice. A sob caught him.

Elliot swiped at her face. Dress torn and dirty from the driveway, hair tangled, she was beautiful, like the muddy little girl in Olivia's arms, and Ash wanted to cry again. "She picked," Elliot said. "She couldn't pick otherwise. She had to—" Elliot's grip tightened, and she dissolved into tears.

The fire glowed the garden into orange and yellow, and the house gave a convulsive shudder, but whether from the fire or another cosmic shift, Ash wasn't sure. Red-tongued flame swallowed the first floor and that fire roared like God's own judgment. It would burn now. The flames would take it back to the earth finally, and something else could grow there—something different, not the house and its blood-soaked legacy but a different kind of blossoming.

"Rhys and Sullivan—" Elliot managed.

"They're coming," Ash said, hope snagging, frail. He prayed he was right. As those flames writhed, he doubted anything could escape them—not his father's ghost, not his brother and cousin. Ash hugged Elliot tight. He couldn't cry. He couldn't cry because

Elliot was crying, and one more time, he would be the strong one. He was a Trenholm, and she was family. As he held her, as he watched, those orbs glittering in the trees lifted, rising like soda-bubbles; something like a star streaked improbably sideways, then vanished. Despite the smoke, the air in Ash's lungs seemed to expand. It felt like nothing so much as the end of his childhood asthma attacks, but unphysical, cosmic, and for the first time, Cypress Bend became nothing more than another piece of South Carolina: shimmered with everyday lunacies of poverty and grief, racism and history, but of a piece with reality. His little cousin wept against his chest. She would not grow up bowed by Cypress Bend's absurdities, and he finally let himself cry with her.

They'd lost the quilt, too, Ash realized. Returned to the house by whatever unearthly forces moved it, it would burn with everything else. The loss almost broke him. He'd tried. But that wanton destruction had taken so much—

The flames roared too tall, too hot. His brother would not return. Sobs choked Ash. Sullivan had said he loved him. And Rhys—for once, they'd gotten along; for once, they'd acted together. He hoped his cousin had felt that solidarity while it lasted. *I love you*, he wished he'd shouted to them both. *I love you for this, for saving Elliot.*

"The ghosts disappeared," Elliot told him through her tears. "I felt all that sadness lift up and disappear."

"I know," Ash said.

"All that emotion was stuck." Elliot sniffled; she swiped her face, and ash streaked her cheek. "You unstuck it, Ash. Everything can go forward now."

"I hope so."

Flames crackled, seethed. The wind shifted, and smoke billowed toward them; Ash pulled Elliot back. Sullivan and Rhys were trapped, perhaps fallen through to that other time. He had to get his little cousin out.

"C'mon," Ash said. "Let's—"

"No." Elliot held her ground. "We have to wait for Sullivan and Rhys."

"They aren't—" He choked, unable to form those words.

"They're coming," Elliot told him. "I know they are."

Ash squinched his eyes shut. He prayed they had avoided his father's ghost. "They aren't, honey. Come on."

But Elliot pointed. "I told you," she said.

Footsteps grated the pebbles. Ash whirled. Sullivan ran to them, Rhys right behind. His brother was sooted, sweating, seersucker torn but bow tie somehow perfect. In his arms, he carried the quilt, pristine, unburnt. The world smelled like smoke and ashes. The house was burning, burning. But the dogs were barking joyfully, running from Elliot to swarm at his brother's feet—

"Sullivan!" Ash ran to meet him in that desolation of smoke. They would have to get out. They would have to pray the drive was still clear, that the fires didn't rage into wildness, but they met in a crashing, fierce hug, not as Trenholms finally but brothers instead. They had no words. Cypress Bend burned, and time unspooled like a ruined sweater.

"You got her out," Sullivan finally said, voice hoarse, and Ash opened his arms to Elliot, to Rhys. They were Trenholms, and they were free.

"You got the quilt," Ash said, almost giddy. "You got it out."

"Now we have to get ourselves out," Rhys told them, and as the house crumbled behind them, they ran, dogs leaping around them. Truluck Trenholm would be rolling in his grave—or perhaps screaming in that fire. Ash no longer cared. He ran with his brother, his cousins, his dogs, and the plantation burned. There would be time to regret, to tally loss, to mourn. They would have to take care of their suddenly jobless relatives. But as they raced down that driveway, Ash could manage nothing but exultation in the end. Or, perhaps, in the beginning.

EPILOGUE

Sunrise came as a red maul in the east, as insistent, discordant birdsong. All night, Ash had herded people—mostly relatives—like fuddled cattle, had triaged disaster from the immediately physical to the bafflingly existential. His brother had tried to help. But Sullivan had careened wildly from exultation in their destruction to devastation at Olivia and Henry's loss. Finally, Ash had dispatched him to a Columbia AirBnB with Rhys, Elliot under his arm. The dogs had refused to leave her side.

But the long, moonless dark had ended. New dawn broke with Cypress Bend a smoldering ruin, the house torched, the cousins fled, their primary wedding venue a jagged, ashen heap. Sun shafted through the wreck of that Federalist home which had stood through more than two hundred years of time's ravaging violence. Soot-stained, shirt sleeves rolled and white bucks ruined, bow tie dangling, Ash stood before the wreckage of his own smoking mansion. It struck him as a kind of burnt offering.

The Trenholms were free.

Though freedom also meant unhomed and unemployed. All night, as Ash directed wailing firetrucks and clumps of pale, bewildered cousins, the knowledge tightened like a vise: when they'd burnt Cypress Bend, they'd consigned sixty-three relatives—at last count—to penury, not including themselves. Smoke hazed over the house's black-wet ruin. He would never rinse the stink of its burning. Ash wanted to weep. Fuck the house. He'd destroyed his family.

This land was never meant to be mine, he wanted to scream to the ghost of his father, the specter who'd tried to stop him. *It was never meant to be any of ours. Why did you do this to me?*

He had his inheritance: a heap of ashes, a land of relics. Cypress Bend was finished. Ash spared no regret for the house. But his relatives—the museum—the displays and the history behind them—

The sun bullied through those last wisped clouds. The cabins had not burned. No flying sparks had ignited them; that precious heirloom quilt was tucked there, safe. It wouldn't go wandering again. Both Black and white cemeteries lay intact. Legare County firefighters had doused the brush fires, saved the gift shop and the Pavilion, even the gardens. Ash regarded that dismal heap of a house, a monument to what Alexander Parrish had so long ago called "the mad Trenholms." Cypress Bend wasn't gone, Ash realized. The *white* part of Cypress Bend had burnt. Its history and artifacts remained.

Hope rose with that feathering smoke, and Ash glimpsed it in a moment, whole and entire. He knew what he had to do. Maybe his brother and cousins would kill him. Maybe, for once, it didn't matter.

Ash caught a ride back to the gatehouse with the last of the Legare County firefighters. Dreadlocks tied back, seersucker jacket long discarded, Lewis was helping the last of the confused guests find rides home. Ash crossed the drive, newly rutted by the fire trucks, and laid a hand on his cousin's shoulder. "Can we talk?" he asked.

Lewis nodded once. "Parker's gonna help you out for a minute," he told the bedraggled wedding guests, then followed Ash to the base of a shambling live oak. Away from the crowd, they sat like small boys spying on a grown-up party. Cousins, they were separated by only a few years. Ash ached. He and Lewis had never played together as children.

"What's up?" Lewis asked.

The firemen loaded their truck. The guests were all accounted for. Lewis had made sure of it. "I had an idea," Ash began.

"I'm listening," he replied.

Spanish moss hung limp, dead; monesterial stretches of tobacco hunkered like a blasted green waste. No tourists swarmed the gatehouse, and no cars paused to photograph that once-grand vista, which ended not in a proud mansion but a charred shell. For once, no TV cameras tracked them. Ash counted it as an unaccustomed grace.

"This is—this feels weird," Ash said. "The house is ours. The land is ours—on paper, I mean. Legally. It doesn't feel like ours. I mean, it doesn't feel like it should be. And I was thinking how Cypress Bend was gone, and all our people were unemployed. But then I realized that it wasn't all of Cypress Bend, just the *white* part of Cypress Bend, and—"

When Ash said the word *white*, heat crept up his cheeks. Attempting to span that long, bitter gap of race felt like a step onto a rotted bridge, sure to shatter underfoot. His tread fell clumsy and roughshod. Surely, he'd say something stupid. But Lewis watched him steadily. Rather than break under that brown-eyed gaze, Ash blundered on.

"The Black part of Cypress Bend, it's still here. The cabins and the quilt and the most important parts. They haven't left. And it feels dumb and condescending, to say—God, I hate talking, it never comes out right—" Ash trembled on the brink of tears, frustrated with himself, with his own limitations, with a world that had never taught him the right words to say or how to say them. "It feels weird to offer because it doesn't feel like mine, or like it should be mine, I mean, to give you, but Cypress Bend should belong to people who sweated for it. Not white people. It should pass to you. Like, a trust or something. To preserve what's still here. This feels wrong." He dropped his head in his hands. "I don't want it to be like a white savior thing. And white steward isn't any better. That's wrong. I just wanna do the right thing."

A long, dead silence stretched. Ash thought he might crumble. He wanted Lewis to tell him it would be okay. He knew that was wrong, too. *Why are we like this?* he wanted to cry. *I don't want to be like this. I hate this.*

"You're trying to do the right thing," Lewis said finally, and Ash lifted his head. Relatives flitted around Boo like shoaling fish as firefighters rounded up their equipment. Morning had broken into full honeyed day. "This is one of those tests where your grade takes effort into account." He paused. "But you really are pretty bad at this."

Ash scuffed his feet in that undying earth which he never wanted, which belonged to him and yet didn't. "What d'you think?" he ventured.

Lewis was also watching those relatives. He was a Trenholm too, and he cared about them. "I have to talk to some people," he said. "It'd take a lot of work. We'd need some of the insurance money for clean-up. And we'd need everyone's help. It's not a walk-away-and-done job, Ash."

"I know," he said, probably too eagerly. He sounded like a stupid kid. But better naive and ridiculous than fat and satisfied in hate. "I'll help. But it's your—your—" Enthusiasm died at the feet of embarrassment again, fear of those rotten boards. "It's your land and you lead," he said carefully. "I'll help and do what *you* ask."

Lewis gave him something like a smile. Maybe it said, *poor white boy*, or maybe *thanks, cousin.* Perhaps it could be both at the same time. "I'd like to see this place preserved and in Black hands," he said, shoving up from the branch. "We can try to work this out. But let's get these people home. Now's not the time to talk about it."

"I just..." Exhaustion dragged at Ash, as if the night's adrenaline had finally worn off. "I don't want everyone out of a job, y'know?"

"No," Lewis said. "Me either. Let's start there, huh?"

Ash got up. He followed Lewis to the crowd of cousins. *You are not doing the right thing,* he told himself. *You are instead doing the thing that should have been done a long time ago. If you were a better man, you would have done this already.* But he couldn't change the past. He could only move forward.

Do better, Olivia would have said.

The circling of blood and madness broken, Ash could try.

READER'S GUIDE QUESTIONS

1. The Trenholm cousins suffered through an abusive childhood. In Chapter 4, Rhys thinks, *Olivia carried herself like a perfect Southern lady; childhood had left her practiced in the art of pretense. They had all come through it differently... Sullivan found solace in alcohol and art; Ash had faded into stage lighting. Rhys had emerged with genetic liver disease, with exhaustion and the looming terror of a transplant waiting ahead. His psychic damage remained untallied. If he dared ask, Sullivan could add it up. He was always best at that.*

How accurate do you feel Rhys's assessment is? What does he get right about his cousins' damage, and what does he get wrong? What does he fail to see about himself? Why do you think it's easier for him to see his cousins' trauma rather than his own?

2. The three men, Sullivan says, are time. How does the past intrude at Cypress Bend? How do the cousins enable its intrusion, and how do they finally stop it? What are some ways that you allow the past to intrude on your life?

3. *Ninety-Eight Sabers* is a novel about white people trying to reconcile their racial legacy as historical oppressors, and the ways that oppression continues into the present day. How do the characters attempt to talk about race throughout the novel? Why do you think they find it so difficult? What do they do wrong? What

do they do right?

4. Why doesn't Sullivan want to forgive Henry for his past? Why does he finally decide that he should? Do you agree or disagree with his decision?

5. Mute ghosts populate the corners of Cypress Bend. What do you think they add to the story? What does it mean to you that Truluck Trenholm forbade people from mentioning them? Why do you think the Trenholm cousins kept that taboo, even after he died?

6. Ash makes a display using a quilt made by an enslaved person, Aunt Hera. Why is the quilt so important, and why do you think its display causes such conflict between Ash and Sullivan? Do you think that conflict is merited? Why do you think Sullivan saves it?

7. The epigram for *Ninety-Eight Sabers* is "South Carolina is too small for a republic and too large for an insane asylum." It comes from James Louis Petigru, a noted South Carolina jurist who opposed secession. Why do you think it was chosen, and what do you think it says about the book?

8. What do you think it's like for the Black Trenholm cousins to work at Cypress Bend? How does Lewis, in particular, seem to manage its awful legacy with his own talents, passions, and projects as part of Ash's paranormal reality show?

9. If you were a wedding guest at a function held in Cypress Bend's Barn event space, how do you think the bleak history of the venue would affect you? What do you think of plantations-turned-tourist-traps? Have you ever been to one, and if so, how did you feel while you were there?

10. Though *Ninety-Eight Sabers* sits comfortably in the Southern Gothic Horror genre, it also has strong elements of eco horror. How do you see the environment being championed? How do you see the changed landscape of Cypress Bend being mourned?

11. The concept of family and familial loyalty for the Trenholms is both bolstering and suffocating. How do these cousins and siblings draw strength from one

another? How do they wound each other most deeply? And, after the stunning events at the end of the book, do you think Ash's and Sullivan's truce will hold? Why or why not?

12. Both Aunt Alda and Elliot are important family members who live at the "big house" at Cypress Bend, though we do not get their direct perspectives in individual chapters. What role does Aunt Alda serve for the family, and what does she symbolize for them? What about Elliot? Her older cousins attach so much hope to her, raising her so that she doesn't feel trapped by traditional feminine roles the way Olivia does. Do you think Elliot escaped as unscathed as Ash and Olivia think she did? In what ways do you think Elliot will always carry Cypress Bend with her?

13. There are plenty of animals at Cypress Bend—Ash's loyal dogs, Uncle Wade's patio parrots, invasive tegus, horses, swamp alligators. What do you think the animals add to the story? How do they relate to the paranormal happenings? Do you think it's fair to keep animals at Cypress Bend? Why or why not?

ELIZABETH BROADBENT

Elizabeth Broadbent left the South Carolina swamps for the Commonwealth of Virginia, where she lives with her three sons, two dogs, two cats, and patient husband. She's the author of Ink Vine (Undertaker Books), Ninety-Eight Sabers (Undertaker Books), Blood Cypress (2025 from Raw Dog Screaming Press) and Breaking Neverland (2026 from Sley House Publications). Her speculative fiction has been published with The Cafe Irreal, Tales to Terrify, Penumbric, If There's Anyone Left, and Haven Speculative, among other places. During her long career as a journalist, her nonfiction appeared in places such as The Washington Post, Insider, The Daily Mail, and ADDitude Magazine.

ACKNOWLEDGMENTS

*N*inety-Eight Sabers begins with Truluck Trenholm's death for a very simple reason: I started the novel the morning after my own father died. In a very real way, I am a Trenholm child. My father was an alcoholic who terrorized his children; I learned of his death through a phone call. While he flew no Confederate flag, he fell prey to the racism that plagues many members of the white working class, once telling my brother that his Black friend couldn't play at our house.

I grew up well-schooled in the ways of white supremacy. The n-word was spoken at our kitchen table; Black stereotypes were presented as self-evident and logical. Black history was a waste of time, and Martin Luther King Day a sham. I was told that affirmative action let Black students steal my place at an Ivy League university. You know what it looked like—American racism is nothing if not predictable and unimaginative.

That makes it no less destructive.

My reckoning came in a hundred small moments; to detail them would take another novel. But primarily, I owe the attempts at unraveling and examining my racism (an ongoing process) to two of the most important people in my life, Smith King and Joey Oppermann. Both fierce warriors for social justice, they showed me the human face behind the hate my father handed me. While Smith was taken from this world more than twenty years ago, his effect lingers in every friend he touched. Joey battles for justice as a public defender in Oconee County, South Carolina, and this book is dedicated to him, my oldest friend, and one of its first readers.

I say "one of the first," because I can't recall if he or my husband read it first—Chris is my biggest cheerleader, my constant support, and my best friend. I couldn't have written this book without him. He solved a hundred small problems and listened to a hundred rants. He tolerated a hundred writer highs and a hundred writer sulks. He brought me coffee and kittens. I love you, Bear.

When this novel was in its very early stages, I said to my oldest son Blaise, a dedicated amateur cryptozoologist, "I need something really scary." He said, "You should use the mirrored men." Because of our accent, it came out something like, "mere men," and after about five minutes of "What?" "I said, 'Mere men!'" I made him write it down.

"Oh, *them*!" I replied.

The mirrored men are a phenomenon first reported by Derrick Hayes on his podcast *Monsters Among Us* (please give it a listen—truly spectacular). A huge thank you to Derrick for his tireless hard work in bringing this formerly unknown phenomena to light. If you're interested in learning more about the mirrored men—they're utterly terrifying—he dedicates all of Season 7, episode 15 to them.

This book wouldn't be what it is without the endless work of my editor, Rebecca Cuthbert. I thank her every time, and it's never enough. She's spectacular at her job, and an incredibly talented writer in her own right. I wake up every day delighted to work with her, and even happier to call her a friend. She picked up this manuscript, and like she did with *Ink Vine* before it, started making suggestions that made the book infinitely better. If you liked *Sabers*, well, thank her. She made it what it is.

After her first read-through, she said we needed a sensitivity consultation. I was terrified: it's one thing to write a book confronting that you're racist. It's another to hand that book to a Black person and say, "Hey, can you point out how I'm being racist?" Of course, you *want* to know, but you're so scared; we're schooled to believe that talking about these things is damning and awful. But Rob Grimoire was a tremendous help. This book owes him an enormous debt of gratitude for his advice—Rebecca would agree that it wouldn't be the book it is without his suggestions. If you liked *Sabers*, thank Rob.

And I'm grateful, one more time, to work with the entire Undertaker Books team. *Ninety-Eight Sabers*, like all their books, is a group effort. Cyan does our formatting and so much else, from research to pricing to web design. Joe did the final proofing—thank you to my favorite former mortician for the accuracy of the casket falling scene! My cover artist, Erick Worthington, came to Richmond to draw the Wickham House, and even added the extra story to the top. So many people gave their best selves to this book, and it shows. I'm so grateful to every one of you, and *Sabers* is more special because of it.

Thank you to everyone who offered me a blurb, who reviewed, who helped me to promote the book and get it in the hands of readers. There are too many of you to name.

And finally, to South Carolina itself—what do I say? If this is a novel about my father's death, it's also a novel about homesickness. There were days while writing that I'd call Joey and cry about how much I missed it. Is it a terrible thing to miss a land so soaked in blood and violence? Maybe not, if you called it home. We Southerners never quite get over that one.

People said that I seemed to deal so well with my father's death. I didn't realize until a year later that I had written a novel instead. You hold in your hands my own Cypress Bend.

Thank you for helping me set it aflame.

QUILTS AND THEIR PART IN THE UNDERGROUND RAILROAD

The first public mention of quilts and their role in helping enslaved people escape came in 1998, when Jacqueline Tobin and Raymond Dobard published *Hidden in Plain View: A Secret Story of Quilts in the Underground Railroad.* They tell us that enslaved seamstresses would make a "sampler" quilt, then ten different quilts of various patterns, usually starting with a wrench pattern. These quilts, hung in a certain order, gave enslaved people directions about when and how to flee.

As evidence, Tobin and Dobard cite oral history tradition passed down to Ozella McDaniels, a descendent of enslaved people. However, detractors of their research note that neither antebellum slave narratives, nor 1930s WPA interviews with former enslaved people, cite quilts as an aid to escape. Therefore, they claim, Tobin's and Dobard's conclusions are doubtful. However, other descendents of enslaved people, including retired teacher Connie Martin, also report oral traditions about quilts' use in escaping captivity.

Oral history is notoriously difficult to verify, particularly when divulging these codes (i.e., pre-Civil War) would have destroyed their utility. In *Ninety-Eight Sabers*, Rhys, as a historian, would stake his claim on methodology. However, these assertions stumble into difficulty: Who has the right to determine another person's story? Who has the ability to judge the veracity of an oral tale? Tradition is compelling, and questions arise about who exactly determines academic veracity. Who makes up the academy? What voices does it lift up, and which does it suppress? Who invented the methodology we use, and what voices does that methodology prioritize and favor?

LEARN MORE ABOUT THE EXHIBITS AT CYPRESS BEND

The Vesey Rebellion:

"Denmark Vesey." National Park Service. Last updated 17 July 2020. (Accessed 14 Sept 2024)

Hansen, Victoria. "Denmark Vesey Is Honored. His Slave Rebellion Was Thwarted and He Was Executed." National Public Radio, 10 August 2022. (Accessed 14 Sept 2024)

Robertson, David. *Denmark Vesey: The Buried Story of America's Slave Rebellion and the Man Who Led It.* Vintage: First Edition. 2000

Schipper, Jeremy. *Denmark Vesey's Bible: The Thwarted Revolt That Put Slavery and Scripture on Trial.* Princeton University Press: Princeton, NJ. 2022

Waxman, Olivia B. "The Most Important Slave Revolt That Never Happened." *Time Magazine.* 15 March 2017. (Accessed 14 Sept 2024)

The Stono Rebellion:

"Jemmy." *Peoples of the Historical Slave Trade,* Enslaved.org. (Accessed 14 Sept 2024)

Pearson, Edward A. "'A Countryside Full of Flames': A Reconsideration of the Stono Rebellion and Slave Rebelliousness in the Early-Eighteenth-Century South Carolina Lowcountry," in *The Slavery Reader* (2003).

Smith, Mark Michael, ed. *Stono: Documenting and Interpreting a Southern Slave Revolt.* (2005).

Sutherland, Claudia. "The Stono Rebellion (1739)." *Black Pasts*, 18 September 2018. (Accessed 14 Sept 2024)

"The Stono Rebellion of 1739: Where Did It Begin?" Charleston County Public Library, 2024. (Accessed 14 Sept 2024)

"Two Views of the Stono Slave Rebellion." Becoming American: The British Atlantic Colonies, 1690-1739. *National Humanities Center*, (Accessed 14 Sept 2024)

Potter David Drake:

Burtseva, Sandra. "David Drake's Poetic Pottery Was Resistance." *National Gallery of Art*, 16 June 2023. (Accessed 14 Sept 2024)

Channey, Michael, editor. *Where Is All My Relation? The Poetics of Dave the Potter*. New York: Oxford University Press, 2018.

Finkel, Jori. "The Enslaved Artist Whose Pottery Was an Act of Resistance." *New York Times*, 17 June 2021. (Accessed 14 Sept 2024)

Leonard, Todd. Carolina Clay: *The Life and Legend of the Slave Potter Dave*. New York: W. W. Norton & Company, 2008.

Rothschild, Jill Vaum and Leslie Umberger. "David 'Dave' Drake: Potter and Poet." Smithsonian American Art Museum, 1 February 2023. (Accessed 14 Sept 2024)

Spinozzi, Adrienne, editor. *Hear Me Now: The Black Potters of Old Edgefield, South Carolina*. New York and New Haven: The Metropolitan Museum of Art, distributed by Yale University Press, 2022.

Robert Smalls:

Gates, Henry Louis Jr. "Which Slave Sailed Himself to Freedom?" WNET, 2013. (Accessed 14 Sept 2024)

Lineberry, Cate. "The Thrilling Tale of How Robert Smalls Seized a Confederate Ship and Sailed It To Freedom." *Smithsonian Magazine*, 13 June 2017. (Accessed 14 Sept 2024)

Miller Jr., Edward. *Gullah Statesmen: Robert Smalls from Slavery to Congress, 1839-1915* (University of South Carolina Press, 2008)

"Robert Smalls." *National Park Service*, 2024. (Accessed 14 Sept 2024)

"Smalls, Robert." History, Art, and Archives. United States House of Representatives. (Accessed 14 Sept 2024)

Zuczek, Richard. *State of Rebellion: Reconstruction in South Carolina* (University of South Carolina Press, 1996)

The Orangeburg Massacre:

Bass, Jack. "Orangeburg Massacre." South Carolina Encyclopedia, University of South Carolina Institute for Southern Studies. 8 June 2016. (Accessed 14 Sept 2024)

Bass, Jack and Jack Nelson. *The Orangeburg Massacre*. Mercer University Press, 2017.

History.com Editors. "The Orangeburg Massacre." 6 April 2018. (Accessed 14 Sept 2024)

Manos, Nick. "Orangeburg Massacre (1968)." Black Past. 31 Dec. 2018, (Accessed 14

Sept 2024)

Sellers, Cleveland. *The River of No Return: The Autobiography of a Black Militant and the Life and Death of SNCC.* William Morrow Paperbacks: Reprint Edition, 2018.

The Shooting at Emmanuel Baptist Church:
Elliott, Debbie. "How a Shooting Changed Charleston's Oldest Black Church." *All Things Considered*, National Public Radio. 8 June 2016. (Accessed 14 Sept 2024)

Horowitz, Jason, Nick Corasaniti and Ashley Southall. "Nine Killed in Shooting at Black Church in Charleston." *The New York Times,* 18 June 2015 (Accessed 14 September 2014)

US Justice Department, "Justice Department Announces Multi-Million Dollar Civil Settlement in Principle in Mother Emanuel Charleston Church Mass Shooting." Office of Public Affairs, 28 Oct 2021. (Accessed 14 Sept 2024)

Von Drehle, David. "How Do You Forgive A Murder?" *Time Magazine*, 12 Nov 2015. (Accessed 14 Sept 2024)

Zapotsky, Matt. "Charleston Church Shooter: I Would Like to Make It Crystal Clear, I Do Not Regret What I Did." *The Washington Post*, 4 Jan 2017 (Accessed 14 Sept 2024)

BIBLIOGRAPHY

12th South Carolina Infantry Regiment, The Civil War in the East. Hawks, Steve A., 2024. (Accessed 14 Sept 2024)

The 1812 John Wickham House. National Trust for Historic Preservation, 2024. (Accessed 14 Sept 2024)

Belle-Kite, Diana. "Quilting Part I: 18th Century to Antebellum Era." *NCPedia*, North Carolina Museum of History, 2015. (Accessed 14 Sept 2024)

Betts, Vicki, "Paper Manufacturing and Paper Shortages in the South, 1861-1865" (2016). Special Topics. Paper 18. (Accessed 14 Sept 2024)

Bryant, Marie Claire. "Underground Railroad Quilt Codes: What We Believe, What We Know, and What Inspires Us." *Folklife Magazine*, 9 May 2019. (Accessed 29 July 2024)

Charleston County Public Library. "The Ghost of Christmas Past: Joy and Fear During the Era of Slavery." Charleston County Public Library, . (Accessed 14 Sept 2024)

The Charleston Museum Staff. "The Charleston Museum's Slave Badge Collection." The Charleston Museum, (Accessed 14 Sept 2024)

The Church of Jesus Christ of Latter Day Saints. 12th Regiment, South Carolina

Infantry. Family Search. https://www.familysearch.org/en/wiki/12th_Regiment,_South_Carolina_Infantry (Accessed 14 Sept 2024)

Clyde, Wanett I. *Clothing the Black Body in Slavery: What They Wore and How It Was Made.*

The Graduate Center, City University of New·York, May 2019 (Accessed 14 Sept 2024)

DocSouth Staff, "The Slave Experience of the Holidays." Documenting the American South, (Accessed 2 Aug 2024)

Educational Broadcasting Corporation, "Slavery and the Making of America." 13/WNET New York, 2004. (Accessed 14 Sept 2024)

Foster, Thomas. "Sexual Exploitation of the Enslaved" Encyclopedia Virginia. Virginia Humanities, 2022 (Accessed 14 Sept 2024)

Fretwell, Sammy. "Angry Crowd Blasts Westinghouse over Nuclear Leak Few Knew About." *The State.* Aug 14 2018. (Accessed 2 Aug 2024)

Fretwell, Sammy. "Holes Found in SC Plant's Protective Liner." *The State.* Feb 16, 2020. (Accessed 2 Aug 2024)

Fretwell, Sammy. "Radioactive Groundwater Found at South Carolina Nuclear Fuel Facility." *The State*, Nov 9, 2018. (Accessed 2 Aug 2024)

Fry, Gladys-Marie. *Stitched from the Soul: Slave Quilts from the Antebellum South.* University of North Carolina Press, Chapel Hill, 1990.

Fulghum, R. Neil. "The Southern Homefront: 1861-1865." *Documenting the American South.* (Accessed 2 Aug 2024)

Harris, LeBron. "Confederate Adversity Covers from Paper Shortages." Linn's Stamp News (2015). . (Accessed 2 Aug 2024)

Ives, Sarah. "Did Quilts Hold Codes to the Underground Railroad?" *National Geographic*, 5 Feb 2004. (Accessed 2 Aug 2024)

Kromash, Wendy. "How Pre-Civil War Quilts Hid Secrets to the Underground Railroad." Evanston Roundtable, 27 March 2023. (Accessed 2 Aug 2024)

Mallory, Laurel. "8 More Non-Native Tegu Lizard Sightings in South Carolina Have Wildlife Officials Concerned." WIS10, 10 Sept 2020. (Accessed 2 Aug 2024)

McCray, Shamira. "SC DNR Documents State's First Confirmed Tegu Lizard Sighting, in Lexington County." *Charleston Post & Courier*, 24 August 2020. (Accessed 2 Aug 2024)

Mills, Chad. "We Don't Trust You, Some Tell DHEC After Nuclear Leak." *WISTV*. August 13, 2018. (Accessed 2 Aug 2024)

Morris, Bilal G. "What Was Christmas Like for Slaves in America?" NewsOne, Dec. 15, 2023. (Accessed 2 Aug 2024)

Museum of Early Southern Decorative Arts. *Slave Cloth and Clothing Slaves: Craftsmanship, Commerce, and Industry*, Madelyn Shaw Journal of Early Southern Decorative Arts. (Accessed 14 September 2024)

National Park Service. 12th Regiment, South Carolina Infantry. National Park Service. https://www.nps.gov/civilwar/search-battle-units-detail.htm?battleUnitCode=CSC0012RI (Accessed 14 Sept 2024)

The Pinckney Papers Projects. "People Enslaved at War Hall Plantation," 8 February 1771 https://exhibits.library.sc.edu/peopleenslavedbythepinckneys/people-enslaved-by-the-pi nckneys/(Accessed 14 Sept 2024)

Rigdon, John. "South Carolina 12th Infantry Regiment." Research Online. (Accessed 14 Sept 2024)

Smith, Sam. "Moments in Time: The Battle of Second Manassas - The Railroad Cut, Part 2." American Battlefield Trust. (Accessed 14 Sept 2024)

Spivey, William. "What Did Christmas and New Year's Mean to the Enslaved?" OHF Weekly, 9 Dec. 2023. (Accessed 2 Aug 2024)

Stachura, Sea. "The Enduring Story for Underground Railroad Quilts." NPR, 3 March 2024. (Accessed 2 Aug 2024)

Stevenson, Brenda E. "What Love Got to Do with It? Concubinage and Enslaved Women and Girls in the Antebellum South." , Vol. 98, No. 1, Special Issue: "Women, Slavery, and the Atlantic World" (Winter 2013), pp. 99-125 (Accessed 7 July 2024)

Thomas Jefferson Foundation, "Colonoware." *Digital Archive of Comparative Slavery*. Thomas Jefferson Foundation, (Accessed 3 Aug 2024)

Thomas Jefferson Foundation, "The Hermitage/The Triplex." *Digital Archive of Comparative Slavery*. Thomas Jefferson Foundation, (Accessed 14 Sept 2014)

The Valentine, 2023. *The Wickham House*. https://thevalentine.org/explore/exhibitions/the-wickham-house/ (Accessed 1 Aug 2024)

Vlach, John Michael. *Back of the Big House: The Cultural Landscape of the Plantation*. George Washington University, 1995. (Accessed 2 Aug 2024)

Wilson, Richard Guy et al. Society of Architectural Historians. *Wickham House, Valentine Museum*. SAH Architpedia. (Accessed 2 Aug 2024)

If you are a fan of horror stories and tales,
you'll want to follow Undertaker Books.

We're bringing you stories to take to your grave.
SIGN UP FOR OUR NEWSLETTER ONLINE

www.ingramcontent.com/pod-product-compliance
Lightning Source LLC
Chambersburg PA
CBHW021023310726

48969CB00006B/1512